Coach Dad

A Novel

Work hard to achieve your hopes, dreams,
and aspirations—but remember,
sometimes fate has other plans.

Frank Agin

ISBN: 978-1-967521-32-6

Published by:

418 Press, A Division of Four Eighteen Enterprises LLC
Post Office Box 30724, Columbus, Ohio 43230-0724

Author's Notes & Acknowledgements

I began writing this novel in late 2008—shortly after finishing my second, *Rival*. I was in a creative mood and had a unique spark of inspiration.

At the time, voters in a local school district had defeated a tax levy, and the school board responded by cutting sports as a cost-saving measure. Some students suffered without their beloved extracurriculars, while others found ways to transfer to different high schools.

But I wondered: *What if parents had the opportunity to rise up and coach their sons and daughters? And what if one of those teams was the defending state champion?*

With that single thought, I got going. But I quickly stalled. I had never been on a team that won a playoff game, let alone a state championship. And my kids were still in grade school, so I had no experience on the parental end of teenagers navigating school life—something that was going to be a big part of the story.

Then, in November 2009, I pulled my kids early from school to attend a state championship soccer match involving St. Francis DeSales High School. That day, my children decided they would one day attend—and play soccer at— DeSales: a great Catholic school, a state championship machine, and a perennial soccer power. Through that experience, I gained an almost front-row seat to a title run and, later, to the defense of that title.

More on the DeSales experience another time—perhaps in another novel? For now, however, I want to thank Coach Domenic Romanelli, the iconic soccer coach, for allowing me to serve as team photographer and for giving me the chance to be within earshot of him and his trusty sidekick, Ben Brooks.

Like *Rival* and *Out of the Comfort Zone*, the backdrop of this novel is football. But the story is not really about the sport. *Coach Dad* is about parental love. It's about pursuing hopes and dreams. It's about navigating young relationships. It's about how people can enter our lives and change everything. And it's about the reality that, in the end, fate is in control.

I'd like to thank my dad, Michael L. Agin, to whom I've dedicated this book. He was my very first coach as well as my enduring role model and mentor. I made the final push to start this book in March 2023 during one of my many twelve-hour trips to sit with him.

I'd like to thank my wife, Linda, for giving me the space to mentally disappear from time to time to draft this tome—and for encouraging me to further develop the "hot wife" storyline.

And finally, I'd like to thank my three great kids—Lucas, Logan, and Chase. Individually and collectively, you've kept me connected to sports of all kinds: the Packers, the Michigan Wolverines, the British Premier League, Major League Soccer, the National Women's Soccer League—the list goes on and on.

If I haven't said it enough before, let me put it in writing now: I am proud of you and I love you very much.

Frank Agin
September 20, 2025

To My First Coach
Michael L. Agin

Head hockey coach of the Copper Country Motors Mustangs, runner-up in the 1971–72 Copper Country Junior Hockey Association Squirt Division — but most of all, my dad.

Hvala, i s mnogo ljubavi.

Dads Matter

Chapter 1

"Where is it?" Jonathan Reese said to himself as he instinctively grabbed his phone. He was hopeful that what he was expecting had come in, somehow occurring undetected by him.

He was looking for a single email. And that would alert him that a series of documents had been modified and were sitting on a proprietary internet cloud owned by the law offices of Eisenberg & Anders. Jonathan could then access those documents.

He activated the backlight and studied the large display screen. The phone indicated that it was getting a good signal. That was consistent with the information he had uncovered on the phone company's website. It indicated that the Canton, Ohio area had solid coverage.

As he pensively waited, he contemplated calling back to the office to determine what was holding up the email and the related documents. He refrained, however. As much as he wanted to get what he was after, he felt a sense of guilt.

It was late afternoon on the first Friday in December. Jonathan had directed a small army of junior associates to be in the office at 7 a.m. sharp and not leave until the work was done—even though he was not there.

While he was not with them now, he had been with them earlier. At 5:45 a.m., Jonathan made the lonely drive into his plush downtown Columbus, Ohio, law firm offices. Ahead of the team's arrival, he spent time organizing the work that needed to be done. Then, for a few hours, he worked with them shoulder to shoulder. But he needed to leave late morning to travel to Canton, which was about two and a half hours away.

While Jonathan needed to leave, the team needed to get work done. The firm's biggest client, Emerald Medical, was on another acquisition binge to further integrate itself vertically. The current acquisition target was a large manufacturer of medical equipment and supplies whose main operations were now scattered across the Far East.

As Jonathan was lead attorney from Eisenberg & Anders on this acquisition, he had his team's attention focused on formulating a formal letter of intent and a series of due diligence requests. The Emerald Medical acquisition team—which was based in Hong Kong—wanted these items first thing Monday morning.

The problem was that the Emerald Medical acquisition team's Monday morning was half a day ahead of U.S. Eastern time. So, the draft needed to be done on Friday so they could have Saturday and part of Sunday to review and edit.

Mindful of the adage "a watched pot never boils," Jonathan slipped the phone back into his pocket and let out an extended exhale. He was officially stressed.

However, no sooner had the phone hit the bottom of his pocket than it vibrated to life. Jonathan dug into his pocket, carefully retrieving the sleek phone. He could feel some of the tension ease out of his body. He felt somewhat back in control. He had the answers to his questions and a secure link to the documents he had to review.

He sifted through the half-dozen emails, looking for one. When he found it, he immediately clicked on the provided link. Almost instantly, he was sent to the cloud. After typing in a username and password, the gateway to the revised documents was initiated.

Pensively, he waited for it to load. He thought to himself, "No matter how quickly these things get, they never seem to be quick enough." Moments later, however, the document he had waited the better part of the day for was on the small screen of his phone.

He squinted to read the tiny text of the document titled "Letter of Intent." His squint, however, became a full-blown wince as he started to review the letter line by line, making mental notes as to what and how he needed to rework it. He gave another extended exhale.

As Jonathan pored through the document, the cries of someone nearby broke his train of thought.

"Jonathan … Jonathan … Hey, JONATHAN? Are you here to work? Or watch football?"

Jonathan Reese broke from his trance and looked around at the handful of people in the stands looking at him. Slightly embarrassed, he slipped the phone back into his breast pocket. The attention on him did not last long, however. It quickly shifted back to the field for the next play in the Ohio High School Division IV State Football Championship at Hall of Fame Stadium, located beside the Pro Football Hall of Fame.

Chapter 2

"Football fans, we're in the final minute of the Division IV state championship," the radio commentator announced.

Anyone who knew anything about Ohio high school football could see this state championship showdown coming long before the playoffs began—the Blacklick Mustangs versus the Cardinal Mooney Cardinals.

These two high schools were different in many ways. Blacklick was public. Mooney, a private Catholic school. Blacklick drew students only from the unincorporated portion of Jefferson Township, which was just east of Columbus, Ohio. Mooney drew students from all over the greater Youngstown, Ohio, area. Blacklick did not even have a decade of history yet. Mooney welcomed its first freshman class in 1956.

While these schools had their differences, it was what they had in common that led people to project their matchup in the Division IV title game: offense. While each school went about it in different ways, each generated a plethora of yardage and points every game leading up to the championship.

Blacklick's offensive production mainly came from a high-flying passing game. Mooney's, however, came through a grind-it-out running attack. In either case, they each averaged over 30 points per game and were seemingly unstoppable.

While anyone who knew anything about Ohio high school football could see this Division IV title game coming, none of them would have predicted that with less than a minute to play, the score would be only 14-10. Prolific as the offenses were for each of these teams, they each had staunch defenses as well— defenses that did not get the credit they were due. Much of the offensive success throughout the season was the result of turnovers, field position and time of possession.

Beyond the fact that these two defenses contributed to the perception that their respective offenses were unstoppable, sheer pride inspired this defensive battle. For the better part of a month leading up to this projected showdown, all anyone talked about was the likelihood that this game would yield lots of points.

In short, neither defense was given much respect, motivating both defenses to come ready to play. They each intended to prove a point and make a statement.

The opening series for each team went according to script: Blacklick—sporting its home navy blue jerseys and gray numbers that matched their pants—scored a touchdown on an eight-play, 90-yard aerial attack. And Mooney—in its away white jerseys, with red numbers and bright yellow-gold pants—answered with a touchdown on a 15-play, 75-yard ground assault. Midway through the first quarter, it seemed as if the Division IV state football championship would be a high-scoring barn burner.

On the next series, however, the Blacklick Mustangs were not able to muster a first down. The red and gold Mooney Cardinal defense made some sideline adjustments, resurrected its pride and held the state's top passing offense on three consecutive plays—a sack, an incomplete pass and a screen pass blown up for a short gain. The Mustangs punted the ball in the first quarter for the first time all season.

From that moment, the game became a defensive struggle. Each offense took the field and attempted to do what had worked for it all season long. And while on a good series they might have been able to muster a first down or two, in the end they had to resort to punting the football. The first half ended with the teams deadlocked in a 7-7 tie.

The second half continued much the same. Blacklick would pass the ball one, two, three times and then punt. Mooney would run some combination of left, right and up the middle and then punt. The defenses felt vindicated. The offenses felt frustrated. Those who came to see a high-scoring affair were disappointed. And the faithful from each side remained hopeful.

Both Blacklick and Mooney faithful knew they were not getting the game they had hoped to see. They remained hopeful that the next time they had the ball, their offense would "find the groove" it had been in all season. That was not the case, however. Strong defensive play, mental mistakes and ill-advised penalties dashed hope time and again.

Despite this, each team was able to muster some additional points. These points were not the result of potent offense but rather special teams. Late in the third quarter, the Blacklick Mustangs were able to return a punt inside the opposition's 20-yard line. While their offense was not able to fully capitalize, they managed to take a 10-7 lead on a 25-yard field goal.Midway through the fourth quarter, the Mooney Cardinals had its own special team's moment. Two of its defenders broke through to block a punt, while a third one swooped in and took the bouncing ball in for a touchdown. The kids from the Catholic high school now had a 14-10 lead in the final quarter of the Division IV Ohio high school state championship game.

Blacklick got the ball back after the kickoff with a little over seven minutes left in the game. Just like the umpteen times since the opening kickoff, it was not able to sustain a drive. All it succeeded in doing was getting a good punt off. The Mustangs pinned the Cardinals deep inside their own 20-yard line—but at the cost of almost three and a half minutes.

Sensing the urgency, the Blacklick defense further heightened its intensity. There was only so much it could do, however. It yielded only six yards on three consecutive plays but then gave up a first down when a defender stepped offside as the Cardinals punted the football. The error was significant in that it gave Mooney a new set of downs, negated a poor punt and essentially wasted another two minutes.

The Blacklick defense again held. This time, it minimized the loss of time to only 30 seconds, but to do so, it had to use all its remaining timeouts. Staying onside this time, the Mustangs made a valiant attempt at blocking the punt. Adding to the agony of narrowly missing the block, however, was the fact that the football landed far from the lone Mustang return man. The misery was further magnified as the Blacklick team and faithful could only watch as the Mooney Cardinals got several favorable bounces as well.

It seemed that fate was not working in the Mustangs' favor. They needed a touchdown but were 63 yards from the end zone. Additionally, they had no timeouts and only 56 seconds to work with. There was every reason for hope to fade—just like the early December daylight.

Chapter 3

"Huddle up, huddle up. Quickly, huddle up," the Blacklick quarterback, No. 12, Mason Jackson, quickly directed. While the clock was stopped, he spoke as if time were ticking away. "It's time to make something happen." Mason went quiet as the team settled into its huddle formation, though he motioned with his hand for them to keep it moving.

The plethora of challenges and shortage of opportunities in the championship game did not seem to daunt the Mustangs' offense. More times than anyone could count, they scored in less than a minute. While points seemed hard to come by, they fancied themselves a team that could score at will. They just had not asserted that "will" yet.

"Get the ball to me," No. 29 blurted over the din of mumbling players, chin straps being buckled, and the knocking of shoulder pads in close quarters. "Get it to me."

"AJ," Mason paused and drew a heavy sigh. "Coach already sent in the play—Rainbow Triple. You're just a decoy on this one. My first three reads aren't even in your direction."

"I don't care. Speed read and throw me the ball," AJ Reese retorted.

"AJ," Mason responded again, pausing briefly to gather his words. "They've been keyed on you since before we got off the bus."

The Cardinals' defensive game plan was simple: In all cases, put double coverage on AJ Reese and pressure Mason Jackson to make hurried passes to anyone else in the Mustang receiving corps. This was the only rational strategy available, as Mason and Reese had been the "dynamic duo" all season.

Both only juniors, they had accounted for almost 1,500 passing yards throughout the season. This potent passing combination connected on 26 touchdown passes and set up countless other touchdowns and field goals. Mason held almost every passing record at Blacklick High School, and Reese was only 51 points from being the Mustang football program's all-time leading scorer. If Youngstown Mooney had any hope of shutting down the Blacklick offensive attack, it needed to stymie the Jackson-Reese combination.

This is what they did. Every play, two Cardinals shadowed AJ. He could usually outrun or juke one, but the other was right there to either break up the catch or limit yards afterward. On occasion, AJ could shake both. This never seemed to happen quickly enough, however.

While two Cardinals shadowed Reese, one or two others had responsibility for chasing down Mason. As a result, the Mustang quarterback was under duress all day. Although he tried to find an opening to get the football to his favorite target—which seldom happened—he had to scramble to get a pass off to his second, third or even fourth option. As such, his throws were hurried, thrown across his body or off the wrong foot. While he avoided being sacked—all but three times—he usually got hit, and his passes were seldom on target.

With good reason, the Blacklick coaching staff directed Mason Jackson to ignore the primary target—AJ Reese—on all plays going into the final drive. They believed it was their only hope to stage a comeback.

Before the quarterback could respond and draw a heavy sigh, AJ snapped, "We don't have time to debate. And we don't have time to waste plays. Throw me the ball. Trust me."

The quarterback said nothing. He shook his head slowly, however, indicating that he would not comply with AJ's command. He then launched into command mode: "Rainbow Triple. Flag, slant, buttonhook. Get that flag. Slant. Buttonhook. Flag, slant, buttonhook. On two ... Two—don't jump." He paused for a moment, then finished with a hearty, "Ready, break," as the 10 other players joined in.

As the huddle broke and team members scurried to the line of scrimmage, Mason caught AJ's attention and mouthed the word "Sorry" to him. AJ mouthed back, "Throw to me." Mason simply averted his eyes, putting an end to the issue.

The Blacklick offense lined up in a similar manner to how it did all game. Mooney match it, as it had—two players poised to cover AJ Reese and a couple others keyed in on Mason Jackson. As such, the play started like most any other—cadence, hut-hut and then chaos. While Mustang receivers streamed down field like any other play, this time Mason Jackson did not even look in the direction of the receiver who has helped him generate career stats this season.

Nevertheless, AJ took off on the snap of the football down the right side of the field as if he were the primary receiver. He sprinted and stopped, cut left and then right, and juked and jived. Whenever he created the slightest separation from his defenders, he waved a hand high in the air as he ran and shouted, "Hey." He hoped his quarterback would see him.

Mason Jackson did not. He was too busy looking to the left, as three other Mustang receivers scrambled down the field according to their prescribed routes. And as if that weren't enough, he maintained partial focus on the scheming defenders who had harassed him all day. Mason pumped his arm once, contemplating throwing the football. Then a second time. The receivers were not getting open. Nothing.

As his protection began breaking down, Mason could feel a sense of panic. The moment he spotted the smallest of openings between the pushing and shoving of offensive and defensive players, he tucked the football and began to run. The moment he did, however, the defenders' mode switched from pass rush and coverage to all-out pursuit.

Mason did not make it far. He got beyond the line of scrimmage, but not much further. Officially, he gained a yard. That was generous, however. The worst part was that Mooney gang-tackled him inbounds, and thus the game clock continued to wind down—45, 44, 43.

Mustang players pulled their quarterback from the mound of red and gold jerseys. Mooney was in no hurry. Time was on their side—42, 41, 40.

Blacklick, however, needed every second. They scurried to the line of scrimmage. Despite all of this, time still slipped away—39, 38, 37.

When all 11 offensive players were back, lined up and set, Mason signaled to the center to snap the football. With one quick motion, he stepped back and used second down to slam the ball against the ground. While he worked out some frustration, his primary intent was stopping the clock—now frozen at 33.

Chapter 4

"Well, that was useful," No. 29 sarcastically yelled as the team made their way back to the huddle. As the huddle took form, he quickly changed tone. "Mason, get me the ball. I can get open. I have been open. Get me the ball."

"I hear you, AJ," Mason responded with a resigned tone. "Coach thinks our best chance is away from you. Not saying I agree, but it ain't my call."

As the players finalized their positions in the huddle, Mason Jackson looked toward his coach, who was signaling in a play from the sideline. The quarterback nodded once to indicate he had it, then turned to address the huddled offense.

Before he could, AJ said, "To hell with Coach. To hell with the play. Throw me the ball."

"AJ," Tommy Frank, a lineman, jumped in. "This is not about you and your stats. This is about us—us getting a touchdown." Other mumbled words followed in support of the lineman.

"Shut up!" AJ responded. "I am not talking to you, Tommy." But then he continued in rebuttal to everyone, "And I am not trying to pad stats ... I am just trying to win."

Before the debate could continue, Mason Jackson took charge of the huddle. "Okay, okay, okay. Enough already. Coach sees something. We have to go with it. Same play—Rainbow Triple. This time slant, flag, buttonhook. Note the slight change: slant, flag, buttonhook. This time on one—one."

"Why don't we just wave a white flag?" AJ quietly said under his breath. "We are abandoning something that's worked all season for something that isn't tested."

"Shut up, would you?" a stray voice from the huddle muttered.

"Go with it, AJ," Mason fired out, looking directly into his receiver's eyes. "Just go with it."

"Whatever," AJ mumbled under his breath and shook his head as he looked away.

The quarterback then refocused on the entire huddle. "Again, Rainbow Triple. Slant, err,"—in his anger, he lost his train of thought.

"Flag, buttonhook," a litany of other players chimed in.

"Yes, flag, buttonhook ... on one. Ready ... break," Mason finished.

As the huddle broke, the players quickly reassembled at their appointed positions. When AJ got back out to the far right, he got in position—one foot on the line of scrimmage and the other bent behind it, as if to prepare to take off on a sprint. He looked up at the two Cardinals poised to cover him and started in, "Ready to try to keep up again?"

Before another word could be said, Mason Jackson had worked through the offensive cadence and set the play into motion, starting the clock—33, 32.

AJ took off, as he had done the entire season. He made it his personal mission to get separation and make himself an offensive target. It seemed that, unlike much of the rest of the season, it was for nothing. AJ's quarterback did not even look in his direction, even when there were moments when he had a step or two on his dual defenders. Nevertheless, he continued to work and occasionally shouted, "Mason," as he waved a hand in the air.

Jackson had his orders and stuck to them. The play called for him to not necessarily look for the best option, but rather check receivers in sequence. He checked the receiver running the slant route. Nothing. He was well guarded and in heavy traffic.

He quickly assessed his situation. Mason knew he could not be sacked, as it was third down—that would be devastating. The offensive line and blocking back were holding out the onslaught of rushers.

Mason then checked on the flag receiver. That situation was worse than nothing. His defender had knocked the receiver to the ground just past the line of scrimmage. The receiver stumbled to his feet but had trouble regaining footing and momentum. For all intents and purposes, he was out of the play.

The line continued to hold the rushing defenders at bay. Mason quickly looked to his buttonhook receiver. He had cleanly made it off the line and had run 30 yards downfield along the left sideline. The entire sprint, however, the receiver had a defender matching his movement step for step. Effectively, the receiver was covered.

At approximately the 35-yard line, the receiver abruptly stopped, leaving the Mooney defender to overrun him. The Blacklick receiver then quickly whipped his body around and took two steps seemingly in the wrong direction. For a moment, he was wide open.

Mason Jackson took advantage of the opportunity and rifled a hard pass on target. The receiver kept his eyes on the ball, careful to catch it before turning toward the sideline and attempting to run downfield. While the route, pass and reception were successful, the yards after the catch were limited.

Before the ball arrived, the defender had recovered. He was back in pursuit, wrapping his arms around the receiver before he could get two steps downfield. While the Mooney defender was successful in preventing significant yards after the catch, he failed to prevent the receiver from reaching to get the football out of bounds, stopping the clock at 25.

Both teams took a collective gasp of air—but for entirely different reasons. The Cardinals were relieved to have prevented significant gain, especially considering the time remaining. Given that the game had evolved into a defensive struggle, 33 yards was an almost insurmountable distance.

The Mustangs were relieved because they had gained enough yards for a first down. Had the pass been incomplete, they would have been facing a dire fourth-down situation. With the time remaining, they could manage to run a couple more plays.

Despite the stoppage, Jackson hustled his team back to the huddle to keep the pace.

Most everyone on the Mustang offense hustled. AJ Reese meandered. While he remained silent, his demeanor communicated his frustration.

Mason called the next play. Again, it was clear the coaches were not going into the double coverage that AJ drew. Though he wanted to do otherwise, AJ remained relatively quiet. He mumbled under his breath words of disdain toward his coaches. While he was not disruptive, he was loud enough that everyone in the huddle could hear him. No one responded.

The Blacklick offense quickly broke the huddle and assembled on the line of scrimmage. Keeping with the rhythm of the moment, Mason rapidly went through his cadence and set the play in motion, starting the clock—25, 24. Almost in a panic, he took three steps back and rifled the football, aiming it in the direction of the first receiver to get open. While the pass was on target and caught in tight coverage, the receiver was only five yards downfield. Upon catching the ball, the receiver immediately stepped out of bounds.

The clock was stopped with 19 seconds, but the Mustangs were effectively no closer to scoring. As Mason beckoned players to race back to the huddle, AJ could not contain himself.

"I am no math whiz, but at this rate we'll score two or three minutes after this game is over," he said, emphasizing his sarcasm with an uncomfortable chuckle. "Mason, this ain't working. We have got to take charge of this. And now."

Jackson said nothing. He was focused on the play sent in by the coaches.

"Mason," AJ attempted to get the quarterback's attention. "Mason."

It did not work. Mason called the play and broke the huddle. Within seconds, Mustang players were scurrying to their appointed place on the field. AJ Reese, however, moved at half speed. It was clear that his role was now simply to misdirect the two Cardinal defenders covering him away from the real action.

When the ball was snapped, AJ sprinted forward for about 10 yards and made a hard cut to the outside left toward the sideline. Essentially, he was open. At this point, however, he did not want the ball. That would have been a complete waste. Rather, he could do nothing but watch the intended plan unfold.

When the ball was snapped, Mason dropped back into the pocket and took a deep breath. He knew he had panicked on the last play, and that had cost the team in terms of lost time and potential. He did not intend for it to happen again. He hovered five yards from the line of scrimmage and surveyed the field as four receivers raced to spots downfield.

Receivers were headed toward the end zone from various angles. One receiver had gone down the right sideline and then, at the 10-yard line, turned in, angling across the middle. As he neared the center of the field, he was crossing into the end zone. At that moment, he had half a step on the defender.

Jackson seized on the opportunity and darted the ball toward his receiver. He threw it with the right touch. The football could not have had a better spiral or placement.

As the football sailed toward the receiver, there was a collective gasp heard around the stadium. Blacklick players and fans took a breath with anticipated elation. The Mooney faithful inhaled deeply in hopes of one small miracle.

That miracle was answered. The Mustang receiver took his eye off the ball for a split second. It was just long enough, however, for it to slip through his fingertips, hit his facemask and ricochet to the green turf.

The Mooney following cried out in jubilation. Blacklick matched it with sounds of frustration and lost opportunity. While the game was not quite over, it was slipping away quickly. There were only seven seconds left on the clock. Time for only one play.

Chapter 5

"Run that play again," the head coach told Mason Jackson. The Blacklick coaching staff had motioned their quarterback to come to the sideline to some quick instructions. Mason then raced back to the huddle and made the play call once. He started to repeat himself when he was abruptly interrupted.

"What? Are you kidding me?" AJ Reese interjected. "This is crazy."

"AJ, this is what Coach called. He is the coach, you know." Mason's words lacked conviction. Nevertheless, he further reasoned, as if he were trying to convince himself, "He sees something."

"Mason, throw me the ball. I will get open. I will catch the pass. I will get us in the end zone." AJ spoke calmly and confidently, sensing an opportunity to convince his quarterback. "I have not let you down all season."

"AJ, I can't," Mason sheepishly responded. "Coach ..."

"Yes, you can," AJ blurted out before Mason could finish. Silence hung in the air.

Sensing that the debate was cutting into the time they needed to get to the line and run the play, Mason defiantly took a stand. "AJ, I can't, and that is it." The quarterback then proceeded to call the same play they had previously run and broke the huddle.

AJ, however, was not done with the issue. As the huddle broke and players dispersed, he held his position. "Mason," he semi-shouted. When he had his quarterback's attention, he grabbed him by the facemask and said, "I am not going to say it again. You know."

Mason grabbed his receiver's facemask in return and pulled it close. AJ pulled back tighter. In a defiant tone, Mason carefully choked out a single word: "Blueberry."

AJ eased up on his tugging, let go of his quarterback's facemask and inquired, "Blueberry?"

"Blueberry," Mason quietly confirmed as he let go of AJ's facemask and moved to take his position behind center.

AJ slowly meandered to the outside left, toward his position. As he did, his head was down, and he continued to mutter slurs against the game plan. As he approached the line of scrimmage, he enunciated his disdain aloud to those on the opposition set to cover him. "This is such crap. You guys did it. You shut me down. They've cut me out of the game plan."

The Mooney Cardinal defenders did not know how to respond. They ignored AJ's banter and prepared to do what they had been doing all day—shut down AJ Reese.

AJ got himself halfheartedly set into a stance to go out for a pass. Nevertheless, he continued, "What's the point? We might as well phone this one in. Why waste the energy?" He paused for a moment, then abruptly turned right and began walking. "Screw it. I quit. Congratulations, boys." Walking away, he undid one of the four snaps securing his chin strap in place. His demeanor clearly indicated that he was officially taking the play off.

As AJ walked away, the two Mooney defenders dumbfoundedly looked at one another. This was a contingency for which they had not prepared. In a natural reaction, they stepped down their readiness a tad. They could not help but chuckle in uncertainty and astonishment.

Meanwhile, Mason had gotten the team set and started through the cadence. Midway through, however, he stopped and started to audible a change of play.

As he did, the Blacklick coaches became demonstratively agitated on the sideline, jumping up and down, waving their arms, trying to get the attention of Mason Jackson. The head coach began screaming, "No, no, no." What was happening was not part of what they intended. They were, however, powerless to stop it.

Players on the field were not agitated, but rather perplexed. While it was not their place to question, they could not help but wonder what was happening. Nevertheless, they listened carefully to the change of plan and made a mental note of their adjusted responsibilities.

At the defined moment, Mason signaled for the football to be snapped—7, 6.

The Blacklick Mustangs had dozens of players on the sidelines, another 11 on the field, and a whole slew of coaches, trainers and statisticians. Of all those people, only two—Mason Jackson and AJ Reese—had any idea what was about to happen.

Chapter 6

"Fans, it appears that the game is coming down to this one play," the radio commentator shared.

In a tightly contested state championship game, it's a shame that any team must lose. At this point, each team has navigated a variety of potential threats across a long football season.

First, a team needs to be fortunate enough to minimize the impact of injuries. Football is not just a contact sport—it's a collision sport. Injuries are going to happen. You must hope they don't happen to key players or deplete the team's depth at any particular position.

Beyond injuries, it's just a matter of keeping the team healthy. Football is a long season. It starts midway through summer and continues well into the fall. Just as young bodies are getting worn down by the continual grind of practices and games, the football season collides with cold and flu season. One sneeze or cough can quickly work through an entire team—and that could prove disastrous depending on the opponent.

High school football coaches also need to contend with the antics of teenage boys. The team staff and athletic administration need to be on guard for players who might not think about the consequences of a particular action—or know but act anyway.

Beyond injuries, illness and off-field issues, there is the season itself. Unlike many other team sports, in Ohio high school football, not every team makes the playoffs. There are seven divisions—Division I for the largest schools and Division VII for the smallest.

Each division has about 120 schools, which are divided into four regions. Only eight teams from each region make the playoffs—32 total. So, only about 25% of all teams make the playoffs.

As a result, competition to get into the playoffs is fierce in and of itself. Which teams the OHSAA selects is determined by a point system, with each team earning points based on their wins and losses, as well as the record of the teams they've played. So, accumulating wins is important—but wins against winning teams are paramount.

But getting into the playoffs is just the start of the state championship journey. Starting with 32 teams means that it takes four wins to make it to the championship game. And with each victory, the competition gets more difficult. The margin of error becomes smaller.

And should a team get beyond all of that, it is then pitted against another team that has run that same gauntlet and is arguably one of the two best teams in the whole state in that division. It's unfortunate that one team must lose. But that's the entire notion of the word "champion"—only one team can be it.

Often, the difference between being a football champion and being the team left wondering "what if" hinges on one small moment, on one play of an entire game.

Chapter 7

The Mooney defenders were perplexed by AJ's demeanor. Throughout the game, they seemed to have taken Blacklick's star receiver out of the game. Slowly, they appeared to have drained the energy from AJ. But it was stunning that he would just give up altogether—especially on the last play of the game.

Nevertheless, that is what AJ's body language indicated, as he still seemed to be meandering toward his own bench—head down, shoulders slumped.

That all changed in an instant. When Mason Jackson gave the signal for the center to snap him the ball, AJ immediately planted hard on his right foot, turned abruptly left, and began sprinting across the middle of the field. The ruse gave him a head start, as his defenders scrambled to recover.

No. 12's mid-cadence change sent the other Blacklick receivers on shallow routes or behind the line of scrimmage. This effectively took their defenders out of the plan. AJ was wide open in the middle of the field at the 15-yard line.

Mason Jackson wasted no time in taking advantage of the situation. He set his feet and carefully lobbed the football ahead of AJ's path.

Blueberry was a code word between AJ and Mason. It indicated they were ignoring the official play call. Instead, AJ would operate in a schoolyard fashion—go out for a pass and, however or wherever, get open. Mason would then throw him the football.

The scheme started merely as a teenage lark that Tommy Frank, one of the linemen, came up with: "Wouldn't it be crazy if everyone thought that ... and we did this instead?" AJ, Mason and a few others had great fun, more or less fantasizing about pulling off the stunt. Those musings evolved into, "We should try that sometime." Blueberry was just a silly name they attached to the plan. It was the first word that came to mind—teenage boys being silly.

As much as they talked and joked about running a Blueberry, they had only dared do it once before. It was in the waning minutes of a game. It resulted in inquiries from offensive coaches along the lines of, "What happened? We called a running play." The quarterback-receiver combination of Reese and Jackson played off their deviousness as a misunderstanding in the huddle. Everyone laughed it off with a hearty chuckle, especially since it resulted in a 49-yard touchdown pass that only further lopsided a victory.

Calling an audible was not officially part of the Blueberry plan, but then by definition, everything about it was unofficial. Mason changed the original play call at the line on his own. It was a whim he acted on to simply clear defenders from downfield.

Nevertheless, he knew AJ was right—the coaches didn't really have a feel for the game like they did. Once he audibled, however, Mason knew he was beyond the point of no return.

AJ turned his body back toward the line, where offensive and defensive linemen were smashing into one another. Almost on cue, the football came floating over that commotion. Essentially alone on that part of the field, he intently focused on watching the football into his hands. AJ firmly grabbed it with both hands and then cautiously secured it to his side.

Once AJ had the football secured, tucked into his left side, he turned up field. Several defenders pursued from various angles off to the side and behind. None of them was a threat.

There were, however, two defenders between him and the end zone. It was their responsibility to freely roam downfield as the last line of defense and to guard against trickery and shenanigans such as this. Shoulder to shoulder, they confidently closed the distance between themselves and the approaching receiver. Together, they had the angles and the advantage.

As the defenders closed in, AJ lowered his right shoulder and accelerated toward the left inside corner of the end zone.

As he did, the clock continued—3, 2, 1. The game was effectively over. All that was left to decide was who would win. Victory depended on one of two mutually exclusive events: either a tackle or a touchdown. Both couldn't happen.

AJ continued to angle left, signaling that he intended to score going that way. He leaned forward and pushed off the balls of his feet. He was single-minded.

The Mooney defenders adjusted their angles. They pushed forward and prepared to create a collision. The moment the defenders committed, AJ planted his right foot and ...

Chapter 8

"Go, AJ!" Mason Jackson shouted to his main receiver. They both needed this to work.

Championships can hinge on one play. But most people at the contest—fans, coaches, staff, sideline players, and even many of those on the field—are helpless as to the outcome. They only get to bear witness as the situation unfolds.

AJ Reese, however, was living the moment. But he wasn't thinking. He didn't need to. He had played football for years. That translated into dozens of games, hundreds of practices, workouts and times just messing around with friends—and countless moments of just thinking about football and all that went into it.

All of that led to dozens and dozens of individual scenarios and maneuvers where reactions and muscle memory were completely set. As the Mooney defenders committed, AJ planted his right foot and pivoted hard to the left, spinning around and reversing direction in a single motion.

The Mooney defenders knew in an instant that they had bitten on a fake. They had been operating on muscle memory too—but it failed them. They tried to redirect their energies. In so doing, they got tangled with one another. Nevertheless, they desperately reached out toward AJ. They grasped for and clung to his jersey, which was now moving away from them.

AJ spun three-quarters of a turn, firmly planting on his left foot. He felt hands tugging on his jersey. The grasp was not firm, but it hastened his forward progress, jerking his shoulder back slightly. He quickly shifted the football from his left to his right hand, relying again on muscle memory to secure it.

As he did, AJ turned his torso slightly left, back toward the defenders who were hoping to parlay their tenuous grasp into something more. Before they could, however, AJ used his left hand to quickly brush away their hold. He was free. AJ casually jogged into the end zone.

The game was over. Blacklick was not going to attempt an extra point. There was no need. The Mustangs had come from behind to win, securing a state championship.

Chapter 9

"There you have it—the Blacklick Mustangs are your Ohio Division IV high school football champions," the radio commentator stated before going to commercial break.

In any game, there is a fixed amount of energy. It ebbs and flows—up and down, back and forth—between teams and fan bases as the game plays out.

As AJ crossed the goal line, the energy held by the Mooney players and faithful rushed out, creating a sense of gloom and depression. In that instance, that very energy rolled over to the Blacklick side, creating an explosion of jubilation.

Fans roared with excitement. Coaches congratulated one another with hugs and high-fives. Sideline players rushed onto the field, heading toward the end zone to join AJ.

Emotions were high. The Blacklick team celebrated wildly. There was a main scrum of players on the ground. Others completed choreographed mini-celebrations, and a few just did their own thing—shouting, pumping fists, throwing arms in the air.

As these minutes wore on, the Mooney players sauntered to their sideline—dejected, dumbfounded. They were left to wonder how their command of the game had fallen apart. Their parents and fans applauded their effort, even though they fell short of their goal.

Eventually, the respective consoling and celebrating settled enough. The coaches, school administrators and teams made their way to midfield.

There, almost magically, a couple of tables appeared. Each had a tablecloth with the Ohio High School Athletic Association insignia on it—OHSAA. Each was covered with a trophy and a litany of individual awards—medals, each with a red, white and blue neck ribbon. One trophy was slightly larger than the other. One set of medals was gold, the other silver.

Once the teams were sufficiently gathered, the OHSAA football commissioner produced a microphone that was tied into the stadium public address system. He clicked it on, endured a few seconds of loud crackles and annoying feedback sounds, and then launched into a litany of polite pleasantries.

He thanked everyone for attending, being great fans, and demonstrating civility and sportsmanship. He remarked on the epic contest everyone had just witnessed and congratulated both teams. He then introduced the OHSAA football commissioner.

As he continued, he gave more details about each team— their coaching staffs, schools and respective journeys. After all, neither team just showed up in Canton, Ohio, for a game in early December. He started quickly with the champion Blacklick Mustangs, then segued to the Mooney Cardinals.

While the game was a story unto itself, so was the season. This gave the commissioner much to share about the runner-up. After working through that, he called forward the Mooney head coach and athletic director. The commissioner added a few additional kind words, then awarded the athletic director the runner-up trophy. The Mooney team and fans clapped and cheered with pride; the Blacklick faithful clapped respectfully.

Following that, the public address announcer took over. He carefully pronounced the name of every young man on the Mooney team. As he did, each player stepped forward to his athletic director and had a silver medal placed around his neck.

He then shook the hand of the commissioner and went down the line, receiving a conciliatory hug from the head coach and each of the various assistant coaches.

Just when it felt as if the whole ceremony had stalled, the football commissioner again took charge with his handheld microphone. He shared from his notes about Blacklick's season and touched on the short but successful history of the Mustang football program. At both appropriate and inconvenient times, the Blacklick fan base roared to life.

Patiently, the commissioner persisted—smiling, laughing. It was a spirited time. They had earned it, so he let it play out. When his monologue was done, he called Head Coach Pete Fisher. The team and fans cheered, interrupting the ceremony again. When it subsided, the commissioner simply said, "Athletic Director Gary Studer." Everyone applauded more.

As that commotion stirred the atmosphere, Coach Fisher and Studer quickly gave one another a manly embrace. While Fisher worked for Studer, it was clear they were friends. Their relationship had gone back to before Blacklick High School was even a thought.

Again, things settled. Not another word was spoken by the commissioner at this point. The ceremony simply moved forward according to script. However, rather than awarding the championship trophy, the public address announcer began introducing each Mustang team member.

One by one, each player came forward and allowed Athletic Director Studer to place a championship gold medal around his neck. Cheers broke out for each. The fans gave heightened applause for various players—seniors, as well as Mason Jackson, AJ Reese, Tommy Frank and a few other standouts.

With a medal proudly around their necks, the players moved on to shake hands and hug the litany of assistants who had stepped forward to congratulate them.

When all medals were awarded, the Blacklick players and fans cheered loudly. But it wasn't over. The commissioner let the mood settle a bit, added a few additional kind words, then awarded Athletic Director Studer the Division IV state championship trophy.

Then, without a word, Studer motioned over Coach Fisher. Again, they quickly gave one another a manly embrace as best they could. Then, together, they held the massive trophy and hoisted it into the air. They smiled broadly. The players and fans cheered even louder.

Chapter 10

"Team let's quickly confer," Coach Fisher suggested.

When the award ceremony was over, he huddled his dozens of players near midfield. Next to him was Athletic Director Studer. Each had a few words of praise and congratulations.

The players had a pensive energy. They could hardly contain themselves. The moment Fisher and Studer were done, they raced to the area behind their bench. Just up from there, their friends and classmates were waiting in the stands.

The young faction of players and students erupted even more. Players reached up to touch or hand-slap their peer fan base, who were reaching down over the railing that kept them in the stands. Some players hoisted up teammates so they could get into group phone selfies with friends. The mood couldn't have been more celebratory.

As the players and students carried on, Athletic Director Studer, Coach Fisher and the remainder of the coaching staff gathered closer to where the team had been moments earlier.

While Fisher was the head coach of the football team, Studer was the alpha coach. He addressed the staff and congratulated them on the overall great season and championship.

Studer also commended them for the creativity of the winning play. They awkwardly accepted the accolades. After all, the result was positive, and the season was over. There was little point in dissecting how it unfolded.

The lights were still on at Hall of Fame Stadium, and the Division IV championship final outcome—16-14—was still on the scoreboard. Yet the athletic director was already looking ahead to next season: who they had returning, who they needed to develop, and who they might attract into the school district (or who was already there but needed to be drawn away from one of the area Catholic schools—St. Francis DeSales, Bishop Hartley or St. Charles).

For some coaches, this seemed a little odd. For Fisher, he had come to expect it. He had answered to Studer for years. Fisher wasn't totally comfortable with the tactics, but he loved to win. And win, they did.

For the Studer-Fisher duo, this was not their first state football championship. They had coached together at two other high schools around the state. Like hired guns, they had been sought after to win championships.

The newly formed board for the Jefferson Township School District recruited Studer to work his magic on the Blacklick Mustangs. After all, the new district had new, state-of-the-art everything. Why not do the same with its football coach? Fisher was part of the package.

While this was not the first championship in football at Blacklick, it had been a few years. And for such a young high school, it felt like an eternity.

They had a formula—source solid talent and develop it. That was easy in years one and two. The Jefferson Township district had broken away from the massive Gahanna-Jefferson district. The seniors and juniors who lived in the township had the choice to stay at Gahanna Lincoln High School or come to Blacklick High.

For football players, the choice was easy: new facilities, a much-heralded coach, a chance to dominate at the Division IV level. They tore through the competition, going undefeated in two seasons. In year three, they suffered a loss midseason. It felt like the world had ended. For Studer, it was merely a speed bump he could use to inspire a "three-peat."

Year four, things got a little more challenging. The allure of Blacklick High was not as strong. The facilities were no longer new. And there were demands from other interests. Not everyone can be a star on the football team. In fact, most people can't. They wanted—and deserved—something else.

But in any system or organization, there are only so many resources. And those resources create a zero-sum game. One faction's gain results in a loss for another. Thus, the growing popularity of other sports—such as soccer, volleyball and lacrosse—pulled money and players from football. And to avoid multiple, overlapping and competing fundraisers, the then-athletic director mandated that the net proceeds of all athletic fundraising be directed to the general athletic fund.

The football program was not dying. Far from it. But Studer had limits on what he could do. And he didn't like limits. He didn't like rules that stood in the way of his football ambitions.

This was nothing new. He'd faced it a couple of times before. Each time, he found a new school and moved on. But this was different. Jefferson Township was different. It had a rural feel, but it was connected to Columbus, Ohio—a large, growing, white-collar city. He liked both of those things. He wasn't planning to move on.

While he wasn't planning to move on, he wasn't planning to simply accept the situation as is, either. So, he began to subtly put pressure on the athletic director—creating challenges, both direct and indirect. Fanning the flames of other athletic department issues, even if they had no relationship to football.

Stirring up anger within the community over anything and everything.

Within 18 months, the athletic director moved on to another opportunity—same job, different school, a little less money and a lot more peace. Studer then jumped at the chance to become the next athletic director and turned the day-to-day football operations over to Fisher.

As athletic director, he was creative, crafty and arguably underhanded in improving the football situation. For starters, he quickly allowed for a football-only booster club—which immediately gathered substantial funds that did not need to be shared. Studer also shifted the existing budget toward football whenever possible. Additionally, he pushed the boundary of Title IX, which requires equal spending between girls' and boys' programs.

Again, in any system or organization, limited resources create a zero-sum game. And football started to win that game—again and again. While people were upset, it was hard for those outcries to be louder than the cheers associated with football dominance. It took only two seasons to bring a football championship trophy back to Blacklick High. And if that came at the expense of other kids and sports, to Studer, that was an expense worth making.

And there seemed to be nothing that could stop it.

Chapter 11

"Where are some scissors?" AJ inquired of the lone student trainer left on the field.

When the Blacklick players raced to the area behind their bench to celebrate with friends and classmates, they didn't go around the bench. They went over and through it, creating a chaotic mess of water bottles, balls and equipment. This included makeshift toolboxes that athletic trainers used to cart around gauze, tape and other quasi-medical supplies.

The official team trainer—Nathan Rogers—was not around. He was off in the locker room, preparing to tend to the injuries and pains associated with a hard-fought football game. Left to deal with the mess, however, were a small core of student managers and assistant athletic trainer Shea Brooks.

She wasn't really an assistant athletic trainer. The title was strictly unofficial. Officially, she was just a team manager. However, her intelligence and willingness to learn made her far too useful. So, Nathan Rogers dubbed her his assistant and protected her from having to fold towels and other menial tasks. Instead, he kept her busy with related athletic training activities.

Rogers taught her to tape ankles, wrists and other body parts. He taught her about various treatments for strains and contusions. He took advantage of the expanded football budget and had the team send her to courses and certifications related to CPR, concussions and mental health.

For an outside observer, Shea Brooks—only a junior—was fast-tracking to become an athletic trainer one day. Though, her quiet, internal aspirations were much bigger—perhaps medical school.

As the lone female around the team, she was not one of the boys. But she was far from being one of the girls, either. When she was only 3, her mother walked out of the family and moved away. No explanation was given. And the situation was never discussed. This left Shea to be raised by her father.

He was a tenured astronomy professor who was engrossed in his research and little else—including appearance. He resembled more of a mad scientist than an academic type.

This was the example that Shea grew up with. She wore thick, out-of-style glasses. She'd simply had lenses added to frames her father no longer used.

Those glasses worked to her advantage, however, as from a distance the large frames hid her bushy eyebrows. But up close, one could see her eyebrows were nearly one.

Her clothes were functional, but she made no attempt to be fashionable. Similarly, makeup was not part of her routine. And even if it was, she wouldn't have known what to do.

Her hair was long, sandy brown and in a style best described as "bed head." As a result, she often wore it pulled back in a ponytail.

She wasn't a complete abomination when it came to personal hygiene. She showered daily but didn't get caught up in any frilly shampoos or conditioners. And she didn't shave her legs—or any of that.

As such, she didn't fit in. But she was not a threat to anyone. So to her face, she was largely left alone. She busily kept busy. Behind her back, however, she was mocked and snickered at as "Shea-squatch."

As no one is ever completely insulated from this sort of ridicule, she somewhat knew. Though she was never fully aware of the extent of the scorn. But even if she were, she would not have known what to do about it. What she was, was all she knew. There had never really been a feminine role model in her life.

So it didn't bother her to be a girl among a bunch of rambunctious football players. Besides, she was interested in science. And being involved as a quasi-athletic trainer—where dozens of human bodies were colliding and breaking down— was a great experience.

As the team managers were busy picking up water bottles, footballs and miscellaneous gear, Shea was doing her best to reassemble the athletic training kits that were scattered in the celebratory melee. Tape. Gauze. Iodine. Bandages. Rubs. Sprays. Everything had a place, and she was ensuring that each thing got there.

As she was mindlessly tending to that task, a lone, barefoot football player came walking out to the sideline.

Ever impatient, AJ was tired of waiting for Mr. Rogers to make it around to all the players who needed attention. "Surely, a state championship football team has more than one pair of scissors," he remarked with a giggle.

He caught Shea's attention, and she jumped to her feet. "They're over here. In this kit." She knew exactly where she'd put the various cutting implements. She raced over, whipped open the kit and produced a pair of scissors specifically designed to cut athletic tape off body parts.

"Great. Let me get this stuff off my ankles." AJ reached for the scissors.

But before he could get them, Shea pulled them back. "I can do it." She was on her knees by the kit, inviting him to give her a foot so she could cut the tape around his ankles.

"Okay," AJ complied. He would have had Mr. Rogers do the same if he'd had the patience. He gently stepped his left foot on her right thigh.

AJ stood there still in his game pants. His shoulder pads were off, but he'd put his No. 29 jersey back on to provide some protection from the early December evening chill. Nevertheless, his body was still hot, steaming into the air.

As Shea busied herself cutting the tape on AJ's left ankle, she finished and pushed it away. Without a word, she indicated that she would now deal with the right ankle.

AJ dropped his left foot, repositioned and put his right foot on her left thigh. Shea quickly got to work.

Moments later, she remarked, "All set," as she balled up the cut tape, intending to discard it. "Anything else?" she inquired, looking to further serve.

AJ indicated, "Nope. But thanks." Shea then quickly put the scissors back in the appropriate kit and shackled the toolbox shut.

Then AJ asked, "Are you done with that?" He motioned to the cutting-implement kit.

"Yes," Shea replied, not knowing why he was asking.

AJ then bent down and picked it up. "How about this one?" He pointed to a second, similarly looking toolbox. Shea nodded yes. AJ bent down and picked it up with his other hand. He then started to walk back toward the locker room.

Shea watched him walk away. She was thankful for the help, but somewhat taken aback that it was happening. She gathered herself and said, loud enough to be heard, "Thank you, AJ."

No. 29 didn't respond. He continued back toward the locker room.

Chapter 12

"Here you go," AJ said aloud to everyone and no one as he ventured back into the locker room and dropped the training kits just inside the door.

As Rogers was still making the rounds, players were in various stages of changing. Many who had not seen any action were back in street clothes and ready to depart. Others were in the shower, washing away the sweat and grime from the game. And a few, like AJ, were in the early stages.

Everyone, however, was reliving aspects of the win—the final touchdown, this play or that. Not surprisingly, they had forgotten about those plays that had less-than-favorable outcomes.

But soon enough, all players were changed, and the locker room cleared. They brought their equipment bags—neatly tethered to their helmets and shoulder pads—to the team bus. Rather than getting on the bus, the players detoured to "the team spread."

After each game, the team families coordinated food and drink for the players and staff. These weren't three-course, sit-down meals. Rather, the spread was a grab-and-go buffet—placed as reasonably close to the team bus as possible—to allow hungry players to refuel after a long game and the hours pregame where they simply had no appetite.

The families ensured that each spread offered somewhat sensible options—sandwiches, pizza or boneless chicken tenders. But there was also a plethora of pure, empty, salty and sugary calories: pretzels, chips, cookies, and the like. Usually, one or two well-meaning parents would bring a few bags of apples or oranges—and often, they'd go home with the same.

Throughout the season, one or two parents coordinated the spread effort by assigning team parents into groups of six to eight families. Each of these clusters was then assigned to a game. That game was the cluster's responsibility—to organize who was bringing what and how it would unfold.

This system ensured that every family—like the team itself—did its part. And this continued throughout the playoffs. With the state championship game, however, the situation was a little different. Win or lose, there were no more games. And almost every family wanted to take part. So, the spread was well provided for from the start.

In addition, most families arrived early to tailgate. And those who could invited others—after all, state championships don't come along every day. Certainly, none of these people wanted to be deemed a mooch, so they brought something to share as well.

The reality, however, was that the "something to share" everyone brought was upwards of three times as much as they could individually consume. Thus, there were tons of leftovers, which all got added to the spread.

Because there was so much, everyone was invited to eat. This welcoming vibe attracted a gracious and celebratory army of people picking over and through the massive feast. This would ensure that, in time, all the food would be gone—except for perhaps a few bags of fruit.

But this sharing of food, coupled with the euphoria of ultimate victory, created a heightened sense of camaraderie. Everyone was in a great mood. They were to the point of being giddy.

And this spurred everyone to share hugs. Families hugged. Friends hugged. People who didn't normally care for one another hugged. Complete strangers hugged.

Hugging was the love language of the moment, as mere handshaking was simply not enough to express feeling.

Chapter 13

"Thank you," AJ reflectively responded as pockets of people—generally holding paper plates of chips and chicken wings—offered congratulations to the newly minted state champions as they moved along the spread.

AJ quickly dumped his mound of equipment under the team bus and turned to enter the crowd. Immediately, he heard, "AJ!" A cheerleader shouted to him, and without another word, she approached and hugged him.

"Awesome game! Congratulations!"

He hugged back, smiling ear to ear, and said, "Thanks."

That was the entirety of the exchange. AJ moved on but was met by a litany of others that played out much the same way. Greetings. Well wishes. Hugs. Repeat. Cheerleaders. Classmates. Other parents. Random fans. Nothing really registered. But it didn't matter. He was happy. Fulfilled. Accomplished. He smiled broadly. Winning and adulation felt great.

Then he encountered someone who broke the monotony.

"AJ! What a game!"

"Thanks, Mom," AJ said as his mother walked up, giving him a hug and kiss on the cheek. AJ hugged her back.

"Seriously, what a game. We're so proud of you." Dr. Samantha Reese hugged him again.

"Thanks," was all AJ could say. What else could he say?

"Go find your dad, AJ! He's so excited. So proud!" Samantha watched AJ glance off into the crowd. But it was obvious he wasn't looking for anyone. He just wanted to avoid the conversation. Sam continued, "I know he doesn't make it to many games, but he was at this one—and what a game to see."

AJ's smile was gone. He just stared off. He had nothing to say.

His mother just looked at him, trying to understand what was going on in his mind. She quickly kissed him on the cheek and calmly remarked, without any sort of pressing tone, "Go find your dad. And get yourself something to eat."

Jonathan Reese didn't get to many games in the last several years—JV or varsity football, basketball, lacrosse, nothing. He was heads down working at Eisenberg & Anders, trying to make a name for himself and make a case that he deserved to be a partner. Plus, he felt a sense of obligation to provide for his family. With two older children working their way through college—and then graduate and professional school—and leaner years leading up to it, he felt as if the money was necessary—actually, vital.

Nevertheless, he knew this win was special. His older son had been on the team when Blacklick High School won its first state championship. That had a similar, but different, feel—similar in that a championship is a championship. Winning at this stage has a distinctive euphoria to it.

The situation was different, however, in that now he didn't really know any of the players. Almost a decade earlier, he knew all the players—names, numbers, nicknames and how they liked their pizza. He felt like he had seen many of the kids grow up, helping coach them in middle school before they headed off to various high schools. With this team, he was only familiar with one player—AJ—and it was arguable whether he even knew him.

And equally different was that he didn't know the other parents. In the current celebration, he couldn't carry much of a conversation, as he didn't know which player was associated with which parent. Jonathan didn't want to be embarrassed saying, "Your son did great," when that son never played—or worse, when the person was a random fan who didn't have a kid on the team.

He found himself tagging along as close to his wife, Sam, as possible. She could then casually whisper to Jonathan as they headed into an encounter: "Their son is Mason Jackson, the quarterback." Or, if that didn't happen, he could pick up clues from the conversation: "John really booted those kickoffs."

But when Sam excused herself to find something other than an overflowing porta-potty, Jonathan was lost. He felt as if he had traveled to a foreign land where he simply could not understand the language.

But he saw a familiar face emerge from an opening in the crowd near the spread tables. He called out, "AJ. AJ." Then louder: "AJ! AJ!"

The human brain is fascinating. In a noisy crowd, it can pick up on familiar sounds. So, AJ heard his name—all four times. And he knew who was calling out, so he pretended not to hear. He knew he couldn't keep that up.

AJ felt a sense of panic. He quickly surmised that he could simply disappear back into the crowd and worry about getting something to eat another time. But before he could, someone tapped him on the shoulder.

"Hey, AJ. Your dad is calling to you."

AJ now felt as if he had to acknowledge his dad. He quickly smiled at the well-meaning parent, muttered a quick thanks and turned to face his dad. While AJ was able to avoid disappearing, the smile on his face did—as he reluctantly walked toward him.

The same was not true for Jonathan. He was beaming from ear to ear, looking at his son. As AJ approached, he raised his right hand and extended three fingers—the little, ring and middle—while holding his index finger and thumb close to his palm.

AJ saw the signal but didn't acknowledge it.

"Hi, Dad." His tone was void of any emotion or energy.

Jonathan sensed the chill in AJ's demeanor. With the big win, he had been hopeful for something different. He was disappointed it didn't come—but he wasn't surprised. His relationship with AJ had become more and more estranged in the last few years.

Nevertheless, Jonathan resisted matching AJ's energy.

"Great game. An amazing game. Wow! You should be excited."

"Yeah. We are." AJ's words lacked conviction. His eyes were down and to the right. It was evident he didn't want to be in this situation.

"Well, congratulations," Jonathan said, extending his hand.

"Yeah. Thanks," AJ barely enunciated. He kept his eyes down and made a feeble attempt to shake his father's hand. His energy was emblematic of someone who had just suffered a disappointing loss.

This led to an awkward silence. Jonathan couldn't think of anything else to say. AJ didn't want to put any effort into a conversation with his father. He just wanted to go—but he wasn't going to be rude.

"Well, thanks for coming to the game," AJ finally said, breaking the silence.

"Sure. Of course. I … uh." Jonathan struggled to find words.

Before he could, AJ interjected, "Well, I've got to go and get something to eat."

"Yeah, you do that. Get something good to eat," Jonathan said, hoping to add value.

AJ didn't acknowledge the words. He kept his head down, turned and walked away.

Jonathan could do nothing but watch his youngest son head toward the spread.

Before AJ arrived, another team dad approached, intending to hug him. AJ enthusiastically smiled and engaged the man with a hug. They exchanged words and each let out a laugh.

Jonathan could not make out what was said. It didn't matter. He simply felt uneasiness and hurt. To mask his feelings, he reached for his phone and began reviewing work emails.

Chapter 14

"Are we going to stay in touch?" Sam asked Jonathan very early on in their relationship.

But eight years ago, their roles had been reversed. During Blacklick High's inaugural season and first state championship run, Sam was missing games due to her low seniority as an ER doctor. She often worked weekends, making game attendance rare. Back then, Jonathan worked at the Ohio Attorney General's Office, a job with lower pay but flexible hours. That allowed him to attend almost everything their older kids—Kelly and Jonathan Jr.—were involved in.

Jonathan and Sam both grew up in Point Place, a small Toledo neighborhood known by locals as "the best place, any place." It had a small-town charm, but they hadn't really known each other growing up. Sam, from a devout Catholic family, went to St. John's and then Central Catholic High School. She pursued medicine, attending Notre Dame and then med school at Case Western.

Jonathan's life was different. His father was mostly absent, and by age 13, all Jonathan received from him were occasional postcards. His mother, with help from her parents, raised him with resolve and pride—so much so she refused to give him his father's last name. He attended public schools, graduating from Woodward High the same year Sam graduated from Central Catholic.

Though both families were Catholic, Jonathan's grandfather joked they were "B-minus Catholics," showing up mostly for Christmas and Easter. But his grandfather's advice stuck: "Use your mind, not your back." After his grandfather's death during his freshman year, Jonathan redoubled his academic focus, eventually earning a spot at Case Western, where he played Division III football and studied psychology. From there, he went to law school at Capital University in Columbus.

Despite their different paths, it was Point Place that eventually brought them together. The summer before Jonathan started at the prestigious Belden & Schmidt law firm, and between Sam's third and fourth years of med school, they both found themselves home, relaxing and reconnecting with old friends.

Their social circles had begun to merge, thanks to mutual friends from college or work. Sailing was the summer pastime in Point Place, and it was at the yacht club that they kept running into each other.

They weren't strangers, but assumptions lingered. Sam had always seen Jonathan as a typical loudmouth Woodward kid, and he assumed she was one of those rigid Catholic schoolgirls. But as they listened to each other talk in the group, those stereotypes faded. She saw he was more thoughtful. He realized she wasn't uptight. They discovered shared experiences: higher education, time at Case Western, and for once, no pressing schedule.

Often, they were the last two left at the Toledo Beach Yacht Club, sitting around the firepit, sipping drinks in near silence. It wasn't flirtation or chatter that deepened their connection—it was comfort.

On Jonathan's last night in town before heading to Columbus, Sam surprised him with a simple question.

"Are we going to stay in touch?"

"Sure. We can," Jonathan replied, unsure of how it sounded.

"That sounds noncommittal. You're just saying that, aren't you?"

"No. I mean it," he said, though it came out defensively.

Sam pulled out a notepad and scribbled down her contact info. "Here. My address and phone number at school."

Jonathan accepted it. "I haven't even set up my phone yet," he admitted.

Sam wasn't sure what to make of his response. "You won't reaching out, will you? Typical."

Jonathan protested. "No, I will. In fact, I bet I reach out before you do."

"What's the bet?" Sam asked.

"You set the stakes," Jonathan fired back.

"Pizza," she replied. "Loser buys."

"Deal," Jonathan said with a smile. They shook on it.

"And I like sausage and pineapple," she teased as she walked to her car.

"Pretty confident, aren't we?" he called after her.

"We'll see," she said over her shoulder.

Jonathan turned back to the fire, heart racing and thoughts swirling. He wasn't sure what to make of the moment—until Sam came running back from the darkness.

Without a word, she kissed him. Long, deep, and certain.

Then just as suddenly, she pulled away, smiled, and sprinted off into the night without a word or a backward glance. Jonathan stood there, stunned—heart thudding—now with a clearer sense of how she felt.

Chapter 15

Med school for Sam was typical: long hours and heavy coursework. The first two years were packed with sciences—anatomy, pharmacology, microbiology—while the third shifted to clinical rotations in hospitals and clinics. Her fourth year would focus on emergency medicine and applying to residency programs.

But for now, she was home in Point Place, enjoying the rare luxury of sleeping in. At 10:37 a.m., she woke up—only to be hit by anxiety over the bold move she'd made the night before. She had kissed Jonathan, rationalizing it as a no-risk gamble. But now she worried—had she come on too strong?

She considered going back to explain herself but couldn't think of the right words. So, she went home, fell asleep, and forgot about it—until the next morning. "Samantha, you messed this up," she muttered to herself.

Heading downstairs, she expected her usual breakfast routine with her parents. Instead, her mom pointed to a bouquet of flowers on the table that "some boy" had dropped off earlier.

Sam stopped in her tracks for a moment. She then stepped forward and broke into a wide smile, as she read the card "You lose. When do I get my pizza? X! Jonathan."

Jonathan had been equally unsure what to do after the kiss. His grandmother advised him to get her flowers and write a note. A friend told him where Sam's parents lived, and Jonathan dropped them off on his way back to Columbus.

Sam didn't care that she lost the bet; she just couldn't stop smiling. She told her parents about Jonathan—yes, he came from modest beginnings, but he clearly had his life on track.

Four days later, Sam returned to Cleveland and found a card from Jonathan waiting in her apartment mail. It said the same thing as the flower card, plus his address and a note: "As soon as I get a phone, I'll call. I promise."

An hour later, the phone rang. It was Jonathan. "I'd like to order a pizza," he joked.

They laughed. Jonathan explained he was calling from a friend's house and reiterated that the pizza had to be paid in person. From that day on, they talked daily. Jonathan visited that weekend—and many weekends after.

By Christmas, he proposed—on one knee, in the snow, near the Toledo Yacht Club firepit where they'd first kissed. They married in May, just after Sam graduated and began her emergency medicine residency at Ohio State.

A month later, Sam learned she was pregnant. Soon came their son Johnny, then daughter Kelly, and—after a six-year pause from family planning—Anthony James "AJ" Reese.

Money was tight. The early years were challenging. But with love and support from both families, Jonathan and Sam were rich in everything that mattered — love and happiness.

Chapter 16

"Did you find AJ?" Sam asked Jonathan. While she made a beeline back toward Jonathan, she did not make it back in time for his conversation with AJ. She was able to witness it, however. Judging by body language, the encounter was not going well, which was typical.

When she finally made it back, Jonathan was head down, engrossed in reviewing a document on his phone. Sam leaned in and kissed him on the cheek. He broke from his work trance, looked up and smiled. Without looking, he clicked the phone screen off and placed the device in his coat pocket.

"I see you talked with AJ," Sam remarked with a dry tone.

"Yyyeeaa," Jonathan replied. "If you wanna call it that."

"Come on. Let's head home." Sam bumped her hips against her husband's, nudging him toward where they had parked their car. She then grabbed him by the wrist and accelerated his momentum in that direction. "I've got to work the graveyard shift tonight … and judging by how you're looking at your phone, you do too."

Jonathan said nothing. He moved ahead of Sam, grabbed her hand and picked up the pace.

As they walked, he shared his thoughts. "I don't get it. My relationship with Johnny and Kelly couldn't have been any better. But with AJ … with AJ … I can't seem to get on the same page. Heck, I'm not even in the same book."

"Honey, that was then and this is now." Sam let those words hang. Then continued, "And between the two, we've encountered circumstances—and opportunities. Everyone does." She went quiet and took a moment to catch her breath, as they were moving along.

When she did, Sam continued. "And with every circumstance or opportunity, we made decisions."

"And your point?" Jonathan inquired.

"Simple, honey," Sam quickly jumped in. "Each decision created changes. And so, things are different now compared to then."

At this point, they were back to the car. Without a word, they loaded blankets in the trunk and got situated in their seats.

As soon as they did, Sam continued. "As a result, you're just not in AJ's life like you were in Johnny's and Kelly's."

Jonathan just listened. He knew that once they got on the road, Sam would be fast asleep. He teased that she suffered from car narcolepsy.

"Honey, the reality is that you were around Johnny and Kelly a lot. That hasn't been the case with AJ. Your career has become like a fourth child for you."

"I know," Jonathan conceded. "I admit it. And I feel bad." He let out a heavy sigh. "But once I make partner—when I make partner—I feel like I can downshift a little bit. Just a little. And then ..." Jonathan searched for words.

Sam interjected, "I understand. But AJ won't be around forever. He needs to know that you love him."

"Sam! Really? I do. I work really hard for us. For this family. That includes AJ." Jonathan made an emotional protest.

Sam continued, "You do. You have. No question. I know that." She allowed a moment to pass to let the emotions settle a bit. "Jonathan, you have done everything possible to provide for and love our kids. Everything—everything but take the time to tell them. Johnny and Kelly didn't need it, however. They didn't need it because they felt it. AJ hasn't, though, because you haven't been around. He just needs something from you. Time. An expression of love. Something."

"I'm just not good with that. Sam, you know that." Jonathan pleaded.

"I do," Sam replied and let out a chuckle. "The record is very clear that you're not good at all. I don't need to be reminded that your first words of affection to me were, 'You lose!'"

Jonathan laughed. Sam had made her point. Her car narcolepsy was setting in. She adjusted her seat back, grabbed the pillow she brought and within minutes was fast asleep. Jonathan was on his own for the duration of the two-hour trip home.

As he drove, he could not help but reflect on his recent conversation with Sam. He certainly faced circumstances. The firm that gave Jonathan his first opportunity—Belden & Schmidt—imploded eight years after he arrived and just before AJ was born. All Jonathan's work into making partner was lost. The salary was gone. And that experience—being part of the failed firm—served as a sort of black mark on Jonathan's résumé for years. From there, the best positions Jonathan could find were with small firms, none of which were very stable.

This resulted in a series of starts and stops to his legal career over several years. Occasionally, when it seemed like they needed it most, a great client would contact Jonathan out of the blue. But it never lasted. And it was never enough to sustain his legal practice.

It seemed like the best days of his professional life were behind him. He was just another lawyer—often as a solo practitioner—trying to eke out a living, billing his time doing anything that a client needed: wills, divorce, personal injury, small claims, whatever. But even in good years, he couldn't earn as much as his first year starting salary with Belden & Schmidt. And that mattered.

At this point, there were three great kids at home and a young doctor wife who had not hit her stride financially yet. And there was lots of other need for money: student loans from years of education, Catholic school for the kids, mortgage, car payments, sports and activities, braces. It felt like there was no end.

Jonathan wasn't happy with his professional life. And worst of all, he could not see a path to change things. But like any husband and father, he was willing to endure. As his grandmother told him years earlier, "Parenting is a team sport." Jonathan rationalized that he simply did not have a glamorous position, but he was doing what he could so the team could win.

Then, almost like magic, he caught a break. Out of seemingly nowhere, Jonathan got a call from the Ohio Attorney General's Office. He was told that the newly elected attorney general—the top legal officer in the state—was putting an emphasis on enforcing business and corporate matters. And when the office was looking to build its team, Jonathan's name kept coming up as a "must-have" attorney.

Jonathan was floored. He thought, "Really? I've done some business work. But I wouldn't say it's been my emphasis."

He dared not share that thought, however. He couldn't see how he could turn the position down. There was stability, no crazy hours and earning near the top of the pay range, as they gave him credit for all his years as an attorney.

Furthermore, he would focus exclusively on business matters as well as be exposed to lots of influential people. Best of all, he would again be part of a team where he mattered, and others cared about his well-being and development.

This would help fill their family's financial holes. But more importantly, with the non-demanding, flexible schedule, Jonathan could help fill the holes at home. As Sam was trying to build her name in and around the emergency room at the Wexner Medical Center, she had unique demands on her time. This opportunity could not have had better timing.

Then shortly after Blacklick High won its first state championship, Johnny's senior year, the fast-paced, high-flying firm of Eisenberg & Anders recruited Jonathan. The firm's largest client, Emerald Medical, was going public and would be using the investment monies to make acquisitions around the world. There would be lots to be done, and the firm felt that Jonathan would be well suited to help.

The jump in salary from the attorney general's office was staggering. And with Johnny heading off to college—and Kelly shortly thereafter—the extra money was hitting at the right time.

Moreover, Jonathan could get back on track to becoming a partner. This would allow him to earn an equity position within a firm. That would help cement the long-term financial security for the family.

But it would come at a cost: time. Long hours. Weekends. And travel—domestic and international. He and Sam would have to figure out a new plan on the home front. Johnny would be off to college, and Kelly, now a senior, could take care of herself. AJ, however, was only 10.

At this point, Sam and Jonathan's respective families were enjoying full-on retirement and could not be called upon to help. They contemplated hiring a nanny or sitter to help when needed. And Sam toyed with sidelining her medical career to allow Jonathan to fully pursue the Eisenberg & Anders opportunity.

Before they needed to decide, however, fate seemed to intervene again. Sam's boss received a position with the State Medical Board. Sam was promoted to fill his position. More important than the bump in pay was a shift in responsibilities. Sam now had more of an administrative role and would have less of a hands-on role in the emergency room.

Additionally, she would have more control over her hours. While she still needed to spend time tending to emergency patients, she could pick and choose hours. Whenever possible, she would grab the overnight shifts, allowing her to sleep while AJ was in school. This made it so that Sam could become the soccer mom—or football mom, or basketball, or lacrosse, or whatever season was up.

Circumstances and opportunities necessitated that Jonathan and Sam make decisions. And those decisions served to change their family dynamics—especially Jonathan's relationship with AJ. It was not the same as Jonathan had with Johnny and Kelly. It was strained at best. And for now, there was nothing that Jonathan could do about it.

Chapter 17

"Let's get on the buses and head home," the various assistant coaches shouted at the team.

After devouring much of the spread and mingling with family and friends, it was time to make the trip back to Jefferson Township, where Blacklick High was located.

Jefferson Township is unincorporated and situated on the eastern edge of Franklin County. To the east is Licking County. In the other directions are Ohio cities: New Albany to the north, Reynoldsburg to the south and Gahanna to the west.

For a time, there was only one high school in the area: Gahanna Lincoln High School, part of the Gahanna-Jefferson School District, established in 1928. Originally, there was just a single building. But as nearby Columbus, Ohio, grew, the Gahanna suburb grew with it—along with neighboring Jefferson Township.

Eventually, Gahanna Lincoln became one of the largest high schools in the state of Ohio. But the area continued to grow. Something needed to happen. Residents and the school district discussed various options.

They could create a second high school. They could create separate campuses in different parts of the area. Each seemed like a simple enough solution. But when the school board and administration started to consider the logistics of busing, class offerings and more, neither option would work.

The best option was to create a separate school district for Jefferson Township. After all, much of the population growth was happening on once-farmland situated along nearby watersheds—Blacklick Creek, Big Walnut Creek and Swisher Creek.

Plus, there was property for schools, as that's where a second high school or additional campus had been contemplated. In fact, local billionaire Robert O'Farrell purchased and donated the acreage at the corner of Havens Road and Dixon Road, which bordered Licking County.

O'Farrell, known as Bobby O, was the founder and CEO of Emerald Medical. He could easily afford and justify the donation, as it ensured that the neighbor to his wooded estate on McOwen Road would be a quiet school campus rather than a tract of homes or condos. This would better ensure that he could shuttle in and out of his residential compound in his metallic Gaelic green Leonardo AW139 helicopter—known as Emerald One—with minimal opposition.

In fact, Bobby O was so committed to the new school district that he donated additional funds to help underwrite certain luxury purchases: technology, playground equipment for the adjacent elementary school, and even athletic funding that, among other things, allowed the district to bring in Gary Studer, the acclaimed high school football coach.

This commitment inspired others in the community—even those without children enrolled in school—to support the district. And why not? The school buildings and education programs would be state of the art, and the sports programs were built to win. All in all, it was good for housing values.

As the Jefferson Township School District was coming into being, this created a decision for Sam and Jonathan. Just as Sam had enjoyed a complete K-12 Catholic experience, so would Johnny, Kelly and AJ.

Johnny and Kelly were enrolled at St. Matthew, a K-8 school affiliated with the Catholic church of the same name on Havens Corner Road. When they graduated from eighth grade, they headed off to Bishop Hartley High School.

But Hartley was not Toledo Central Catholic in lots of ways. Johnny and Kelly were disenchanted with the Catholic education experience. Sam was disappointed, too. Jonathan didn't really have a frame of reference—he just wanted a happy family.

So the decision was made. Johnny would transfer into the first graduating class at Blacklick High, and Kelly would join as a junior. AJ would continue at St. Matthew through eighth grade, then go from being a St. Matthew Mustang to a Blacklick Mustang. Sam and Jonathan would invest the Catholic school tuition savings into the collective college fund.

Chapter 18

The team bus departed Canton, Ohio, and took the quickest route back to the school. Waiting there were fans. Everyone just enjoyed the moment. The hugs continued. The cheers echoed in the night sky. And parents casually talked off to the side.

While Sam and Jonathan made it to the parking lot celebration, they only attended briefly. Sam had to work—officially from midnight to 8 a.m. Jonathan did too, unofficially though—from the time Sam left for work until about 2:30 a.m., when AJ made it home.

Despite getting to bed late, Jonathan was up and hunched over his laptop by 7:40 a.m. He had a strong black cup of coffee and two or three more in reserve in the coffee maker.

Within 40 minutes, Jonathan had reviewed the notes and critiques he had written just a few hours earlier. He poured a second cup of coffee and was ready to start creating due diligence assignments for the small army of Eisenberg & Anders associate attorneys meeting him at noon. Before he could, Sam arrived home.

As she settled in, Jonathan quickly made her a cup of chamomile tea. This allowed her to get some sleep, even though her circadian clock was telling her it was time to get up.

As she sipped from the steamy mug, Jonathan and Sam visited.

"How was work?" Jonathan inquired, as he had hundreds of times before.

"Unusually quiet for a Friday night to early Saturday morning," Sam said after taking a sip. "But then, if I recall from past December weekends, it was probably typical."

Sam let out a yawn. The tea was working.

"What time did AJ make it home?"

"Right around 2:30-ish, I believe."

"Did you two talk?" Sam asked.

"Yes. Yes, we did," Jonathan quickly responded with an upbeat tone.

Sam raised an eyebrow as if to say, *tell me more.*

Jonathan continued, "I asked if he had fun, he responded 'yeah,' and then he walked up to his room."

Sam scrunched her nose.

"Yep, it was pretty heartfelt," Jonathan said, laughing. Then he added, "Well, at least he came home."

Sam remarked, "Yeah. He's a good kid. You two are out of sync, but he's a good kid."

"He is. He's a great kid. Friendly and kind," Jonathan agreed. "That's because he wastes all his cold, nastiness on me," he added with a chuckle.

Sam smiled and politely ignored the humor before she changed the subject again.

"Who did you talk with at the high school last night?"

"No one, Sam. I don't know anyone," Jonathan said with a defensive, embarrassed laugh. "I'm still a little irked you abandoned me," he added, but only half serious.

"Well, I had a couple of interesting conversations," Sam said, lifting the mug to her face and taking a long, satisfying sip of tea.

Jonathan was quiet. He knew she was dying to share.

Sam continued, "Do you know that student trainer, Shea?" Jonathan just listened. "She's really sharp. She's interested in going to med school. I think she's got the smarts, you know? We talked medical, and she held her own. In fact, she rivaled conversations I've had with our interns and residents."

Sam nodded to accentuate her point.

"Hmmm?" Jonathan said, trying to be polite.

"Here's something else. Something we need to keep an eye on," Sam prefaced.

Jonathan perked up with intrigue and leaned in.

"One of the moms shared with me that there's a movement afoot to defeat the tax levy this spring, and it might impact sports next year."

"Sam!" Jonathan jumped in. "Sam, Sam, Sam!" He then let out a heavy sigh. "Come on. You're educated—highly educated. How can you get caught up in these rumors?"

Sam allowed Jonathan to finish and then responded, "I'm not sure it's a rumor. This is real. A few others had heard the same thing."

"Sam, that's the very definition of a rumor," Jonathan said with a laugh.

"Jonathan, it's more than just talk. Apparently, there is someone—some retired guy—who recently moved in just down from the school and is leading the charge on this. In fact, he's posted on social media. I could show you that on my phone. That's real, for sure."

As Sam reached for her phone—fired up to defend herself via social media—Jonathan rolled his eyes. He put his hand on Sam's, which now held her phone, gently pushed it down on the table and patted it.

"Sam, fine. Someone is not happy about the tax levy. And fine, that person posted about it on social media. But where you lose me on this is getting stirred up that it might be a credible threat."

Now Sam just listened. Jonathan tended to be logical—the ying to her emotional yang.

Jonathan continued, "Think about it. The school just won another state championship. The community is high with pride."

Sam rebutted, "Yes, the football program is flying high, but there is little sports pride beyond that. I can't think of any other team that I would call successful at Blacklick."

Sam stopped to think, then continued, "No, not one since about after Kelly graduated."

Jonathan jumped in with a eureka-like response: "Susan Isaacs! She was a state champion. Two years in a row."

"Jonathan, she won individual championships in swimming. Beyond her, there was not much to the team," Sam clarified. "Football is king. Yesterday and last night, everyone there was excited and happy. But beyond football, there is little happiness—and maybe not as much support for the school as you might think. You haven't been around. Blacklick sports are just not the same as when Johnny and Kelly were there."

Jonathan sat and thought. He took it all in, then exhaled and slumped his shoulders.

He quietly shared, "You got me there. I haven't been around, so I can't compare then to now." He paused and thought some more.

Then Jonathan came to life with a thought. He sat up straight and confidently said, "I do know this: We have Gary Studer. As the coach or athletic director, he seems to be able to make magic happen." Jonathan pointed a finger to emphasize his point. "Other than Warren Scott, Studer is the most devious, manipulative, conniving S.O.B. I've ever witnessed."

"I'm not sure any of those things are positives," Sam said. "Certainly, any comparison to Warren Scott isn't."

"Perhaps not," Jonathan conceded. "Unless those things are on your side." Then he let out a confident chuckle and continued, "If it comes down to some unknown, newbie retiree to Jefferson Township and Gary Studer, my money is on the guy who's brought two—now three—state championships to Blacklick High."

Jonathan got up to get some coffee. As he did, he looked back toward Sam and said, "This might be real, Sam. But it's not a real threat."

Sam let it drop and moved on to another topic.

"So, what are your plans for today?"

"Well, I plan to be around here for a few more hours. I'm really productive here. But I need to get to the office and coordinate with the team." Jonathan sipped his fresh cup of coffee. "We've got to get things turned around and over to the other side of the world."

"Work, work, work," Sam interjected with a playful pout.

"I know. It's not forever," Jonathan said, with a hint of fatigue. "How about you?"

"Me?" Sam took a final drink, finishing her tea. "I'm going to get some sleep."

With that, she got up. She put her mug in the dishwasher, gave Jonathan a kiss on the cheek, and then headed toward their bedroom.

Chapter 19

Right after Sam went to bed, Jonathan got busy. The house was quiet. His phone was off. These distraction-free times didn't happen often, and he needed to take advantage of it.

For as long as he'd been with the Eisenberg & Anders firm, its biggest client—Emerald Medical—had been in serious growth mode, going public mode, or acquisition mode. The upside for Jonathan was lots of interesting work: contracts, tax, securities, environmental, human resources. Every day was a little different.

And Jonathan never had to worry about where he billed his time—or how much. Emerald Medical, or one of its growing number of subsidiaries, was all Jonathan worked on. And Emerald Medical paid its bills—it seemed as if it printed money. No questions asked.

The downside for Jonathan was the same as the upside: work. And lots of it. He felt like he was always under the gun. There were always boxes and boxes of records to pore over. Financial statements and tax returns to review. Negotiations to undertake. Offers to make or respond to. Contracts to write and rewrite.

Part of Jonathan always felt ongoing pressure. He wanted to become a partner at Eisenberg & Anders. This would allow him to buy into a small ownership stake in everything the firm achieved. And that could be quite lucrative, depending on the year.

But becoming a partner wasn't about the money. He and Sam weren't rich—other than in love and happiness—but money wasn't an issue. They were two successful professionals with a conservative financial mindset. Sure, the money would be nice, but they didn't need it. For Jonathan, at this point, it was a matter of pride. Pure ego. He felt that becoming a partner would be the final confirmation of his success.

To become a partner at Eisenberg & Anders was relatively simple: get 75% of the existing partners to vote you in. Simple, but not easy. Jonathan had to make a case for himself as someone worthy of admission to the partnership in each of several areas:

- **Make it rain**: Bring in work to the firm.
- **Work ethic**: A willingness to put in the time.
- **Technical competence**: An understanding of the law.

- **Team player**: Others enjoy being around you.
- **Community involvement**: Creating positive exposure for the firm.

In thinking through the criteria, Jonathan was reasonably certain he could become a partner. But he wasn't totally sure. And it was that scintilla of doubt that drove him to be almost singularly focused on Eisenberg & Anders every waking hour—and at times, even when he slept.

Chapter 20

At about 10:30 a.m., Jonathan felt great about what he'd gotten done from the kitchen table. He wanted to make one more check of his email before heading into the office.

In his mind, going to the Eisenberg & Anders offices served three purposes. First, he needed to coordinate with his team to ensure that all the T's were crossed, and I's dotted relative to the formal letter of intent and a series of due diligence requests.

Second, he needed to model the appropriate work ethic. Jonathan could not expect those on his team to do things he wasn't willing to do. Right or wrong, if he stayed late, they would. If he came in on Saturday, they would. If he worked while on vacation, they would.

Finally, Jonathan felt a need to be at the office merely to get facetime. While he couldn't be sure who would be there, if there were one or two partners, they would see him. And from there, he was hopeful those few would tell other partners when it came time to vote on whether Jonathan should become a partner.

Just as Jonathan started to review his email, AJ quietly emerged. Stealthily, he entered the kitchen, grabbed a box of Pop-Tarts and started to exit as silently as he'd arrived. He saw Jonathan but pretended not to.

"Good morning," Jonathan said to his son.

"Mmmrn," AJ couldn't be bothered to enunciate.

"How was last night?" Jonathan called out, essentially repeating his earlier question.

There was no reply. AJ heard him. He paused for a moment, contemplating a response. But he was outside the kitchen, out of sight. It would just be easier to keep moving. A response might lead to another question—or, God forbid, an actual conversation. So AJ moved forward, back into his room to play video games, gently closing the door behind himself.

Jonathan sensed that AJ had paused to respond. He felt a sense of hope. Then—nothing. No response. Just the sound of a bedroom door closing. Disappointment set in, but none of this was unusual.

He returned his focus to email and quickly responded to the few messages that needed his attention. Then he got himself showered, shaved and suited up with a casual but professional look.

Before jumping in his car and driving downtown, he figured he'd make another attempt to connect with AJ. Jonathan approached his son's bedroom door and gently knocked on it with the back of his hand. There was no response. He could hear activity—the clicking of the video game controller. He contemplated knocking again.

AJ heard his dad knock. It had a distinctive sound, different from his mother's. He considered ignoring it. But if his mom found out, that would disappoint her—and that mattered.

He said, "Come in," without being distracted in the least from the game he was engaged in.

Jonathan slowly opened the door and tentatively entered. As he did, he said, "I just wanted to check in before I headed to the office for a few hours."

"Okay," AJ said, not taking his eyes off the gameplay on the screen.

"So, how was last night?" Jonathan repeated his earlier question.

"It was good. Fun," AJ replied with a monotone. He wanted to respond, but he didn't want to encourage conversation.

Jonathan could sense the same. Although he wasn't willing to give up, he wasn't sure what direction to take to engage. He watched the screen as AJ played. He noticed that AJ was not playing alone—there was a series of others working in conjunction or against him.

Curiosity got the best of Jonathan, and he blurted out, "Who are these other people?" Before AJ could respond, Jonathan fired off a few more questions. "Do you know these people? How does this work?"

AJ remained focused on the screen and addressed the most recent questions. "Some people I know. Others I don't."

"Like, who is who? Do you know?" Jonathan was genuinely interested.

"We just play. Those I know, I talk to at school. Others? I'm not sure. It doesn't matter. We just play." AJ didn't really have to think too much about what he was saying.

"Well, who do you know?" Jonathan inquired.

"T-Frank is Tommy Frank from the team," AJ shared. He looked at other player tags. "QBMaJack is Mason Jackson." He continued to search for answers. "Ummm?"

"How about Skylar3?" Jonathan asked.

"I don't know. Some I don't know. They're new anyway." AJ casually answered. He was a little more engaged in the conversation. His dad nodded, indicating he accepted the answer.

"How about JSevans?" Jonathan continued to quiz.

"That's our kicker. John Evans. Number seven. Think about it—Sevens, Evans." AJ kept his focus on the screen.

Jonathan tried to keep up with the action on the screen to find more people to ask about. "And SpartyBT10? Who is that? Is he on your team?"

"No. Not on our team. SpartyBT10 is usually on, though. But I don't know 'em."

"What's yours?" Jonathan fired out.

AJ took a deep breath. He was annoyed. Nevertheless, he quickly barked out, "A2J9R."

"How about—" Jonathan started to ask.

AJ quickly took his eyes off the screen and glared at his dad in a manner that said, "Enough."

"Okay. I need to get to work anyway." Jonathan moved toward the door. AJ resumed his trance on the video game. As Jonathan started to close the door, he said, "I'll talk to you later."

While still engrossed in gameplay, AJ let go of the controller with his left hand and gave his dad a quick thumbs-up. Then he quickly got back to the video game.

Jonathan closed the door and headed to work. He considered the exchange a win.

Chapter 21

The impromptu parking lot celebration for the state championship football Mustangs was just the beginning.

A pep assembly followed that Monday, and later in the week, players were fitted for rings and took extra yearbook photos. Before Christmas, the team rode in a holiday parade on trucks and floats.

The celebration continued after New Year's with a banquet hosted by parents, boosters and the athletic department. Highlights included a season yearbook, a 15-minute video and custom state championship jerseys.

In January, a gym assembly was held to raise the team's banner alongside the school's other two titles. Parents, local officials and representatives from Congress and the State House attended.

Finally, in February, the team received their championship rings at halftime of a packed home boys basketball game.

Besides football, other sports at Blacklick were not doing well. Boys and girls soccer had horrible seasons. Cross-country teams could hardly field enough runners to compete. And the girls volleyball team finished with a .500 record.

While the boys basketball team had a record crowd for the ring ceremony, after halftime that throng dissipated. The football players, parents and coaches abandoned the basketball Mustangs as the team suffered a ninth straight loss.

Football was king. It had resources and opportunities. And all other sports were paupers. Collectively, they just made do. And Athletic Director Gary Studer was not concerned with the inequity; he was largely the architect of it.

No one shared their frustration with the unfairness within football circles. But outside of that community, players and parents of other sports were not happy. They felt powerless, however. Rumor had it that nothing good came from challenging the football machine.

Jonathan was oblivious to all this drama. Other than the impromptu parking lot celebration, he did not attend anything else related to the champion Blacklick Mustangs. Circumstances and opportunities pulled him deeper than ever before into life at Eisenberg & Anders.

Shortly after the state championship game, he learned that he did not get enough support to be admitted to the Eisenberg & Anders partnership.

The managing partner—Ari Eisenberg—met with him personally. Ari shared with him over lunch at the Huntington Club that everyone felt he was a team player—they loved having him around. And there was no question that he'd demonstrated technical competence and work ethic. The problem was that some partners wanted to see more development in the areas of bringing work into the firm and Jonathan's involvement in the community.

Jonathan had mixed feelings about everything. Sure, he was disappointed. He truly thought he'd done enough. His frustration related to the reasons.

Over the past several years, he'd been head down traveling, working and mentoring younger attorneys on his team. While that wasn't new client money for the firm, it served to bring in lots of revenue. And being as busy as he had been, where was he supposed to find time to get involved in the community? He was hardly involved at home.

But as disappointing and frustrating as it was, Ari Eisenberg put such a positive spin on the situation. "Jonathan, this is not no, it's just not now."

Beyond the pep talk, Ari announced to Jonathan that in his paycheck that week there would be a very generous bonus. It more than fairly compensated him for the last few years.

Additionally, Ari shared with Jonathan that he was going to hand him a couple leads for some prospective new clients. With all the exposure that Emerald Medical was getting, the firm was mentioned several times. With that, there were other growth-oriented companies interested in making Eisenberg & Anders their attorneys of record.

Ari shared, "I'm 70 ... something." He stopped himself as he laughed. Then he continued through his chuckle, "Okay, I'm much closer to 80 than 70. I don't need to be bringing in more clients, Jonathan." He took a drink of water. "I need to empower the likes of you—the younger, but experienced face of the firm—to bring in clients." He raised his water glass as if to make a toast. "That is how the firm of Eisenberg & Anders lives beyond me."

Reflexively, Jonathan raised his glass slightly off the table and smiled. He had nothing to say other than "Thanks." Yes, he still wanted the moniker of partner after his name. And he would have to deal with the self-perceived shame of failing on this attempt. But he could see a clear path to make it happen in the coming year.

Mostly, he felt as if he had the unwavering support of the managing partner. But he could not let Ari Eisenberg down. So as soon as they returned to the office, Jonathan followed him back to his office. He got contact information for the prospective clients and immediately started reaching out.

Ari coached him a bit. He shared that landing these sorts of corporate clients was an exercise in patience. It started with the initial contact and then might entail writing proposals and making presentations—some online and then eventually in person. There would be meetings with the initial contact, then that person's boss, and then the boss's boss, and then maybe a CEO or corporate board or venture firms. It might be all of the above.

The lead time on converting a lead to an actual client was generally not measured in weeks, but rather months—potentially years. And it involved lots of non-billable time as well as travel. Jonathan needed to be prepared.

In the meantime, he needed to continue to remain productive—billing hours and leading his team. It was as if he needed to double down on the incredible pace he was already on.

But Jonathan felt like he had no choice. This was part of the price of becoming a partner. He tried to comfort himself with the thought that this was not forever. He told himself, *just push through. A year from now, I'll be a partner. Then I can relax some.*

Chapter 22

"Where are you? What time is it?" Sam asked as she answered her phone, walking into the house.

"Well, I'm somewhere near Tokyo," Jonathan remarked, then checked his watch. "It's 9:35 p.m. here. I'm 13 hours ahead of you. A better question is, what day is it? I've been back and forth across the international date line and in time zones I didn't even know existed."

"It's March 14th … no, 15th. I seem to have my own issues, crossing over from yesterday to today while at work." Sam laughed, then asked, "How are things going?"

Jonathan let out a heavy sigh. "You know, I'm not sure. The Japanese are hard to read. I think I'm doing a good job, but everything is so stoic and void of feedback. I feel like I'm talking to AJ." Jonathan let out an uncomfortable laugh. Sam joined in. Jonathan paused, then continued, "Speaking of him, how is he?"

Sam smiled and replied, "He's doing well. He's a good kid. Studies. Works out. And—"

Before she could finish, Jonathan chimed in, "And games online."

"Yes, games online," Sam agreed. "But he's a good kid."

"A2J9R is," Jonathan chuckled. "He just loves his online life with the likes of T-Frank, JSevans and SpartyBT10 … whoever those people are."

Sam laughed. "I have no idea." Then added, "You should call AJ sometime."

"I will," Jonathan responded, though he didn't sound confident. "No, I will," he said again, sounding more positive, as if psyching himself up. "The last few days have been busy—last few weeks. Who am I kidding?" There was a momentary pause, then he asked, "What's going on with you? How's work? Johnny? Kelly?"

Sam jumped right in. "Work is work, you know? Another day, another accidental poisoning, drug overdose or heart attack.

"As for Johnny and Kelly, both are doing well, honey. Johnny calls occasionally and gives me a full review of things. Kelly texts two or three times a day, giving me a play-by-play rundown of her world. Either way, I hear it all." Then Sam let out a big sigh.

Jonathan picked up on it and inquired, "What was that?"

Sam gathered her words and responded, "This tax levy thing. I don't know. It is real. And may well be a real threat."

Jonathan interjected rhetorically, "Really?" Then followed up with, "Why do you say that?"

"Jonathan? It's just a feeling," Sam struggled with her words. "No, it's more than a feeling. I'm involved with the parent committee to help ensure the passage of the levy. I have a front-row seat to everything."

Jonathan indicated he was listening, so Sam continued, "First of all, this retiree guy—he's not just some dumb senior citizen. And he didn't just move to Blacklick from the farm. He's sharp. He knows what he's doing. He seems to have a plan, and he's executing it with precision."

Trying to catch up on details, Jonathan asked, "What's this guy's name?"

"Ummm," Sam rustled through her notes. "Walter ... Walter Bachman."

"Hmmm? Walter B. When you say he has a plan, what do you mean?"

"Jonathan, he knows what to ask for—records, documents, financials. Things I didn't even know existed. Moreover, when the school board tries to stonewall, he seems to know exactly what to say and do to get them to cave." Sam briefly paused. "I wish you were here. This Walter guy throws around terminology and names of court cases. It makes my head spin."

"Is it administrative law-type stuff?" Jonathan jumped in.

"I don't know," Sam sounded frustrated. "I'm a doctor. I was married to an attorney, but he seems to have moved to the Far East."

"Hey, hey," Jonathan chuckled. "That was low."

Sam giggled, then got back to her serious tone. "He knows how to figure out where the vulnerabilities are. He seems to be one step ahead—on everything."

"What about Studer and the school board? Aren't they helping?" Jonathan squinted, trying to envision the situation.

"NO!" Sam abruptly responded. "Walter shut that down from the start. They're not permitted. According to my notes…" Sam flipped through a small notebook. "They—the school board or anybody with the school—can provide information on the levy. They can encourage people to support it. But they cannot be involved in our campaign efforts."

"That makes sense," Jonathan added.

"Well, it's stupid," Sam replied. "I feel like this jerk has dropped in from I don't know where and…" She paused, then moved to another thought. "And he's built a staggering coalition of support. He's even won over some families whose kids attend Blacklick High."

"WOW! That hurts," Jonathan interjected.

"It does. I feel like we're totally outnumbered, outflanked and outfunded." Sam thought for a moment. "I don't know where they're getting their money. There is just a plethora of 'Vote No' signs. Banners. Plus, mailers a couple times a week… emails and robocalls."

"Really?" Jonathan was amazed. "All for a stupid tax levy."

"I know. And we simply can't match it—no matter what we try," Sam sounded defeated.

"Someone should reach out to Bobby O'Farrell," Jonathan postulated. "Blacklick is the school that Bobby O—and his Emerald Medical fortune—built, after all."

"Jonathan, we've tried, believe me," Sam declared. "But we've gotten nowhere."

"Well, in his defense," Jonathan rationalized, "life has changed for him in the last eight, nine years. His focus is on multi-billion-dollar acquisitions, not a multi-million-dollar tax levy."

"That's right. He's over in Asia with you," Sam giggled.

Jonathan let out a laugh. "He isn't with me, Sam. Trust me. He's not staying in the hotels I'm at." Then his tone became more serious. "Don't give up on Bobby O swooping in with assistance. I have faith that things will work out in the end."

"Honey, I'm not so sure. You're a world away. You're not on social media. You don't feel the vibe." Sam sounded down. "The levy passing is not a sure thing at all."

"Well, if the campaign needs money, use some of the Eisenberg & Anders bonus money."

"No!" Sam protested. "That's for the kitchen. Remember?"

"It is. I said some," Jonathan clarified. "I'm not telling you to underwrite the entire campaign. Just some." Jonathan laughed, prompting Sam to do the same.

From here, the conversation lost momentum. They were each tired and needed to get some sleep.

Chapter 23

Very few knew anything for sure about the man leading the charge to defeat the Jefferson Township School District tax levy. But because Walter Bachman was at the center of a contentious community issue, curiosity ran high. That interest sparked plenty of rumors and speculation—reinforced within the local echo chamber.

People believed he lived in a large house about a half mile from the school. That was the address listed in Franklin

County's voter registration rolls. And it was where people had seen his car—a late-model, gold Lexus SUV—disappear down a long drive behind a tall iron gate.

That house, however, wasn't registered in Bachman's name. It had been purchased years ago, in cash, by a corporate entity with an address in rural Nevada. That entity was wholly owned by another based in the Bahamas, whose address belonged to a law firm known for creating layers of secrecy.

No one knew exactly when Bachman moved in. Some claimed to have seen him around, here and there, for years. But it was hard to separate fact from the speculation dominating recent conversations. What was clear—according to Franklin County records—was that he registered to vote a little over a year before he began showing up at Jefferson Township School Board meetings the previous spring, asking pointed questions.

A few local contractors said they had done work at the property—built-in bookshelves and other custom touches to make a house a home. Their unconfirmed and frequent trips to the mini mansion only fueled the rumor mill.

Bachman reportedly had lots of big, heavy hardcover books covering a range of subjects. History books detailing the rise and fall of nations, and the regimes of third-world countries. Volumes on wars—strategies and battle tactics—about the Spanish-American War, the two World Wars, Korea, Vietnam, the Gulf Wars, and even lesser-known armed conflicts.

There were books on technology: computer science, programming, surveillance, security—and infiltrating security.

And there were books on stained glass art. Its history. Photo collections. How-to manuals. That seemed odd and uncharacteristic until contractors discovered a basement workshop devoted to it: tools, supplies, and projects in progress.

He also had a room overlooking the outdoor pool that served as a home gym. Light weights. A treadmill and rowing machine. Yoga mats. And judging by the odorous humidity and shifting of hand weights from day to day, the room was used often.

How people described Bachman's appearance and presence largely depended on which side of the tax levy debate they were on. Some saw him as a white knight. Others looked at the same man and saw something closer to satanic.

He was in his mid-seventies, six-foot-two, and fit. He never wore a suit, but no one could recall seeing him without a crisp pair of slacks and a tailored sport coat over a dress shirt.

When he entered a room, people noticed. He stood tall — shoulders back, head high, chin out. Even seated, he sat upright, almost at attention. He carried an air of confidence—always smiling, always appearing in control.

Even those who opposed his stance on the levy couldn't deny that he was remarkably personable. He engaged with genuine interest, remembered conversations and details, and never made it personal. Though he worked tirelessly to defeat the levy, he clearly valued people—regardless of which side they were on.

Still, even those who admired him sensed an edge. They felt that, if pushed or provoked, he could become something very different.

This wasn't the first time the Board had gone to voters for a tax levy. The first was two years before the district opened—a simple question of whether the community supported separating from the Gahanna-Jefferson School District. The result was overwhelming: 75 percent in favor.

The second came three years later, when the Board requested additional funds to meet the needs of a growing school system. Again, support was strong—67 percent voted yes. At the time, the Jefferson Township School District was still in its honeymoon phase, with the high school only a year old.

But those funds weren't permanent. The levy had to be renewed three years later. Voters approved it a third time, but this time made a portion permanent. The rest would be up for renewal again in three years—in May.

This was the first time, however, that passage of the levy wasn't a sure thing. Yes, there was support. There were always opponents. But this was the first time someone as formidable as Bachman was leading the opposition.

Not only did Bachman oppose the measure, but he was also vocal about it—attending meetings, seeking information, requesting documents, challenging the board, questioning decisions past and present, and scrutinizing those that could impact the future. Most of all, he was building a coalition within the community.

No one opposed the idea of the Jefferson Township School District itself, but a growing number questioned how its funds were being used and managed. The information Bachman uncovered fueled that doubt. He shared his findings with a small core of opponents, who then spread the message organically— via mail, social media, email, and phone.

The movement was growing, as well as motivated, organized and well-funded.

Chapter 24

In the early evening of the same day Jonathan called Sam, AJ was sitting in his room playing video games. In fact, after dinner most nights, AJ typically retreated to his room to pass the time this way. He, Tommy Frank, John Evan, Skylar3, SpartyBT10 and a host of others would engage in mock battles against zombie invasions or some other popular online game.

What wasn't typical, however, was for his phone to light up with a text during these moments. Most of the people he texted were, like him, already online—and why text when you could just message within the game?

Curious, while still trying to stay engaged in the online battle, AJ grabbed his phone and opened the texting app. Almost immediately, a picture appeared: the sun just rising over the horizon. Moments later, a message followed.

Curious, while still trying to engage in online battle, AJ grabbed his phone and opened the texting app. Almost immediately a picture appeared: the sun just rising over the horizon. Moments later a message appeared.

> **The day is winding down there. But here's a preview of what tomorrow looks like. It's shaping up to be a glorious day.**

AJ knew immediately the message was from his dad—partly because he always texted with near-perfect punctuation. He hesitated, wondering, *Should I respond? What should I say?* Before he could answer either question for himself, another message came in.

> **Japan is one of the first places to see the sunrise each day. Which is why it's called the land of the rising sun.**

Jonathan was attempting to engage in small talk. AJ continued to stare at the screen. He had paused the online game, prompting SpartyBT10 to goad him to get back in the fight. AJ was torn about whether—or how—he should respond. Then another message appeared.

If you are up and available, give me a call.

AJ froze. He could make time—it was his dad. But there was really nothing he wanted to share and pretending otherwise felt uncomfortable. The best he could offer in response would be: *Fine. Okay. I will.*

Meanwhile, T-Frank and Skylar3 sent playfully chiding messages, encouraging him to "carry his weight" against the zombies. He felt the urge to pick up his controller.

Then he remembered that his mom would want him to call his dad and "make an effort." AJ clicked over from the text thread to his dad's contact and was just about to initiate a call when another message came in.

It was a simple symbol—meaning "okay" to most. But within the Reese household, it carried an entirely different meaning. It immediately filled AJ with resentment. He quickly clicked the screen on his phone dark, laid it face down, and covered it with a pillow.

Without a second thought, he resumed his role in the online game.

SpartyBT10 quickly messaged, "'Bout time!"

Chapter 25

Just after the previous school year ended, the receptionist at the law offices of Joseph Thompson led an elderly man into the conference room. He shuffled in—slow, cautious, hunched over. His clothes were dated and disheveled: worn work boots, wrinkled khakis, a grease-stained black windbreaker over a gray sweatshirt with sweat stains at the collar, and a sun-faded Ohio State football hat.

He had already completed the standard check-in forms and paid the consultation fee—peeling it from a wad of 20s, 50s, and 100s. Once seated in one of six cushioned chairs, he slouched and closed his eyes, as if needing rest. As she shut the door, the receptionist said, "Mr. Thompson will be with you shortly."

As soon as the door closed, the man opened his eyes and pulled three sheets of paper from an inside pocket. Torn from a spiral notebook and hastily folded in thirds, he placed them— still folded—on the table in front of him and sat quietly.

Moments later, a second door opened. A sharply dressed man in his fifties entered, carrying the intake paperwork. Pressed dress shirt, tight-knotted tie, tailored pants. He moved quickly, closing the door behind him.

He dropped the forms on the table and extended a hand. "Don't get up, please. I'm Joseph Thompson."

After a firm handshake, he took a seat across the table. "So, what are we talking about today, Mr....?" He glanced at the form. "Bachman. Walter Bachman."

Bachman smiled nervously. "Mr. Thompson, you can call me Walt."

"Okay, Walt—then please call me Joe." Thompson smiled. "It looks like you're interested in estate planning?"

"Yes," Bachman said, unfolding the papers. They were filled with handwritten notes and numbers, which he quickly turned face down. "But I'm a little nervous sharing certain information."

Thompson gave a reassuring nod. "Totally understandable. Everyone's a little uneasy sharing their—" he made air quotes "—life secrets and after-life plans. But let me assure you, anything you say is covered by attorney-client privilege. I cannot—and will not—share anything you tell me. If I do, I could lose my license."

Bachman nodded, turned over the papers, and slid them across the table. "Excuse my handwriting."

Thompson glanced through them. "No problem. I've seen worse," he chuckled.

He then asked a series of clarifying questions. Bachman struggled to recall some details, but together they muddled through.

"I've got a good sense of how to proceed," Thompson said finally. "Let me review everything and I'll get back to you." Bachman nodded.

"Is there anything else? We've still got time."

Bachman hesitated. "Well, yes… there is something. What do you know about school funding?"

Thompson gave a puzzled look. "What do you mean?"

"I'm looking for help challenging an upcoming tax levy," Bachman said. "I want to know what I'm legally allowed to do. And where I can find real financial information to dig into."

"Okay, I see," Thompson said. "May I ask which district?"

Bachman looked around, as if checking for eavesdroppers. "Jefferson Township School District. Out in Blacklick—east of Gahanna."

Thompson paused. Then raised both palms. "Let's stop right there, Walt. I'm happy to help with your estate planning."

"Great," Bachman said.

"But I can't help with anything involving the Jefferson Township School District."

Bachman looked confused. "I don't understand. Isn't this communication privileged?"

"Walt, yes, it is," Thompson said, holding up a hand. "But there's another legal rule: I can't represent people on opposite sides of an issue."

"But I don't understand," Walt said, frustrated.

"In addition to being a lawyer," Thompson explained, "I'm also President of the Jefferson Township School Board. My job is to work in the district's best interest. Representing you would be a conflict of interest."

"Ohhh," Bachman said, nodding. "I get it. I'm sorry. I'm really embarrassed." He looked down, shaking his head.

"Don't worry about it," Thompson said kindly. "You didn't know." He paused, waiting for eye contact. "What's your issue with the district?"

"Simple. Taxes are too high," Bachman said.

"Perhaps," Thompson replied, "but it takes a lot of money to run a school."

"Sure. But there's so much waste and abuse."

"Waste? Abuse? Where?"

"Athletics," Bachman said, slightly more confident. "Too much money goes there—especially to football. It's bloated. It just needs to be pared back. Don't you think?"

"No, not at all," Thompson laughed.

"What's so funny?" Bachman's confidence wavered.

Still chuckling, Thompson replied, "I can't represent you, but my advice is not to waste money on another attorney either. Everything's fine—with the district, the high school, and especially the sports programs."

"Really?" Bachman asked, uncertain.

"Yes, really," Thompson said firmly. "Especially football. Football is the crown jewel of Blacklick High."

"Yeah… but—"

"Yeah, but what?" Thompson was growing agitated. He paused, collecting himself.

Shaken, Bachman continued, "Isn't football prioritized at the expense of other sports? I mean, I hear the athletic director— former football coach—has things… well, skewed toward the program."

Thompson took a slow breath, clearly irritated. "Walt, I don't know where you're hearing this, but everything is fine. Trust me."

"Really?" Bachman's voice trembled.

"Yes. First, there's no truth to what you're saying. We have oversight. Checks and balances. No abuses. Second, the tax levy will pass—easily. I haven't heard a whisper of discontent. And Gary Studer—the athletic director—is beloved. He might be more popular than Bobby O."

"Who? Bobby who?"

"Bobby O'Farrell. The billionaire who…" Thompson stopped himself. "Never mind. The point is, people love Studer. They'll vote yes just for him."

"Wow. Again, I'm really embarrassed," Bachman said with a nervous laugh. He looked up and grinned. "Attorney-client privilege?"

Thompson gave him a curious look, then smiled. "Yes, Walt. Attorney-client privilege. No one will ever know of your embarrassment."

Thompson stood and walked to the door, waiting as Bachman slowly rose and shuffled toward the exit. They made small talk on the way to the reception area. At the door, they shook hands. Thompson held it open as Bachman carefully stepped outside.

Once the door closed, Thompson turned to his receptionist, rolled his eyes, and muttered, "Oh boy."

Out of sight, Bachman pulled out his phone and tapped a button. Then he yanked off the Ohio State football hat, stuffed it into his windbreaker, straightened his back, and walked briskly to his car.

He'd gotten what he needed.

Chapter 26

"Do you have a minute?" Jonathan Reese inquired as he simultaneously knocked on the doorframe of the corner office.

"Of course, Jonathan," Ari Eisenberg responded immediately, punctuating his answer with a hearty laugh. "Warren and I were just talking." He nodded toward the man seated across from him. "Nothing official."

Warren, a small, sharply dressed attorney, turned toward the door. He didn't acknowledge Jonathan—his face blank, creating an uncomfortable tension.

Jonathan stepped inside. He offered Warren a brief, polite smile, trying to ignore the cold reception, then turned to Ari and broke into a wide grin. "I wanted you to be the first to see this." He handed Ari a printed email.

Ari took the page and adjusted his glasses to read the tiny print. As he scanned it, his expression shifted from focused to faintly amused—then he erupted in laughter. "Warren, it appears our boy Jonathan just landed another fish—and this one's bigger than the last." He handed the printout to Warren, then stood and moved around his desk to greet Jonathan.

Warren gave the paper a cursory glance, then set it face-down on Ari's desk without comment.

Jonathan remained oblivious to Warren's disinterest. He was too focused on Ari's reaction. Seeing his boss's hand extended, he reached out eagerly.

"Jonathan, this is great," Ari said, letting out another hearty laugh. "We're very proud of you." Jonathan beamed.

"But your first-quarter hours are off pace," Warren muttered—not quite under his breath. Just loud enough to take the air out of the room.

"Warren, Warren," Ari said, motioning downward with his hand, gently chiding him. "Jonathan, you're fine." He turned toward Warren, though still addressing Jonathan. "We need this. Eisenberg & Anders always need new clients and additional work." He faced Jonathan again. "And we need people like you who know how to bring it in. So ignore Warren. You're fine. No—you're great. We're all very proud of you."

Warren went silent. He stared out the corner office window, as if he weren't part of the conversation.

"Thank you," Jonathan replied, likewise ignoring Warren.

"Tell you what," Ari said, placing an arm around Jonathan's shoulder and guiding him toward the door. "Go bill some hours," he added with a broad smile and a wink. "Then around noon, we'll have lunch and catch up. It's a beautiful April day—I think spring is finally here to stay. We'll grab a table at an outdoor café. I want to hear all about your adventures... Sam... the kids... everything." Ari let out another deep laugh. "I've missed having you around." He gave Jonathan a firm pat on the back as he sent him on his way.

There was little question that Eisenberg & Anders was one of the most prestigious law firms in Columbus, Ohio. But there was no question that Ari Eisenberg was the ultimate authority—and had been since founding the firm just over 20 years earlier. That it existed at all was, frankly, miraculous.

In high school, all Ari wanted was to play football and get out. At Bexley High, he took only the required coursework and put forth just enough effort to stay eligible. Once he played his last game, he was ready to drop out—and did, to the deep disappointment of his father.

Ari didn't understand why it mattered so much to the man who always seemed to be working. And he didn't care to. Like many teenage boys, he was constantly at odds with his father— feeling he could never measure up, while his father believed he never really tried. Both were true. One drove the other.

Ari wanted to escape the constant judgment. But life with only a high school diploma is tough; without one, nearly impossible. It took him seven years to learn that lesson.

At 24, his girlfriend Alison became pregnant. They got married and decided to see it through. The pregnancy, however, was complicated. While the baby—a boy—was born near full term, it was clear he wouldn't survive long.

Ari and Alison poured everything into loving their son, whom they named Alan. But love wasn't enough. Alan died on his fourth day.

It was devastating—but it brought Ari and his father back together. And it inspired Ari to change his life. He earned his GED and enrolled at Columbus State Community College. For the first time, he developed a thirst for learning. He was determined to finish college and then go to law school.

He did just that. Community college led to The Ohio State University, where he entered the College of Business as a late-20s student. He worked evenings to help support a life with Alison.

Ari was a good student, but not a great one. On his own merit, he likely wouldn't have made it into OSU's law school. But kindness opened the door.

Midway through his first semester in business school, Ari showed up early to turn in an assignment. While waiting, he noticed a struggling freshman—Robert O'Farrell—battling with an entry-level accounting course. Ari jumped in to help, walking him through the basics of debits and credits. That tutoring continued informally for weeks.

Eventually, their mentor-protégé relationship became a genuine friendship, despite nearly a decade between them. When O'Farrell—whose family ran several small businesses across Ohio—started branching out as a young entrepreneur, he turned to Ari for guidance.

It was during one of those early meetings that Ari said, "I just can't keep calling you Robert. Bobby O fits so much better."

Bobby O loved spending time with Ari. But it was Bobby's parents who truly appreciated Ari's maturity. So much so that they called in favors to get Ari into OSU's law school. Later, they helped him secure a job at Belden & Schmidt.

By then, Bobby O had launched a business sourcing and distributing medical supplies to doctors and urgent care centers. A proud Irish Catholic from Dublin, Ohio—alma mater of the Shamrocks—he named the company Emerald Medical.

Who handled the legal work for Emerald Medical? Ari Eisenberg. And as Bobby O's business grew, so did his influence. Over time, he directed more and more clients to his trusted friend—and best man.

To Belden & Schmidt, Ari was both a blessing and a curse. A blessing because he brought in work—something most associates failed to do. That work fueled firm-wide profits. But once Ari became a partner and kept bringing in business, it exposed the complacency of others. The managing partner barked constantly: "Why can't anyone else bring in business like Eisenberg?"

That pressure bred animosity.

Ari wasn't considered a "blue blood." He hadn't graduated high school. He came from community college. He got his job through a favor. To the old guard, he didn't belong—and they didn't let him forget it.

They excluded him from black-tie fundraisers. They assigned him the least desirable tasks, like conducting "go-nowhere" interviews at Capital Law, while others traveled to Harvard, Michigan, and Yale.

Ari wasn't oblivious. He just took it in stride—confident, happy, gracious. He worked hard and never asked for anything. Except once.

He lobbied hard for the firm to hire a young candidate from Toledo who deserved a chance: Jonathan Reese.

But everyone has a breaking point. Ari reached his after Jonathan's first year. A group of senior partners conspired to reassign Ari's clients to themselves—internal politics that would drastically impact his income.

Outwardly, Ari said nothing. As usual, he seemed unfazed. Internally, he began to plot. And he didn't plot alone—he brought in Bobby O.

Together, they orchestrated Ari's exit from Belden & Schmidt.

The first step was reaching out through the O'Farrell network to Richard Anders, a seasoned attorney who'd long held a grudge against the firm. Behind the scenes—slowly, methodically—they laid the groundwork for what would become Eisenberg & Anders.

While the senior partners at Belden & Schmidt smugly carried on, Ari prepared his exit. Anders searched for the perfect office space downtown. Bobby O met with clients who'd been wrongly reassigned.

Six months later, the plan was ready. Ari submitted his resignation. But he wasn't leaving empty-handed. He took with him a slate of clients—amounting to 17 percent of Belden & Schmidt's total revenue. And he hoped to recruit one person: Jonathan Reese.

In the end, every client followed him. But Jonathan—newly married, expecting a child, with a wife in medical residency—couldn't risk leaving the security of one of Columbus's top firms.

Ari was disappointed, but he understood. As he left Jonathan's office to turn in his resignation, he hugged the young associate and said, "I'll be around. I'm here to help when you need it."

Chapter 27

In the first three-plus months of the year, Jonathan could not remember being at home for one complete week. Europe. Asia. South America. East Coast and West. Chasing new clients and serving existing ones. It all melded together in his mind.

And when he was in Columbus, he couldn't remember coming home during daylight hours. Today was no different. He had a very productive morning—logging billable hours to appease Warren Scott. And that led to an uplifting lunch with Ari Eisenberg, who was endlessly and genuinely curious about everything Jonathan Reese.

But when he returned to his desk, there was still a litany of things he had to accomplish. He was only in town for a few days. There were valuable face-to-face "touch base" meetings with his team of young associates to coordinate action items. There were meetings with the other teams to ensure there were no gaps or overlap in serving large clients like Emerald Medical. And there was just doing work. He never felt like he could get out of the office at a decent hour.

So, it was not at all strange that Jonathan rolled into his driveway under the cloak of darkness. This had become somewhat normal.

What was also not strange was finding the garbage bins still out by the curb. The Reese family had hired out much of the household chores. Weekly cleaning. Yard work. And snow removal when needed.

There was no service to get the garbage bins to the curb and back, however. So Jonathan and Sam expected AJ to handle this one simple household responsibility. And somehow, AJ always seemed to forget or outright fail to come through.

For Jonathan, it wasn't worth the battle anymore, especially being home so infrequently. Neither was homework. Nor was getting AJ to pick up his room, or a dozen other things.

Jonathan was exhausted from work and travel. He didn't have the energy to confront AJ. Besides, their relationship was tense enough. He simply parked his car, then walked to the curb to retrieve the large, rolling garbage bin.

Rolling the bin back to its place on the side of the house, he could see that AJ was up. Judging by the flashes of blue light coming from the window, it was easy for Jonathan to deduce that his son was engaged in virtual mortal combat alongside the likes of T-Frank, JSevans, SpartyBT10 and whoever else had nothing better to do.

When he finally made it inside, Jonathan went to AJ's room and poked his head in. He smiled and merely said, "I'm home."

AJ barely reacted. He just flashed a quick thumbs-up without taking his eyes off the screen. He spoke. However, he yelled in communication with his compatriots playing the game with him: "Zombies at three o'clock!"

Unduly unacknowledged, Jonathan slowly backed out, gently closed the door and ventured toward the kitchen. This was not his first mere thumbs-up from AJ.

As he shared with Sam when the thumbs-up was becoming commonplace: "Well, at least I'm not getting another single digit."

The relationship between Jonathan and AJ had seemed to be getting more and more estranged. Worst of all, Jonathan felt hopeless in repairing the situation. It was a conundrum, of sorts. When he wasn't able to communicate, he couldn't work on the relationship. And when he was, he seemed to only make it worse.

Jonathan entered the kitchen without the main light on. The digital clock on the stove provided enough light for him to safely navigate to the refrigerator. And once he opened that door, he was temporarily blinded by the light.

When his eyes adjusted, they immediately centered on an airtight plastic tub with a couple of pieces of leftover pizza. Sam had texted him about it before she ventured into the ER for a shift. He grabbed the container and turned toward the kitchen table.

Now, Jonathan knew what Sam meant when she texted, "Sorry about the mess." From the refrigerator light, he could sort of make out that the kitchen table was strewn with materials in support of the tax levy campaign.

With no refuge at the table, Jonathan set the now-open container on the counter in a somewhat open space. Biting a piece of cold pizza, he found the remote to the television hanging in the corner. Clicking it to life, he closed the refrigerator door.

With light from the glowing TV, he could now better see everything that was on the table. Letters to be signed. Flyers. Yard signs. He thought, *A portion of the Eisenberg & Anders bonus has gone to good use.* Sam had gotten herself knee-deep in the politics of fighting for the levy.

Holding the container, Jonathan maneuvered toward all the "Vote Yes!" propaganda. In their daily communications—via text or phone—Sam had shared all the details. He had a hard time understanding why this was such a battle.

Who was this Walter guy? Where was his support coming from? Why did he have such a problem with the schools? He was new to the area. He never had a kid in the district.

And a more perplexing question: Why were people joining ranks behind him? On the surface, the district seemed to be a wonderful model for public education. Racial and socioeconomic diversity. A strong curriculum. A solid graduation rate, with students headed in the right direction for the most part.

As Sam shared in one frantic conversation: "Even parents who have children in the schools are dead set on defeating the levy. This is not looking good."

She also shared with Jonathan that the school board made public what would go without the levy passage: transportation to middle and high school buildings, nonacademic-related clubs and sports. And Board President Joseph Thompson declared in a letter to all district residents that "none of this is a bluff."

Jonathan understood the situation. The levy pass-fail margin was small, and the stakes were high. But just like trying to reconcile with his son, he felt helpless and useless, knowing his time in the Eastern time zone was usually measured in hours and not days.

Chapter 28

Once Walter Bachman left, Joseph Thompson couldn't wait to reach out to Gary Studer to share with the school's athletic director what "some old geezer" suggested. He texted:

> **Up for a beer?**
> **Got a funny 1 to share.**

As school was out and all sports were over, Studer arranged to meet Thompson within days. They agreed to go to a small establishment in a neighboring community and took a seat outside on the edge of the patio.

Once settled, with beers in hand and small talk out of the way, Thompson related his encounter with Walter Bachman — completely violating the attorney-client privilege.

Thompson didn't care. He didn't respect the "old geezer" and figured that his conversation with Studer would never get back to Bachman. And even if it did, the "geriatric simp" would likely not remember the notion of attorney-client privilege. And even if that happened, Thompson could deny the conversation. After all, who would anyone believe? An established attorney and board president or "some old tard who can't remember what he had for lunch"?

So Thompson shared every bit of the conversation with Studer. He'd quote Bachman, pretending he were him with a shaky, elderly voice — "Way too much money goes to football ...

football is at the expense of other sports ... oh, I'm really embarrassed."

As Thompson spoke, he and Studer would interject with laughter. The whole situation was hilarious to them. One old-timer, who they'd never even heard of, was going to upend the Blacklick High football machine? Completely preposterous.

The two laughed the evening away. And that continued over the following weeks, as they randomly sent each other texts making fun of the "geriatric simp." They were completely amused, and they carried on like teenagers with their first phone.

It was all very humorous until the next school board meeting. Moments before it commenced, Walter Bachman walked through the door. It took a minute for Thompson to realize who it was. It wasn't the same guy who came limping into his office.

Bachman waltzed in with an air of confidence. Smiling. Moving effortlessly. Standing tall. Shoulders back. Head high. Chin out. Wearing a nice pair of slacks and a tailored sport coat over a dress shirt.

Once Thompson realized who it was, he could feel the blood rush from his head. His instincts told him that whatever was going to happen was not good. And the board president was further unnerved as Bachman sat in the front row of public seating directly opposite him.

Thompson's intuition was correct. At the first opportunity, Bachman started to ask probing questions about financials as well as how and why decisions were made. He was also not shy about making requests for additional detail — some they had, but much they would have to get back to him with.

And that was just the beginning. Bachman continued to attend meetings — month after month, asking and requesting. But he did not limit himself to official board meetings. He did the same at committee meetings. And he reached out to board members individually.

Privately and in closed session, board members would ask, "What's this Bachman fellow up to?" Of course, Thompson knew. But he dared not say. In fact, at one point, he texted Studer:

> **You cannot tell anyone about our conversation! I could lose my license.**

Bachman single-handedly took on the board president. When Thompson attempted to limit his attendance at meetings, Bachman won an emergency injunction from the courts.

When Thompson had the board deny his request for information, Bachman found other ways to get it.

When Thompson would attempt to have the board act in closed session, Bachman let the masses know — and they challenged it.

When Thompson sought to get Studer, faculty and staff to act in support of the tax levy, Bachman quashed it on legal grounds.

Through this, Bachman was able to occupy the board with his presence and antics. They were tentative with everything they did and said — routinely stopping to correct or clarify the official record.

But Bachman's real aim was to get information and review it. And the more information Bachman received, the more questions he had. And that led to uncovering irregularities and inconsistencies. This created an air of suspicion, and word of that started to get out in the community. Soon, interest in and attendance at school board meetings started to grow. Many simply attended to support Walter Bachman.

And he never had to point out the obvious. Others did it for him. Funds were skewed toward football and expenses diverted away. At best, monies were being wasted. At worst, there was corruption. Even other members of the board became enlightened by certain revelations.

Beyond Studer and Thompson, it was unclear who knew what. What was clear, however, was that legitimate uncertainty began to build within the community. Suspicions led to mistrust, and mistrust morphed into quiet conversation. In time, those whispers became shouts: "Why should we approve more monies for the district, when it doesn't have a handle on the monies it already has?"

The tax levy, which a year earlier was a shoo-in to easily pass, was now anyone's guess. The district started to have real conversations regarding what would happen if the levy failed.

If the vote was close, they'd seek a recount. If that failed to change the results, they would quickly move to put the levy back on the ballot in August — hoping to secure passage before school was in session. If the levy didn't pass then, the board made it clear that there would be a litany of cuts to programs — including sports.

Chapter 29

Jonathan's phone flashed and vibrated to life.

call ASAP!

It was Sam. He sensed that there was an urgency to her request. He sat up in bed, rubbed his eyes with one hand and reached for the phone with the other.

It was Thursday, 4:23 a.m. local time. He quickly reminded himself where he was and then did a simple time conversion in his head. As much of the United States was amidst daylight saving time, Columbus, Ohio, was 12 hours behind Perth,

Australia. It was 4:23 p.m. for Sam — but only Wednesday. *Perth is an easy conversion*, he thought.

Even though Jonathan was busy with meetings and travel, he and Sam had been texting more than usual over the last few days. Tuesday had been the election day in Ohio, and it was decision time for the voters of the Jefferson Township School District.

Sam was relaying information as she received it. Some of it was idle rumors and conjecture.

> **I bet the maples vote against**
> **Their kids r at bishop hartley.**

Other texts contained more official information and important revelations.

> **studer released an official statement today stating**
> **that bachman met w/ thompson months**
> **ago … made it known that he coming after**
> **football. hopefully, that that rallies support FOR.**

And then on election day itself, she fired off a litany of quick updates.

> **voted! one of first**
>
> **...**
>
> **10 AM … long lines still**
>
> **...**
>
> **not looking good**
> **need a 4q comeback**

Much of Jonathan's replies were simple words of support and affirmation. He had voted absentee. She'd voted. They'd contributed money, and she'd invested significant time in support of the levy. That was all they could control.

By 11:55 p.m. Eastern on Tuesday, it appeared that defeat was inevitable. The hope was that the vote was close enough to trigger a recount — though that didn't seem likely either.

can you get recount to find votes for official recount?

That was the last message he'd received from Sam until now. She'd likely been exhausted or angry at his response to her question — "No! That makes no sense." Maybe it was a little of both. Either way, Jonathan dutifully called Dr. Samantha Reese.

She picked up on the first ring. "Oh, honey. Thanks for calling."

"What's going on there? Have there been some positive developments?" Jonathan infused enthusiasm into his tired voice.

Sam launched into a response. "There has been so much going on here since last night. It's just too much to text." She paused for a moment. "Wait. What time is it there?"

"About 4:25 a.m.," Jonathan said in a tone that indicated it was early.

"Oh shoot. I'm sorry. Do you want me to call you later?" Sam asked.

"Nope. I'm up. What's going on?" Jonathan replied, sitting up further. He turned on the light and grabbed the pen and paper.

"Well, there will be no recount," Sam stated.

"Well, we can get it back on the ballot for August, right?" Jonathan asserted positively.

"Yes, but no," Sam responded. She then quickly clarified. "Joe Thompson just came out with an official statement from the board that they would not attempt to get on the ballot in

August. Isn't that odd? He indicated that they need to devote time and energy to operating the school within its new means, as opposed to trying to push through a tax levy."

"Why is that odd? That seems reasonable," Jonathan stated.

"You're right," Sam conceded. "It's just odd because of how adamant Joe was about stating it. And Mason Jackson is transferring high schools.'"

"What? Where?! How?!" Jonathan became more alert. Mason was a longtime friend of AJ. This was big.

"Upper Arlington." Sam paused to let Jonathan take it in. Then she addressed the "how" with, "His dad lives in that district, so he can do it."

"Are there any others?" Jonathan was now out of bed, pacing. He had so many questions.

"I don't think there is anyone else at this point," Sam responded. "Upper Arlington needed a quarterback, so this was likely in the works for a bit."

"What does AJ think?" Jonathan stopped pacing, listening intently for the answer.

Sam thought for a second and then answered, "I'm not sure." She thought some more. "I just don't know. This is all so fresh. We haven't really had a chance to talk. Like everyone, he's stunned. We all thought this was a possibility, but no one really comprehended what it meant. But AJ has no option to transfer, anyway. And I'm not sure he would. Up until today, his focus has been on next season, repeating, and breaking the scoring record."

"Fair," Jonathan conceded. "What did Studer say?"

"Studer?" Sam then started in on an angry rant. "He's gone. Or soon to be. Rumor has it he — and his whole gaggle of coaches — are off to coach some team in Illinois. They were nothing but hired guns. Yeah, they won, but I don't think they ever really cared about the kids. They certainly didn't care about non-football players. Or football players who weren't the stars."

"Wow, that's quite a condemnation. Where did that come from?" Jonathan asked.

"This whole process has been enlightening. People talked, Jonathan. And they all had stories they weren't willing to share before. One thing I will say is that as much as I despise Walter Bachman, his presence — and actions — gave lots of people the courage to say what they really think. It was shocking."

"What do you mean?" Jonathan was pacing again.

"I can't get into it all right now, honey. I will get too worked up. And I need to get a nap before I head into work." Sam gave a big exhale. "But I will tell you that the developments are not all bad, Jonathan."

"How's that?" Jonathan remained curious but changed the focus.

"Well, Bobby O came through," Sam was upbeat.

"What do you mean?" Jonathan stopped what he was doing. Sam had his attention.

"While we're disappointed that he wasn't able to help with the levy — and I'm not sure it would have mattered anyway ... Walter Bachman was evil, slick, and slippery ... but we got word from Bobby O ... well, someone on his team, anyway ..."

"Sam!?" Jonathan tried to rein in his wife's wandering answer, and she knew it.

"OK, Bobby O is going to underwrite some of what the school board is cutting — sports in particular." Sam's tone was giddy.

Jonathan went quiet for a moment. He wanted to make sure that what he thought he heard was what Sam said. Then he blurted out, "Well, that's great."

"Isn't it?" Sam responded with delight. "He's sort of our white knight coming out of nowhere to save the day. Like the time he had his helicopter hover over the field to dry it."

"Yes, yes," Jonathan reined Sam in again. "But I'm confused then. So why did Studer and his ... gaggle? ... leave?" He was perplexed.

"Well, here's the thing. Bobby O stipulated that he would not cover the compensation for any coach. He'd cover uniforms, yes." Sam glanced at her notes. "Equipment. Transportation. Meals. Insurance for the school. Nathan, the athletic trainer. But he was clear, he would not pay for coaches' salaries." Sam paused. Jonathan said nothing, so she clarified. "More or less, parents — or someone — is going to need to step up to coach."

"Wow! Sam, you buried the lede. That's the big news." Jonathan thought for a moment. "For some sports, having a parent coach might be an improvement." He giggled and then asked, "Are people stepping up?"

Sam shared, "I believe so." She paused for a second, then continued. "There is nothing official, but the word is that there are people looking to step up." She glanced at her notes again. "Volleyball. Cross-country. Soccer. Those are important as they are fall sports."

"Football?" Jonathan interjected.

"Nothing yet." Sam paused. "Again, this just happened a few hours ago."

"Interesting." Jonathan was thinking about who might step up. He drew a blank, as he really didn't know any players' parents.

"You should do it, Jonathan." Sam quickly put it out there.

"Sam?" His tone called for her to be reasonable.

"No, you should." Before Jonathan could rebut, she laid out her case. "You were a good coach for Johnny — and even Kelly's teams. The kids loved you. Those kids still call you Coach. You'd be great."

"Sam? No!" He wasn't mad, but he was firm in his response.

"You'd be great. I know it." With that, Sam rested her case.

"Sam, there are so many reasons why that is a silly notion." Jonathan gathered his thoughts. "Now, hear me out. First, I didn't coach Johnny and Kelly beyond middle school ... this is high school football ... defending state championship high school football."

"So, no other parent has any more experience," Sam interjected.

"Second," Jonathan debated for a second what his second point should be. "Second, I don't think that AJ would be keen on me coaching at all. And things are already tense enough."

Sam refuted his second point with, "Yes, things are tense, but maybe — just maybe — this allows you two to reconnect."

"Sam, you watch too much Hallmark Channel, you know?" Jonathan chuckled and then launched into his last point. "Finally, right now, I'm not even in the same hemisphere. And I can't tell you when that will be or where I'd be going next. And you know that. And you know that is what it's going to take to become a partner. And I really want that. And I've worked hard for it. And the football team deserves better."

That ended the debate. They talked for a few more minutes and headed off to contend with their days, a world apart.

Chapter 30

Joseph Thompson found himself in his office early the day after the failed levy vote. He didn't sleep well. How could he? It wasn't an overwhelming defeat, but it was still a defeat. And it shouldn't have been. That ate at him.

While the vote was not close enough to trigger a recount, there were options. They could always petition the election commission or the Franklin County Municipal Court for a recount. And if that didn't work, the board could get the levy back on the ballot for August. Maybe that levy request would be a "watered-down" version of the one that failed.

The thought of either of those options — or potentially both — was bewildering. They would take time to formulate. And they would require effort to see through. And there were so many people who had done so much in support of the levy. Could they be rallied to do it again? Could the reality of the cuts inspire others to have a change of heart?

It was too much to think about in the moment. He had a law practice to run. As soon as he started to work, his mobile phone vibrated to life. The number appeared as "UNLISTED." He ignored it. "Likely just a robocall," he thought. Then just as soon as it stopped, it vibrated again — same unlisted indication. Thompson still didn't intend to answer. But he clicked a button to push the call directly to voicemail.

He thought that was the end of it. But then, moments later, a text came in from the same unlisted caller.

Answer please!

That's unusual, Thompson thought. He waited for the phone to vibrate a third time. When it did, he answered and said, "Hello, attorney Joseph Thompson."

"I'm sorry the levy failed," the male voice on the other end said. There was a pause, and then the person continued with, "It was inevitable, though."

"How did you get this number?" Thompson knew immediately who it was — Walter Bachman.

"Joe don't be so surprised. I'm resourceful," Bachman interjected, then briefly paused. He continued, "Listen, I didn't call to gloat. I come in peace. The township citizens voted. This is over. Time to move forward."

"Over!?" Thompson was angry. He was sleep-deprived and stressed — a horrible combination. "This isn't over. Not at all. You won round one, sure. But we're not done."

Bachman remained calm. "It's done, Joe. Move on. Devote your time and energy to how to operate with less."

"Who do you think you are?" Thompson wasn't yelling, but he was projecting anger into the phone. "We'll get a recount. If that doesn't work, there will be another election. We will see this through."

"Joe, none of that is going to happen," Bachman remained adamant but calm.

"Yes, it is!" Thompson fired back. The conversation went quiet.

"Joe, you violated our attorney-client privilege," Bachman calmly stated. "I hate to do this, but either this is over or I'm going to play that card."

Thompson knew Bachman was right, but he felt confident in his position. "What privilege? There is no record of us ever meeting. We have nothing in our file. You paid a retainer in cash and have no receipt. None. The only evidence you have is the word of some dumb football coach who is two states away."

Bachman said nothing. He set his phone down and calmly clicked a button to replay a recording.

> *"But let me assure you that anything you share is covered under the attorney-client privilege. What that means is that anything within this meeting I cannot ... and will not ... reveal to anyone else. These are ethical standards that attorneys take very, very seriously. In fact, if I do reveal ANNNYTHING I could lose my license to practice law."*

Thompson recognized his own voice. He felt dizzy. He ended the call without another word. It was over, as Bachman suggested — or his standing in the legal community. His thoughts then turned to how he could backtrack on his pledge to fight on.

Chapter 31

never mind

That was the entirety of Sam's text. He hadn't heard from her in a day, and in the week since the failed levy vote, there had been a flurry of communication between them on a litany of things. "Never mind" could relate to any number of topics.

Never mind, what?

Jonathan fired back. As he hit send, he noted the time. And with that, he almost automatically did a time conversion in his head. He was now in Sydney, Australia. It was 10 a.m. local time on Thursday. That made it 8 p.m. Wednesday in the Eastern time zone.

they found football coach

Among the "litany of things" Sam had continued to press Jonathan on was coaching the football team. She didn't debate; she simply continued to remind Jonathan that she believed in him. And there were plenty of opportunities to do so, as no one was stepping up to take on the role of being the sideline field general for the defending state champions. Even lowly boys tennis — a seldom-mentioned spring sport — had a volunteer coach. It was beginning to feel as if football would not happen.

That's great. Who?

Sam wasted no time. In fact, she was typing before Jonathan even asked.

derrick maven

To Jonathan, the name was not familiar. But then, he didn't really know any of the parents, so the name begged the question.

Who is Derrick Maven?
What year (or position) is his son?

Jonathan hit send. Though Sam was a world away, his message arrived at the speed of light. His wife immediately began typing a response. A few seconds later, it dropped.

not parent former grad asst …
looking 2 break into coachn.

Jonathan had questions, but he could see that Sam was still typing.

this is good opportunity
has own gaggl of assts

She kept going. Jonathan patiently waited for the next thought to drop.

they just met team,
great connection with kids

Jonathan was somewhat following what Sam was texting. So, he let her.

**hope they r good role models
kids/aj needs it**

That was odd. "Need what?" he thought. As he had time, he decided to just call.

Sam picked it up immediately. "Oh! Hey, honey. I wasn't sure if you were in meetings."

"Soon," Jonathan responded. "Sam, this coach thing sounds great. Actually, perfect. But what do you mean, 'AJ needs it'?"

There was a pause, as Sam gathered herself, shifting her brain from text to speaking mode.

As she did, Jonathan waited, but anxiously. He almost spoke to ensure that call had not dropped. Then he heard a deep breath, a heavy sigh, and then Sam broke the silence.

"Honey." She took in another breath of air. Then she began to share her frustration. "Jonathan, AJ is different." She then caught herself, wanting to re-phrase. "Not completely different, but with everything happening here, there has been a shift as to who he aligns."

"What do you mean?" Jonathan felt more confused.

"Well, with the whole question as to would someone step up to coach, the players have sort of drawn together to support one another." Sam took a quick breath and then quickly interjected, "Circled the wagons to coin a phrase."

Still confused, Jonathan asked, "And what's wrong with that?"

"Well, with Mason Jackson leaving the team, AJ has filled that void with a new friend group," Sam clarified.

"And ...?" Jonathan probed for more.

"And I don't like it," Sam emphatically stated.

"I gathered that ... but why? Who are we talking about? It's the football team. Good kids from good families. Right?" Jonathan stared off, focused on understanding an explanation.

"Jonathan?" Sam fired out rhetorically. "You've said it yourself. You haven't been around. Yes, for the most part there are good kids from good families."

"Again, and?" Jonathan pressed for more.

"There are pockets of trouble. And with the departure of Mason, his former back-up — Sebastian Sullivan — is filling a leadership void and it's not good. The kid is trouble, with a capital T. And so are the kids who run with him."

It didn't take much prodding from Jonathan to get Sam to share a rundown of Sebastian Sullivan. From the moment he arrived at Blacklick High, he was almost constantly in trouble. His parents were largely hands off — unless his behavior inconvenienced them.

Like attracts like. Mason Jackson and AJ, two good kids from good families, attracted others like them. That nucleus even drew in Tommy Frank, who, despite a tough home life — raised by a single mom with a father living three counties away — was influenced by Mason and AJ to stay on the right path.

Mason's departure not only opened the door for Sebastian to be the starting quarterback, but also left a leadership void. Sebastian was eager to fill both — and he didn't come alone. He brought others cut from the same troubled cloth: Noah Turner, Aiden Davis, and a few more from the football team.

This shift was informal but real. And parents — especially involved ones like Dr. Sam Reese — could feel it. Yet as much as they noticed, there was little they could do except worry. And there was plenty to worry about. Sebastian and his crew had a long history of trouble — with little deterrent.

From its inception, Blacklick High athletics operated under an honor code requiring players to maintain good conduct in class and in the community. The code barred cheating, truancy, substance abuse, and legal violations.

Acknowledging that teens make mistakes, the code offered a "three strikes" system:

- **Strike one**: sit out a week — practices and games.
- **Strike two**: forfeit the rest of the season.
- **Strike three**: total ineligibility.

Sebastian and his group were caught cheating at the end of freshman year — strike one. They sat out the first week of sophomore conditioning, more reward than punishment.

Then, with two games left that fall, the sheriff's department conducted a drug sweep. Sebastian and others were caught with illegal contraband — strike two. Football was over.

But they didn't stop. Once more their sophomore year and twice their junior year, they arguably hit strike three. Each time, their parents — and allies — rallied to their defense, offering excuses:

"That first violation shouldn't count."

"It's not that bad."

"They're just kids having fun."

"Other schools let worse kids play."

"Don't ruin a young man's future over this."

"Think about the stigma this creates."

Each time, the athletic department — led by Gary Studer, with Coach Fisher's input and support from board president Joseph Thompson — caved. Strike three became a stern warning or a slap on the wrist. Why? Some of them made a difference on the field. All of them boosted the team's roster count. And under Studer's skewed funding system, every name on the roster meant more money for football.

In practice, the honor code had no teeth. Parents and students outside of Sebastian's circle scoffed at it. Behind the scenes, they jokingly referred to the violators as the "foul tip club" — a nod to the baseball rule that a batter stays alive if the third strike is just barely tipped.

Sam summarized her rundown with, "I'm just worried as to where this might lead. You can only be around fire for so long without getting burned."

"Um, Catholic school girl, it took a while, but welcome to the dirty underbelly of public education," Jonathan sneered. "I would say we've been pretty blessed by not having to deal with this for this long."

"That's easy for you to say. You're a world away … and not eager to deal with it when you're not," Sam snapped back.

"True. I know. I know. I know," Jonathan tried to calm the situation. "I'm not much help wherever I'm at. It's just how it is right now. Maybe something will change. I just can't envision it, though."

Chapter 32

As Jonathan worked through his morning exercise routine, he mulled over the busy day ahead — assessing what was important, what could be delegated, and what could wait.

Sitting on the weight bench, removing his shoes and wiping away sweat, his phone vibrated to life. Sam was calling. He answered.

"What's up, honey? Are you coming home soon?" Jonathan asked, wiping his face again.

Sam sounded panicked. "Are you still at home?"

"Yes. I just finished working out. Why?" Jonathan's tone shifted to match hers.

She didn't acknowledge the answer. "Is AJ still home?"

"Yes. I think. I'm not even sure he's up yet — it's still early." He checked the time. "Why? What's going on, Sam?"

"I can't tell you," She cut in.

Jonathan immediately assumed it was related to her work at the Wexner Center ER and went quiet.

Sam filled the silence. "There's been an accident. You need to go to the school and run football practice."

"What? Why? Sam?" He was completely perplexed.

"Jonathan! No one is going to be there. That's all I can say." Her words carried more than she was legally allowed to explain.

Jonathan tried to piece it together. "Why me? Isn't there someone else?"

"Jonathan, I don't know anyone else who knows anything about football," she said, her panic softening into logic. "Please, just go. Practice starts at 8 a.m."

"Okay. Okay. I will," he said, relenting. "Let me jump off and get moving."

They ended the call. Jonathan quickly changed out of his workout clothes and took a fast shower. He texted his assistant to let her know he'd be a few hours late — though in truth, his absence wouldn't be noticed. He'd been gone so much lately.

It was now 7:30 a.m. The high school was only minutes away. He had plenty of time.

Instead of dressing for work, he hung slacks, a dress shirt, and a sport coat in a garment bag — like he was prepping for a short trip. Then he threw on a T-shirt and a pair of khakis he typically wore for housework — something he hadn't done in years. He raced out to hang the bag in his car.

When he came back inside, AJ was up and emerging from the bathroom. With less than 20 minutes until practice, he was clearly behind. Seeing his father's casual attire, AJ stopped and eyed him up and down.

Jonathan was about to explain the situation, but before he could, AJ made a smug face and asked with a snark, "What? Did you get fired?"

Jonathan swallowed what he'd intended to say. AJ would find out soon enough. He simply stepped past him and said, "Don't be late for practice."

He grabbed his workout shoes, slipped them on, and headed out the door to Blacklick High.

Chapter 33

The trip from the Reese household to Blacklick High School was short — about a mile and a half. Jonathan arrived at 7:50 a.m. The parking lot buzzed with activity as the band drilled on the blacktop, using the lines for spacing and shape. There was little sign of varsity football.

Junior varsity players were off in the distance on their corner of the practice facility, surrounded by parent coaches prepping to lead their sons. But across the varsity field, only a handful of players stood around, chatting. They leaned on or sat atop the blocking sled. None wore shoulder pads. Two were still barefoot.

Jonathan wondered if he had the wrong time. Anxious for answers, he approached the nearest person.

"Excuse me. Is there football practice this morning?"

"Yes," the young woman replied quickly, looking up from organizing ointments, tape, and wraps.

"Eight o'clock?" he asked.

"Yes," she said again, this time without looking up.

"A.M.?" He checked his watch.

The young woman chuckled. "Yes. Football seems to be on 'ish' time."

"Ish time?" Jonathan was confused. Another teen slang he didn't understand?

She stopped what she was doing, stood, and smiled. "Ish time. You know — eight-ish. Start time is loose. Whenever the coaches show up."

"And when does practice usually end?" Jonathan asked. Before she could answer, he added, "Ish time?"

She laughed. "Practice ends precisely at ten o'clock. There's no 'ish' to that."

"Great! What's your name? I'm Jonathan Reese — AJ's dad." He offered a handshake.

"Oh, hi. I'm Shea Brooks." She reached out, then paused. "Sorry — my hand might have dirt, or Vaseline, or both on it."

"Shea Brooks? I've heard of you. My wife, Sam, says you're super smart." Jonathan gave a respectful nod.

Shea looked down, trying to hide the blush she could feel on her cheeks. She pushed her glasses up and brushed back her unruly hair. "Thank you. Please tell Dr. Reese thanks, too."

An awkward silence followed. Shea broke it. "Where's AJ? Or are you looking for him?"

"AJ should be here. I just saw him at home," Jonathan replied, skirting the question. "I'm supposed to run practice this morning."

"Really?" Shea's face showed genuine surprise.

"That was my reaction, too," Jonathan said, then pivoted. "What time do you get here?"

"About 6:30," she said proudly.

"Six-thirty-ish?" Jonathan teased with a chuckle. "Why so early?"

She laughed. "Lots of sports in August — volleyball, soccer, cross-country, football…"

"And the band," Jonathan added, glancing at the students across the lot carrying instruments.

"And band," Shea echoed, laughing. "They need water and get injuries, too."

"Well, Shea Brooks, I'll let you get back to it. Nice meeting you. I need to figure out this practice thing."

Jonathan made his way toward the field. It was now 7:58. More varsity players had trickled in — still no AJ. When Jonathan got far enough onto the grass, he called the players in.

They moved slowly. The unspoken thought: *Who is this guy?* Even those who knew he was AJ's dad were unsure why he was calling them. But out of respect for adults, they gathered. As more joined, Jonathan's authority grew.

At 8:02, he told them to get ready — shoulder pads on, cleats laced. As that got underway, AJ arrived, casually ambling in with a few others. After all, it was still "eight-ish."

He spotted his dad and did a double take. Realizing it was the same man he'd seen at home, his pace quickened. He jogged ahead of the others still sauntering toward the group.

Within earshot, AJ shouted, "What the hell are you doing here?"

Jonathan flinched but kept his cool. "I'm here to run practice. Why? Ask your mother. Just get ready."

He saw AJ's annoyance but ignored it. There was nothing he could do about it. Sam asked him to run practice — that was his focus. AJ would get over it.

"Okay, bring it in," Jonathan called, channeling his old college football coach. As the team gathered, he began explaining the situation: he was running practice — didn't know why.

Then he noticed a lone player standing at the edge of the parking lot, facing away as if waiting for someone.

Jonathan waved. "Hey! Come on into practice!"

The team turned to look. Then, all at once, they burst into laughter — some rolling on the ground.

Jonathan ignored the joke and kept calling. The player ignored him. Frustrated, Jonathan turned to one of AJ's friends.

"Tommy, what's that kid's name?"

Through laughter, Tommy Frank said, "Mr. Reese, I'm not sure. Brandon? Brody? Bryan?" He was barely able to get it out.

"Doesn't really matter." Then he dropped to the ground, cracking up.

"Okay, okay," Jonathan said, trying to restore order. "If you've got that much energy, burn some of it with a few laps."

"How many?" Tommy asked, still grinning.

"What's your favorite number between one and ten?" Jonathan asked as he walked toward the parking lot.

"Seven!" Tommy shouted without thinking.

"Then give me seven laps of the whole field!" Jonathan called back.

A collective groan followed — "Seven laps!"

Chapter 34

Jonathan ignored the team's protests, focusing instead on the stray player lingering near the parking lot. As he trotted over, he stopped calling out. The player wasn't responding and continuing to shout felt pointless.

Before Jonathan reached him, the player turned and saw him approaching. His expression was panicked. He quickly looked down, turned away, and scanned the lot — as if searching for someone, hoping for rescue.

The player wore number 38. Jonathan assumed it was his number — AJ wore 29, and his practice jersey matched.

When Jonathan reached him, he tapped the player on the shoulder pads. "Hey, what's your name?"

The player turned and locked eyes with Jonathan — his face full of fear. He motioned with his hands but said nothing, then turned away again.

Jonathan was completely confused. Before he could try again, someone called out, "Coach! Coach! Coach!"

He turned and spotted a petite woman in her 60s, walking briskly in flat dress shoes. She was motioning and trying to speak, clearly out of breath.

As she neared, she gestured toward the player and said, "Sorry I'm late, Coach. Traffic was horrible."

Jonathan quickly deduced: the player was deaf, and this woman was his interpreter. The confusion lifted.

"Hello," he said. "I'm not the coach — just a dad who got hoodwinked into running practice this morning." He chuckled, still a bit uneasy. "Jonathan Reese. What's your name?"

The woman signed his words to the player, then continued signing as she replied, "Thanks for helping out. This is certainly a unique high school. I'm Joyce Yocheim."

"Joyce, it's so nice to meet you," Jonathan said, reaching to shake her hand.

She grasped just his fingertips, then quickly pulled away so she could sign again.

A short silence followed. Jonathan looked between her and the player, then asked, "What's his name? What's the best way to communicate with him?"

Joyce signed Jonathan's words to the player, then replied, "Thanks for asking. This great young man is Brady Troy."

Jonathan turned to Brady and extended his hand. Brady — tall, athletic, about 6'2" — met it with a strong, meaty grip and a broad smile.

"Wow! What a grip," Jonathan said. He turned back to Joyce. "Could you tell Brady it's nice to meet him?"

"Of course," she said, signing quickly. Then she addressed Jonathan directly. "If you don't mind, here are a few etiquette tips for communicating through an interpreter."

Jonathan nodded.

Joyce gently turned him toward Brady and began:

"Speak directly to Brady, not me.

"Maintain eye contact and speak naturally.

"Don't exaggerate lip movements — it makes reading harder.

"Use normal gestures and expressions, but don't overdo it.

"Speak in short, clear sentences and pause so I can translate.

"Be patient.

"If you need clarification, ask Brady. He might ask you to repeat or rephrase.

"And most importantly, respect his desire to be communicated with — and heard."

Jonathan, now more confident, turned to Brady. "Welcome to Blacklick High, Brady. I'm Mr. Reese. My son is on the team, and I'm helping out this morning."

Joyce signed the message. Brady signed back.

"Thanks, Mr. Reese. It's nice to meet you. I'm excited to play football here," Joyce translated.

Jonathan responded naturally. "That's great. I'm sure the team will be happy to have you." He paused for Joyce to translate, then added, "They're doing warmup laps. Why don't you join them and finish when they finish. I'll meet you at midfield."

Joyce signed again. Brady nodded, smiled, and took off toward the group.

"Thank you," Joyce said softly, without signing.

"You're welcome — but for what?" Jonathan asked.

"For welcoming Brady. For shaking his hand," she replied. "In two or three weeks of practice, no one's done that. No one."

"You're kidding," Jonathan said, stopping to look at her. "Not even the coaches?"

"No, not even the coaches," she said firmly. "They barely tolerate our presence. The way they treat Brady, you'd think he had leprosy. Deafness isn't contagious, Jonathan."

"Has he always been deaf?" Jonathan asked.

"Yes," Joyce said. "He was born several weeks premature. His auditory system never developed. But everything else about him is perfectly normal. He's just a red-blooded American teen who loves sports, video games, pizza — the usual."

She shared that Brady lives in the Jefferson School District but had attended the Ohio School for the Deaf. He chose to transfer to Blacklick High after learning Mason Jackson was transferring — hoping there'd be a season. He had been a standout at OSD but wanted to test himself in a bigger pond.

Jonathan remained mostly quiet as they walked. He gave the occasional nod or gesture of attention. He wasn't sure why he needed to know all this — but he could hear his grandfather's words echoing: It never hurts to be kind and respectful.

By the time they reached midfield, the team was finishing their seven laps — Brady now among them. Players arrived, feigning exhaustion and joking that the warmup was more of a workout. Jonathan ignored their groans and gestured for Shea to hand out water.

Once the team had caught their breath, Jonathan stepped forward. "Okay, listen up." He motioned to Brady to come forward. Brady hesitated but complied. Jonathan turned him toward the team, Joyce at his side.

"Okay, settle down," Jonathan said. As they quieted, he put his arm around Brady. "I want to introduce your new teammate — Brady Troy." Joyce signed. Brady smiled. "He transferred here from the Ohio School for the Deaf."

Jonathan paused. "He wanted to trade his…" He turned to Brady. "What's your mascot at OSD?"

Brady signed. Joyce translated: "Spartans."

Jonathan continued, "He wanted to trade his Spartan jersey for a Mustang one."

The team was quiet, unsure how to respond.

Then someone asked, "What position do you play?"

Brady didn't hear. Jonathan repeated the question, Joyce signed, Brady responded, and Joyce said, "Quarterback."

Half a second later, Sebastian Sullivan chimed in, "Third-string quarterback," patting the number 10 on his chest. Laughter followed. Brady smiled, unaware of the joke. Jonathan and Joyce ignored it.

Jonathan then shared the respectful communication etiquette Joyce had taught him. Point by point, Joyce signed. Brady nodded.

When he finished, Jonathan asked, "Did I cover everything?"

Joyce signed the question to Brady, then replied, "Coach — I mean, Jonathan — you did great." She added, "If you want to make things easier, the best way is to learn some basic sign language."

Sebastian quipped, "What's the second-best way?" then muttered, "I'm not learning any of this shit." His friends, Noah Turner and Aiden Davis, laughed and gave him high-fives.

Brady smiled again, not catching the slight. Jonathan didn't ignore the disrespect, but he didn't confront it either.

"Brady's your teammate," he said. "He's here to help you win. Welcome him. Respect him."

Joyce signed. Brady smiled. The group broke. Practice began.

Chapter 35

Jonathan had mixed feelings about being the substitute coach for the Blacklick Mustangs. On one hand, he was completely unprepared.

He didn't know the players, their positions, or the playbook. He had no idea what drills to run. It had been years since he coached and even longer since he played. Still, he tried to dig into the recesses of his memory for anything productive.

The players weren't much help — not even AJ. They listened as Jonathan suggested ideas, but no one offered input. Instead,

AJ, Sebastian Sullivan, and his crew — Noah Turner, Aiden Davis, and others — chimed in with comments like, "That's stupid" or "We don't do that." Jonathan didn't have the authority to push back. He was just the sub.

Then there was the challenge of involving Brady Troy. Jonathan had to communicate through Joyce while keeping her safe from the chaos of colliding bodies. It was a long couple of hours.

But in some ways, it was good for Jonathan. After months of meetings and travel, the sun and fresh air were a welcome change.

The experience was oddly exhilarating — the clash of pads, the scent of fresh-cut grass and sweaty gear. It brought back memories of his playing days at Woodward High and Case Western Reserve. Despite the chaos, he felt alive.

As 10 a.m. approached, Jonathan spotted Nathan Rogers, the athletic trainer, talking to Board President Joseph Thompson on the sideline. Rogers being there was normal — Thompson was not. Their body language felt ominous.

Jonathan sensed they were looking for a chance to speak with him, so he called the team in, hoping to keep them busy while he broke away.

"Good practice. Let's finish with some light running — nothing crazy."

He paused to let them groan, then grinned. "It won't kill you."

When the complaints died down, he caught Brady's attention. "What's your favorite number between one and ten?"

Brady turned to Joyce. As he did, the team erupted: "Say one! Say one!"

Joyce may have heard, but she didn't translate. Brady smiled and held up ten fingers.

"There you have it, boys — ten laps," Jonathan said, laughing. The players groaned louder. "No walking. Keep a steady pace." He tapped his watch and started the stopwatch. "Fifteen minutes. Go!"

As the players stampeded off, Jonathan called, "No cutting corners. Joyce is watching."

He jogged toward Thompson and Rogers, who stepped forward to meet him.

"Gentlemen," Jonathan greeted.

"Thanks for pitching in," Thompson said. "You're a natural."

Jonathan chuckled. "You sound like my wife. Speaking of which — can one of you explain what's going on? She sent me here but said nothing."

Rogers shrugged, deferring to Thompson.

"There was an accident," Thompson said, choosing his words carefully.

"I figured," Jonathan said. "How bad? Will... what's the coach's name again?"

"Derrick Maven," Rogers supplied.

"Will Coach Maven be back later?"

"No," Thompson said flatly.

At that moment, the players ran past, panting. Jonathan called out encouragement, then turned back. "Look, Joe, I get it. Everyone's trying to C-Y-A. But these kids deserve to know if they've got practice this afternoon."

Thompson exhaled. "Derrick Maven was in an accident. Broken femur, internal injuries. He won't be coaching anytime soon. His assistants — who were with him — have minor injuries. They'll be fine."

Jonathan was relieved. "Okay, so one of them will take over then?"

"No," Thompson said, firmly.

Jonathan gave him a puzzled look.

"There was alcohol in the car," Thompson said. "And ... a couple teenage girls."

"Oh," Jonathan muttered, then, "Ew. Yeah — none of them can coach here." He paused. "Now what?"

Thompson looked down. "I think ... I hate to say it ... but we might have to cancel the season." He cleared his throat. "I don't see any other way."

Rogers looked away, ashamed.

"Cancel?" Jonathan repeated, stunned. "There's no one else?"

"You'd think someone would coach the defending state champs. But apparently not," Thompson said. "This whole Maven crew — it came out of nowhere. Some say parents pooled money to bring them in. I don't know. But before that, we had no one. So no — we don't have a coach."

"Why not you, Jonathan?" Rogers asked. "You seem to know what you're doing."

Jonathan hesitated. "Thanks, Nathan ... but it's not that simple."

"I understand," Thompson said. "I started in a big firm too. They own you."

"Come on," Jonathan said, walking toward the field. "If it's over, someone needs to tell the team — now."

"Me?" Thompson asked.

"Yes, you," Jonathan snapped. "I'm just here — how'd you put it? — 'pitching in.'"

"Shouldn't we wait for them to finish running?" Thompson asked, unsure.

Jonathan looked back. "We're not making them run seven more laps for a season that just ended." He waved him forward. "Come on."

He called to the players. They quickly broke stride and sprinted in, eager not to miss good news.

They formed a loose semicircle around Jonathan. Joyce stood at one side, ready to sign for Brady. Thompson stood on the other, fidgeting. Behind them, Rogers looked at the ground, unable to meet their eyes.

The players, still winded, didn't settle right away. Some bent over. Others drank water Shea handed out.

"Okay, have some water. Catch your breath," Jonathan said, buying time. "Take your helmets off. Cool down."

As the players complied, Jonathan scanned their faces. They were tired — but happy. None of them had to be there. They wanted to be. Football energized them. He saw it in Tommy Frank's jokes, Brady's beaming smile, and AJ's bright demeanor.

This was going to hurt.

"Okay, listen up," Jonathan said. He waited for Joyce to catch up. Then: "Today, I want to introduce Mr. Joseph Thompson." He motioned to him. "He's here today… he's the school board president … and he's here to … well … thank you and wish you well this season."

Thompson froze for a second, then nodded, playing along.

Jonathan continued, "Obviously, with the levy failing, this year will be different — but that doesn't mean it can't be great."

"Where's Coach Maven?" Tommy asked.

"To be honest, I'm not sure," Jonathan said. "But you have practice today at 5 p.m. sharp. Be here. It'll be sorted out by then."

He paused, let Joyce translate, then added: "Hydrate. See Nathan or Shea if you're banged up. Eat something healthy. And go easy on the video games. Rest those thumbs."

Everyone laughed. The meeting broke. The players headed toward the locker room. Joyce and Brady walked to the lot. Shea cleaned up.

Jonathan stayed at midfield with Thompson and Rogers.

When they were alone, Thompson asked, amused, "What are you doing, Jonathan?"

"These kids have been let down — by Maven, the voters, Studer. I'm not sure how I'll manage, but I'm going to coach them. I'm not letting this team down."

"Really?" Thompson asked, surprised.

"Really."

Rogers' eyes widened. "Jonathan, I'll help however I can. Just say the word."

"Thanks, Nathan," Jonathan said, placing a hand on his shoulder. "I'm going to need it."

"Yes! Me too!" Thompson added. "I don't know what I can do — I was in the band — but I'll help." They laughed.

"Well," Jonathan said, "I need a roster and basic info. Beyond that, just support me when things get tough. I know there'll be bumps."

Thompson asked, "Want me to call Ari and explain this to him?"

Jonathan exhaled. He wasn't looking forward to that conversation. "Thanks, Joe, but this is something I need to do myself." Then he smiled and joked, "Who knows? I might need a job by the end of today."

Chapter 36

Jonathan walked off the field at Blacklick High, hopped in his car, and drove to his office downtown. On the way, he worked in a couple of quick calls with associates on his team, as well as a few clients — just quick touch-base stuff.

It was hard to focus on work, though. His mind was consumed with how to approach Ari about fitting coaching football into his path toward partnership. Various versions of the conversation played out in his head. While Jonathan remained optimistic, he knew not all of them ended well.

Nevertheless, he was committed to asking and exploring the possibilities. After all, other firm attorneys pursued outside interests — arts, humanities, charitable and civic causes. The question was whether coaching high school football was noble enough for a preeminent law firm.

When he arrived, he parked in the garage adjacent to the Huntington Center, a 37-story building across from the State Capitol. It housed various legal, accounting, and marketing firms — including Eisenberg & Anders.

Years earlier, when Ari was starting his firm and had no cachet, his good friend Bobby O arranged for a subsidiary of Emerald Medical to lease space in the Huntington Center, with an option to expand. It then sublet the space to the fledgling Eisenberg & Anders firm. As the firm grew, Emerald Medical exercised its expansion rights.

It was the perfect setup. Emerald secured favorable lease terms thanks to its business stature. Bobby O shared those benefits with Ari while ensuring Emerald got a reasonable return. Meanwhile, the legal fees Emerald paid Eisenberg & Anders made sure the sublet rent got paid.

Rather than going straight up to the firm's offices, Jonathan detoured to shower and change in the Huntington Club — the swanky, exclusive dining and workout facility on the lower levels of the building. As warm water washed away the football field grime, he zeroed in on how he would approach Ari.

Once clean and dressed, he took the elevator. Though he wasn't alone on the ride, he was alone in thought — confident in his approach but unsure how it would be received.

Jonathan exited on his floor, quickly greeted the receptionist, and went straight to his office to drop off legal files and hang his suit bag. Then he headed directly to Ari's office — down the hall, around the corner, up a set of internal stairs, and along a corridor to Ari Eisenberg's spacious corner suite.

As he approached, he saw Warren Scott inside with Ari. He considered coming back later, but Warren always seemed to be around. Jonathan decided to push forward.

"Do you have a minute?" Jonathan asked, knocking on the doorframe.

"Jonathan, Jonathan, Jonathan! Come in!" Ari said warmly. "Here. Catch." He tossed Jonathan an umbrella.

Jonathan caught it, puzzled. "What's this?"

"You're making it rain at Eisenberg & Anders. We all need an umbrella." Ari laughed at his own joke. "At this rate, we might need to build an ark and march the animals in two by two." He laughed even harder.

Warren Scott was not amused. He never enjoyed others' accolades. Especially when they stole attention from him.

Ignoring Warren, Jonathan politely laughed and stayed on task. "I wanted to talk with you about our conversation regarding..." He hesitated, glancing at Warren. "... my path to partnership."

Ari looked over his glasses. "It's okay, Jonathan. Warren's privy to most things. When you're a partner, you will be too." He smiled. "Yes, when. You're doing all the right things, my friend."

"Thank you," Jonathan said, though a flicker of anxiety ran through him. He now felt like he had something to lose. Still, he pressed on. "You said there were two things I needed to work on — making it rain..." He held up the umbrella, "...and getting involved in the community."

Ari nodded. Warren did too, eager to cite that "deficiency" come partnership review season. He had already worked to undermine Jonathan's bid last year — and was ready to try again.

Jonathan swallowed hard. His heart rate rose. He could feel sweat along his back. Still, he continued. "I have an opportunity to coach the football team at Blacklick High. They had a coach

— actually coaches — and I'll spare you the details… but now they don't."

Warren jumped in. "What are the details? Don't withhold information. We need to consider everything."

Jonathan fired back, "Sheesh, Warren. I'm asking Ari, not you. The information's not public. It was shared in confidence." He paused, trying not to escalate. "And it doesn't really matter. It has no bearing on what I'm asking."

Ari remained quiet. Warren's face turned red. He stood, squared up with Jonathan, and snapped, "If it involves the firm and its good name, it is my business. And the details always matter. We're accustomed to sharing and keeping confidences here — so out with it."

Jonathan shook his head. The details didn't matter. Warren was just asserting power — again. But sharing wouldn't hurt. He just hated giving in to "that short, balding, Napoleonic loser."

Still, it wasn't worth the fight. He relented. "Okay, fine. Summary: car accident, broken femur, alcohol, underaged girls. What part of that really matters, and do you want to explore, Warren?"

Warren had no retort. He pivoted. "Well, nothing. But coaching sweaty teenage boys doesn't really meet the standard for community involvement at this firm."

Jonathan turned back to Ari. "What do you think?"

Warren bristled. Jonathan was going over his head — appealing to the firm's supreme authority. He hated it.

At the firm, everyone knew Warren Scott was despised. He kissed up to those above him and kicked down at those below. He flattered those in power, and belittled associates and staff. Even when he sucked up, you had to watch your back. He was always looking to gain the upper hand — highlighting mistakes, spreading rumors, even fabricating lies about drug use, mental health, or personal failings.

And when caught, he'd feign confusion. "Oh, that's not what I meant," or "I didn't realize…" He was slippery, calculating — and utterly untrustworthy.

Warren also had a knack for abusing junior staff. "Take my car for an oil change." "Wait at my condo for the cable guy." "Take my labradoodle to the vet … and don't forget the fecal sample."

He was notorious for gaslighting new associates into thinking their suits weren't firm worthy. Then he'd refer them to a tailor, collecting a free custom suit for every ten referrals. Ari, in contrast, used the same tailor for years — always paying full price, in cash, and often leaving a tip so the tailor could "take that beautiful wife of yours to dinner."

Ari's generosity was the only reason Warren ever made it into Eisenberg & Anders. Warren's father, Raymond Scott — a friend of Ari's from law school — sold his estate planning firm to a Chicago-based firm. But the Chicago firm didn't want Warren.

Raymond called in a favor. "Could you take on my son, Warren? He's mine, but… he's not me. He takes after his miserable ex-mother-in-law." Ari laughed and agreed. Raymond retired to Costa Rica. The rest was history.

Warren joined four years before Jonathan and started manipulating from day one. Ari remained hopeful he could mold him into a good attorney — maybe even a better person. But progress was slow, and some days nonexistent.

Warren resented Jonathan from the start. Before they even met, Ari was elated to bring Jonathan in — calling it a huge win. At one gathering, Warren claimed Emerald One — Bobby O's green AW139 helicopter — could break the sound barrier. Jonathan laughed, "That's not even close. The speed of sound is 700 mph."

Jonathan had worked extensively with Emerald Medical, including tax implications of Bobby O's fleet. He knew Emerald

One topped out around 190 mph. The room fact-checked and confirmed he was right — again tarnishing Warren's self-proclaimed expertise.

Jonathan also shrugged off Warren's fashion criticisms. Later, he began showing up in custom suits — made by the same Italian tailor but referred by Ari himself.

So, as Warren awaited Ari's response to Jonathan's request, he rooted for disappointment. He couldn't help but smile as Ari finally spoke.

Still in thought, Ari said, "You know, Jonathan ..." He paused. "To be honest ... um ... I don't like it. Not one bit."

Chapter 37

In medical school, Dr. Sam Reese learned that one never truly acclimates to working the graveyard shift — late at night into the early hours of the morning. Despite this, she found that, with practice, she could develop the ability to fall into a deep, restful sleep under almost any conditions. So, it was not surprising that she didn't hear Jonathan's text come in just after 11 a.m.

Hey, Honey! Guess What?

What was surprising, however, is that he didn't reply to her 12:33 p.m. response.

what?

Or the follow up text at 12:50 p.m.

what??? r u okay?

Or another text at 1:30 p.m.

dont leeve me hang'n

Or the three other text messages and the eventual phone call that went immediately to, "You've reached the personal cell phone of Jonathan Reese ..."

Chapter 38

"To be honest ... um ... I don't like it ... not one bit." Those words rang in Jonathan's ears as his heart sank and stress filled his body. His mind raced. He was stuck between letting down a team or potentially abandoning a pursuit he'd worked so hard for. Warren Scott could sense Jonathan's angst. It brought him great joy.

"Yeah, I don't like it," Ari repeated, still staring off. Then, in an instant, he snapped out of his trance, stood up, and roared to life: "I don't like it. No, I love it. Every bit of it. Love it." He let out a bellowing laugh.

He reached for the phone on his desk, pushed a button, and eagerly inquired, "Theresa, could you come in here, please?" Then he looked toward the door, waiting for her to enter. Both Jonathan and Warren stood in stunned disbelief. Neither said a word.

"This is great ... really!" Ari could hardly contain himself. "Think about it, Warren." He didn't wait for a response. "This will be great for the firm."

Warren and Jonathan remained silent. Neither looked at the other. They simply watched Ari pace and fidget.

"Oh, where is she?" Ari muttered, then walked to the door, looked left, and called out, "Where's Theresa?"

"I'm right here, Ari," came the reply. Theresa was approaching from his left, a file in hand.

Ari turned and quipped, "Don't sneak up on me." Then he laughed at his own joke and waved her in. "Can you come in really quick?"

"Sure," Theresa replied with her usual smile as she followed him into the office.

Theresa had been with Ari for years. She had a twin sister, Tessa, who was now an impressive assistant to Bobby O. The Emerald Medical boss raved about her. When Ari once asked Tessa if she knew anyone like her, she replied, "Yes! She's identical."

"Theresa, can you get with the PR people at Walker Communication?" Before she could answer, Ari continued, "Coordinate with them to get some press for the firm on Jonathan. He's the head football coach at … drumroll, please … Blacklick!" The excitement rang in his voice.

"Oh, that's wonderful, Jonathan," Theresa chimed in. "My twin daughters graduated from there."

Her daughters and Tessa's twins had played soccer together — four girls from the same athletic gene pool. There had been plenty of optimism about what that "duo double" could accomplish. And it was all unfolding — until just before their senior season. In a move that diverted funding to football, their veteran coach was replaced with a rookie. What should have been a state championship run ended in a complete debacle. The new coach moved on shortly after.

"Wait," Theresa said, suddenly remembering. "You had me book Jonathan on a trip to the Far East this fall — for the Emerald acquisition. I can't remember the dates. Late October, maybe?"

Ari paused, the excitement draining from his face. He thought for a moment, then lit up again. "That's okay. Warren can cover that. He'd be a wonderful replacement."

Warren was stunned. He had no interest in going to the Far East — or anywhere. He also knew his usual office manipulations didn't work well outside the building. Either way, he'd had enough of this scene. He politely excused himself and left the room.

Chapter 39

As he drove away from the office, Jonathan finally responded to his wife.

"Sam, where are you? I'm sorry I haven't responded. I've been tied up all day."

"I guess," she replied. "So, what's up?"

"Good news, bad news. What do you want first?" Jonathan asked playfully.

"Um, give me the good."

"I'm going to be the football coach at Blacklick this season," Jonathan said.

"ARE YOU KIDDING ME?" Sam screamed into the phone. "Oh my God! Really? This is so awesome." She rattled off thoughts of excitement, then launched into a queue of questions. "How did it happen? How are you going to work it out with work? Wait, what's the bad news? Did you quit your job?"

Jonathan laughed. "No, everything is fine at work."

"Then what's the bad news?"

"The bad news is that I'm going to be coaching AJ for his senior season," Jonathan chuckled.

"Oh, it won't be that bad." Then Sam corrected herself: "It won't be bad at all. Actually, it'll be good. Does AJ know?"

"Well, I assume he doesn't. You can tell him, Sam."

"I can't. I just parked. I'm headed into a meeting … actually I'm late," Sam said. "You can tell him. He's at home. We dropped off his car at Don's Car Care — the back right tire has a slow leak or something, again. Then I left him at home about an hour ago. He was going to take a nap, and Tommy was going to bring him to practice."

"Well," Jonathan paused to think, "if he doesn't know yet, he'll find out soon enough. I've got to get to the school, get keys, a roster, the playbook, and a bunch of other things before practice kicks off at five."

"Before I go," Sam said, stepping one foot out of her car, "how do you feel?"

Jonathan thought for a moment, then said sincerely, "Like a new dad, to be honest. I'm so excited. But also terrified of what I don't know or what I might screw up."

Sam reassured him, "Just like our kids — it'll be great."

As Jonathan continued on to Blacklick High, he replayed the previous five or six hours in his mind. Much of it had been a whirlwind of football-related and semi-related activity, starting with calling Joseph Thompson. There were basics they needed to cover. Thompson pledged to call the school to alert the appropriate people to be expecting Jonathan and get him what he needed. The board president ended the call with, "Thank you. On behalf of these kids, the parents, and the whole school — thank you. You've got my full support."

From there, Jonathan gathered whoever from his Eisenberg & Anders team was in the office. Together, they meticulously coordinated project completion and reassigned responsibilities. While Ari was behind him, the work still had to get done and clients needed to be served. Jonathan's coaching opportunity also created growth opportunities for other attorneys.

He then spent 90 minutes on the phone with coaches at his alma mater — Case Western Reserve University.

"Um, hi … my name is Jonathan Reese. This might sound strange, but I played football at Case, and … well … I was hoping to pick someone's brain."

The voice on the other end responded, "Jonathan? Jonathan Reese?"

Jonathan was caught off guard and had nothing to say.

"I'm Coach Connor," the man said. "You graduated a few years before I arrived to play here. My coach … your coach … our coach — Coach Nelson — shared lots of impressive, almost legendary, stories about you." Jonathan was still silent. Connor asked, "How can I help?"

From there, a conversation unfolded. The veteran coach got the rookie coach up to speed on jargon, drills, and protocols. Soon enough, Jonathan's brain — and email inbox — was full of enough to give him confidence to lead the team.

Connor closed the call with, "Contact me whenever. I'm happy to help."

Then Jonathan turned back to legal work — reviewing documents, drafting letters, and talking with clients. But it was hard to focus. Football was on his mind. He couldn't wait to leave the office — earlier than he had in a long time — to run practice. It had been a busy, productive afternoon when he stepped onto the elevator at 4:05 p.m.

It had been a busy afternoon for Warren Scott, too. It took some effort, but he figured out how to weasel his way out of going to the Far East — and who to dump the trip on.

Shortly after lunch, Warren gave a firm directive.

"Stephenson, Ari told me earlier that he needs you to go to the Far East in late October to oversee some Emerald acquisition due diligence."

"Um, Warren, are you sure? My wife is due to deliver twins mid-October. They'll only be weeks old," the senior associate said, shaken by Warren's pressure.

"Listen, this is not a request. This is a firm assignment from the top," Warren snapped. "I'm not going back to Ari to tell him you can't … or won't. At this point, he doesn't want you bothering him with these trivial matters." Warren let the words hang. Then he piled on: "Besides, your hours are down. Moving to a larger house. Doctor appointments. Couples baby showers. Those may well be career-limiting moves."

Stephenson stood frozen with fear.

"Just figure it out if you want to keep working here."

Not long after, Warren circled back to Ari to complete the manipulation.

"Ari, funny thing. Stephenson heard I was getting to jet off to the Far East in place of Jonathan. He practically begged to go instead. Crazy, huh?"

"Stephenson? Really?" Ari asked, looking over the top of his glasses. "Isn't his wife expecting twins?"

"Yes," Warren laughed. "That's probably the reason he wants to get away so much."

"What a team player. We need to commend him ... in some special way," Ari said.

"I agree — and I have. No need to do any more, Ari. He's the shy sort. It'll only embarrass him to mention it again."

Chapter 40

Prior to the five o'clock rush hour, it was a quick trip from downtown Columbus to Blacklick High — out I-670 eastward, through the city of Gahanna. Jonathan pulled into the school parking lot at 4:35 p.m.

He looked out onto the practice field. It wasn't empty. Shea Brooks was weighed down with a litany of kits, water bottles, and bags of balls. Briefly, they made eye contact. Jonathan didn't wave or say a word. He made a beeline into the school and down to the office.

Waiting for him were some papers to sign, a set of keys, and materials from Coach Maven — the briefly tenured replacement coach. There was the roster with proposed position assignments. That would be helpful.

He also found the playbook. The was vital. Jonathan asked the staff to make copies of the several page document for each player and place them in a three-ring binder. He intended for everyone to have a copy.

He also found a notebook of drills. That he intended to discard, as Coach Connor and other friends from Case Western Reserve University had already given him plenty.

He exited the office, intending to leave the building the same way he came in. As he rounded a corner, he nearly ran into Shea Brooks, once again laden with equipment.

"Whoa! Excuse me. I'm sorry," he said reflexively.

"Oh, sorry," Shea replied in kind. She'd clearly been out in the heat — her shirt was soaked at the collar and down her back, and beads of sweat dotted her forehead and upper lip.

Her hair was pulled into a chaotic bun atop her head, though one clump had fallen onto her face, resting on her thick glasses and intermingling with her brows. With a quick puff of air, she blew the hair back into place — temporarily.

"Can I help you? Shea, right?" Jonathan asked.

"Yes … and thank you," Shea replied, handing him an item. They started walking together toward the practice field.

As they walked, Jonathan asked, "What time do you get here?"

"6:30 a.m.," she said without hesitation.

"No — this afternoon?" he clarified.

"Oh. I get here at 6:30 a.m., and I stay until practices are done," Shea explained.

Jonathan's eyes widened. "Wow. That's a long day."

"It is," Shea agreed. "But there are a lot of sports going on now. It eases up in a week once school starts. There'll be others to help, and teams will only be practicing once a day."

"Still — wow," Jonathan repeated. "I'm going to get some of the football players to help you … at least with football gear. You know I'm going to be coaching?"

Shea smiled and giggled. "Yes, I'd heard. Word is getting around."

"I hope it's a good word," Jonathan said.

"It is. There's a buzz of excitement," Shea told him.

They continued chatting until they reached the practice field at 4:50. Then they went their separate ways — Shea attending to trainer duties, and Jonathan greeting players as they trickled out from the locker room.

As 5:00 approached, Jonathan called the players in. At precisely 5:00, his watch chimed. He blew his whistle to officially start practice and directed them to take a brisk warm-up lap.

When they gathered again, Jonathan surveyed who had arrived on time. It was obvious who hadn't.

"Tommy? Where's AJ?" Jonathan asked with a stern voice. "I thought you were supposed to bring him to practice."

"Mr. Reese. I was. I tried," Tommy Frank answered, a hint of panic in his voice. His unease didn't quite match his stout, six-foot-three frame. "I stopped at your house. I beeped. I rang the doorbell. I knocked. I texted. Nothing. No response. I assumed he got a ride from someone else. I'm sorry."

"It's okay. I was just asking. He's not your responsibility," Jonathan said, softening his tone.

Just then, Sebastian Sullivan, Noah Turner, Aiden Davis, and a few others from the "foul tip" crew wandered out and joined the rest of the team.

Jonathan shook his head in disbelief. They acted like their tardiness was no big deal.

"You're late. Give me two laps," he fired off.

"Are you serious? Late's not a problem here," Sebastian replied for the group.

"It is now. Two laps!" Jonathan snapped; his tone sharp.

"Well, who do you think you are? When is Derrick coming back?" Sebastian challenged.

"He's not," Jonathan said. Then he addressed everyone. "This season — like it or not — I'll be coaching."

As soon as Joyce signed that, Brady Troy's expression shifted from concern to a happy smile.

"I'm not going to get into it all right now," Jonathan continued. "I believe the school is communicating with your parents ... I don't know for sure. But what I do know is that I have a lot to learn, and we have a lot to cover before the first game. So, Sebastian, I need you and the others who were late to take two fast laps and then get into practice. We're starting now."

The debate was over. The "foul tip" crew conceded and began their laps. Sebastian was the last to leave, taking a path behind Jonathan. As he passed, he flashed a single-finger gesture in sign language. Everyone who saw it understood — and was shocked.

As they departed, AJ arrived — still in street clothes, drenched in sweat. He barked at his father, "What are you doing here again?"

"Coaching," Jonathan replied matter-of-factly. "Where've you been? Why aren't you dressed?"

AJ looked toward Tommy Frank. "I fell asleep and missed my ride."

"So, how did you get here?" Jonathan asked.

"How did I get here?" AJ repeated sarcastically, as if the answer was obvious. He glanced at Tommy again. "I ran ... the whole mile and a half."

"I'm sorry, AJ," Tommy offered sheepishly.

"Enough," Jonathan cut in. "AJ, go get some water from Shea, get dressed, and get back out here ASAP. You owe me five laps."

"Five laps?" AJ protested. "I just ran a mile and a half!"

"You did," Jonathan agreed. "But you're late. So — five laps. Save the excuses."

Without another word, AJ sauntered off, resigned to his penance.

Chapter 41

AJ was late. He was resolved to that. But he was also tired and parched. Racing the mile-and-a-half distance in the August heat made that inevitable. So, he walked toward where Shea Brooks had the water set up.

As he walked, he tried to shake off his confusion. *Why is my dad here again?* It felt like a dream — not necessarily a bad one, but weird. If he told anyone he'd overslept a nap, sprinted to practice, and found his dad coaching, they'd assume it was all imaginary.

"Here, AJ!" Shea eagerly called out, meeting him with a water bottle.

"Thanks," AJ said, taking the clear plastic bottle and spraying water into his mouth. After a quick blast and swallow, he asked, "Where's Derrick and the others?"

Having been around the school most of the day, Shea had heard plenty — some rumor, some speculation, and some verifiable facts. She distilled what she knew into a few short sentences.

AJ said nothing. He rotated between shooting water into his mouth, splashing it on his face, and pouring it down the back of his neck. Other than "thanks," he stayed silent. He handed the now-empty bottle back to Shea, turned, and trotted away.

A short while later, AJ returned to practice — changed out of sweat-soaked street clothes into dried-sweat football gear. He dutifully ran his five-lap penalty, then jumped into drills, where his dad now seemed remarkably prepared.

Despite that, AJ and Sebastian occasionally challenged his instructions: "That's not what we do," or, "This seems pointless." Jonathan confidently met each challenge: "It's what we're doing now," or, "Just go with it — these are college-level drills." The responses didn't please them, but they had no recourse.

AJ shook his head. The situation seemed surreal. He didn't want to push back too hard — he had to live with his coach.

Sebastian, however, didn't have that limitation. He pushed harder, often asking "why?" Jonathan held firm. But when his view was blocked or he wasn't looking, Sebastian — to the amusement of some and the disgust of others — would flash a middle finger gesture.

By the time Jonathan was ready to talk about offensive formations and game plan, the school office bought out the litany of three-ring binder playbooks, with Coach Maven's offense. He distributed them out, explaining that there wasn't time to create a new one. "It'll have to work," he told himself. He relied on the team to identify who played where.

All in all, the team gave Jonathan Reese a spirited first official practice. Aside from the occasional challenge and Sebastian's covert gestures — which Jonathan never saw — the team accepted him. As a quiet reward, he ended practice with light conditioning, then called them in for a debrief.

As the players circled around, Shea handed out water bottles, and the players passed them among themselves.

"Okay, get some water and listen up," Jonathan called, positioning himself with Joyce at his side and Brady Troy across from him.

Once everyone was settled, he continued. "Good practice. We've got a lot to work on, but we made progress today — and that's what matters."

He let that sink in before moving on. "A couple things. First, school starts in a week and a half. While we're doing two-a-days,

I'm going to adjust practice times — some of us have jobs. So tomorrow, the second practice will be at 6 p.m."

No reaction.

"And that'll help us avoid the worst of the afternoon heat."

Jonathan took a breath, then added, "Starting tomorrow morning — until school starts — practice is at 7:15 a.m."

His announcement was met with a chorus of groans.

"But … but … but," Jonathan said, holding up a hand. "You need to be here by 7:00 a.m. sharp to help Shea get all the equipment out."

The groans grew louder.

"Listen," Jonathan said, "a lot goes into football beyond practices and games. And with the levy failure, everyone is shorthanded and stretched thin. We need to help out."

"That's not our job," Sebastian Sullivan snapped. "I'll be here at 7:15 — not 7. I'm happy to run a few extra laps to avoid hauling stuff. Shea-squatch can handle it. She doesn't need us — or at least not me."

"And we don't need Shea-squatch," Noah Turner added with a laugh.

Aiden Davis echoed the term with amusement: "Shea-squatch."

Much of the team stood in silence, unsure how to react. Joyce Yocheim struggled to respectfully convey to Brady the meaning behind the nickname. Shea was visibly hurt, uncomfortable with the attention.

Jonathan said nothing at first. He let the moment hang. His expression remained stoic. Inside, he was angry. But it wasn't worth expressing in anger.

He calmly spoke: "First — her name is Shea. That's how she's to be addressed. To her face. And behind her back. Understood?"

No one replied, and Jonathan wasn't looking for confirmation.

"Second — we're a team. And Shea is part of the team. She's as important as anyone here."

He paused. Let it hang.

Sebastian broke the silence. "Yeah, she's first-string homely."

He said it just loud enough to be heard, but quiet enough to maintain deniability. While meant to be funny, no one laughed. Noah Turner and Aiden Davis muffled their amusement. Joyce pretended not to hear and conveyed nothing to Brady. Most of the team stared blankly at Jonathan, avoiding eye contact with Sebastian.

Jonathan heard it. It made him angry. But again, he didn't show it. He simply pointed at Sebastian and said, calmly, "Take a lap."

Sebastian obeyed without protest, grinning as he started off — proud of himself. As he passed behind Jonathan, he once again raised a single-finger salute.

Chapter 42

Jonathan directed Sebastian to take a lap as punishment for being mean and disrespectful. That, however, sent a clear message to everyone: he was serious about supporting Shea. Player after player quickly jumped in to take direction from the student trainer. In no time, kits, jugs, and blocking pads were put away — ready for 7 a.m. tomorrow.

Even though it was AJ's fault for oversleeping, Tommy Frank felt bad about stranding him. He apologized profusely and offered to take AJ home — with a detour to McDonald's.

Before that plan could be set in motion, Jonathan intervened. "Thanks, Tommy, but I've got him."

AJ rolled his eyes, resigning himself to riding with his father. He sulked to the car, quickly got in, and nonchalantly hid his face with his right hand.

For AJ, the run from home to school — a mile and a half — had been long. The ride home, however, seemed even longer. The only consolation was that his mother was waiting in the driveway, inviting him and his father in for pizza.

As soon as everyone was seated, blowing on hot pepperoni slices, eager to bite in, Sam Reese asked, "So, AJ … what do you think of your new coach?"

Both Jonathan and AJ gave her the same look. Neither wanted to talk about it. She quickly changed the subject, sharing a cute but completely unrelated story about ordering the pizza. They all laughed. That led to other non-football small talk.

In short order, AJ had devoured five slices. He grabbed a sixth and excused himself, indicating — in so many words — that he was morphing into A2J9R and meeting up with the likes of SpartyBT10, JSevans, TFrank, Skyar3 and QBMaJack.

As soon as he was out of earshot, Sam turned to Jonathan. "Sooo, tell me all about it."

That launched an entire conversation: the morning practice; the talk with Nathan Rogers and Joe Thompson; the meeting with Ari Eisenberg and his lapdog, Warren Scott; then the afternoon practice. There had been plenty of developments over the course of 12 hours.

Sam fired off another open-ended question. "So, what do you think?"

Jonathan thought for a moment, then responded, "You know, I like it. I can't believe I'm saying that, but it's true." He smiled broadly.

"Coach," Sam said, "you gonna do great."

Chapter 43

Sam and Jonathan talked for a couple of hours, delving into the details of the big picture they'd already covered. Sam shared what she could about Derrick Maven. The specifics didn't really matter. They agreed the situation was just stupid.

Eventually, their pizza party broke up. Sam needed to nap before work, and Jonathan needed to finish some Eisenberg & Anders tasks before bed.

He, however, had trouble concentrating. Football thoughts and ideas churned in his head, distracting him from billable client matters. Jonathan was less efficient with his time, but nonetheless productive.

After a few hours, exhaustion set in. He could no longer form coherent sentences. He had trouble focusing his vision between words on the computer and handwritten notes from earlier. Continuing was pointless.

No sooner had he gone to bed than Sam was getting up to begin an overnight shift at the Wexner Medical Center Emergency Room. This allowed Jonathan to sprawl out and fall into a deep sleep.

There, his brain sorted out his thinking — like crafting negotiation terms for an Emerald Medical acquisition target and brainstorming a football teambuilding exercise. These thoughts worked like a jolt of caffeine. At 5:30 a.m., Jonathan was back at his computer, alternating between billable work and Mustang football.

Forty-five minutes later, he hit print. As the printer churned out a single-page document with the heading "Making a Team," Jonathan roused AJ, got himself dressed for practice, and packed a bag so he could shower and change into work attire downtown. At 6:45 a.m., they were out the door for the short trip to practice.

When they arrived a few minutes later, Brady Troy, Tommy Frank and a slew of other varsity players were already there. They sported bedhead hairdos and let out yawns, but they were ready to help Shea.

The moment she got out of her car, Tommy yelled, "We're here, boss. Put us to work."

Shea couldn't help but smile. She was ready. As she keyed into the training and equipment area with a couple dozen players behind her, she politely shared out assignments. Young men scattered here and there, helping to set in motion everything needed to successfully run a football practice.

As the players ran about, she grabbed two large orange Gatorade jugs, placed them under waist-high water bibs, and started to fill them. As the jugs filled, she doled out more assignments to players offering a second round of help.

"What's next?" AJ asked loudly, compensating for the gushing of water. He was into the spirit of the undertaking.

Shea didn't respond right away. She looked around, scanning the room for anything else that needed to go out to the field.

"Hang on. I'm thinking," she said as she dumped into each jug a few scoops of moon-shaped nuggets from the ice machine.

"What about those?" AJ asked, pointing to the jugs she was working with.

"These?" Shea echoed, motioning toward the containers. AJ nodded yes.

"How do you get those out to practice? They've got to be — what? — 100 pounds each." He kept talking, not waiting for a response. "I'll go get a few linemen."

Shea didn't say anything, but shot him a look that said, "I can't believe you just said that."

AJ innocently looked back, as if to say, "What?"

Shea rolled her eyes and replied in a playfully exasperated tone, "Just go get suited up for practice and meet me back here in five minutes."

Chapter 44

Jonathan checked his watch. It was 7:13 a.m., but the seconds were quickly advancing toward 7:14. He had every intention of starting practice punctually. And why not? Much of the team had been there at 7 a.m., helping Shea.

As he scanned the group of players, it was nearly a full roster. A couple of notable names were missing. Sebastian and the "foul tip" club were still not there—but that wasn't surprising. He checked his watch again … 7:14:10, 11, 12.

Then it dawned on him: "Where is AJ?" He was obviously on the premises … 7:14:20, 21, 23. "Maybe I missed him among the masses of helmets," he thought. He scanned the field again. Nope. Not there … 7:14:30, 31, 32. *Oh well. I'm coaching the team, not just my son*, he rationalized.

"Okay, bring it in," Jonathan yelled. Players began moving closer to him … 7:14:49, 50, 51. "Thanks for being here. I appreciate you helping out."

The night before, Jonathan had set his watch to beep when it hit exactly 7:15:00. At that moment, he gave a quick burst on his whistle. Practice was underway.

Before he could say anything else, a series of beeps erupted off in the distance—and they were getting closer.

As Shea continued filling the water jugs, AJ left the training room, quickly suited up for practice, and returned. When he did, Shea was waiting—but the jugs were gone. She motioned for him to follow and led him down a short, little-known corridor that opened into a small garage. Inside was a golf cart with the water jugs loaded, secured and ready for transport.

Shea instructed, "Get in. I'll drive you to practice."

"Okay," AJ responded, hopping in.

She pressed the accelerator and the cart lurched. As it did, she shouted over the engine and the sloshing of the jugs, "First of all, don't be sexist. I'm fully capable of lifting the water jugs. How do you think they've been getting to practice?"

AJ said nothing. The words were indicting. The question, rhetorical.

"And second …" She stopped the cart and looked over at AJ. "Don't be stupid."

"Stupid?" AJ looked mystified.

"Yes, stupid," she clarified. "We were in chemistry together last year, right?"

AJ nodded.

"Well, H_2O … water … is approximately 8.34 pounds per gallon."

"Approximately?" AJ gave her a quizzical look.

"Yes. One gallon of water is 3.785 liters, and the density is about 1 gram per milliliter, so—"

"Shea!" AJ cut her off. "I'm kidding. I believe you. Water is roughly eight pounds per gallon. What of it?"

"Well, if water weighs eight pounds per gallon and a jug holds five gallons …" Shea started.

"Precisely five gallons?" AJ teased.

"Roughly, AJ. I'm keeping the math simple for you," she shot back. "So, five times eight is only 40. The jugs combined don't even weigh 100 pounds."

"What about the ice?" AJ asked without thinking.

Shea let out a long sigh, rolled her eyes, and punched the accelerator. As AJ was thrown back into his seat, she casually remarked, "Don't be stupid. Ice is lighter than water."

The exchange had only taken a fraction of a minute—but it was critical. As they rounded the corner toward the field, AJ saw his dad lifting the whistle to his lips.

He reached across Shea's lap for the golf cart horn, hoping the beeping would make his presence clear. He kept tapping it until they were close enough.

As the cart rolled to a stop, AJ stepped out while it was still moving. He stumbled slightly but quickly found his footing.

"I'm here!" he shouted.

"Well, you're late," Jonathan responded.

"What are you talking about? What time is it? 7:15," AJ protested.

"It was 7:15 about a minute ago," his father replied, holding firm.

"Are you serious?" AJ was incredulous. "I was helping out. Those things are heavy." He motioned toward the Gatorade jugs. Shea nodded to confirm.

"Water weighs like 8.43 pounds per gallon," AJ added.

"Point three-four," Shea corrected.

"Yeah. 8.34 pounds per gallon," AJ said. "Times five ... times two." He was clearly reaching for leniency.

"Save it, AJ. I appreciate the help, but you're late. You owe us a lap after practice," Jonathan said, matter of fact.

AJ let out a heavy sigh. Shea quietly muttered, "Sorry, AJ."

"Well, I might be late ... but I'm not last," AJ said, pointing toward the parking lot.

Sebastian and the "foul tip" club were just getting out of their cars, casually heading inside.

Jonathan didn't react. He simply moved forward, giving instructions and getting practice underway.

He was growing more confident in his new role. He had drills from Case Western Reserve University. He was piggybacking on the playbook left by Coach Maven. And he was beginning to assert himself as a leader. There were challenges, yes, but he took them in stride.

As his watch clicked from 8:59:59 to 9:00:00, it beeped again. Jonathan blew his whistle and called the team in.

"Good practice," he said as players gathered. Shea passed out bottles of water. "Remember to help Shea put everything away. Then we're back at 6 p.m. to do it all again."

The group groaned, offering lighthearted complaints. Jonathan just smiled. He wasn't budging.

"Okay, one more thing," he added, holding up the "Making a Team" document. "Everyone's paired with someone. I want you to get to know each other—like, really get to know each other."

He paused, making eye contact.

"This is in person. Sit down over pizza, coffee, whatever. Spend some time together."

Players looked at one another, curious but attentive.

"Here's the rundown. This list will also be posted in the locker room," he said, then began calling out names.

"AJ Reese and Brady Troy."

AJ rolled his eyes and sighed. Of course, his dad would give him the toughest pairing.

Brady lit up with a big smile as Joyce signed the name.

"Tommy Frank and Noah Turner." A simple nod passed between them.

"Aiden Davis and Steve Stapleton. Tim Stephens and Paul Mandrake …"

Jonathan kept going. As names were read, players acknowledged their partners—even AJ and Brady.

Almost done, Jonathan read, "Sebastian Sullivan and David Roberts."

"Yo, David!" Sebastian shouted. When David Roberts, the backup quarterback, looked his way, Sebastian added, "Okay. We're done." Then, just loud enough to be heard, he muttered, "This is stupid. I'm not doing it."

The group went quiet, watching for Jonathan's response.

He didn't take the bait. Instead, he addressed the team.

"I can't force you to do anything. No one can. I'm just trying to put things in front of you that can help you succeed. What you do with them is your choice."

Then he turned to Sebastian. "Practice is over. You're paired with David Roberts. Do what you will. But you were late—so take your lap and help Shea."

Sebastian said nothing. He jogged off, hiding a middle finger behind the crowd.

Jonathan addressed the team again. "If you've been paired, you're free to help Shea. And if you owe me a lap … AJ Reese, Aiden, Noah, who else? … get that done first."

Then he continued reciting the remaining names.

AJ and several others caught up to Sebastian, who was giving half effort on his lap.

Once they matched his pace, Sebastian didn't hold back.

"That guy's a complete ass, you know?" he said, looking at AJ. "No offense, but your dad has no idea what he's doing."

AJ stayed quiet. He had his own frustrations with his dad, but he wasn't ready to jump on Sebastian's train. He just kept running.

"You know, Reese," Sebastian continued. "You should hang with us. Between practices. We're all …" he gestured to Noah and Aiden, "… going to my place. Movies. Hydration."

"Sure. Maybe. I have to pick up my car from the shop," AJ offered noncommittally.

"So? How long does that take?"

"I don't know."

"Well?"

"Okay. I'll stop over. I know where you live."

Before they could say more, Shea pulled up in the golf cart.

"AJ, I'm really sorry."

"It's okay, Shea. I'm getting used to bonus laps," he joked.

"Hey, Squatch," Sebastian yelled. "Why don't you let me drive?"

She ignored him.

But before she could react, Sebastian yanked a five-gallon jug from the cart. It hit the ground with a thud, rolled, and split apart—water and ice everywhere.

Shea slammed the brakes and let out a guttural sound. She glared, stormed toward the mess.

Sebastian jumped into the cart, laughing, and drove it forward 20 yards.

"Come on, guys," he shouted. "Coach said help Squatch!"

Everyone but AJ jumped in. Noah tried to set down the second jug carefully, but Sebastian hit the gas. It rolled and burst open just like the first.

"Come on, Reese!" Sebastian shouted. AJ waved them off and walked to the first jug.

With the bottom in hand, AJ joined Shea. "I'm sorry. Sebastian can be a bit of an idiot."

"No, he's a complete asshole," she snapped.

Her face was beet red. With her wild hair and thick eyebrows, she looked nearly demonic. AJ said nothing—better to let her fume.

He helped reassemble the jug. Then they did the same with the second and carried both back toward the field.

They were quiet. After a few minutes, AJ broke the silence.

"I don't want to sound stupid, but approximately how much does the air in these things weigh?"

The question cracked her. Shea smirked, laughed, and gave AJ a playful punch on the arm.

Chapter 45

Saying little, AJ walked with Shea to the training room, carrying the empty water jugs. While she cleaned out the containers and put away gear others had returned, AJ went to retrieve the golf cart. It was parked among the cars in the school lot—presumably near where Sebastian and his crew had parked.

AJ took a wide, fast loop across the practice field, enjoying the ride while scanning for any forgotten items. Satisfied nothing had been left behind, he drove the cart back and parked it where Shea had originally found it.

He then made his way to the locker room, where a few teammates were still lingering. Without saying much, AJ showered, changed into street clothes, and sat by his locker, waiting.

He was waiting for Tommy Frank, who was taking one of his famously long showers. Tommy was always the first in and the last out—something he said he couldn't enjoy at home.

AJ, however, was getting antsy. He needed Tommy to drive him to Don's Car Care.

"Come on, Frank!" AJ shouted playfully. "This is Blacklick High, not a Russian bathhouse!"

That moved Tommy along. Soon he was dried and dressed. Together, they headed off to fetch AJ's hopefully fixed car. On the short ride, they caught up on a mix of football and random topics.

"Wanna come hang out?" AJ asked. "After I get my car, I'm stopping by Sebastian's."

Tommy glanced over and hesitated, searching for words. "I really can't. My mom has some stuff for me to do—laundry and all that," he said. Then, after a pause, added, "And I don't know about hanging with that group. They're trouble. Trouble just looking for a place to happen."

AJ couldn't argue. Tommy wasn't wrong. He let the subject drop. A short while—and a few more quick topics—later, AJ got out at Don's Car Care.

After practice, once he was satisfied everyone was helping Shea, Jonathan jumped in his car and headed to the office. On the way, he called his team of attorneys to check in and ensure projects were moving forward.

In no time, he was parked at the Huntington Center. After a quick detour to shower and change in the Huntington Club, he was at his desk and quickly in the flow of work—as if he'd arrived at 7 a.m.

Interestingly, knowing he had a hard stop at 5 p.m. to get back to practice, Jonathan found himself more intentional with his time. He didn't overthink what or how to delegate—he just decided and acted. All in all, he was more productive than on many previous 12-hour days.

Still, his mind occasionally wandered to football—an idea for a drill, a tweak to a play, or something motivational to say. Whenever a thought struck, he jotted it in his phone, then quickly returned to firm matters.

After all, coaching aside, his professional goal remained unchanged: making partner. And to get there, he needed to keep his billable hours up, manage his team, and bring in more business.

It was a lot. The pressure was real. He could feel it in his elevated heart rate. But Jonathan had set this goal years ago, and now he was on the cusp of achieving it.

Losing focus wasn't an option.

When AJ arrived at Don's Car Care, his car was ready. He paid with his father's credit card and was on his way. Rather than going home as he normally would, he redirected his path to Sebastian Sullivan's house.

He parked on the street and walked to the door, which was slightly ajar. AJ rang the doorbell and listened for footsteps. Nothing. He rang again and waited. Still nothing. Then he pushed the door open. As he did, he heard a toilet flush in the bathroom just off the front hall. Noah Turner emerged.

"Hey, you probably don't want to go in there for a bit," the beefy lineman said with a sheepish grin. "Come to think of it, you might want to avoid the one in the basement too … Aiden wrecked that one earlier."

"That's okay. I'm good," AJ replied. He was a little uncertain. He'd spent time with Sebastian, Noah, and Aiden Davis in the weight room, out for pizza, and at school events. But being in Sebastian's home felt different. Still, he followed Noah to the finished basement.

"AJ's here," Noah announced as they reached the bottom of the stairs. The others—Sebastian, Aiden, and a few other football players—barked out a chorus of welcomes.

AJ said nothing, still uneasy. The air smelled of beer, though it was cool and refreshing.

"Take a seat, AJ," Sebastian said, motioning to a bean bag on the floor. "Can I get you a beer?"

"Hey, Sebastian? What are you doing?" Aiden asked, concerned. "He's the coach's kid."

"Davis, stop being a little old lady," Sebastian shot back with a chuckle.

AJ raised his hands and opened his palms, motioning for everyone to relax. Then he said, "I'm good. I'm sticking with water."

"You sure? Beer's great for hydrating," Sebastian joked. Everyone raised a can that had previously been hidden. "My dad said there's a study proving it."

"Thanks. A bottle of water is fine," AJ said.

"There might be one or two left in the fridge," Noah added. "We were trying to clear space for more beer." He chuckled and cracked open another can.

AJ grabbed a water bottle from the fridge and sat down. As he did, Sebastian addressed the group.

"Relax, everyone. Reese isn't going to say anything—he's one of us now." He laughed, and others joined in. "Besides, no one's kicking us off the team. We are the team. Sideline us, and you basically tank the whole season."

He took another sip, let out a loud belch, and added, "Think about it. Sitting here is the starting quarterback and three-fifths of the offensive line."

No one argued. He pivoted topics.

"So, who's met their team buddy yet?" He exaggerated "team buddy" with air quotes. "No one?" Everyone laughed.

Aiden jumped in. "I don't even know who I've got." He laughed, then turned to another player. "Stephens, who do you have?"

"Paul Mandrake," the lineman replied.

"Man-drrrraaaake," Noah said in an exaggerated tone. More laughter.

"AJ, who you got?" Sebastian asked.

"Brady Troy," AJ said, unenthusiastically.

"Wow! That'll be scintillating," Sebastian said with mock excitement, flailing his hands before flipping everyone off.

The conversation drifted to other topics, then eventually gave way to a movie. One by one, players nodded off—including AJ.

Midway through the second movie, AJ woke up, disoriented. Once he gathered his bearings, he stood up and said, "I need to go home for a bit. I'll see everyone at practice. Don't be late."

Sebastian, half-asleep, replied, "Oh, we will be." The room let out a chuckle through their slumber.

AJ arrived home in the early afternoon. His mom had been up for a couple of hours after her morning sleep and was sitting at the kitchen table, enjoying a cup of coffee.

Hey, honey. How was morning practice? How did Dad do?" Sam asked with a big smile, clearly hopeful.

"It was okay. He did fine," AJ replied, guarded.

"I see you got your car," she continued, still smiling. "Did you just pick it up?"

"No, Tommy dropped me off this morning," AJ answered without thinking.

"Then where have you been?" Samantha Reese's curiosity was piqued.

Being honest, as he always was with his mom, AJ admitted, "I was over at Sebastian's house."

Her face dropped. "Oh, AJ." Her tone was heavy with disappointment.

"Mom … it's okay," AJ tried to reassure her.

"AJ, really?" she said, gently shaking her head.

"Mom, I know. I know," he repeated. "It's okay."

They didn't say anything more on the matter. The conversation shifted, then quickly wrapped up as they each turned to other things.

Jonathan had an extremely productive day. It had to be—there were always deadlines looming at Eisenberg & Anders. But he needed to be out the door by 5 p.m. at the latest.

His trip home usually took about 20 minutes—but that was when he left the office between 7 and 8 o'clock. At 5, it was a different story: an extra five-minute ordeal just exiting the parking garage, and the short expressway would be choked with traffic. He might need every minute of the hour to make the 15-mile trek to Blacklick High School. He couldn't be late.

At 4:45 p.m., Jonathan began packing what he needed to stay productive from home later that night. As he focused on gathering files and his laptop, a light tap on his office door pulled his attention.

"Are we ready?" asked Ari, the firm's patriarch, poking his head in.

Jonathan looked up, smiled, and nodded before turning back to his briefcase. "Well, I've got a few more leases to review, and…"

"No, no, no, Jonathan," Ari cut in with a laugh. "Are you ready for practice?"

Jonathan chuckled and replied, "I don't know, Ari." He paused, then repeated, "I really don't know. There are a lot of kids. A lot of different personalities. Oh—and then there's this other complication—the X's and O's of football."

Ari took a deep breath, clearly preparing to offer some sage advice. "Jonathan, you're a great person, and you're well intended. But you're only human. My completely unsolicited advice? Give yourself some grace. It's OK to make a mistake here and there."

With that, Ari walked Jonathan to the elevator and gave him a gentle pat on the back as the doors closed.

The most senior partner of Eisenberg & Anders looked on fondly as Jonathan Reese descended toward a different kind of leadership challenge.

Chapter 46

As expected, Jonathan hit traffic leaving the parking garage. It made him anxious. But once he was on the road—though moving slower than usual—he took solace in the fact that he was moving. He used the time productively, calling the office and touching base with clients.

After stressing about being late, Jonathan rolled into the parking lot at Blacklick High School at 5:40 p.m. He raced into the locker room, changed, and joined the team in helping Shea. By 5:55, he was on the field, talking with players already assembled.

Two minutes later, AJ came barreling in with the golf cart, hauling two five-gallon water jugs—and Shea, holding on for dear life. He skidded to a stop and shouted, "I'm here!" Everyone laughed.

At 6 p.m., Jonathan blew his whistle to start practice with a warm-up lap. That rolled into AJ and Tommy Frank leading the team through stretches and calisthenics.

Five minutes in, Sebastian and his crew casually pulled into the parking lot. Ten minutes later, they emerged in practice gear, cracking jokes as they joined drills already underway. Jonathan ignored their lateness; stopping to confront them would only waste time. The first game was just weeks away, and there was a lot to cover.

The team was learning both the offense and defense that Jonathan had inherited from Coach Maven. Everything was new, and every minute counted. Jonathan's focus: learn, walk through, drill. Offense. Defense. Repeat.

Time moved fast. Jonathan ended practice as promptly as he'd started it, blowing his whistle and calling the team in. He stood opposite Brady Troy, with Joyce nearby to sign.

"Good practice," Jonathan began. "We got a lot done, but there's still more to do. Quick show of hands—who's met with their Making A Team partner?"

No hands went up. Some players looked down. Sebastian made a quiet quip to his crew, drawing laughter.

Jonathan ignored it. "Okay, who's at least arranged a time to meet?"

Five hands went up.

"How can there be an odd number?" Jonathan asked.

Tommy Frank replied, "Mr. Reese, I texted my person but haven't heard back."

Jonathan nodded. "Thanks for the effort. Everyone—do the same. Make the effort. You need to be more than just teammates."

Sebastian muttered another joke under his breath. Some snickered, but others stayed silent, following their coach's lead.

"So, tonight—eat well, hydrate, and get some sleep. Before we leave, let's help Shea put everything away. And those who were late—Sebastian, Noah, Aiden—get going. You owe us a lap."

The latecomers jogged off. As Sebastian passed behind Jonathan, he flipped him off—again—and shouted, "Hey, Shea! Come give us a ride!"

Practice dispersed. Players helped clean up, got changed, and headed home.

Jonathan returned home too. Over dinner, he and Sam debriefed as they always did, reviewing highs and lows, progress and frustration. AJ eventually arrived, joined them silently, and devoured food.

"So, how was practice?" Sam asked.

AJ didn't speak—he just made a sound that indicated it was fine, avoiding eye contact with his dad-turned-coach. Sam asked a few more questions, but AJ remained brief and evasive. Eventually, he excused himself and left with his plate, off to play video games.

Jonathan and Sam continued their conversation as they cleaned up the kitchen. Then Sam went to nap before her overnight ER shift, and Jonathan settled in for Eisenberg & Anders work. He finished just before Sam left.

In less than 48 hours, Jonathan had become Blacklick High's head football coach, completely upending his routine. But the disruption was quickly becoming a new rhythm.

Each morning, Jonathan woke before dawn, worked out, made sure AJ was up, and headed to practice. Most of the team arrived early to help Shea, and AJ always called dibs on driving the water—along with Shea—out to the field. Players horsed around until practice started, Joyce signing to Brady in the middle of the chaos.

Jonathan began promptly at 7:15 a.m.—even as Sebastian and his crew typically rolled in by 7:30. Practice was efficient, with Jonathan working through a mental checklist: install, drill, review.

Sebastian often challenged him—questioning drills, second-guessing decisions. But Jonathan no longer wavered. Football, he reminded himself, isn't a democracy. It's not a committee. The coach is in charge. And he was that coach—period.

He started on time. He ended on time. And when he blew the final whistle, he always brought the team in for a quick recap, encouragement, and a reminder about the Making A Team initiative.

That part frustrated him. The players weren't engaging. They weren't meeting. They weren't even pretending to care. The concept—getting to know each other beyond football—was mocked, largely by Sebastian. The initiative had no traction.

As usual, late players — "the foul tip club"— ran laps, often flipping a gesture behind Jonathan's back as they did. They also avoided cleanup duty.

But that hardly mattered. With 50-plus players helping, teardown was quick. And working together created camaraderie—something Jonathan valued.

Once satisfied that Shea had enough help, Jonathan dashed downtown, stopped to shower and change, and got to work. He remained focused, productive, and driven—interrupted only by a daily 15-minute pep talk from Ari Eisenberg.

By 4:45 p.m., he was wrapping up: delegating work, packing files, and preparing to leave. By 5, he was in the car—fighting traffic, cursing slowdowns, and heading back to Blacklick for practice.

After evening practices, he and Sam ate dinner and caught up. AJ would join briefly, grab snacks, and disappear to his game console and online crew.

After morning practices, AJ still spent time at Sebastian's house. Although that group had a questionable reputation, AJ enjoyed the midday downtime with teammates. He knew his mother wouldn't approve, so they seldom discussed it. And when it came up, he downplayed it. "I don't participate," he told himself. That was how he justified staying.

The routine lasted about a week. Like most Ohio school districts, classes resumed in mid-August. Blacklick High shifted to one practice a day. That eliminated AJ's midday visits to Sebastian's—and let Jonathan start work three hours earlier, which was even better.

Considering how Jonathan had become coach — and had implemented a playbook that was different from the Studer regime — he had done well preparing the team for the season opener. Except for one thing.

Just after practice began on the Wednesday before the first game, a startling thought struck him. Moments later, he said it aloud:

"Oh crap. We've done nothing regarding special teams."

Everyone could sense the alarm in his voice. Many shared that feeling. Special teams are arguably a third of the game. AJ looked down and shook his head, embarrassed—as if his father's oversight somehow reflected on him.

Sebastian seized the moment.

"You're stupid," he bellowed. "And so out of your league."

Jonathan said nothing. He was coaching the team alone and felt overwhelmed. The oversight was his fault. For a moment, he was frozen. Bewildered. But then he remembered some sage advice from Ari:

"The mistake has been made. You can't change that. But you 100% control what's next."

That snapped him back to focus.

"Yep. I'm sorry. Let's take some time and put special teams in place."

Quickly and confidently, he assembled the kick return and punt return units—blending starters and reserves to give some benchwarmers a role.

Then he moved on.

For the punt and field goal teams, he wanted to keep most starters in to preserve the option to fake. But one thing was missing.

"Okay, who's our kicker and/or punter?"

Silence.

Tommy Frank finally spoke up: "He quit, Mr. Reese."

"Who? When?" Jonathan asked, startled.

"John Evans. Technically, he didn't quit. He just didn't come out this season," Tommy said sheepishly. "It's a long story."

"I can kick. I can punt. It's not a big deal," Sebastian volunteered, smug and condescending. "Evans is a loser, anyway."

Jonathan ignored the attitude and turned to the backup quarterback.

"Roberts, can you hold for extra points and field goals?"

David Roberts, only a sophomore, answered honestly. "I can try. I've never done it before."

Just then, Brady Troy stepped forward and raised his hand confidently. He signed to Joyce, who had been translating the whole exchange. Everyone waited.

"Brady said he did this for three years at the School for the Deaf," Joyce reported, her tone matching Brady's quiet confidence.

Sebastian scoffed. "I'm not learning any of that hand stuff."

"You don't need to," Jonathan said, cutting him off without turning to look. His eyes stayed on Brady. He smiled.

"Great. This is great," Jonathan said, stepping forward to shake Brady's hand. Brady smiled back. He now had an official role—albeit a minor one.

With special teams finally assembled, Jonathan dedicated most of the remaining practice to drilling those units.

The team was now fully set. And just in time. The first game was only two days away.

Chapter 47

There seemed to be heightened excitement about the season. Although much about the team was new—starters, system, and coach—they were still the defending state champions. And for that reason, every opponent would be gunning for them.

This was especially true in Game 1. Blacklick traveled to the small Dayton suburb of Kettering, about 90 minutes west of Columbus. The opponent: Archbishop Alter High School.

Like the Mustangs, the Knights were a perennial powerhouse in football. In fact, these two teams had squared off in the state semifinals the previous year, en route to Blacklick's championship. This added another layer of excitement to the game, as Alter had revenge on its mind.

That was obvious from the moment the teams took the field. The Alter fans roared with electric fury—and grew louder with every early success. The Knights won the coin toss. Cheers erupted. They elected to receive. More cheering.

Then the home team returned the opening kickoff 45 yards. The stands exploded. Four plays later—run, pass, pass, run—the Knights completed a 55-yard drive and went up 7-0.

Alter's fans were wild in celebration. Just when it seemed the noise might subside, something else would happen. The Knights pinned the Mustangs deep on the kickoff, and the crowd noise triggered a false start—pushing Blacklick back to its own two-yard line.

From there, Blacklick could do little. Three plays and a cloud of nothing. They were forced to punt.

Standing deep in the end zone, Sebastian waited for the snap. But he bobbled the ball and accidentally stepped on the end line.

Safety.

Alter led 9-0, and now Blacklick had to kick the ball back. The game was only minutes old, but it already felt like it might be over.

Eventually, Blacklick caught a break. With Alter facing first-and-goal from the 8-yard line, the Mustangs gave up just a short gain before a holding penalty and two incomplete passes ended the drive. But Alter still nailed a 35-yard field goal to go up 12-0 midway through the first quarter.

Still, holding the Knights to three tempered the crowd. They quieted further when Blacklick returned the kickoff to the 40. And they went silent as the Mustangs mounted a methodical drive—short passes and three-yard runs pushing down the field.

The drive stalled at the 9-yard line. Jonathan realized Sebastian had distance on kickoffs but was unreliable with field goals. Sebastian blamed his holder, Brady Troy, but the issue wasn't the hold—it was accuracy.

Though still down 12-0, Blacklick had settled the momentum. For the rest of the half and into the fourth quarter, both teams traded modest drives and punts.

Other than that opening possession, Blacklick's defense was stout. The offense, however, struggled—due to inexperience, a new system, and a rookie coach.

Jonathan was overwhelmed. He was calling both offense and defense, leaving little time to coach either group between possessions. Adjustments and corrections were limited.

To make things worse, his quarterback often ignored him. Sebastian routinely changed plays in the huddle, saying things like, "That's stupid. We're doing this instead." And he was often wrong.

Jonathan tried to rein that in at halftime.

"Don't change the plays I send in, Sebastian. I'm calling them for a reason."

Sebastian listened but didn't plan to comply. "I'm on the field," he reasoned to himself. "I know best."

It was incredibly frustrating. But with no backup plan—only a sophomore QB with zero game experience—Jonathan was stuck.

Still, they were only down 12. One score could shift momentum.

And things were trending that way. Starting from their own 10-yard line, the Mustangs moved the ball in chunks—eight, nine yards at a time—over seven plays. Now they were inside the Alter 30.

Jonathan's calls were working. But Sebastian grew impatient. He wanted the end zone now.

When a teammate brought the play in from the sideline, Sebastian waved it off. "I've got a better idea," he said.

The play he called swept everyone left. But before AJ took two steps in that direction, Sebastian pulled him close and whispered, "Blueberry. Quick block, then fade right. I'll hit you."

AJ nodded and grinned.

Watching from the sideline, Jonathan knew immediately the play had been changed. Again. He cursed under his breath and debated calling a timeout—but decided against it, wanting to save timeouts for later. All he could do was hope the improvised play worked.

The play unfolded. Everyone went left—except AJ, who drifted back toward the Blacklick sideline. Jonathan, confused and furious, muttered, "What the …?"

Sebastian faked the handoff and pivoted. He turned right and threw a wide-open pass to AJ, who caught it in stride with no defender in sight.

He should've sprinted to the end zone. But AJ, flooded with pride, let it turn into cockiness.

He began high stepping. Then, trying to showboat, he planted hard and spun—pivoting left, reversing direction. But his foot slipped. He fell backward, lost control of the football, and hit the turf.

Before he could recover, three Alter defenders were there. One scooped up the ball and sprinted the length of the field. None of Blacklick's players were close enough to stop him.

Touchdown, Alter.

With the extra point, it was 19-0.

Just like that—midway through the fourth quarter—a complete reversal. Any hope of a comeback vanished. And Alter's crowd roared back to life.

The game was over. The clock hit 0:00. Players shook hands, and the Mustangs sulked into the visitors' locker room in stunned silence.

Five minutes later, their coach walked in.

Jonathan exhaled, despondent, before beginning. "I don't know what to say. We were in it. We had momentum."

He paused.

"I'm still trying to unpack what happened when they scored their last touchdown."

Another pause.

"Sebastian, I told you not to change the play. I don't understand. And what play did we even run?" He looked around. "That's a question. I expect an answer. Sebastian? AJ? Anyone?"

Tommy Frank spoke quietly. "I think it was a Blueberry."

Several players rolled their eyes.

"Blueberry?" Jonathan repeated. "What's a Blueberry?" Silence. "Tommy?"

"It's where the quarterback calls one play but secretly runs another—with just one or two players in on it," Tommy explained. "I came up with it a couple years ago. As a joke. I've never run one. I'm just a lineman." Then he added, "It usually works."

"I don't care," Jonathan snapped. He turned toward Sebastian. "We don't do this. I send in a play. We run it. Period. Do you understand?"

Sebastian didn't look up.

Then Jonathan turned to AJ.

"And AJ? What were you thinking? Just get into the end zone. Don't do some prima donna celebration 20 yards from it. That and your fumble crushed us."

As Jonathan focused on AJ, Sebastian looked up—and raised both middle fingers behind his coach's back. The only problem was a mirror on the opposite wall. Jonathan saw the reflection.

He took a breath, slowly turned, and asked calmly, "What's your problem?"

He didn't wait for an answer.

"Your antics aren't productive, Sebastian. Not one bit."

Sebastian fired back, defiant. "You're not a real coach. You don't know football. We don't need you. This team doesn't have a real coach. You should leave—and not come back."

The locker room went silent. No one talked to adults like that.

Jonathan held his composure. A younger version of him might have lashed out. Instead, he responded evenly.

"Well, I don't know what to say. Like it or not, without a coach, this season ends. And I don't think any of you want that. So I'm the coach. And you'll need to get used to that."

Sebastian wasn't done.

"No one cares what you think. You're a substitute coach with a borrowed offense. Your drills aren't original. And no one cares about your stupid buddy thing. I'm not doing it. No one is."

Jonathan just listened.

"You can't make us," Sebastian added. "You need me more than I need you."

Jonathan took a long breath.

"Maybe, Sebastian. Maybe," he said, then turned to the team. "I may not be a real coach—but if you don't meet with your

'Making A Team' partner by Monday, the sprints will be very real. Ev-er-y-one of them."

Then, without another word, he told the team to shower, dress, and get on the bus. He turned and walked out of the locker room.

Chapter 48

Inside the locker room, after Jonathan left, no one moved at first. Then one player began untying his cleats. Another peeled off tape. The motion cascaded into action—equipment clattered, showers ran, bags were zipped. The room became a low roar of postgame routine.

But there was little real conversation. No one dared—except Sebastian. He was unfazed by the exchange with his coach and had already moved on from the loss.

After a few minutes, he walked over and sat next to AJ.

"Hey, Reese," he said in a half-whisper. "I'm sure your dad's a good guy … and good at whatever it is he does. But he's not a football coach. And he needs to hear that. I'm just the only one willing to say it."

AJ said nothing. He was confused. He'd never seen anyone challenge his dad like that—let alone some teen. His instincts told him there had to be consequences. But none had come.

"Anyway," Sebastian continued, his tone shifting to something more casual. He paused, glancing around to make sure no one was listening. Then he leaned in. "Tomorrow night. My house. Seven. Buckeyes play Pitt in primetime. Perfect night to hit campus—blend in with the chaos, right?"

AJ nodded slightly but stayed quiet. It didn't feel right. But at the moment, nothing did. He thought, *why not?*

"Just come over. Seven p.m.," Sebastian said, standing. "Actually—bring a bag. Plan on crashing. My dad's out of town on business, and my mom's in Cleveland till Sunday with her college roommates." He added air quotes around the last part. "We'll have the run of the place."

After Jonathan issued his edict to the team, he stepped out of the locker room and found a small alcove—just far enough from the players but not quite out among the lingering fans and Alter officials. He needed a moment. A moment to calm down. To think. To get control of his emotions and gather himself. The situation was overwhelming.

When he felt steady again, he left that space and made his way to the buses. Nathan Rogers and Shea Brooks were there, loading player gear and team equipment into the smaller bus. Jonathan jumped in to help. As a staff, they were a laughably thin crew.

Once he was no longer of use, Jonathan stepped away and walked over to the player bus, standing outside the door. One by one, players began trickling in—first dropping their gear with Nathan and Shea, then stopping at the table where team parents had laid out a spread of food, snacks and drinks to refuel their teenage, football-playing bodies.

As they boarded the bus, few players said anything beyond a quiet "hey" or a nod. Eye contact was rare. The tension from the game—and its aftermath—still lingered. Jonathan checked off each player's name, accounting for the roster. Inside, the players filed into their seats and sat in silence.

Tommy Frank was one of the last to arrive—and one of the few to speak.

"Hey, Mr. Reese," he began quickly, as if rushing to say it before getting cut off. "Please don't be mad, but I might not be able to meet with my partner before Monday. Tomorrow morning—like, early—I'm driving up to spend the weekend with my dad. He lives near Findlay. I won't be back until late Sunday night … like eight o'clock."

He paused, then added, "I will get it done, though. Maybe Monday. Maybe before practice, but I'll make it happen."

Jonathan nodded, his voice calm. "Thanks, Tommy. It's okay. Just do your best."

"Thanks, Mr. Reese. My partner's Noah … Noah Turner," Tommy added, just in case there was any doubt.

Jonathan nodded again. "All right. Thanks for letting me know. Go ahead and get on the bus. Let's get home."

Tommy climbed aboard, and Jonathan followed. After a quick head count and roll call, he took the seat behind the driver and gave the instruction to head back to Blacklick High.

As the bus rolled out into the night, Jonathan stared out the window, lost in thought.

The team wasn't bad. There was a good foundation in place. But within that foundation were cracks—players like Sebastian Sullivan and his crew, who weren't aligned with him. Still, for every one of them, there were a dozen others—good kids who wanted to learn, work hard and win. And then there were a few Jonathan wasn't sure about at all—like Brady Troy … and, sadly, his own son.

His mind churned as he searched for an approach, a way to connect with all of them. But the thought process was maddening. No single tactic was going to work with everyone. And as one person, it was nearly impossible to tailor multiple approaches. Idea after idea hit dead ends.

Eventually, he accepted that he wasn't going to solve the problem tonight. He needed to step away from it, let his subconscious do the work. He kept looking out the window, but let his thoughts drift—to clients, to matters waiting for him at Eisenberg & Anders.

The 90-minute ride back to Blacklick went quickly. Once at the school, Jonathan ushered the team inside and enlisted them to help Shea and Nathan unload. He gathered everyone briefly, reminding them they'd just lost to a great program—and if things went well, they might face that team again in the playoffs. He told them to rest up and be ready to get after it on Monday. Next Friday, they hosted Utica, a team they'd never lost to.

After the impromptu meeting, Jonathan headed home. Sam was waiting at the kitchen table. She'd been at the game but was eager for the behind-the-scenes rundown. Jonathan dished up two bowls of ice cream and shared the frustrations—especially the defiance.

"So, everyone's just not meeting with their team partner?" Sam asked, seeking clarification.

"Not everyone, no," Jonathan replied, scooping another bite. "But the ones who are openly defiant seem to influence the rest."

"What about AJ? Who's he paired with? Is he defiant?" she asked quickly.

Jonathan swallowed before answering. "He's not openly defiant. More … passive aggressive. This whole team is like one big psychology experiment—every personality type imaginable."

"Well, let me help with this one," Sam said, standing up. She walked to a spot where she knew AJ could hear her—headset or not—and shouted, "AJ! Come here, please!"

She returned to the table and gave Jonathan a look that said, Watch this.

A few minutes later, AJ appeared. "Yeah, Mom? What's up?" Seeing his dad at the table, his posture stiffened.

"Come sit," Sam said, calm but firm. Once he did, she asked, "Who on the team are you assigned to meet with?" Her tone made it clear she wasn't playing.

AJ glanced at his dad, trying to gauge what had already been said. But he didn't dare stall too long.

"Brady Troy," he muttered. "Why?"

"Have you met with him yet?"

"Um…"

"Why not?" Sam cut in before he could answer. "You're not too busy—you spend plenty of time gaming."

"Mom—" AJ tried.

"What?" she said, pressing again. "Why haven't you met with…"

"Brady Troy," Jonathan supplied.

"Brady Troy," Sam repeated. "Why not?"

"Mom, he's deaf. I don't know how to talk to him," AJ said, hoping it would pass as a reasonable excuse.

"So what?" Sam replied without hesitation. "You talk to people halfway around the world when you game—some of them barely speak English."

AJ looked at her, unsure what to say.

"Listen," she continued, softening slightly but staying firm. "Your father assigned you to Brady because he believes you can handle it. And maybe—just maybe—he's hoping others will follow your lead."

She paused, locking eyes with him. "AJ, like it or not, we're a family. And families support each other. Your father has always supported us. So now, you're going to support him."

"But Mom—"

"But nothing. You're going to meet with Brady Troy. Tomorrow. And until you do, no more gaming."

"Mom!" AJ groaned.

"Yes," she said firmly. "Go tell your friends whatever you want—I don't care. But if you have time to game, you have time to meet with …"

"Brady Troy," Jonathan chimed in, smiling.

"And if you can talk to people online, you can figure out how to talk to someone in the same room," Sam finished. "Once you're done signing off, I want your headset and controllers."

AJ let out a sigh and left without another word.

Jonathan looked at Sam and gave her an approving nod. She didn't say anything—just kept eating her ice cream.

About a minute later, AJ returned with a small box of gaming gear. He set it on the table.

"This is all of it," he said sheepishly.

"Thank you," Sam replied. "You can have it all back—as soon as you meet with…"

"Brady Troy," Jonathan finished, grinning.

Without a word, AJ turned and walked back to his room.

Jonathan raised three fingers in silent admiration—pinky, ring, and middle—while holding his thumb and index finger together in a loose circle.

Sam smirked and took another big spoonful of ice cream.

Chapter 49

AJ was fuming when he dropped off his gaming gear. Deep down, he knew he was in the wrong—but emotionally, he scrambled to justify his actions, or lack thereof.

Still, the anger didn't last. He was exhausted. Between a long day of school, a tough road loss, the confrontation with his parents, and the sudden loss of digital stimulation, fatigue took over. He laid down and quickly fell asleep.

He slept soundly and didn't wake until almost 10 a.m. No one else was home, which wasn't unusual. Both his parents had a relentless work ethic. He didn't fully understand it, but he respected it—and saw it reflected in his older siblings too.

He could've easily grabbed his gaming gear off the kitchen table and snuck in a few hours of play. But he didn't. As frustrated as he was with the punishment, AJ wasn't defiant. And he certainly wasn't deceitful.

Instead, he grabbed a bowl of cereal and sent a text to Brady Troy.

Brady replied quickly, and the two had a typical teen exchange—misspelled words, sentence fragments, emojis, and zero punctuation. They made plans: Brady was going to a football game at the Ohio School for the Deaf but would be home by four. AJ could stop by then to hang out and meet his parents.

"Perfect," AJ thought. He could check off his team obligation, then head to Sebastian's to hang out and eventually go down to campus. Sunday, he figured, he'd be back online—fighting an alien horde with QBMaJack, T-Frank, SpartyBT10, and whoever else.

After breakfast, AJ cleaned up and went to his room. Without gaming, there was a void. He tried to fill it with homework.

By noon, he moved to the family room, still tinkering with schoolwork while flipping through college football games on TV. At 3:30 p.m., he showered and got dressed. He left a note on the counter:

Going to Brady's so I can get my stuff back. Then watching football with Sebastian and others. -AJ

By 3:50 p.m., he was out the door, pulling up to Brady's house at exactly four.

It was just another house, in another Jefferson Township neighborhood. AJ wondered why he'd expected anything different. He rang the doorbell. Ding-dong.

Moments later, a kind-looking woman opened the door.

"Hello, AJ. I'm Brady's mom. Come on in—we're excited you're here." She held the door as AJ entered. "Transferring to a new school, a mainstream school, has been a challenge for Brady. So we really appreciate you coming by."

"No problem, Mrs. Troy. Happy to be here," AJ said, his tone polite but guarded. Deep down, he just wanted to check the box and move on.

"Wait here, AJ. I'll go get Brady." She disappeared upstairs, returning about 30 seconds later with Brady, who was grinning from ear to ear.

AJ smiled back and extended a hand, then hesitated. He looked Brady in the eye and carefully enunciated, "How was the game?"

Brady gave a thumbs-up. The moment hung, awkward and silent.

Mrs. Troy jumped in. "They lost. Badly. Wisconsin has those big farm boys. And the team's just not the same without Brady." As she spoke, she signed the words so Brady could follow along.

Brady signed something in response. She laughed, then signed and said back, "Well, it's true. They miss you." Brady signed again, and she waved him off. Then she looked at AJ and suggested, "Why don't you show AJ around?"

Brady gestured for AJ to follow him. He gave a quiet, thorough tour of the house—living room, kitchen, bathrooms, basement.

Eventually, they realized they could just text. It made things a whole lot easier.

They ended up in Brady's room. It wasn't all that different from AJ's—computer, bookshelves, trophies and awards from the Ohio School for the Deaf. On the walls were photos of Brady on the field: running over defenders, throwing passes, wearing number 10 and a Spartan-logo helmet.

As they texted, AJ also received messages from Sebastian— reminders and a heads-up: grab food before you get here, we picked the kitchen clean. AJ didn't reply.

After a while, the boys went outside to shoot hoops. Without their phones, the game became their language. They played a quick round of one-on-one, then several games of HORSE. Just two teen athletes, playfully trying to outdo each other.

Two hours passed quickly. AJ glanced at his watch—he had to get moving. He needed food before heading to Sebastian's.

He pointed to his wrist. Brady nodded.

They walked inside together, where Mrs. Troy waited in the kitchen.

"Thanks for having me over. This was fun," AJ said, facing Brady out of courtesy.

"No, AJ, thank you," Mrs. Troy said, speaking and signing. "You're welcome here anytime."

Brady got his mother's attention and signed something quickly, then smiled wide.

Mrs. Troy turned to AJ. "Brady is giving you a sign name."

AJ tilted his head in confusion.

She explained: "In the Deaf community, it's common to give people a 'sign name'—a kind of nickname. It's more efficient than fingerspelling someone's whole name, and it's usually based on something unique about the person."

Even though fingerspelling "AJ" wasn't difficult, Brady wanted to give him a sign name — "First Friend" — because AJ was that at Blacklick High.

AJ didn't know what to say. He felt two things at once: flattered and guilty.

Flattered that he meant something to Brady. Guilty that he hadn't wanted to come in the first place. And guilty again— because now, he was leaving to hang out with people he knew wouldn't be as welcoming of Brady.

But he had made plans. And at that moment, he intended to keep them.

Chapter 50

Jonathan got up early Saturday morning and quietly showered and dressed. He planned to be at his office by seven, so he skipped breakfast. Though he was typically the first to arrive, he knew someone would eventually show up with coffee and baked goods—part bribe, part ritual to lure staff in on weekends and generate more billable hours.

But Jonathan wasn't there for pastries. He was there to work. There was plenty of client business to handle—which always seemed to be the case at Eisenberg & Anders. The job paid well, but it demanded even more, especially if you had ambitions of making partner.

At his desk, Jonathan immediately settled into a rhythm—drafting documents, reviewing emails, outlining strategies for clients, assigning tasks to his team, coordinating with other departments. He stayed locked in, breaking only to grab food or use the restroom. He didn't lose focus—except once.

"Tough loss, Jonathan." Ari stood in the doorway of his office. "Hang in there. We're all really proud of you. Right?" He turned toward Warren Scott, who had followed him in.

Caught off guard, the junior partner nodded reflexively. But inwardly, he was gloating. Warren resented Jonathan's close bond with Ari and secretly hoped this football experiment would implode. A stumble on the field, he thought, could be used to block Jonathan's path to partner.

"Thanks," Jonathan said simply. "We've got some things to work on." He didn't elaborate—football was out of his mind, replaced by deadlines and deliverables.

Ari and Warren didn't linger. Ari had a firm to run. Warren had his usual agenda—doing little but appearing busy while staying in Ari's good graces.

Jonathan dove back in and worked straight through the day. As usual, he was among the first to arrive and the last to leave.

That evening, back home, he sat at the kitchen table and scavenged a quick dinner from the fridge while watching the Buckeye pre-game show. After eating, he cleaned up, muted the

TV, and returned to work, glancing up at the game now and then while logging billable time for Eisenberg & Anders.

After the game, he unmuted the TV to catch the post-game commentary while organizing files one last time. He'd racked up 15 billable hours. Mentally, he was drained.

He went to bed and fell asleep quickly.

The next morning, he was up early again, working at the kitchen table when Sam got up and began making coffee. Just as Jonathan was finding his groove again, his phone buzzed with a text.

can u talk?

Jonathan saw that the message was from Nathan Rogers. Rather than texting back, he called the athletic trainer, who picked up almost immediately.

Nathan spoke fast, clearly agitated. "Jonathan, sorry for calling on a Sunday, but you need to know something."

"What?" Jonathan's expression hardened.

"I have a friend with Columbus police. Early this morning, Sebastian Sullivan was arrested … along with two others. A couple more got away."

Jonathan's mind raced. "How did they know to call you? What did Sebastian do? Who were the others?" Before Nathan could answer, Jonathan added, "Can I put you on speaker so Sam can hear?" He didn't wait. "She can hear you now."

"Hi, Nathan," Sam said, jumping in.

"Hey, Dr. Reese," Nathan responded quickly.

Jonathan jumped back in, holding up AJ's note from the night before:

Going to Brady's so I can get my stuff back. Then watching football with Sebastian and others. -AJ

"Okay," Nathan began. "My friend's a Columbus officer. He was working overnight near the OSU campus. A group of what they thought were students set a dumpster on fire. The fire spread to an apartment complex. No injuries, but the building was evacuated and there's serious damage."

Jonathan cut in. "How was Sebastian involved?"

"Apparently—allegedly—he set the fire. That's what the video shows. My friend called me because Sebastian was wearing a Blacklick football T-shirt. And apparently, he was also intoxicated."

Sam's eyes widened. Jonathan looked at her, then asked, "Who were the others?"

Nathan hesitated. "Two ran off. The two they caught—well, I'm technically not supposed to know, since they're minors. But I do. They weren't Blacklick students. That's all I'll say."

Jonathan exhaled, shaking his head. "Thanks for letting me know, Nathan. I guess we'll find out more soon."

"Yeah. Keep me posted. I'll do the same." Nathan ended the call.

Sam and Jonathan stared at each other in silence. Finally, Jonathan broke it. "This is bad." He held up AJ's note.

"Let's slow down," Sam said, trying to stay calm. "We don't know for sure."

"Sam, it doesn't take a genius to connect the dots. We need to talk to AJ. Now. Is he even home?"

Sam moved to the window. "No. His car's not here."

"Then let's call him," Jonathan said, clearly expecting Sam to do it.

She began dialing but stopped. "Never mind. He's pulling in now."

Together, they watched as AJ parked and walked to the house. His clothes were wrinkled; he looked like he hadn't slept.

He stepped inside and immediately sensed the tension. His parents stood still, saying nothing. He spoke first. "I know. I know. I'm sorry. I should've told you."

"AJ, what's going on?" Sam asked gently.

AJ looked down, guilt creeping over him. He said nothing.

"AJ, this is serious," Jonathan said, anger tightening his voice. "We're here to protect you. But we can't do that if you don't tell us the truth. We need to know what happened last night. What were you and Sebastian doing? Who else was there?"

AJ looked up, confused. "What are you talking about?"

"Oh, come on," Jonathan snapped. "Don't play dumb. There's video. Sebastian's in custody. This is all going to come out. What were you thinking?"

"I wasn't with Sebastian last night," AJ said calmly, still clearly confused.

Sam and Jonathan froze. Sam asked, "Then what were you doing ... all night?"

AJ looked down again. "I was playing video games."

Sam turned her head toward the kitchen table, where AJ's box of headsets and controllers still sat untouched. Her eyes narrowed. She looked back at him. "How? Where?"

AJ had every intention of meeting up with Sebastian. Before he could leave, however, Brady's father showed up with a couple of pizzas. They invited AJ to stay and "help minimize leftovers."

AJ reasoned, *why not? I need to eat anyway.*

Over slices of pepperoni and sausage pizza, Brady's parents made an effort to include him in their conversation, doing their best to keep Brady engaged as well.

At one point, Mr. Troy asked casually, "So, AJ, do you play video games too? Brady seems to be obsessed." He laughed, and everyone joined in.

"Yes. Yes, I do," AJ replied. "My parents might say I'm obsessed too." He smiled toward Brady.

Mrs. Troy then asked, "Have you ever encountered a SpartyBT10?"

At that moment, everything clicked. Sparty—the mascot for the Ohio School for the Deaf. BT—Brady Troy. 10—his jersey number.

AJ turned to Brady and carefully mouthed, "Is that you?"

Though he couldn't hear, Brady instantly understood and nodded.

AJ picked up his phone and texted Brady:

Im A2J9R

The moment Brady got the message, he looked up and smiled broadly. He stood, high-fived First Friend, then signed an explanation to his parents. They all laughed.

When the laughter subsided, he signed another message. His mother looked at him and said, "Brady, you shouldn't even ask." Then she turned to AJ and asked, "Have you ever been grounded from gaming?"

AJ laughed and came clean. "Actually, I'm grounded right now. I was procrastinating too much in setting this meeting up, so my mom took my gear until Brady, and I got together."

Mrs. Troy smiled, thought for a moment, then turned back to Brady. "Do you promise you'll keep up with your homework?" Brady nodded. "Okay then. You can get back to playing online."

Brady shot a look to First Friend that said, Come on! Let's go!

AJ hesitated. "Mrs. Troy, I'd love to play, but technically I'm still grounded."

She didn't miss a beat. "No, you're not. You're here. I'd say you've officially fulfilled your requirement."

AJ went with it. He and Brady got set up and launched into a marathon gaming binge.

"Mom, I'm sorry. I know I should have checked in. I know. I'm sorry," AJ said, his tone remorseful. "We just got caught up gaming. I didn't even respond to all the texts Sebastian was sending."

"You mean, you were gaming all night?" Sam asked for clarification.

"No. At one point, we just fell asleep," AJ replied.

"Oh, AJ," Sam said as she stepped forward and hugged her son. "That is such a relief. We thought you were caught up in this Sebastian thing."

AJ hugged his mom back, then grew curious. "What's going on with Sebastian?"

Jonathan jumped in. "Sebastian? He's a dumpster fire—literally." He gave a nervous laugh.

"Jonathan," Sam chided.

AJ looked on, confused but intrigued.

Jonathan let out a heavy sigh. The situation clearly unsettled him. "Apparently…" he started, but the words caught in his throat. "He and a few others were down on campus and set a fire in a dumpster."

"Whoa," AJ said. "Sounds like Sebastian."

"Oh, there's more," Jonathan added. "The fire spread to an apartment building."

AJ's eyes widened as his father continued, "Sebastian and two others got arrested. And there are two more they're still looking for."

He paused, then asked, "Do you know who they might be? Tommy? Aiden? Noah?"

"Dad, I don't know," AJ said quickly. Then, thinking for a moment, added, "Could be Aiden and Noah. They go where Sebastian goes. Hmmm... It wasn't Tommy, though. He's up north with his dad."

"That's right," Jonathan recalled.

"Don't worry about it, AJ," Sam said gently. "We're just relieved you weren't involved. I was so worried."

"Mom!" AJ began. "I told you. Don't worry. Yeah, I watched TV with them once. I was bored. But being bored doesn't mean I'd be stupid."

No one said anything. They just looked at each other.

AJ finally broke the silence. "What happens now?"

His mom and dad exchanged glances and shrugged slightly.

"I don't know, AJ. I really don't," Jonathan admitted. He paused, then added, "But I'm going to have to find out."

"Dad, we can't lose those guys," AJ said urgently. The room went quiet again. "We can't. We just can't."

"AJ," Sam said softly, gently correcting him like a mother speaking to a child who didn't yet understand the weight of the situation.

"Mom, that's our starting QB—and most of our offensive line," AJ protested.

"AJ," Jonathan said firmly to get his attention. "I don't know what's going to happen. I don't even know how Blacklick handles situations like this. And let's forget about the alcohol for a second — arson is a serious crime. And it sounds like this one caused serious damage."

"Dad," AJ repeated, more quietly this time, "we can't lose these guys."

Chapter 51

The debate about what consequences Sebastian and his crew might face didn't last long. AJ was tired, and there wasn't much more to say.

Two things were true at the same time: Sebastian was important to the team, and he had allegedly committed a serious crime. In doing so, he had once again violated the athletic honor code. Reconciling those facts seemed almost impossible.

As Sunday progressed, more details emerged about the incident on the Ohio State campus. Aiden David and Noah Turner had also been involved. Initially, they ran off but later surrendered to police and were now awaiting arraignment.

Unlike the American justice system, the court of public opinion didn't wait. News of the situation spread quickly through the Blacklick High community. Like the Reese family, many were now debating how this might impact the "foul tip" club's standing on the team.

Years earlier, in the early days of the Jefferson Township School District, the school board empowered the athletic department to create an honor code. It was designed to ensure that student-athletes conducted themselves appropriately in the classroom and in the community. The gist was simple: there was no room in sports for cheating, truancy, smoking, drinking, or breaking the law.

Recognizing that teenagers can make mistakes, the code allowed for three strikes. Strike one: sit out a week—practices and games. Strike two: forfeit the rest of the season. Strike three: ineligible for good.

Initially, the athletic director created a small committee of teachers, coaches, and a few community parents. The committee would gather facts and decide if an infraction had occurred.

But when Gary Studer became athletic director, things changed. He claimed there was still a committee, though no one really knew who was on it. He claimed it still gathered input—but it became clear you didn't dare offer input that opposed his desired outcome.

If a student was involved in a non-football sport, the honor code was applied fairly. But when it came to football—especially a star player—things were different. "Anonymous input" often appeared to justify special consideration. As a result, serious issues were overlooked or downgraded to avoid triggering an honor code strike.

But Studer was gone now, and so was the athletic department. It wasn't clear who should handle the situation. The principal wanted nothing to do with it. The general message was: "Athletics are parent-run now. Let the parents deal with it."

Sensing trouble, a small group from the school board—led by Joseph Thompson—called for an informal meeting at 7 p.m. Sunday night. It would be a chance for parents to have an organized conversation.

Leading up to the meeting, Jonathan hoped to get some firm work done. Instead, he was consumed by calls and text messages from people lobbying on behalf of the foul tip club. As coach, they saw him as someone with influence — "The board always supported the coach on honor code matters."

Jonathan listened politely and read the messages carefully. Most people pushed for the same outcome: ignore whatever allegedly happened on campus. Their supporting arguments varied.

At one point, Jonathan turned to Sam with a smirk. "These people are 'should'ing' all over me. I *should* do this. I *should* do that."

By 6:30, Jonathan was antsy and headed to the high school. He had no idea what to expect and wanted to get a read on the atmosphere. Sam chose to drive separately, planning to arrive closer to the start.

When Jonathan arrived, several parents were already gathered—somehow knowing to head for the cafeteria, which was best suited for a large, informal meeting.

To Jonathan, most everyone was a stranger. He recognized Joseph Thompson, a fellow attorney, but that was it. The rest were just concerned faces. He wondered: *Who are team parents? Who are just curious?*

Most people seemed to recognize him. He could feel it in the glances. A few approached to introduce themselves, referencing prior messages or calls. Jonathan thanked them but quickly forgot their names—and what exactly they'd said.

As 7 p.m. approached, the cafeteria filled to standing room only. Sam rushed in just before the meeting began, finding a bare spot along the wall to lean against. As she settled in, she turned to her left—and was startled.

"Hello, Dr. Reese," said Walter Bachman politely, with a slight, friendly smile.

Sam gave an awkward smile back. Her instincts told her to step away from her tax levy nemesis, but there was no time— and no space. Joseph Thompson was already calling for quiet. Even if she had wanted to leave, she couldn't.

"Thank you, everyone, for being here," Thompson began. He caught a glimpse of Bachman and was visibly surprised. Still, he pressed on.

He gave a brief history of the honor code, the strike system, and the incident under consideration. Then he opened the floor for comments.

A small group of parents quickly began making the case for Sebastian, Noah, and Aiden. Some challenged the premise of action: "They're innocent until proven guilty. Let the legal process play out."

Others dismissed their prior infractions. "Those are ancient history—or minor stuff. Let's wipe the slate clean and treat this as strike one."

Together, they pleaded for leniency.

"We need to consider the consequences of declaring them permanently ineligible."

"These kids need our support, not judgment."

"We have to think about the message this sends."

"These kids, these kids, these kids…" The group seemed to filibuster.

Among them were the boys' parents—including Sebastian's father, who stood out with a gruff, don't-mess-with-me swagger. He ran a successful HVAC supply company and carried himself like the big dog in the room. He said nothing but bobbed his head approvingly as others spoke. It was clear: Sebastian was his father's son.

Once it seemed every argument had been voiced, Joseph Thompson asked, "Jonathan, you're the coach. What do you think?"

Jonathan stood. He wasn't surprised to be asked to speak—just surprised that he wasn't prepared with anything specific to say.

He took a breath and scanned the room. He heard the support for the foul tip club and saw its advocates sitting in a tight cluster.

But he also saw the rest. Dozens of parents who had said nothing. Their silence wasn't apathy—it was discomfort. Jonathan could sense it. The tension in their eyes. The anxiety about what might happen next.

Jonathan took in the room once more, gathered himself, and began.

"You know…"

He trailed off, scanning the crowd again. The silence began to grow heavy. He glanced at Sam. For a moment, he wondered what Ari might say if he were standing here.

"You know, I completely agree."

Another pause.

"We should consider the impact this will have on these kids."

He drew a breath.

"And I agree—these kids need our support."

The room remained quiet. Attentive. Jonathan could feel every eye locked on him.

As he paused again, Sebastian's father resumed nodding, a bit more assured now.

Jonathan went on.

"And I agree that we need to send the right message to these kids."

Another beat.

"But do you know what?" He scanned the room again. "I don't think we're talking about the same kids."

The energy shifted. The room stirred. Subtle movements—furrowed brows, turned heads—spread across the crowd. A collective confusion settled in, as if everyone was trying to catch up to what had just been said.

Sebastian's father stopped nodding. His face stiffened.

But near the edge of the room, Walter Bachman began to bob his head, slowly but deliberately.

Sam noticed the motion and turned toward him. Joseph Thompson noticed it too—and held his gaze, eyes narrowing in thought.

"When I say *these* kids," Jonathan began, "I'm referring to the 50-some who are not the subject of this… this… this tribunal."

He let out an uneasy chuckle.

"Those are the kids we have to make the right decision for. We need to worry about the impact on them. They need the message that being good—and doing well—matters."

A low murmur rolled through the room. Jonathan turned toward the board president but didn't wait for the noise to settle.

"Joe, I respect you. You can tell me that you're giving those three a pass—that they're back on the team, and back to practice, whenever that might be. I'll follow your directive on that. You're the board president. I will honor that."

Then Jonathan leaned forward, locked eyes with Thompson, and continued—his tone firmer, colder.

"But I'm telling you right now—and I mean this with all seriousness—those three are not going to play. Not a down. Not special teams. Nothing. We can lose every game 100 to nothing—and they will not see the field."

"Jonathan," Thompson stood up. "I respect you too—and there is no 'but' following that." He then turned to address the room. "When Coach Reese took this on, I told him I would support him. And right or wrong, I've always backed the coaching staff. There's no reason to change that now. These kids are struck out. I consider this meeting over—and the resolution final."

With that, the gathering began to disband. People filed toward the door, chatting in low voices.

Among the small factions supporting the foul tip club, there was a mix of betrayal and disbelief. Sebastian's father stood, caught Jonathan's eye, and pointed at him with restrained fury— an unspoken threat: *I'll get you.*

But beyond that group, there was another feeling—no cheers, no celebration, but a quiet, shared euphoria. Something important had just happened.

Jonathan stood still, ignoring Sebastian's father and watching the crowd disperse. In time, his eyes found Sam's.

She smiled. Then, slowly, she raised her right hand and extended three fingers—the little, ring, and middle—while folding her index finger and thumb into her palm.

Jonathan smiled back.

Chapter 52

Kelly Reese was barely seven when Jonathan coached her in soccer. Whenever she did something great, rather than shout, Jonathan would raise his hand and extend three fingers—the little, ring and middle—while holding his index finger and thumb close to his palm. It formed a "W," his shorthand for "WOW!"

That hand signal carried over to Johnny's athletic exploits. It was a small, fun gesture Jonathan shared with his kids. Even young AJ tried to make it work with his tiny fingers.

But by the time AJ was truly active in sports, Jonathan was headlong into life at Eisenberg & Anders. He had no time for coaching—barely even for showing up at games. As a result, AJ felt slighted. Over time, he grew to resent the WOW signal. To him, it represented something he never really got.

Jonathan wasn't the last to leave the school cafeteria, but he was among the final few. As he walked out, he received a couple of pats on the back and quiet words of affirmation. Sam waited for him outside.

"Jonathan, that was really great." She hugged her husband and kissed him on the cheek. "I mean, WOW! I'm not sure what else to say. I get the sense that a lot of people really appreciate what you did. *A lot.*"

"Yeah. I know not everyone's going to be happy," Jonathan said, shaking his head.

"Don't worry about Sebastian's dad. That whole crew isn't grounded in reality," Sam reasoned.

"Sam, I'm not worried about them. We have locks on our doors at home," Jonathan said with a dry laugh. "I'm more worried about the other person who lives with us behind those locked doors."

"Jonathan, AJ will just have to understand." Sam hugged him again.

As she did, Jonathan looked over her shoulder toward his car. A single, stout figure stood beside it. He quietly said, "Well, there might be an unhappy camper camped out by my car."

Sam turned quickly; her voice tinged with concern. "What should I do?"

"Nothing, Sam. Go home. Talk to AJ. I'm sure he knows by now." Jonathan leaned in and kissed her. "I'll handle whatever this is."

Sam walked off in the opposite direction as Jonathan calmly made a beeline toward his car. Despite his cool demeanor, his heart was racing. He didn't know what he was walking into.

The man near his car had a stoic expression. He wasn't watching Jonathan directly but slowly scanned the area, glancing this way and that.

As Jonathan approached, the man turned to face him. "Hey man, that was great."

"Thank you," Jonathan replied, still unsure where this was going.

"I'm just out here making sure no one scratches a love note into your car," the man said with a hearty laugh. "Sebastian's old man is a little… well, tetched. Actually, a lot tetched. The whole clan is."

"I appreciate that," Jonathan said, then asked, "Excuse me… you are?"

"Oh, sorry, buddy. I'm Norm. My son Paul—Mandrake—is on your team. He's a senior. On the line." Norm still hadn't smiled.

"Norm, right?" Jonathan asked. Norm nodded. "Paul's a nice kid. I'm glad to have him on the team." Jonathan extended a hand. "I'm Jonathan Reese."

"I know. I know," Norm replied, shaking his hand with enthusiasm. "Seriously, you said what most people were thinking. Dog, you became a freaking hero tonight."

"Tonight, sure. Come Friday, there might be a whole new feeling about me," Jonathan said with a half-laugh. "I've got to backfill a quarterback and most of the offensive line."

"Yeah, it'll be tough. But if you'll have me, I'd like to help coach," Norm offered. "It's been a minute, but I coached a lot of these kids at St. Matthew—Paul, AJ, Tommy, lots of them."

"Are you kidding? Yes. Yes!" Jonathan laughed. "I'll take whatever help I can get."

"Awesome, dog. This'll be fun," Norm said with another hearty laugh.

"Great. But it's late. I'm fried," Jonathan said, sounding drained. "Practice is tomorrow at six. Can we talk more then?"

"Sure, but do you have time in the morning?" Norm asked. "I'm downtown most days. I spend a lot of time at the Statehouse, which I believe is across the street from your office—Eisenberg & Anders, right?"

Jonathan nodded.

"I could pop over for a cup of coffee," Norm suggested.

"That actually sounds great," Jonathan said, smiling. "I'm at the office early. What works for you? Earlier the better."

Norm shrugged, then said, "Seven-thirty?"

"Perfect," Jonathan replied. "I'll meet you at the security station in the lobby. We can head to the Huntington Club from there."

Chapter 53

As Jonathan drove home, he replayed the last couple of hours in his mind. Sebastian's father had unnerved him—and he knew, somehow, he'd have to deal with that again. The thought was unsettling.

Still, in thinking it through, Jonathan felt confident he'd done the right thing. And it gave him comfort that his decision seemed to resonate with a large number of others.

As much as the support from others helped, connecting with Norm was the true high point. Jonathan needed help—running practices, making in-game decisions, talking X's and O's. The thought of no longer coaching alone was uplifting.

That feeling, however, evaporated the moment he walked through the front door.

"What did you do, Dad?" AJ shouted. He was in the middle of a heated argument with Sam, who was trying to reason with him. As soon as Jonathan entered, AJ's anger redirected. "I told you—we need to keep those guys. I told you!" His face was beet red. "You did this on purpose. I hate you!"

The words cut deep, but Jonathan stayed calm. "AJ," he said evenly.

Before he could say more, AJ snapped again. "We aren't going to win a game this season. Not a single game."

Jonathan stood silently, not wanting to escalate the situation.

Sam stepped in with her calm, rational-mom voice. "AJ, this isn't about football wins. What your dad did was about life wins. And those will matter a lot more in the long run."

That logic caught AJ off guard. "Well," he said, hesitating for the first time, "I'm not even sure we'll play another game. Guys are already talking about quitting. No one wants to get embarrassed by what's coming." He turned to storm off but stopped a few steps away. "And I might be one of them." Then he disappeared into his room, slamming the door.

Jonathan finally spoke. "Well, that went well," he muttered, sarcasm heavy in his tone. He let out a long sigh, turned toward Sam, and asked, "Is this what you meant when you said coaching would improve my relationship with AJ?"

Sam ignored the sarcasm and instead said gently, "It'll be fine, honey. He's just upset. None of this season is unfolding like he hoped. You have goals and aspirations. So does AJ."

Jonathan nodded, then said quietly, "I can relate." He paused, reflecting on moments when his own dreams had felt out of reach. "But honestly, I don't even know my son. Other than playing football, I don't know what he wants to achieve."

"It's okay, Jonathan," Sam said softly. "We've been through this. Your support for us has just looked different."

"Still, I should know," Jonathan insisted. "Especially now that I'm his coach."

"They're simple," Sam said. "Since his breakout season sophomore year, he's talked nonstop about breaking the school scoring record. He's only 45 points away."

Jonathan nodded, listening intently.

"And of course," she continued, "all the boys wanted to— still want to—repeat. You know, win another state title. And AJ wants to get a scholarship to play in college."

Jonathan jumped in, "He doesn't need a scholarship. We have the money."

"Honey, it's not about the money," Sam said. "It's about pride. He just wants the acknowledgment. To know he's good enough. He'd take a partial scholarship. He'd settle for just a pencil. Anything. Just something to prove he got noticed."

"Well, all of that is still in front of him," Jonathan said. Then he added, "Assuming the whole team doesn't implode in the next 24 hours."

"It'll be fine," Sam said again. "It's a bunch of teenagers venting over text. They're frustrated. They're facing a lot of change and feel out of control. But it'll pass."

"I guess we'll find out tomorrow at practice," Jonathan said.

Chapter 54

At 5:35 p.m. on Monday, Jonathan stood alone on the practice field at the high school. No players were out yet. That made him anxious. He had to remind himself that he was early. Still, he was pensive. He kept checking his watch. Maybe football wouldn't continue. A lump formed in his throat, and he swallowed hard—repeatedly.

At 5:50 p.m., the scene shifted. Players emerged from the locker room as they always had, carrying equipment and supplies to help the trainers. AJ rode the water jugs out with Shea, and the air was filled with teen frolic and laughter.

Then, at 5:55 p.m., Norm arrived—right on time. But he wasn't alone.

Earlier that day, Jonathan met Norm and they sat down for coffee as planned. He assumed the meeting would last only about an hour—just enough time to get acquainted and update his new assistant on team particulars. It didn't unfold like that at all.

As they walked to the Huntington Club, Norm started right in. "I'm really excited about this, dog. I was up late thinking about it. I can't wait to share some ideas—if that's cool?"

"That'd be great, Norm," Jonathan replied, not knowing what else to say.

"I've got an idea for the offense. You … we … have a depleted line and no quarterback. But there's a stable of good athletes, right?" Norm didn't wait for a response. "Well, I've got a buddy out in California. A few years back, we were at a conference, talking football. He told me about his son's team— they had a similar problem. You following me?"

Just then, the server brought coffee, briefly interrupting Norm's flow. But once the cups were topped off, he picked right back up.

"Anyway, they were in a tough spot—just like we are." Norm paused to take a long, savory sip of his coffee.

"And?" Jonathan prompted.

"Yeah … this is good coffee," Norm said, taking another sip.

Jonathan waited politely.

"Okay, focus, Norm," the assistant muttered to himself in the third person. "So, their situation was our situation. And what did their coaches do? Guess."

"Norm, I don't know," Jonathan said, a hint of impatience in his voice.

"Guess," Norm prodded again.

"Norm!" Jonathan snapped, making his impatience clear.

"Okay!" Norm relented, then launched into a rapid explanation. "They invented an offense called the A-11. Very creative, Jonathan. The idea was to create formations where, potentially, all eleven players were eligible to catch a pass." He took a quick breath and continued. "It used spread formations, misdirection—completely confused defenses. No one knew who was going out for a pass."

"Interesting," Jonathan said, leaning in.

"I know, right?" Norm grinned and took another sip of coffee before diving back in. "Unfortunately, high school rules have since tightened to limit how fully it can be used. But … but … even with restrictions, the A-11 still has teeth. It's strategically complex—unconventional formations, creative plays, built-in mismatches. In short, it would be perfect for us."

"Sounds great, Norm," Jonathan said, though his tone didn't quite match his words. "But a conversation over a beer a couple of years ago isn't exactly an offense we can duplicate."

"Oh, I know, buddy," Norm reassured him. "That's why I called my friend last night. He's in Cali—three hours behind us. So guess what, dog? He connected me to one of the innovative coaches. Me!" Norm grabbed his now-lukewarm coffee and took a big swig. "And at ten, I've got a phone call with him. Are you in?"

Without a word, Jonathan motioned to their server and held up his cup. "Can we get a couple of these to go?"

Back at Eisenberg & Anders, Jonathan led Norm to a small conference room near his office. He then got to work moving around meetings and clearing his calendar.

At 10 a.m. sharp, Norm stepped into Jonathan's office. He closed the door, pulled out his phone, and placed the call. As it rang, he turned on speaker mode.

"Steve Humphries," a voice answered on the other end. "Hey, coach. Norm Mandrake, here. And I've got Jonathan Reese, our coach, on here too. Thanks for taking our call, especially at this early hour."

"No problem. Happy to help," Humphries replied. "I've got Kurt Bryan here as well. He's the co-originator of the offense."

From there, Norm and Jonathan gave a quick rundown of their situation and the players they had. Then they let Humphries and Bryan take the floor. As the two coaches spoke, Jonathan and Norm feverishly took notes, exchanging nods and impressed looks throughout.

Over the course of 90 minutes, Humphries and Bryan laid out the fundamentals of the A-11 offense—what was legal under current high school rules and what to avoid. They also emailed supporting documents to help with implementation and offered to assist further if needed.

When the call ended, Jonathan and Norm sat back, wide-eyed in astonishment. Jonathan buzzed his assistant and asked her to order lunch in—they had a lot of work ahead compiling notes and mapping out the offense.

Over sandwiches and coffee, they reviewed the players on the roster and began matching personnel to roles within the A-11 scheme. Norm, having coached or followed many of the boys in youth football, offered detailed insights that proved invaluable.

"What do we know about this Brady Troy?" Jonathan asked.

Norm shrugged. He didn't know but excused himself to tap into his network and find out.

"I spoke to the team doctor for athletics at the Ohio School for the Deaf," Norm later reported. "His kids went to St. Matthew."

"What do you mean, spoke?" Jonathan asked, curious.

Norm chuckled. "He's the doctor—but he's not deaf."

Then he shared what he'd learned. "Playing football, Brady was a man among boys, according to Dr. Bryan. Apparently, he's already committed to playing college ball at Gallaudet University."

"Gallaudet?" Jonathan asked.

"It's a private deaf university near Washington, D.C. They play Division III football," Norm answered.

"So why is he at Blacklick? I don't get it," Jonathan said, clearly perplexed.

"I think he's looking for a new challenge. After just three years, he basically owns every offensive record at OSD," Norm replied. "According to Dr. Bryan, he's only got one weakness."

Jonathan bit: "What's that?"

"He's deaf," Norm said with a laugh. "That's it. Apparently, he's a stud."

Jonathan didn't laugh. "I don't know, Norm. To me, he's still an unknown. And I have no idea how to communicate with him—or how he might communicate with me. I mean, he doesn't talk at all, and I can't sign." Jonathan gestured with his hands. "And I can't exactly put his interpreter on the field with him."

Norm nodded, reluctantly agreeing. "Yeah, I get it, dude."

"I feel bad," Jonathan admitted. "But he does have a role. He's David Roberts' backup—though I'm not sure I want to get to that point. And he's our holder for field goals. That's not nothing, right?"

Jonathan paused. He suddenly realized that without Sebastian Sullivan, Brady Troy had no one to hold for. That shifted the conversation.

"What happened to the kicker? Evan or something? He quit?" Jonathan asked.

"John Evans. Great kid," Norm said. "The coaches never had confidence in him—and openly shared that."

"What do you mean?" Jonathan was puzzled.

"There were a lot of things. Some were just unnecessary. Downright mean," Norm explained. "Here's an example: In the playoffs, we were up two late in the fourth. It was fourth and three, just inside field goal range—but too close to punt. You following me?"

Jonathan nodded, tracking the story. "Go on."

"So John Evans does what any good kicker would do. He stands by Coach Fisher—you know, puppet Pete. He did everything Studer commanded." Jonathan waved for Norm to keep going.

"Yeah, yeah … anyway, John asks, 'Do you want me to go kick a field goal?'" Norm paused for dramatic effect.

"And?" Jonathan urged.

"Dude, puppet Pete says, loud enough for everyone to hear, 'Do you want to go in, or do you want to win?'" Norm widened his eyes and dropped his jaw. "Man, that's harsh. He's just a kid."

Jonathan shook his head in quiet disgust.

"Coach, that's just one example. There are others—lots more," Norm added. "The kid was probably demoralized. Decided not to come back. I mean, who needs that?"

"Do you think we can get him back?" Jonathan asked.

"I dunno," Norm said, shrugging. "We can ask."

"Let me work on that … tonight," Jonathan said, jotting down a note to himself.

As he did, Ari Eisenberg knocked and entered.

"Hey, Jonathan, word's out that you ruffled some feathers last night."

Jonathan hung his head, unsure of what to expect.

"What did you hear? Or better question—how did you hear?"

Ari let out a laugh. "I received a litany of emails and a few calls complaining about you."

"Saying…?" Jonathan hesitated to ask but felt obligated.

Ari broke into a hearty laugh and said through it, "Relax, Jonathan. I was born at 10 o'clock in the morning—just not this morning." The firm's patriarch laughed even harder.

Uncertain, Norm chuckled along and offered a hesitant smile.

"Jonathan," Ari said, attempting to reassure him, "you have to know that some people just aren't happy unless they have something to be unhappy about." He paused, then added, "And besides, if you aren't pissing off a few people, you're probably doing something wrong."

Ari then turned his attention to Norm, extended a hand, and said, "Hey … I'm Ari Eisenberg."

Norm shared his name, and the two men shook hands. Jonathan offered some context about Norm's presence at the firm and explained that he worked across the street at the Statehouse.

"Are you a lobbyist?" Ari asked.

"That's the plan most days, anyway," Norm replied with a wry grin.

"Do you know Ronald Chamberlain? He's the executive director at the Ohio Oil and Gas Association. They're always in need of lobbyists."

"Ari, I don't. I'd love to, but I don't," Norm admitted.

With that, Ari pulled out his phone and began composing a text.

"Norm, spell your last name for me." Norm did. Ari typed a bit more, hit send, and said, "You're all set. Ronnie's expecting your call when you have time later today." He scribbled Ronald Chamberlain's name and number on a scrap of paper and handed it to Norm.

The lobbyist was dumbfounded, but managed to say, "Thanks!"

Ari added, "I told him you and I had coffee this morning." With that, the head of Eisenberg & Anders grabbed a cup of coffee from what Jonathan had left over. After a few more words of polite conversation, Ari exited the office.

It took the two coaches a little time to get back on track, but Jonathan eventually did by saying, "Back to John Evans … how many kids do you think quit over this Sebastian thing?"

"None! What you did last night, Jonathan, was big. I mean, *big*," Norm said, taking a sip of coffee. "A lot of parents weren't sure about you. They didn't know if you were just more of the same—you know, football above everything. Well, you're not. And after last night, everyone knows it. So I don't think there's a kid left whose parents would let them quit now."

Jonathan had nothing to say. He wasn't sure if Norm's statement was accurate or just Norm being Norm. After all, he wasn't even sure if his own son would show up to practice.

Then Norm continued, "In fact, do you remember saying you could use all the help you could get?"

Jonathan nodded slightly, unsure of where this was going.

"Well, when I got home, I called some team dads—guys who coach at St. Matthew or in youth football." Norm nodded and winked. "Dog, I've got a small handful of them coming out to help today, if that's okay."

"Great," Jonathan responded.

Norm and Jonathan spent a couple more hours working through details, discussing coaching roles and player assignments. They adjourned at 3 p.m. to each get some real work done but pledged to reconvene at practice.

Norm ran a little later than planned, having had a 45-minute conversation with Ronald Chamberlain and setting up lunch later in the week. But when he showed up at 5:55 p.m., he wasn't alone.

Chapter 55

On Sunday night, following the impromptu meeting at the high school, Norm drove off the parking lot and immediately started working the phones.

He'd spent years coaching his son, Paul, and many of the other Mustang players in youth football and at St. Matthew School. But Norm hadn't coached alone. There was a litany of other dads who had volunteered their time and lent their talents to the young players—some of whom now had sons on the Blacklick High football team.

Norm reached out to invite them to help him and Jonathan coach. Using his signature style—"Hey, dog, let's get the band back together"—he made it hard to say no. He also assured them that Jonathan was a "good egg" and someone they'd be proud to coach alongside.

Before practice started, Norm met the volunteers in the parking lot, and together they walked onto the field.

As they entered, Jonathan felt a rush of relief. Norm's help was already comforting. But reducing the coach-to-player ratio even further made him smile. While they still had a new offense to install and several holes to fill, he no longer felt alone in figuring it out.

One by one, the new coaches introduced themselves to Jonathan and the team. They each shared a bit about their football background—"walk-on running back at Bowling Green"—and where they hoped to contribute.

Then Jonathan addressed the team.

"As you likely know, we lost a few players over the weekend," he said. "That changes our personnel mix somewhat." He scanned the players' faces for a reaction.

There was none.

He moved on quickly, invoking one of Ari's mantras. "The loss of some is a gain of opportunity for others." The room perked up.

"Today, Coach Norm and I revamped our offense into something very unusual." Curious looks spread across the group. Jonathan continued, pausing briefly to let Joyce sign the message to Brady. "The good news? It's going to open things up. Anybody and everybody on the field is a threat to score. The bad news? We've got a lot to learn. We'll be drinking from a firehose all week. Isn't that right, dog?"

He nodded at Norm, who replied stoically, "Absolutely."

Together with the new coaches, they began handing out the playbooks they'd created earlier at Eisenberg & Anders. Jonathan instructed those on offense, "Dump the Maven offense from your binder and add the A-11 material."

Once the A-11 materials were distributed, Jonathan started assigning positions. Paul Mandrake stayed at center. David Roberts was named quarterback. Jonathan filled out the rest of the offensive line with backup tight ends and fullbacks—players who had size and agility.

The moment the line was set, Tommy Frank raised a concern, his voice tinged with worry. "Wait? I'm not starting anymore?"

Jonathan didn't respond. He didn't even acknowledge the question. Instead, he kept going.

"And Tommy Frank is going to be our fullback in this new offense." He walked behind David Roberts, tapping the ground where he wanted Tommy to stand.

Tommy blinked. "You're kidding, right?"

"No, Tommy. We don't have time for kidding. Right here." Jonathan tapped the ground again. "Coach Norm tells me you were once a heck of a back. We don't need you on the O-line. I need you here."

Tommy moved quickly, as if worried the coaches might change their minds. "Thanks, Coach Norm!" he called out, his voice full of giddy excitement. "I haven't carried the ball since junior high."

He landed where Jonathan had indicated but kept talking. "Coach Norm, did you put RB Airstrike in the playbook?" He turned to the group. "It's a great play. I start to sweep with the ball and then pass as the defense closes in."

"Tommy..." Jonathan tried to rein him in.

"I can throw a decent 10- to 20-yard pass with either hand," Tommy continued, oblivious to the disruption. "How about the Boomerang Bomb? That was a flea-flicker! I'd fake the run and pitch it back to David Roberts."

"Okay, okay, big guy," Norm tried to interject. It didn't work.

"How about Hammer Reverse?" Tommy asked, now fully performing. "That one was unstoppable. Right, AJ?" He turned to his friend. "It's where we fake the run off-tackle, and at the last second I flip the ball to AJ, reversing the other direction."

The team and coaching staff were now openly amused. Everyone was smiling. Some were laughing.

Tommy then looked at Jonathan. "It fools them every time. Especially if we've run the Hammer—or whatever we call the off-tackle run—a bunch. AJ just walks in. Everyone's going left. AJ's scoring right."

The reaction gave Jonathan an opening to regain control.

"Well, Tommy, I love the enthusiasm. I'm not sure any of that is in the playbook. With all the new help, Coach Norm and I are going to focus on what we've got. We can talk later. But for now, let's lean into the playbook as it is."

Then, addressing the entire team, he said, "That goes for everyone. Learn the playbook. This won't be easy—at least, not at first—but once we master it, our opponents will be completely befuddled."

Laughter broke out again.

"But it starts with us—every one of us—knowing our responsibilities and what's going on."

Jonathan continued directing players to positions on the field, giving feedback and commentary along the way. But as he did, AJ quietly stewed.

His father had kept him at wide receiver. He'd said everyone was a scoring threat now—but what if that meant fewer chances to score? And if AJ didn't score, he wouldn't break the school's all-time scoring record.

That thought gnawed at him more than he wanted to admit.

Chapter 56

For John Evans, life without football was a mixed bag. He didn't miss all the workouts and practices. He did, however, miss his friends while they were at them.

Online gaming just wasn't the same for JSevans. Playing with relative nobodies wasn't as fun as conquering challenges and defeating zombies with the likes of A2J9R, T-Frank, and SpartyBT10—who he now knew was his new classmate, Brady Troy.

But he looked forward to around 9 each night. Football practice was over, his friends had eaten, and enough homework was done to justify 90 minutes or so of gaming. John sat in his gaming chair, headset on, and waited for his electronic playmates to log on.

He could see that AJ was coming online, but he didn't do so in the usual way. He didn't jump straight into gaming. Instead, he started with a message.

We NEED you on the team.

John read the message twice. "Odd," he thought. Assuming that the "team" referred to the mock combat they were about to embark on, he responded:

alredy on it, aj

A few miles away in Jefferson Township, Jonathan was trying to make sense of how to work AJ's gaming controller. He had labored to create a more complete message: *John, this is Mr. Reese. We need a kicker for the team. Would you please come back out and be on the team.* But he was not willing to hit send, as the message lacked perfection.

"AJ, where's the question mark on this thing?" Jonathan uttered in frustration.

"Dad! Oh my God! This is going to take forever. You don't need it," AJ lashed out. "You don't need punctuation … or perfect English. It's a message, not a legal paper."

"But that seems just wrong. I mean, even my text messages are perfectly spelled out," Jonathan reasoned.

"No, texts don't need to be perfect either," AJ quipped back. "I've been meaning to talk to you about that." He then reached over toward his dad and said, "Give me that." He took the controller and deleted Jonathan's message.

we need a kik'r join us 2moro
@ six you can have 7 still

Sevans perfectly deduced the imperfect message and responded with a thumbs-up emoji.

AJ then said to his dad, "All set."

"Which one is Brady?" Jonathan Dan asked.

AJ motioned to the screen with both hands on his controller and said, "SpartyBT10."

"Why Sparty?" Jonathan quickly followed up.

"Mascot for Ohio School for the Deaf," AJ replied in a matter-of-fact tone, not taking his eyes off the on-screen action.

"Why 10?" Jonathan fired out another.

"That was his number there," AJ responded in a similar manner. Then he took his eyes off the screen long enough to give his dad a glare that said, "You can leave now."

Jonathan took the hint and left.

Chapter 57

Jonathan arrived at Tuesday's practice brimming with confidence. Thanks to contacts at Case Western Reserve University, they had a plan for practices. While untested, they had an offense that seemed as if it would work well for their personnel. Plus, through the efforts of Norm, they now had a stable of quality parent coaches. And they had someone who could kick and punt.

As for that kicker-punter, John Evans fit in well. It was as if he had always been part of the team. He knew everyone, and everyone welcomed him back.

At 6 p.m. sharp, Jonathan blew his whistle and sent everyone on a warmup lap. When they returned and lined up for stretching, it was obvious that two people were missing.

"Joyce, where's Brady?" Jonathan asked.

She shrugged her shoulders and looked around. She had no idea either.

"Where's Tommy?" Jonathan quickly added. Everyone looked around. "AJ?" Jonathan inquired of his son.

"I don't know. I got myself here on time. That's a feat in and of itself," AJ responded with a chuckle.

Moments later, off in the distance, Tommy and Brady emerged from the parking lot. They were walking. They seemed disheveled and exhausted. As they approached, it appeared that their jerseys were scuffed up. The number 8 on Brady's 38 jersey was half torn off. The neck on Tommy's was ripped open like a V-neck, down between the 7 and 4.

As they approached, Jonathan asked — and Joyce quickly signed — "Where have you been? You're late. You look like you've been in a fight."

Brady and Tommy stopped and looked at one another. Then they looked back at everyone without any expression on their faces.

Tommy let out an exasperated sigh and a single word. "Sebastian."

After school, Brady went to study hall with much of the rest of the team. It was a good habit for him — getting after homework right away helped him keep up with his studies and his parents' good graces, allowing him to game online when time permitted.

As 5:40 approached, he headed to the locker room with the others and quickly got ready for practice. He didn't want to put his books and notes in his sweaty, stinky locker, so at 5:55 he detoured to his car before heading to the practice field.

As he was loading his books into his trunk, he was struck violently from behind with a pair of open palms just below his shoulder pads. Startled, he turned quickly and was face to face with Sebastian Sullivan, Noah Turner and Aiden Davis.

As there is the notion of innocent until proven guilty — and they hadn't been — the trio were out of lock-up, awaiting the slow grind of legal justice. They literally had a constitutional right to be at school.

"Where ya goin', dummy?" Sebastian said, pushing Brady again.

Brady wanted nothing to do with this. He turned quickly, closed his trunk and took a step toward the practice field. Aiden blocked his path.

"Where ya goin', dummy? I asked you a question," Sebastian reasserted. "You aren't going anywhere until we get an answer." He grabbed Brady's jersey. Brady knocked the hand away, tearing the number 8 a bit.

"Hey, dummy. You don't hit me." Sebastian punched Brady hard with a closed fist in the stomach, making sure he avoided the football equipment.

Brady dropped his helmet and doubled over, losing his breath. He was terrified. He was cornered and really didn't know what to do.

"No, no, no, dummy. You can't go down there. Up, up," Sebastian said, as Aiden and Noah propped Brady up. Sebastian then tore the number 8 halfway off. "Just tell me where you're going … or I'm gonna punch you again."

Brady was taken by total surprise when Sebastian popped him in the cheek. He didn't make a sound. Primal fear engulfed him. His vision tunneled, fixated on the threat before him.

Aiden and Noah focused on holding their deaf, former teammate tight. Sebastian was focused on where and how to land the next solid blow.

None of them saw beefy Tommy Frank emerge from the side.

"What the hell are you doing?" he shouted. He didn't wait for an answer. As he yelled, he dropped his helmet and grabbed Aiden around the neck.

In an act of self-preservation, Aiden let go of Brady and grabbed Tommy by his practice jersey collar. He tried to hold on, but to no avail.

Tommy yanked Aiden back and threw him down, ripping the number 74 jersey into a V-neck. This actually created momentum that the lineman-turned-fullback used to advance forward. That thrust him between Sebastian and Brady, toward Noah.

In an instant, Noah was engulfed in fear. In a single motion, Tommy forced him down onto the parking lot pavement. Then, he literally stepped on Noah. Not once, but twice. With his foot still on his former teammate, Tommy spun 180 degrees, unintentionally grinding his cleat into Noah's chest.

Sebastian was completely aghast. Tommy had bested his two henchmen in summary fashion. Now, that beast was coming right at him with a demonic stare.

He put up his hands in a defensive, surrendering manner and attempted to rationalize, "Tommy!"

Tommy heard nothing. He grabbed the former quarterback's fingers and started to twist them. He felt his feeble opponent submit, his knees beginning to buckle. His rage urged him to capitalize. That, however, was simply not his nature.

Tommy shoved Sebastian back, sending him rolling across a row of cars.

"Now, get out of here!" Tommy shouted angrily.

The trio complied, scampering away.

Once Tommy was satisfied that they were gone, he turned to Brady, who was clearly shaken by the incident. The fullback took a deep breath to calm himself. He then walked up to Brady, put a hand on his deaf teammate's shoulder and looked him in the eye.

Tommy nodded, not really knowing what to say. Then he held up his other hand and showed an open palm, and carefully enunciated, "It's okay. It's okay." He followed up with, "I … got … you." As he uttered the words, he pointed to himself, then clenched his fist in a grabbing motion, and then pointed to Brady. Then he did it again, repeating, "I … got … you."

Although Tommy's motions weren't standard deaf signing, Brady got the gist. He nodded as he exhaled in relief. Then he patted the fullback on the chest to show appreciation.

They stood there for a moment to gather themselves. Then Tommy picked up their helmets, gave Brady his, and motioned that they should go to practice.

Jonathan shook his head as Tommy shared details about the incident. "I'm sorry, Tommy ... Brady. We're just going to have to deal with Sebastian."

"And his old man too," Norm added.

"Him too," Jonathan agreed. "I can handle that. Everyone else — have each other's back."

At that moment, completely unprompted, Brady began enthusiastically signing to Joyce. Somehow, everyone knew the message was meant for the entire team.

Joyce smiled and said, "While I don't condone violence, apparently Tommy stomped on those kids — he rolled over them. So, with that, Brady has given Tommy a deaf sign name." She quickly explained the purpose of a sign name. "From now on," Joyce paused briefly, "Brady will refer to Tommy as Tank."

"Oh, I love it!" Tommy roared. "From now on, everybody calls me Tank." He patted his chest proudly.

Everybody laughed. Jonathan attempted to rein things in to get practice started.

"Okay then ... Tank, take off that ripped jersey and put this on." Jonathan handed the fullback a number 47 practice jersey.

Tank stepped forward and said, "This makes Tank very happy."

"Good, but you were late, so you and Brady owe us a lap after practice," Jonathan added.

"Really?" Tank was taken aback. "That doesn't make Tank happy at all." Everyone laughed.

"Well, I understand. But that's the point. It's not supposed to be fun. Late is late," Jonathan said.

"But Tank was just protecting Brady," the fullback protested.

Jonathan cut him off. "No excuses. Next time, protect your teammates a little faster." He winked. "And please stop referring to yourself in the third person."

"Tank will consider that," number 47 replied.

Brady then quickly signed, and Joyce relayed, "It's okay, Tank. I will run with you." Tank nodded in appreciation.

"And Brady," Jonathan called out to his deaf player. "Take your jersey off and put this one on." He tossed him a new practice jersey.

Brady caught it as he was receiving the message from Joyce. He was confused by the gesture. But as he opened it up, his confusion quickly turned to amazement and delight — Jonathan had reassigned his number from 38 to 10.

Jonathan smiled as Brady made quick work of changing jerseys. Then he said, "Bring some honor to it."

After getting the message from Joyce, Brady nodded. Then he enthusiastically signed a message.

Joyce translated with a grin: "Brady says thank you very much. And he's given you the sign name of Coach Dad."

Chapter 58

Once everyone settled, Jonathan got practice underway. It was Tuesday. While their next game — against Utica — was very winnable, they still had to install a whole new offense beforehand.

A few coaches worked off to the side with players who were almost exclusively on defense or special teams, like John Evans. Everyone else focused on Coach Dad and Coach Norm as they laid out — in simplified fashion — a complex system of various formations and potential plays.

In their initial meeting, Jonathan and Norm had settled on a logical system for calling plays. The first word indicated the formation — how the team would line up. The second identified who would get the ball. The third described how they would get the ball — pass, pitch or handoff. And finally, "left" or "right" signaled the direction of the play.

Watching on, Shea Brooks worked it out in her head and announced to the team during a quiet moment at a water break: "With 27 different formations, 11 potential ball carriers, 3 ways to distribute the ball, and 2 directions — right and left, for those following along — there are 1,782 potential plays."

That revelation made players' eyes go wide. It was a staggeringly large number compared to any other offense they'd ever been involved in.

Despite that, any and all players associated with the offense were keenly focused on learning. After all, the Blacklick offense, once fully implemented, resembled basketball more than football. Each player knew there were plays where they'd be the primary target or ball carrier — even offensive linemen. That kept everyone's interest.

Nevertheless, at times, the learning was overwhelming. Just as a student could only take so much algebra or chemistry in a single sitting, the same was true for learning the A-11 offense.

At one point, it led Tank to proclaim, half-laughing, "Enough! My head hurts." He grabbed his helmet with both hands. "I say we simplify this. Let's go with either Hammer Left or Hammer Right." The new fullback kiddingly advocated that the offense be whittled down to two plays.

"Give me the ball," he commanded the quarterback. David Roberts complied. Then, feigning slow motion, Tank walked toward the line, three or four yards left of center. When he almost got there, the new fullback slowed and added, "And just to keep them honest, we'll throw in a Hammer Reverse now and then, right AJ?"

Then, just as Tank had done a dozen times in middle school football games — and another hundred or so in practice — he flipped the ball to AJ, who reversed back in the other direction, looping deep behind the offensive line.

As AJ concluded the feigned slow-motion action, Tank remarked, "That's all we need. It works every time."

Sensing that the team was overwhelmed with learning — something he'd encountered time and again studying for the bar exam — Coach Dad sent everyone on a long, slow lap around the field. It wasn't a punishment, but rather a way to clear their minds for more learning. They needed to ensure that practices remained productive.

At 8 sharp, Coach Dad blew his whistle, called everyone in, and offered words of encouragement as he ended practice — except for Tank and Brady, who had a penalty lap to complete.

A necessary evil of high school football is, well, high school. The Blacklick football team had lots of learning in practice, but that did not diminish regular schoolwork. A couple of weeks in, and the academic year was in full swing.

For AJ, there were high expectations. His mother was a doctor. His father was an attorney. And his siblings — Johnny and Kelly — were heading down similar paths. As such, he took a rigorous class load: advanced placement courses and unique college-level offerings at Blacklick.

This put Shea Brooks in class with AJ quite often. Beyond her disheveled appearance, her superior intellect — even in the advanced classes — made her an outsider. She tended to skew any curved grading in the wrong direction, and her know-it-all style made her someone no one wanted to work with on a group project.

Thus, in their Advanced Scientific Methods class, AJ found that he and Shea were the only two people without a partner for a small group project due later in the semester. Though sitting in close proximity, he used his index finger on his right hand to motion across the aisle: "You? Me? Team up?"

To which she replied aloud, "Okay. Fine. But I'm not carrying you."

AJ simply chuckled and rolled his eyes, as if to say, "Whatever."

Later in the week, in senior English, Mrs. Makowski instructed the class to team up with one other student for a semester-long project.

As soon as he comprehended the message, Brady looked back at his rescuer eagerly hoping to pair up. With a nod, Tank agreed.

But then he immediately felt bad that he'd abandoned his longtime friend, AJ. As AJ looked at him, Tommy looked down sheepishly and remarked, "I'm sorry, man."

AJ noticed that Shea Brooks didn't have a partner either. So, in a playful manner, he replied to Tank loud enough for everyone to hear, "It's okay, Tank. I'm going to carry Shea on this project, anyway."

Shea just rolled her eyes, as if to say, "Whatever." Then she waited for AJ to gather his things and make his way over to her. As he approached, she smiled and remarked, "You think you're funny, don't you?"

AJ laughed and responded, "I do. I do." Then added, "But looks aren't everything."

Shea couldn't help but let out a chuckle as she shook her head.

Chapter 59

The team was excited for Friday to arrive — game day. It was a chance to atone for the previous week's loss. More than that, the week had been incredibly intense: new offense, new positions and roles, new coaches, new teammates. All of it required learning and drilling — and drilling and learning. It felt more like a high school musical than a football team.

In addition, there was a new vibe — an energy to the team. Sebastian's divisive presence was gone, which made everyone more relaxed. From that, camaraderie formed. Even Shea became part of it.

The only tension that seemed to remain was between Jonathan and AJ. Like anything in his life, Jonathan was fixated on creating success. It's just who he was. AJ rolled his eyes at that intensity.

He might have been less annoyed if his dad's passion were more focused on him. Sam had theorized that Jonathan coaching would create more time together for father and son. The reality was that while they were now in the same vicinity a couple more hours a day, there was no quality time. AJ was one of dozens of players chaotically moving about.

Moreover, the A-11 offense gave AJ a sense of jealousy and resentment. While the high-flying offense gave others a chance at glory, it diminished AJ's. While most were excited to lean into learning, AJ disliked the idea that, on many plays, he was merely a decoy or blocker.

A popular cliché is that "time heals all wounds." While the amount of time isn't specified, when it came to Jonathan and AJ's father-son relationship, it would take more than a few weeks.

That tension, however, was put aside on Friday. After all, Jonathan and AJ had a common focus. Blacklick was hosting the team from nearby Utica, Ohio. That was a reason for excitement.

The school — in fact, the entire community — was buzzing. The defending state champion Mustangs were at home for the first time. Pageantry surrounded the night.

And their opponent seemed perfect for the occasion. The Mustangs had never lost to the Redskins. In fact, none of the previous meetings had even been close. Jonathan and AJ had no reason to believe that dominance wouldn't continue.

And the game started out that way. Blacklick kicked off to Utica and pinned the opponent — clad in red and white — deep in its own territory. The home crowd roared. That fervor fueled the defense, which stopped the Redskins for no gain on three straight plays.

Utica was forced to punt, giving Blacklick the ball at midfield. More importantly, the Mustangs could now unveil their new offense.

But it didn't start well. On two consecutive attempts to run the first play, the Mustangs committed penalties — illegal procedure and delay of game. Before they could commit a third, Coach Dad called a timeout.

He and Norm called over their young quarterback to review the play and calm David Roberts' nerves for his first varsity start. It didn't work. While Blacklick finally executed a play, David fumbled the snap and fell on the ball for a five-yard loss.

It was now second-and-25. The call was for Roberts to pitch the ball to Tank, who would then throw to AJ downfield. The pitch was late. The pass was hurried. It sailed over AJ's head and out of bounds.

On third-and-25, the Mustangs should have punted. The play — a double reverse — started fine. Roberts took the snap and handed it to Tank, who moved left. The teammate who was supposed to take the second pitch was initially confused and started in the wrong direction. He quickly corrected and ran to where he needed to be, but he arrived a half-second late.

The timing of the pitch was off, and the ball bounced to the turf. No Blacklick player could corral it. A Utica defender scooped it up and easily returned it for a touchdown. With the extra point, Blacklick trailed 7-0.

While disappointing, the team and fans remained optimistic. After all, it was Utica. Surely, the Mustangs would respond quickly.

Blacklick did get the ball back — that's how football works. But they didn't score.

Points had to be earned. To earn points, a team had to gain yards. And to gain yards, it had to maintain control of the football. Blacklick did neither.

Series after series, the offense lost yardage because of poor execution, broken plays or both. On the rare occasion the Mustangs gained yards, penalties often wiped them out.

The new offense had been drilled hard all week. But those efforts weren't at full speed, and they weren't live action. In practice, Jonathan and Norm could stand nearby to offer direction. That wasn't possible during the game. So, it wasn't surprising that chaos led to negative plays.

Negative plays weren't ideal, but they at least got the Mustangs to fourth down — which meant John Evans could punt. And he could send the ball 40 yards downfield.

But it was a problem when the Mustangs didn't make it to fourth down. Including the first drive, Blacklick turned the ball over five times — two interceptions and three fumbles. That put tremendous pressure on the defense.

As shown in the Kettering Alter game, the defense was prideful and stalwart. But when given a short field over and over, it couldn't hold. The usually stagnant Utica offense scored three times in the first half.

Worst of all, the camaraderie the Mustangs had brought into the game began to unravel with each setback. It was frustrating. The results weren't matching the effort — all the learning and drilling.

Players argued. On the field. On the sidelines. And as they walked to the locker room trailing 28-0 at halftime.

Chapter 60

The bickering continued as the players headed into the locker room. All the coaches followed — except Jonathan and Norm.

Norm asked for a minute with Jonathan. He could see the despondent look on Coach Dad's face and assumed it reflected how the head coach was feeling. Wisely, Norm didn't want that to infect the team.

"Hey bud, are you OK?" Norm asked.

Jonathan answered indirectly. "Oh God, what have I done?" He was second-guessing every decision from the past week — including removing the foul-tip club from the team. "I've destroyed the team with my arrogance."

Norm gently interjected. "Hey, dog. It's not 'I.' It's 'we.' I was there Monday with you. We're in this together. I'm with you." He paused briefly, then added, "The other coaches are with you. We're here because we believe in you. We. Are. Here. For. You."

"I know. I appreciate that, but …" Jonathan paused. "The games don't get any easier than this. If Utica drubs us, I can only imagine the scorched earth other teams are going to lay on us." He swallowed hard. "These kids don't deserve that. You coaches don't either."

"Yo, yo, yo. Don't think like that. You can't think like that. Don't worry about other teams or other games," Norm said. He was firm, but still had a gentle tone. "Let's focus on this game. Let's focus on the second half. Let's focus on the next play." He looked Jonathan in the eye. "Yeah, we're down a bunch and a comeback might be out of reach. But we can help these kids finish strong, learn something — and then look ahead."

Jonathan nodded, and his hopeless disposition began to fade.

Norm could tell he was getting through. He switched to a more upbeat tone. "Jonathan, we're not dumb. And we're not arrogant either … we're not smart enough or good-looking enough to be." He added a chuckle.

Jonathan cracked a smile and let out a small laugh.

Norm continued, "We need to stay the course with this A-11 thing. I know it doesn't feel like it or look like it right now, but I sense we can make it work." He paused to gather his thoughts. "It's going to click. I just feel it."

Together, Norm and Jonathan went into the locker room. There were 50-some pairs of eyes staring at them, waiting to hear what was next.

Jonathan jumped right in. "OK, none of that went as planned. First of all — defense — we're sorry. We've put you in an awful position … several times. No more. Offense, take a deep breath. You're going to be fine. We're going to be fine. We just need to clean up the little mistakes. Our offense is complex and requires precision. If everyone executes well, it works. One mistake — one small mistake — by anyone, anywhere, gums up the works."

Jonathan gathered himself and allowed the team to absorb what he'd said — and gave Joyce time to relay the message to Brady. He scanned the room, looking players in the eye.

"OK," Jonathan continued. "We get the ball to start the second half. Let's do something with it. David Roberts?" He searched the locker room to find the young quarterback. "Take charge out there. Everyone, David is our field general. Listen to him. Coach Norm and I are communicating through him. We're going to take this one series, one play at a time."

Jonathan scanned the room again. He could see that the hope Norm had infused in him had now spread to the players.

"Everyone, get some water. Get with Nathan or Shea for any small injury needs. Check in with your position coaches briefly."

He took a deep breath and finished with, "Then let's get out there and see what we can do with the second half."

Chapter 61

When the team returned to the field, they found that much of the crowd had gone home. Parents remained. Friends remained. The band and cheerleaders remained. Most of the fair-weather fans had not.

The few who did stay let Jonathan have it. They worked themselves up to the fence separating fans from the team and coaches and let their foul mouths run, offering obscenity-laced suggestions that Jonathan should stick to practicing law.

Norm placed himself between Jonathan and the few outspoken fans. Serving as a buffer, he sarcastically responded, "Thanks for your feedback."

Despite the stands being relatively empty, the players went through their halftime warm-up drills. Soon, the enthusiastic Utica team returned to the field as well, and shortly thereafter the officials got the second half underway.

The enthusiasm Utica brought to the second half, their kicker channeled through his foot. But instead of booting the ball high and deep, he sent the oblong ball erratically bouncing along the ground. The best the deep man for Blacklick could do before the pursuing Redskins arrived was corral the ball at the 10-yard line and lay on it.

The Mustang offense took the field. And David Roberts, after calling the play in the huddle, lined the team up for a short pass to AJ near the sideline. It was routine. It was simple. It was intended to give them something positive to build on.

Roberts received the shotgun snap at the 3-yard line and let the play develop. Utica players were closing in, but AJ was open. Roberts drew his arm back and smoothly directed it forward —

just as he had 1,000 times before. Except this time, he lost his grip on the ball, and it bounced into the end zone.

Utica defenders shouted "Fumble!" and chased after the ball. So did Roberts. He was closer. Redskin players had the numbers. A scrum of players fell onto the ground and fought for the football.

The officials whistled the play dead and began to peel players off the pile, one by one. There was no question about two things: Roberts did recover his fumble — and the Blacklick quarterback was not moving.

One official indicated that Utica scored a safety. The Utica team and fans celebrated a 30-point lead.

At the same time, another official motioned to the Blacklick sideline for medical personnel. Nathan and Shea came racing to the scene. They prodded, questioned and examined the young quarterback. After a few minutes, Roberts walked unaided to the sideline. He carried his helmet, his head down. Everyone politely clapped.

As the Blacklick punt team raced onto the field to kick the ball back to Utica, Jonathan and Norm approached Nathan. Their faces had one question.

With Roberts at his side, Nathan shared, "He's fine physically, Jonathan. Mentally ... emotionally ... he's taken a hit. He's blaming himself. He's OK to play medically, but ..." The team trainer shrugged his shoulders and scrunched his face to complete the thought.

"Thanks," Jonathan said to Nathan. Then to the young quarterback: "David, this is not your fault. Go take a seat. There's still a role for you on this team. We just need to regroup." Jonathan then turned his attention back to the field.

His team was now punting the ball back to Utica. But he thought, "Perhaps the defense can hold. Then what?" Their original starter was removed from the team. The backup was effectively shell-shocked. And the backup's backup hadn't taken a snap in practice — and was totally deaf.

Jonathan felt a sense of hopelessness in that moment. It filled his face as he looked out onto the field. Norm saw it and quietly chided, "Jonathan?"

Coach Dad responded, "I know. I know." He shouted encouragement to the defense taking the field. No matter what, he had to be positive.

Then he shouted back toward the team, "Joyce, let's get Brady ready to play."

Chapter 62

The Blacklick offense wasn't a week old. The defense, however, was as old as the school. Gary Studer introduced it when he started almost a decade earlier. And since then, the defense had remained unchanged.

Why change it? It worked.

Yes, it had yielded 21 of the 30 points that Utica tallied in the first half, but those were understandable. Over and over, the offense turned the ball over deep inside its own territory. And when it did manage to get to a punting situation, it happened so quickly that the defenders had little time to catch their breath.

But following halftime, the defense was well rested. In addition, John Evans got off a good punt following the Utica safety. The Mustang defense was in a good position to pin its ears back and come after the Redskins.

They stopped the visitors for no gain on first down, then took them for a loss on the second. The third-down play, a pass, fell incomplete. Jonathan watched it all unfold and cheered it on. Finally, something to celebrate.

But he also secretly hoped Utica might get a first down or two. That would evaporate a little more time from the game and delay him from having to insert Brady Troy — untested, ill-prepared and seemingly unable to communicate.

That was not meant to be, however. It was fourth down. Utica was preparing to punt and Blacklick ready to receive. Coach Dad, with Norm at his side, called Brady over via Joyce. When he arrived, Jonathan faced up to the third-string quarterback and began giving instructions.

"Brady, we're going to keep it simple," Coach Dad said, enunciating clearly. "Lots of Hammers. Left and right. Remember?" He waited for Joyce to relay and for Brady to nod, indicating that he understood. "Let's put Tank to work running off tackle. Left, then right. Nothing fancy."

As Jonathan communicated, he caught a glimpse out of the corner of his eye — the Utica punter had boomed the ball. The Mustang return man didn't catch it. Another mental mistake. Instead, Jonathan watched the ball bounce and roll back toward their end zone — inside the 15, to the 10, and beyond. The official finally blew the play dead with the ball around the 7.

Coach Dad turned his attention back to Brady. "Listen, do the best you can. No pressure. Do you understand?" He waited for another nod from Brady. Then continued: "We know we haven't put you in a good position. I'm really sorry. I know this is not fair. Just do the best you can."

Brady didn't nod. He looked Coach Dad directly in the eyes and stepped forward. He was completely expressionless. He raised his hands as if to sign something — but didn't. With his right hand, he secured the chin strap on the right side of his helmet.

As that snapped into place, Brady laid his left hand gently on his coach's chest and uttered, "On't urry, toach."

Coach Dad's eyes went wide with astonishment. He said nothing. Norm, equally amazed, looked at Jonathan.

Joyce sincerely asked, "Do you need me to translate?"

Still looking at Jonathan with wide eyes, Norm sarcastically responded, "No, Joyce. I think we got that."

A split second later, Brady turned and ran onto the field to catch up with the offense.

The offense players knew the sequence of plays – alternating Hammer Left and Right. Hand the ball to Tank. There was no need to huddle. It was no secret. Jonathan just intended to control the football as long as they could. Then they rely on the punting of John Evans and staunch defense.

The team got lined up. There was no confusion. The formation and execution were simple — just block forward and trust sturdy Tank to plow ahead.

Brady lined up seven yards back from his center, Paul Mandrake. The heels of his cleats were on the goal line. He looked left to make sure everyone was set, then right. He quickly reached up to make sure his helmet was securely on. It was.

However, Paul mistook this as a signal to snap the football. Brady wasn't ready. He shouted to the quarterback, but that did no good. He was deaf. The ball hit him in the side of the head.

Sensing the problem, Tank stepped in front of Brady to allow him to get on the football.

On the Blacklick sideline and among the remaining Mustang fans, there was a collective gasp. Jonathan let out a guttural expression of exasperation and wondered to himself, "Can something please go right?"

While the ball hit Brady on the right side of his head, he sensed it was coming before it connected. That allowed him to react in time to grab the ball before it hit the ground. Based on where Tank was now standing, he knew the play was broken — but not dead.

Brady secured the football with his left arm. At the same time, he placed his right hand on Tank's back and shoved him forward hard as if to say, *Go!*

Tank got the message. He didn't think. He simply became the lineman he'd been before this week. He rambled forth and positioned himself so that he blocked one defender. At the same time, he extended an arm to impede the progress of a second.

Tank's action allowed Brady to get to the line of scrimmage. On his left, there was another Utica defender closing in from the outside. Instinctively, Brady shifted his weight to make it appear as if he was going to cut left. The moment the defender adjusted his direction to intercept him, Brady cut right. This allowed him to race past the defender and into the open field. He angled toward the left and up the sideline where Coach Dad, Norm and Joyce were standing — near the 30-yard line.

Jonathan stood there wide-eyed. The fortunate turn of events was almost unbelievable. Norm cheered loudly and openly, jumping in the air as Brady approached. Joyce was completely bewildered, as being caught up in this sort of commotion was something she never contemplated.

As Brady raced past, the entire sideline endeavored to keep up — cheering and motioning for him to continue. And he did — 35, 40, 45, 50. He stormed into Utica territory and continued — 45, 40, 35.

Eventually, one Redskin defender caught up to Brady, slowing him enough so two others could catch up and drag him down. The officials blew the play dead at the 33-yard line. The Mustangs sideline and fans erupted with excitement. Tank, AJ and others on the field caught up to Brady, simultaneously congratulating him and helping him to his feet.

As those players moved inward toward where the official would be setting the football, Jonathan shouted, "Huddle up. Let's call a play." AJ led the team into a circular formation behind the new line of scrimmage. Then, realizing that he had a communication problem, Jonathan shouted, "Where's Joyce?"

Everyone looked down the sideline. Almost 25 yards back, Joyce was slowly moving toward them. She hadn't run since, likely, grade school and was not likely to start now. Norm motioned to a couple of reserve players and instructed them to "go get her." They complied, carrying the ALS interpreter under her arms.

When Joyce was caught up, Jonathan shouted in a play to AJ and asked Joyce to sign it to Brady. When everyone had the assignment, the huddle broke, the teams lined up and set the play in motion.

Brady successfully got the ball from Paul Mandrake and raced to his right, as if he were going on another scamper. However, while still running, he tossed the football to AJ at the 15-yard line. AJ was able to get it to the 10 before being pushed out of bounds.

The team quickly huddled again. Jonathan and Joyce respectively shouted and signed in the new play. This had Brady taking the snap directly from his center and then quickly dropping back for a pass. Defenders flooded into the backfield after him.

The only problem was that Brady didn't have the ball. He'd taken the snap and then immediately handed it back to Paul, who held it tight to his body with two arms and rolled forward as if he were blocking. Eventually, defenders noticed, shouting to one another about the ruse. It was too late. Before they could effectively react, Mandrake was in the end zone.

After John Evans kicked the extra point, Blacklick had seven points.

Chapter 63

On the Mustang sideline, there was a sense of euphoria — they'd scored. They were the defending state champions. As such, they intended to make a comeback.

There was still plenty of time left in the game, but the deficit was substantial. With new coaches focused on defense, Jonathan was now able to work with the offense. On the bench, he gathered the unit around to review.

He and Norm had a challenge. Normally, they'd send the play to the quarterback, who'd share it with the team in the huddle. With Brady, they faced a language barrier. They quickly devised a new system — a player would run into the huddle and call the play, while Joyce signed it to Brady.

They needed to keep Joyce near Jonathan so she could quickly relay instructions. Norm quietly assigned a couple of reserve players the duty of, "Keep her close ... carry her if you have to."

Their next concern was whether Brady truly understood the playbook. He hadn't taken a single snap in practice. Not one under the Maven playbook Not one under the A-11 playbook. And no one had paid attention to what had actually been communicated to him.

That anxiety, however, quickly faded.

Yes, Brady was deaf — but in some respects, that was an advantage. During practices, side conversations often caused confusion. Because Joyce couldn't sign everything, Brady quietly studied the playbooks on his own — the Maven offense, and now the A-11 scheme.

What no one knew was that, in the evenings, he'd been watching A-11 offense videos online. He understood there were flaws in how Coach Dad and Norm had implemented it. He quickly pointed out a few issues, relaying notes through Joyce and tracing his finger across the playbook to explain.

Coach Dad and Norm had a few "how stupid could we be" moments. But there was no time for self-recrimination. They made quick, official changes on the fly.

In a matter of minutes, it felt like they'd overhauled an offense that was less than a week old — and they were relying on a deaf quarterback to execute it. A million things could go wrong.

But they had no choice, and time was running out.

Inspired by the last drive, the defense made quick work of its assignment. Within three plays, Utica was punting the ball back to the Mustangs.

Back on the field, Brady took charge. In many ways, he now understood the offense better than anyone. If there was confusion or a misalignment, he'd get everyone's attention with a clap — two sharp claps, spaced by a beat.

It wasn't a typical applause. Brady smashed his meaty hands together, creating a loud crack. That got attention.

Then he pointed: where First Friend should go, which way Tank should run, and other small corrections. It was chaotic at first. The Mustangs burned a timeout and incurred a couple of delay-of-game penalties.

Still, they moved the ball. In seven plays, they marched down the field and scored — Tank hammering off tackle. With the extra point, they now trailed 30-14.

The team celebrated. Joyce was disoriented from being whisked around, sometimes 20 yards at a time. Jonathan and Norm exchanged a breath of relief. It worked — this time. But there was no guarantee it would continue.

The defense needed to deliver again — no more points for Utica, and quick stops to give the offense another shot.

But Utica played smart. They drained the clock — staying in bounds, taking all the play clock, and grinding out first downs.

Eventually, after three first downs, Blacklick held. The Redskins punted. The bad news: the third quarter was over. Time was not on their side.

Jonathan did the math. They needed two touchdowns and either a pair of two-point conversions or a two-pointer and a PAT. But he didn't need to decide that yet.

The second drive was more composed. If the first proved Brady could play, the second proved it wasn't a fluke.

Still, Utica adjusted. They keyed on Brady. But even as they game-planned around him, the Mustangs gained yards in chunks — 4, 14, 24. They were rolling.

Late in the drive, AJ caught a screen pass and darted toward the end zone. He reached the 7 before being swarmed by defenders. In the chaos, his right pinky got jammed — stuck at an unnatural angle.

He panicked. "Nathan! Nathan! Nathan!" he shouted, looking for the trainer, who was downfield tending to a defender.

Shea Brooks was nearby.

AJ said nothing — just held up his hand, the injury obvious. His face showed fear.

"Relax," Shea said calmly, stopping his forward motion. She took his wrist and repeated, "Relax. Just relax," gently caressing his hand. She maneuvered so her back was to AJ's chest and examined it.

AJ couldn't see the injury, only feel her touch. "Be careful. Where's Nathan? Don't hurt me."

"Oh, shush, you big baby," she teased.

Shea rotated back to face him. AJ's finger was fine. "It was just a dislocation," she said.

Still winded and stunned, AJ said nothing. Shea quickly taped the pinky to the ring finger. "That'll protect it. Ice it later," she advised.

AJ stared at his hand, then looked up. "Thanks."

She smiled back.

Meanwhile, Brady finished the drive, barreling over defenders for a 7-yard touchdown.

They lined up to go for two, but a false start cost them five yards. That made Jonathan's decision easy — send in John Evans for the PAT.

Blacklick now trailed 30-21. Nine minutes remained. They needed two possessions. The comeback now depended on the defense.

But the Mustangs were tired. It had been a long game.

Utica didn't need to score — just keep the clock moving. Run plays in bounds. Avoid risks. And they did.

Six plays into the drive, a Blacklick defensive back tackled a Redskin receiver after a short pass. In doing so, his knee buckled — with an audible pop. Everyone heard it. Officials immediately called for medical attention.

As Nathan ran onto the field, a coach rushed to Jonathan.

The backup defensive back was out with a stomach bug. Thin at that position, they needed someone — fast.

"AJ!" Coach Dad yelled.

No explanation needed. AJ strapped on his helmet and jogged out. As he passed the injured defender, he patted his shoulder.

AJ hadn't played defense since middle school. He felt out of place.

Utica noticed. They targeted him — short passes again and again. The gains were small, but they added up. And the clock kept ticking. With just over three minutes left, Utica was inside the Blacklick 10. The comeback was on life support.

But with each snap, AJ grew more confident. He could see patterns, read shifts, and trust his athleticism.

Then first down, goal to go. AJ sensed it — another pass coming his way.

Enough, he thought.

He waited — lurking, baiting. Then the quarterback threw. AJ stepped into the passing lane, knocked the receiver aside, and became the receiver himself.

He secured the ball. But a pick wasn't enough. He took off.

The Mustangs' sideline erupted. So did the fans. There was no one to stop him. No safety net.

AJ raced 90-plus yards to the end zone. Teammates swarmed him. The comeback was alive.

John Evans converted the extra point. Blacklick now trailed by just two — 30-28.

Chapter 64

The comeback was underway. But Blacklick needed the ball back quickly — and with decent field position.

It didn't start well. John Evans' kickoff was only so-so, and Utica managed a 10-yard return, giving them the ball at their own 30-yard line.

Now it was up to the Mustang defense. They were energized by the pick-six, but it also meant they had to return to the field with little rest — and they were already exhausted from a long game.

Fortunately, AJ was still filling in for the injured defensive back. He hadn't been playing defense all game, so he was relatively fresh. And while not a defensive captain, he took charge.

Directing: "Push up. They aren't going long."

Rallying: "Dig deep. Just a few more plays. We need a stop."

Encouraging: "We can do this."

It worked. The defense held Utica to minimal gains on three straight runs. But the clock kept running between plays. Utica now faced fourth down and had no choice but to punt.

Jonathan had no choice either. He called the team's second timeout with 1:37 remaining. He couldn't allow another 30 seconds to melt away as Utica slowly lined up to punt. But beyond stopping the clock, he could do little — he had no idea where they'd get the ball back.

Utica answered that quickly. The punter launched a booming line-drive kick. It soared over the Blacklick return man and bounced another 20 yards. He chased it down quickly, minimizing clock loss, but Blacklick had to start the drive at its own 15-yard line.

That limited Jonathan's play-calling options — short passes or sweeps toward the sideline to stop the clock. It worked, mostly. They picked up four- or five-yard gains and managed the clock.

The problem: each play used six or seven seconds. Only 19 seconds remained, and they were just across midfield. Even with a first down, it was clear — they were moving too slowly. They wouldn't reach field goal range in time.

They needed one big play. But which one? The offense was new. The quarterback was even newer.

Jonathan needed time to think. He called the final timeout. He pulled Norm close, brought Joyce in, and motioned the entire offense to the sideline.

He gathered them in a circle, placing Joyce directly across from Brady. Then he summarized the situation: "We need one play to get into field goal range — and we have to get out of bounds. Ideas?"

As soon as Joyce relayed that to Brady, the quarterback signed. Joyce turned to the group and said, "Brady has an idea."

She relayed his plan.

Jonathan and Norm looked at each other and shrugged. *Why not?* They confirmed the plan, summarized it for the team, and sent the offense back on the field.

There was no point in huddling. The players lined up immediately.

Brady stood in shotgun, three yards back. Tank lined up to his left. Brady motioned to Paul Mandrake to snap the ball.

At the snap, Brady began to sweep left. The offensive line rolled out that way. Brady held the football in his right hand and used his left hand to guide Tank ahead as a lead blocker.

Utica's defense was ready. They pursued the play, content to give up a few yards and run out the clock. Blacklick looked out of luck.

Brady was running out of room. To his left: the sideline. In front: a wall of players. Whatever he'd intended seemed to be collapsing — or maybe not.

Brady had noticed throughout the second half that defenders were locked in on him. He couldn't hear them, but he could see them pointing, and he could read their lips: "Watch 10. Key on 10. Get 10."

He planned to use that against them.

Just as Utica defenders closed in, Brady stopped suddenly. He spun 180 degrees, planted his feet, and threw a dart 30 yards across the field — to David Roberts.

The starting quarterback, who'd re-entered the game for this moment, was wide open on the far-right side. He calmly caught the ball, turned, and looked downfield.

During the timeout, Brady had proposed calling two plays — one for him and eight others, another for David Roberts and AJ.

AJ briefly played along with the decoy. Then he broke off into a route. A defender stayed with him stride for stride as AJ slanted back toward the right.

David Roberts didn't have the luxury of a soft throw. He stepped into it and fired a perfect spiral.

The ball sailed just ahead of AJ. He leaned into his stride, hit another gear, reached out, and snagged it.

But a catch alone wasn't enough. Seconds remained. He couldn't go down in bounds.

AJ gripped the ball in one hand and stumbled forward, off balance, until he was sure he'd fall out of bounds. Then he let himself crash into the sideline at the 21-yard line.

The Blacklick sideline erupted.

Jonathan called to AJ. When his son looked over, Jonathan raised three fingers — the pinky, ring and middle — signaling the field goal team.

AJ caught the signal, then looked away. His face flashed with contempt. He shook his head.

Jonathan felt the sting. But only briefly — no one else noticed. AJ was soon swept up in the celebration, while Jonathan turned his attention to John Evans.

Utica called a timeout to get their block team set. That gave Jonathan time to talk to his kicker.

He faced him directly. "John, it's time to shine. We need a 38-yard field goal."

John looked uncertain. "I'll try," he said, leaning toward the field.

Jonathan grabbed his shoulder pads. "No, John. We need this. We've come too far to only come this far."

John nodded. "I'll do my best."

He leaned again.

"John, no," Jonathan repeated. "I believe you can. I need you to believe it. I need you to say you will."

He stared into John's eyes. "We can run another play if you'd prefer."

That did it.

Frustrated, John snapped, "Fine! I'll do it." He knocked his coach's hands away. "Can I go in the game now?"

Jonathan smiled. "Yes, John — now you can."

John jogged to the huddle. Everyone was standing, waiting on Utica to finish subbing in. Brady wrapped his left arm around John's shoulders, gave him two firm pats on the chest — *You got this.*

Moments later, they broke the huddle. Everyone took their places — John Evans, the kicker; Brady, the holder; AJ and Tommy Frank flanked out wide.

They were the defending state champions. Winning was what they did.

Paul Mandrake delivered a perfect snap. Brady caught it cleanly and placed it.

John Evans stepped up and kicked the ball cleanly through the uprights — dead center, with distance to spare.

Time expired.

Before the officials signaled it good, Blacklick players and coaches stormed the field in celebration.

The scoreboard read: Blacklick 31, Utica 30.

A tale of two halves — but a win was a win.

Chapter 65

The win was good for the soul of the team. It showed their new offense could work. It revealed Brady Troy. And it instilled a new confidence — a swagger.

Their celebration, both on the field and in the locker room, lasted 90 minutes. Eventually, the players and staff dispersed. AJ, Tank, Brady, and a few others went out for pizza. They did their best to bridge the communication gap. Once the food arrived, there wasn't much talking anyway.

Jonathan got home in time for a congratulatory kiss from Sam and to see her off to work. Then he went to bed. The emotional ups and downs of the week had drained him. He quickly fell asleep and woke up naturally, early as usual. He had work to do.

He arrived at the offices of Eisenberg & Anders shortly before 7 a.m. As the first one in, he used his access card to raise the security gate separating the firm's main entrance from its internal offices — standard procedure to protect sensitive material.

He settled in and turned to the never-ending stream of high-end legal work. The office was quiet, which wasn't surprising — it was Labor Day weekend. Many were taking advantage of the holiday.

With few distractions, Jonathan was productive. He was deep into a case when a gentle knock came at 11:20 a.m.

"Jonathan, I'm sorry to interrupt, but Ari would like to see you in the main conference room," said Ari's assistant.

"Sure," Jonathan replied. He marked his place in the document he was reviewing and followed her down the hallway.

When they arrived, Jonathan saw Ari and about a dozen other partners and associates smiling broadly. On the table was a large sheet cake — vanilla sponge, decorated in Blacklick colors with big, puffy numerals: 31-30!

Ari boomed, "Congratulations, Jonathan!" Others joined in.

"What a win. We're all proud of you."

"Thanks," Jonathan said. "I hope you didn't see the score at halftime."

"Of course, I did," Ari said with a laugh. "But it's not how you start — it's how you finish."

Theresa stepped forward with a knife. "Jonathan, how big a piece do you want?"

"You'll love it," Ari added. "Theresa's nieces — Tamara and Tabitha — they have a baking business. Their frosting is addictive. Honestly, they might be better bakers than soccer players. And that's saying something."

Jonathan smiled and motioned for a corner piece. "Thank you," he said.

At that moment, Warren Scott entered the room with a quiet urgency — a familiar, self-important sort. He had lost track of Ari's whereabouts and had been scouring the office to find him. God forbid another attorney get any face time.

His presence chilled the room. Conversations stopped. Tension rose.

Theresa, unbothered, handed him a plate. "We're celebrating Jonathan coaching Blacklick to a comeback win. Isn't that great?"

To Warren, it wasn't. His face twitched with a brief flash of disdain. He'd been pleased to see Blacklick's halftime score — and had been quietly rooting for Jonathan's failure. The comeback soured his mood.

"I can't waste time here," he muttered and left.

The mood lifted instantly.

An associate said, "This cake is so good. Can we have it after every Blacklick win?"

Jonathan grinned. "We plan to win a lot. Better start wearing stretchy pants."

Laughter filled the room.

"I'm coming to a game," Ari declared. "When's the next one?"

"We play Friday nights," Jonathan said. "The next two are away — Marion and Delaware."

"Nope. Too far," Ari said.

"Just hitch a ride on Emerald One," another partner joked.

"What's after that?" Ari asked.

"September 22 at home against New Lexington. Then Columbus Academy on the 29th."

"Wait — Columbus Academy?" Ari slapped the table. "What day is that?"

Theresa pulled out her phone. "You're off on the 22nd, but you're in town the 29th."

"Book it. Columbus Academy. I hate those—" He looked around and caught himself. "You know what I was going to say."

A younger partner laughed. "It's OK, Ari. We've heard it before."

"I know. I just don't like them. When I played at Bexley, those rich prima donnas always found a way to win. Bunch of cheaters."

Jonathan laughed. "Well, you're invited. And we'll make you an honorary assistant coach. You'll be in the locker room. On the sidelines. The full experience."

Ari lit up. "Theresa, block it. Lock it. Carve it in granite."

"Already done," she said without looking up.

The celebration lasted about 10 more minutes before people began drifting out — kickoff for the Ohio State game was at 12:17 p.m.

As they left, Ari pulled Jonathan aside. "Got a minute? I need a favor."

They walked back to Jonathan's office, still talking about the cake.

Inside, Jonathan shut the door. "How can I help you?"

Before Ari could answer, Jonathan's phone rang. It was Nathan Rogers.

"Sorry, I need to take this," he said. "Might be about an injured player."

"Nathan," Jonathan answered. "What's the good word?"

"Crap," the trainer replied.

"Excuse me?"

"I just came from the school. There's goose crap all over our practice field."

"Really?"

"Yes. This wasn't natural. Someone scattered feed all over, and the geese showed up and did what they do."

"Sebastian and his buddies? That's my guess."

"Thanks for letting me know. I'm going into a meeting. We'll come up with a cleanup plan."

They ended the call.

"Did you hear that?" Jonathan asked.

"I did," Ari said, adjusting his glasses. "Some people's kids, huh?"

Jonathan nodded. "Anyway, what can I do for you?"

"Simple," Ari said with a smirk. "Go home."

He laughed. "I'll see you Tuesday. You've had a busy week. And apparently, literal crap in front of you. Get some rest. Don't burn out — not on me, not on us, not on the team."

Ari grabbed Jonathan's wrist and pressed two $100 bills into his palm.

"Take that beautiful doctor of a wife of yours out for a nice dinner. On me."

He smiled, gave a quick nod, and walked out.

Jonathan sat there a moment, stunned. Then finally said: "Thanks."

Chapter 66

Jonathan would never defy an order, request or even a suggestion from Ari Eisenberg. He put the money in his pocket and prepared to go home. But while he was not going to defy the firm's patriarch, there was work to be done and clients to be served. So he gathered up things he could work on at home.

When he arrived home, Sam was surprised but happy to see him. She was even happier to learn that they were going to have what she called a "schmancy" dinner out, courtesy of Ari Eisenberg.

They had lunch and settled on the couch in front of the television. Over the calls and commentary on the Ohio State football game, they caught up on life and Blacklick football.

"So how's it going with you and AJ?" Sam inquired.

Jonathan let out an exasperated chuckle as he answered, "I don't know." Then he gathered his thoughts and continued.

"He's on the team. I coach the team. Often it feels like we're not even there together."

"It might not feel like it, but you are," Sam said.

"True," Jonathan agreed. "But at times I feel like I'm doing more harm than good." Sam gave him a curious look, so he continued. "Last night, I made him angry by simply signaling." Jonathan mimicked what he'd done — raising his right hand and extending three fingers — the little, ring and middle — while holding his index finger and thumb close to his palm.

"I don't know what to say," Sam said. "Maybe you misinterpreted AJ. Or maybe AJ misinterpreted you."

"No, Sam, this is no misinterpretation," Jonathan said.

"Well, I guess that sign is just not AJ's thing," Sam said.

"What do you mean? Not his thing? It's our thing. Me and you. Johnny. Kelly. And AJ," Jonathan pleaded.

"Perhaps, but AJ just might not see it that way," Sam replied, calmly defending AJ.

"Apparently not, Sam," Jonathan said. "I'll never do that again to AJ."

Quickly the subject changed, and light conversation continued about life at the firm, the Wexner Medical Center and what needed to be done around the house. In time, Sam dozed off, as she was prone to do while watching television.

Jonathan continued watching TV, flipping from game to game. Nothing held his interest. Ohio State was routing a nobody opponent in an early-season game again. Other games on other channels were similar — David versus Goliath without divine intervention. He was not dozing, but merely mesmerized by replays and storylines.

As he sat there, he heard a faint, distant calling: "Coooaaaccchhh, cccoooaachhh, cccoooaachhh." So as not to disturb Sam's slumber, he gently got up to investigate. As he moved out of the TV room toward the front door, the call became louder and clearer. A woman was calling for a coach—presumably him.

Jonathan poked his head out the front door and looked toward the driveway. There was Joyce Yocheim. She had one foot in her car and the other out. It was clear that she was having trouble moving and standing. But she needed to talk to Jonathan.

Jonathan came bounding out toward her. "Joyce, are you OK?"

"Coach, no," the sign language interpreter responded with a pained expression.

"What's the matter?" Jonathan flashed a curious concern.

"Coach, I can hardly move. I'm too old to be running around a football field," Joyce exclaimed as she briefly wobbled. She needed to shift her weight, as it was too painful for her to stand in the same position too long.

Jonathan became confused. "Why didn't you just call me?"

"Because ..." She pulled her light jacket down around her wrists. "I wanted to show you this." Amid a sleeveless top, she revealed bare arms covered in deep, colorful bruises.

Quickly Jonathan flashed back to the previous night's game. They'd whisked Joyce up and down the sidelines so she would be in position to sign in plays to Brady Troy. Caught up in trying to win, they were oblivious to what it might mean for the frail ALS translator.

"Oh, Joyce. I'm so sorry." Jonathan's voice echoed with remorse and sincerity.

"Coach, I can't keep doing this," Joyce pleaded. "I'm too old."

"But ..." Jonathan was at a loss for words. Selfishly, he needed Brady Troy. But rationally, he had to agree with Joyce. She wasn't built for the rigors of football, albeit only on the sidelines.

"Coach, I know what you're going to say," Joyce interrupted. "We have to think about that wonderful young man, Brady."

"Yes, Brady," Jonathan remarked.

But he thought, *Oh, God! How self-centered can I be?* Brady Troy is the real focus.

Before Jonathan could say another word, Joyce said, "Coach, if you trust me, I have an idea that might work even better."

Chapter 67

Ari was right. A few days away from the office did Jonathan good. While he tinkered with client work, he did so relaxed on the couch. He also spent plenty of time with Sam—watching football, going out to that "schmancy" dinner and even shopping. Plus, he caught up on sleep. By Tuesday morning, he was rested and ready to take on life.

He'd messaged the office that he'd be in around 10 a.m., due to a football obligation. Still, he was up at his usual pre-dawn hours to work out and bill time from the kitchen table. As he did, Sam arrived home from her third shift and marched off to bed. AJ slipped off to school without a word.

At 8:45 a.m., Jonathan was packed and ready to head to his football-related appointment. Before he could pull out of the driveway, Nathan Rogers called. Jonathan stopped the car and answered.

"Nathan, what's the good word … and don't say crap," Jonathan said with a chuckle.

"Actually, um, there is no crap anymore," Nathan replied. Before Jonathan could say a word, he continued, "Our school neighbor, Bobby O, probably got sick of the smell. He had an army of people from the Emerald Medical grounds crew here with rakes, shovels and big sucking machines to clean it all up."

"Really?" was all Jonathan could say.

"Yes, really. Jonathan, I'm looking at the practice field right now," Nathan paused to find the words. "It's like it never happened."

"Wow, that's good news," Jonathan said. "Any idea who caused this?"

"Only suspicion," Nathan said with a shrug. "In this day and age, there's likely video somewhere of something, but that's not my concern."

"Good point, Nathan," Jonathan agreed. "Let's move on. I'll see you at practice. I'm headed to Ohio Dominican U to select another ASL signer for Brady."

"What happened to Joyce?" Nathan asked.

Jonathan laughed. "I shouldn't laugh, but she's on injured reserve. All that up and down the sideline was too much for her. So she's networking me into someone in the ASL program at ODU who can fill in for her."

Shortly thereafter, Jonathan ended his call with Nathan and headed toward downtown. Halfway there, however, he got off the highway and worked his way a few blocks over to the campus of Ohio Dominican University. He parked, walked to the designated building and pressed an intercom button on the main door.

"Can I help you?" a young woman's voice inquired via the intercom box.

"This is Jonathan Reese. I'm here to see Joyce Yocheim." Seconds later, the door buzzed, and he knew he could pull it open and enter.

The moment he did, Joyce called out, "Down here, Jonathan."

Jonathan closed the distance quickly and asked as he approached, "How are you feeling, Joyce?"

"Much better, thanks," Joyce responded with a smile. She had much of Saturday, Sunday and Monday to recuperate. Plus, the ASL translator had sent a sub to Blacklick High to chase

Brady Troy from class to class. When Jonathan reached the ASL Center, Joyce led him in.

There, several students were working to perfect their ASL skills by interacting with deaf students from the Columbus Public Schools.

"Thanks for arranging this, Joyce. We appreciate it," Jonathan said sincerely.

"Oh sure, Jonathan," Joyce replied. "There are several energetic people who would work well with Brady."

Jonathan scanned the class. He pointed to a young, athletic woman wearing an Ohio Dominican women's soccer polo shirt. "Who's that? Can I talk to her?"

"That's Casey Kaufman," Joyce responded, then added, "Sure. I guess." With that, she got Casey's attention and motioned her over.

When she arrived, Jonathan pointed to her shirt and asked, "Did you play soccer here?"

"Yes, I did. I'm just a grad student now," Casey replied. "I'm helping out here as I finish up a few last credits."

"What do you know about American football?" Jonathan asked.

Casey's face lit up. "Lots, actually. My dad coached high school near Mentor until he retired two years ago. And my brothers played D-III at Allegheny. We are very much a football family."

"As you might know, Joyce has been helping out at Blacklick High." Jonathan paused briefly, then continued, "We had a player transfer in from the Ohio School for the Deaf and, well, we need help communicating with him in games and at practice. Interested?"

"You had me at football. I'm in," Casey said enthusiastically.

Chapter 68

After Jonathan gave practice details to Casey, he hurried down to his office. That was big law firm life. There were always clients to serve—especially when it came to Emerald Medical.

When he got to his office, however, a printed email was sitting on his desk. It gave him an instant sickening feeling. It was from Sebastian's father and had been directed to all firm partners.

In three paragraphs, it aimed to question Jonathan's character and integrity. It was largely one person's opinion. Nevertheless, Columbus, Ohio, is not Chicago or New York. One's reputation—even if not based in fact—tended to spread quickly. And that might serve to impair Jonathan's case for making partner.

However, in the white space below the email, Ari had handwritten, *JR, this is just an FYI, in case someone says something. Don't worry about it. I got your back.* Jonathan smiled broadly.

As he was about to put the sheet back on his desk, Warren Scott appeared at the entrance to his office door.

"There is an email that we *need* to talk about—*immediately,*" Warren said, with both a serious look and tone.

Jonathan knew it was about the exact thing he'd just read.

"Okay, Warren," Jonathan said as he moved toward the door. "I have a note I need to share with you too." With that, he handed "that S.O.B." Ari's note, and as "that turd" started to read it, Jonathan closed the door on him.

Chapter 69

It was not unusual for Blacklick High to start the week in the fall basking in the glory of a football win. It was expected. How it happened, however, was unusual. The big comeback was legendary—especially for those who stayed until the final whistle.

That alone elevated Brady Troy from largely unknown to superhero roaming the halls. Some students were even inspired to learn a few ASL signs from YouTube tutorials:

"Hello."

"Great game!"

"Do you have a girlfriend?"

But that's the nature of football at Blacklick. Players graduate. New stars emerge. They build a unique lore for that season's team. That fuels a special kind of excitement.

Still, as strong as the football team was, the faculty was equally effective at refocusing the classroom on learning. "Okay, students. Great game. We all saw it or heard about it. Now let's talk science."

Of course, these words were met with futile groans. Education must go on.

In Advanced Scientific Methods, the teacher droned on about the importance and applications of catalysts: "A catalyst is a substance that increases the rate of a chemical reaction without being consumed or permanently altered in the process."

None of this was news to Shea. Bored, she started to doze. AJ nudged her shoulder and slipped her a note. She stirred to full alertness, then smiled and blushed as she read:

Busted! Wake up!

Meanwhile, in Senior English, as the teacher tried to convey the inspiration of "poetic language" and "timeless human emotions," AJ was trying to remember all the team's A-11 formations—each name sounding vaguely similar. As he scribbled out a list, Shea reached over and wrote across it:

Practice @ 6!

AJ smiled, put his pencil down and refocused on the teacher.

They were unlikely project partners in both Advanced Scientific Methods and Senior English, but the pairing proved fortuitous. While others had to juggle multiple group members, Shea and AJ had just one other person to coordinate with. And beyond class, they shared plenty of time together—same study hall, time after school, and time spent getting water ready for practice.

And while those moments weren't always devoted to semester-end projects, being around each other let ideas quietly percolate. Then, out of nowhere, one of them might suddenly offer an epiphany: "Here's an idea on…" or "What if…"

Before long, they were literally shoulder to shoulder, working through the thought together.

Chapter 70

Any more office politics didn't fit into Jonathan's schedule—especially the Warren Scott variety. He sat back at his desk, opened the Emerald Medical due diligence document on his laptop and dug in. Then, what felt like moments later, it was time to head to practice. That looming daily deadline helped him stay focused and productive.

When he arrived, there was a buzz of excitement. Any replacement for 60-something Joyce Yocheim would have drawn attention, but Casey Kaufman turned heads. To help her blend in, Shea had gotten her a Blacklick Football T-shirt. But the seemingly formfitting shirt only accentuated her athletic figure.

As AJ and Shea rode out to practice with ice and water, the sight of Casey stopped AJ mid-sentence. He stared and trailed off: "For Senior English, we should …"

Shea tried to redirect him. "Should what, AJ?"

To no avail—he'd lost his train of thought.

When Coach Dad signaled the start of practice and sent the team on a warmup lap, they quickly returned. He gathered everyone in. Jonathan stood in his usual spot, with Brady directly across. Everyone listened—or pretended to—as this setup was perfect for some low-key ogling of Casey.

"Everyone, this is Casey Kaufman," Coach Dad said.

The team playfully echoed, "Hello, Casey," and she politely waved.

"Be welcoming and respectful. She's here to help us communicate with Brady." Everyone nodded.

Jonathan added, "I want to take a few minutes for you to get to know Brady better." Up to now, most players had little interaction with him. That changed with Friday night. "Any questions?"

Tank blurted out, "Casey, do you have a younger sister?"

The team roared with laughter. Casey blushed but signed the question to Brady. His laughter followed a slight delay.

"No, no," Jonathan interjected. "These are questions for Brady."

"Okay," Tank said, then fired off, "Brady, do you know if Casey has a younger sister?"

More laughter. Brady laughed again, just a beat behind. The deaf quarterback shrugged as if to say he didn't know.

"Nope. Just two older brothers," Casey said quietly.

Tank sighed heavily in mock disappointment. Someone in the group muttered, "Tank, you're no prize. Stop being so picky."

More laughter.

"Okay, okay," Jonathan said, trying to regain control. "To clarify, these are questions to Brady—about Brady."

"Alright," Tank said, like a scolded child. After a moment, he asked, "What are the girls like at your old school?"

Jonathan gave Casey a subtle nod. She signed the question to Brady, who responded instantly.

Casey's eyes widened. She signed back and said aloud, "I'm not saying that."

Brady signed, *Say it.*

Casey shook her head. *No.*

Brady signed again, *Yes.*

She shook her head once more and said, "No, I'm not going to tell them that."

The team watched, highly entertained.

"Say it. Say it. Say it," they chanted.

Tank chimed in: "Well, you can't not say it now."

Casey looked to Jonathan for guidance. He shrugged, as if to say, *why not?*

Brady continued urging her, emphatic and persistent.

"Okay," she finally agreed. "These are his words, not mine." She paused. "Regarding the girls at OSD, Brady said ... Again, these are not my words, but— The asses aren't any tighter, and the tits aren't any firmer."

For a split second, silence.

Then, an explosion of laughter. Players doubled over, some hitting the turf. Brady grinned, satisfied with the chaos he'd created.

Tank got up off the ground, looked at Casey and asked, "How do you sign tits? And maybe nice, too?"

Casey shook her head. *No chance.*

Then she smirked and said, "Tank, if you want to learn a sign to share with your girlfriend, try this."

Tank gave her his full attention.

She held up her right hand, made a fist and raised her pinky finger. "I."

Then, with the pinky still up, she lifted her index finger and extended her thumb outward. "Love."

Finally, she pointed at Tank. "You."

Tank shook his head. "No, no, no. I don't want any of that."

"Enough," Coach Dad stepped in. The Q&A had turned into a distraction. "We've got a lot to cover. We missed yesterday and have a game Friday."

With that, he launched into practice instructions.

There was much to cover—especially on offense. Their execution of the A-11 scheme had been poor. Yes, they'd won in glorious comeback fashion, but it came despite wasted timeouts, broken plays and a litany of penalties born from confusion. And it was only against Utica, a hapless football program. That kind of performance wouldn't hold up against tougher competition.

But there was no going back—or forward to something else. Norm and Coach Dad were committed to the A-11. The problem was, they hadn't yet figured out how to teach it. Their explanations only seemed to confuse the players, which led to questions—questions Norm and Coach Dad might answer differently. Even the coaches were getting confused. It felt like the blind leading the blind.

To reset, Coach Dad sent the team on a friendly lap. As they returned, neither he nor Norm had a clear solution. Shea brought water over and let the players hydrate.

As they drank, Coach Dad said, "Okay, let's back up a bit."

"Coach," Shea said, interrupting gently. "I have a thought… actually a few."

Coach Dad was surprised but receptive. At this point, he'd take any perspective—even from the team trainer. "Can you come over here and share so Casey can sign to Brady?" He motioned her forward.

Shea stepped up between Coach Dad and Casey. She smiled at Casey and greeted her with a casual, "Hey," which was quickly returned.

Then she began. "1,782? That's an absurd number of potential plays. Do we need them all? At some point, there are diminishing returns. You know, as more units of a variable input are added to a—"

"Shea," Coach Dad said, laughing, "I know what diminishing returns are. Please, continue."

"Right. Well, in a quick review online, the bulk of the offense revolves around just six players, right?" She waited for nonverbal agreement. "Okay. Now, Coach, can you and Coach Norm narrow the formations to seven?"

Coach Dad nodded.

"I say seven because studies show that humans can effectively retain three to seven items in working memory."

"Seven it is," Coach Dad replied. "Norm? Can we do it?"

Norm nodded and winked. *Done.*

"Is that it, Shea?"

"No, that's just the start," she said confidently, as everyone watched in awe. "Next, I want to create a seven-letter mnemonic."

"A what?" Tank blurted out.

"I'm sorry," Shea said, then explained. "A mnemonic is a memory aid. Like in second grade—remember HOMES for the Great Lakes?"

She continued, "If we do those two things, the number of potential plays drops from 1,782 to 252. Still a big number—but way more manageable." Sensing some were doing mental math, she added, "Just trust me."

Heads nodded. They were listening.

Shea pressed on. "From here, we work with Casey to create a simple sign for each play."

"Shea," Coach Dad said carefully, "we can't learn signs for 252 plays."

"No, Coach," she said. "It's only 18."

She counted on her fingers. "Seven formations. Three options—pass, pitch, or handoff. Six players. Two directions—right or left. Eighteen. We use those to create the 252 plays."

Casey nodded deeply in understanding, then turned to Coach Dad.

"This can work," she said. "If you give Shea and me the seven formations, we'll have 18 simple signs ready to learn by tomorrow—and easily mastered by Friday's kickoff."

Chapter 71

On Wednesday morning, Noah Turner and Aiden Davis walked over to Sebastian's house—as they did most mornings—to catch a ride to school. Since the "foul tip" club had officially struck out, they no longer had anything to lose. There was little to dissuade them from mischief and mayhem, such as baiting the practice field with feed corn to attract geese.

They were disappointed Tuesday morning to find the mess had somehow been cleaned up—no player would be rolling in bird dung—but they were still proud of the chaos they'd caused. Smugly, they felt untouchable.

They quickly got in the car: Sebastian driving, Noah up front, Aiden in the back. Almost immediately, they were hit with a strong, pungent odor. Still, Sebastian drove on.

"Sheesh, Aiden," Sebastian said. "Don't rip in my car. What have you been eating?" He lowered all the windows.

Davis laughed. "It's not me. Dog smells his own dirty first."

Noah held his nose.

When the smell didn't fade, Sebastian pulled over and they all got out. The scent followed. They checked under the seats—nothing. Sebastian popped the hood. Not the engine.

They walked to the rear of the car. Using the fob, Sebastian released the trunk. It beeped, and he lifted it.

Instantly, the foul odor hit them in full force. They recoiled and turned away.

When they finally looked back, they stared into a trunk coated in layers of goose poop.

Chapter 72

Directly after practice on Tuesday, Shea and Casey got to work on their contribution to the Blacklick offense. They went back to Casey's campus apartment, ordered a pizza and got busy.

Using the seven formations Coach Dad had given them, Shea suggested they ask ChatGPT to create a mnemonic using the word "MUSTANG." Moments later, they had something close to perfect:

> **M – Motion Formation**: A player goes in motion before the snap.
>
> **U – Unbalanced Formation**: More players line up on one side of the offensive line.
>
> **S – Shotgun Formation**: The quarterback stands a few yards behind the center.
>
> **T – Trips Formation**: Three receivers line up on one side of the field.
>
> **A – Ace Formation**: One running back, two tight ends and two wide receivers.
>
> **N – Naked Bootleg Formation**: Quarterback fakes a handoff and runs the opposite direction.
>
> **G – Goal Line Formation**: Used in short-yardage situations.

Casey was blown away and immediately started coming up with simple, random signs. Shea stopped her and suggested they apply a little brain science—something to help players with both learning and recall.

Shea opened her laptop and used another AI tool. Within moments, it generated functional visual signs. They weren't formal ASL, but they'd work.

Once Casey gave her approval, Shea went back to ChatGPT and found a tool to quickly build a two-page PDF displaying all 18 signs. Within 30 minutes—or two slices of pizza—the assignment was complete.

"Wow!" Casey said, genuinely impressed. "I wish I were as smart as you."

Shea looked her directly in the eye. "I wish I were as beautiful as you are."

The comment caught Casey off guard. She struggled to find words. After a moment, she said softly, "Oh, Shea. Honey."

She reached over, gently removed Shea's thick glasses and pushed her hair behind her ears.

"You are beautiful."

Chapter 73

After practice, AJ and Jonathan raced home separately. Sam had promised to have something ready for dinner, and they wanted to support that effort—with both their presence and their appetites.

AJ ate quickly, offering only short responses to his mother's questions:

"Okay."

"Fine."

"I don't know."

Minutes later, he excused himself to tinker with homework, then leaned into video games.

The moment AJ's bedroom door slammed shut, Jonathan lit up, eager to share news about Joyce's replacement. As he spoke, he attempted to sign the word love, using his left hand to guide his right. Even then, he struggled to replicate what Casey had done so effortlessly.

Sam burst out laughing. "Jonathan, you seem utterly incapable of speaking—or signing—that word, huh?"

At school the next day, Shea continued to yawn and nod off. By the time she'd gotten home from Casey's and finished the bare minimum of homework, it was late — bordering on early.

Before AJ could slip her a note, she passed him one:

Busted! Need coffee!

Jonathan didn't have the same issues. He was up early, well rested and out of the house after an abbreviated workout. It was another day of trying to be uber-productive, and he needed time in the office before others arrived to get after it. Plus, that was Ari's mode of operating, and Jonathan wanted a word with the firm's patriarch.

"Ari, do you have a minute?" Jonathan asked, rapping lightly on the door frame.

"Oh, sure, sure, Jonathan. Anytime," Ari said, putting down his pen and looking up.

"Thanks, Ari. I wanted to talk with you about the email that"

Before Jonathan could finish, Ari cut in.

"Oh, Jonathan. I hope you didn't lose sleep over that." Ari chuckled, as he was prone to do. "Let me tell you. I know this, ah … knucklehead's type." He paused to chuckle again. "This jerk is mad at you—for now. But you know what? Tomorrow, someone else will make him angry, and then they'll be in his crosshairs. Really, don't worry about it."

Ari then called out to Theresa for a fresh cup of coffee—and one for Jonathan. He motioned for the partner protégé to pull up a chair and give him a rundown of the team.

After school, AJ made the most of the time before practice to study. He wanted to do well—not just because it was expected at home, but because getting more done now meant more gaming time later. Still, he eventually hit a wall and became "studied-out"—overwhelmed by information. That's when he'd pack up his books and take them to his car.

He had a habit of parking in the last row near the road. Out there, he never had to hunt for a space. As he placed his bookbag in the trunk, an older car drove by, stopped and backed into the spot one space over. Curious who else parked "out in the sticks," as he called it, AJ looked over.

It was Brady's new ASL signer—Casey. She backed in carefully, unaware she was being watched. After maneuvering twice to get it just right, she parked and shut off the engine.

As she stepped out, AJ called, "Textbook parking job."

"Oh! You startled me—I didn't see you," Casey exclaimed, placing a hand on her chest.

AJ laughed. "That's comforting. You could've hit me."

Casey laughed too. Then AJ added, "Hi. We haven't met. I'm AJ." He extended a hand and walked toward her.

She met him halfway. "Oh, I know who you are, AJ. Number 29. First Friend." She smiled. "I've heard lots about you—Brady, Shea, your dad, Joyce. Everyone has something nice to say about AJ Reese."

The usually witty AJ had no comeback. His face flushed as they shook hands. Her grip was firm, her hand warm. He felt a tingle run up his arm. He looked into her eyes, but quickly looked away, afraid his gaze might seem like staring.

There was much to look at. Up close, she was stunning—naturally pretty, not overly made up. Wholesome. She wasn't just another girl. In fact, she didn't feel like a girl at all. She was a woman. And AJ could feel his heart race.

The silence turned awkward. He felt compelled to say something—anything—as long as it wasn't cringy.

"So, why do you back in?"

"Oh," Casey said, glancing at her car. "My dad told me to. He has a friend who's an insurance agent. Apparently, most accidents in parking lots happen when people back out of spaces, so …" She trailed off. Then added, "I know. Sounds stupid."

"Oh, no, no, not at all," AJ said quickly, letting her save face. "Makes sense, actually."

Another beat of silence passed before Casey broke it. "I need to go find Brady—to go over a few things."

"Yeah, I need to go too. I help with water and ice before practice. It's my job," AJ said with a smile.

"Yes, you go help Shea," Casey replied, then turned and walked off.

AJ watched as she walked away—athletic, confident, and very much not just a girl.

Chapter 74

Practice started with great enthusiasm. Coaches and players were eager to see what came next as Casey and Shea unveiled their contribution to simplifying the offense.

Jonathan handed out the few pages that Casey and Shea had created and instructed, "Include this in your playbook binder."

Everyone—offense, defense, even special teams—needed to learn it. Anyone could be called into offensive duty, and the core of what Casey and Shea developed had applications beyond offense, particularly on defense.

As they presented, the team watched in awe. It all made sense. They quickly understood how plays would be communicated. While it wouldn't make them fluent in ASL, everyone immediately began learning the 18 signs.

An unintended benefit was that practices became quieter. Rather than shouting play calls, Coach Dad signed them to

Brady and the offense—ideal for learning and simulating game action.

Another advantage: the team didn't need to huddle. They could line up loosely, receive the play via sign from Coach Dad, shift into the correct formation, and execute.

If a change was needed, Coach Dad would get Brady's attention. Brady would then clap loudly—just twice, clap-clap. It wasn't applause, but a signal. The sharp, meaty sound caught his teammates' attention. They then would mimic the clap and looked to the sidelines for the new call.

The Mustangs drilled this simplified system relentlessly on Wednesday and Thursday. Then they put it into live action Friday night as they traveled north to Marion—the hometown of President Warren G. Harding—to face the Harding High School Presidents.

Blacklick received the opening kickoff and immediately went to work. Coach Dad signaled the play, and the team executed. Casey signed in additional cues, and Brady occasionally signed back to her.

As the Mustangs moved downfield, they faced a third-and-long at midfield. Brady, relying on his sharp instincts, noticed something: a Harding defensive back's feet were set oddly, suggesting he wouldn't drop into coverage.

Brady quickly signed to Casey: *Tell Coach: Trust me.*

He stepped back from center and delivered his clap-clap.

The team rose, repeated the clap, and looked to the sidelines.

Coach Dad shrugged. "What's he doing?" he asked.

Casey replied, "I don't know—but he said to trust him."

Coach Dad pointed and shouted, "Look at Brady!"

Brady signed a new play, shifted the formation, then rolled out and hit AJ in stride across the middle. AJ broke free from defenders and scored. John Evans kicked the extra point.

Blacklick led 7-0 just minutes into the game—and that set the tone for the night.

The Mustangs' offense kept Harding's defense on its heels, scoring 28 in the first half and 14 more in the second. It wasn't perfect, but it was effective and balanced. AJ scored, but so did Tank, Brady, David Roberts, and two non-starters.

The defense, however, was shakier. A previously injured defensive back had returned but wasn't fully healthy. Harding exploited the weakness, scoring twice in the second half.

Outwardly, the Mustangs celebrated a 42–14 road win. Inwardly, AJ stewed.

In past seasons, he might already have scored 20 or 30 points by now. This year, he had just 12—and half of those came on defense. With the balanced scoring of the A-11 offense, he wasn't sure he'd reach the 33 more points needed to break the school's scoring record.

Chapter 75

Eventually, no matter how chaotic, life settles into routine.

Jonathan headed to the office Saturday, continuing his pursuit of partnership at Eisenberg & Anders. Ari arranged for another cake—red velvet this time—and gushed like a proud father about Jonathan and the Mustangs' victory. Warren Scott quietly stormed off, seething with jealousy.

On Sunday, Sam and Jonathan found time to unwind: church, lunch out, grocery shopping, and then home to watch— or nap in front of—NFL games on TV.

AJ picked at just enough homework to justify spending hours gaming. Still, he managed to break away from Zombie Wars or whatever long enough to fuel himself with whatever food was around—and maintain a modicum of personal hygiene.

All in all, the weekend blurred by.

Monday set in motion a more intentional routine. Jonathan left for downtown as early as possible. AJ raced off to school as late as possible. Jonathan leaned into his professional mission. AJ focused on appeasing his parents—which meant listening in class, taking notes, and working on projects with Shea. But not much more than that.

One routine AJ did add was making sure his after-school responsibilities were done in time to be at his car when Casey arrived. Now backed in, he would be busily organizing his trunk as the ASL interpreter pulled in and parked next to him—also backed in, carefully.

AJ would feign surprise, as if their daily arrival was just coincidence. A couple of times, he offered her a cookie or snack from the cafeteria—he "just happened" to have an extra. Casey would playfully accept, smiling and signing *love it* in response. Her presence was intoxicating. His heart would race.

After a few minutes of idle chat, they'd part ways. Casey needed to catch up with Brady. AJ had his duties helping Shea. Somehow, each time, there'd be a moment—a brush of hands, a shared laugh, a passing touch—that sent a warm sensation rushing through him.

Practice had settled into routine. Aside from minor tweaks, the offense was largely set. Now it was about drilling execution—again and again—in pursuit of perfection.

The defense, meanwhile, continued trying to shore up its weaknesses. The fix wasn't obvious. They needed the injured starter to return to 100% or for his backup to elevate his game. Neither was progressing quickly. They could manage against weaker teams, but eventually, the vulnerability would become an Achilles' heel.

By this point in the season, Monday felt like Tuesday, which resembled Wednesday. Thursday stood out—lighter physically and mentally. More fun. It carried the anticipation of Friday night.

The fourth game of the season sent them to Delaware—not as far north as Marion, but still up US 23. As the bus bounced past the commercial sprawl outside Columbus, Tank giggled and quipped, "Weren't we just here?"

The trip felt familiar. So did the opponent—Hayes High School, named for Rutherford B. Hayes, the 19th President of the United States. And the outcome? Also, familiar.

Though the secondary continued to struggle, the offense rolled. Seven touchdowns and a field goal late. The Mustangs outpaced the Pacers, 52–17.

After the game, everyone celebrated—except AJ. He couldn't shake the fact that, out of 52 points, he'd scored none.

Sure, he contributed: long receptions, big runs. They helped move the chains and set up scores. But the actual touchdowns belonged to others.

Brady Troy scored. David Roberts scored twice. Tank turned a short-yardage hammer into a 55-yard sprint to the end zone. Three reserve players even found pay dirt. AJ couldn't believe it. And he wasn't in the mood to celebrate.

Boarding the bus, Casey gently placed a hand on his chest, stopping him. His body paused, but his heart sped up.

With a euphoric smile, she said, "Great game, AJ."

It made him feel better—for a second. He reflexively smiled back and said, "Thanks."

What he wanted to say was: *Seriously? That was not great. In games like this in years past, I'd have had three or four touchdowns.*

He didn't need Shea Brooks–level math skills to realize he probably wasn't going to break the school scoring record. And without the stats, no college—at any level—would come calling. The thought made him sick.

As the bus rumbled back toward Blacklick, AJ sat in silence, sulking, while the celebration buzzed around him. When they arrived at the school, he went straight to the locker room, showered, changed, and headed home.

He said nothing to his dad and offered only polite pleasantries to his mom before disappearing into his room and crawling into bed.

Chapter 76

As soon as AJ shut his door, Sam gave Jonathan a concerned look. Jonathan just shrugged. They both knew why AJ was upset. He'd gotten the ball plenty and made big contributions. The scoring just hadn't worked out—and that can happen in any sport.

An instant later, Sam moved past her concern. "Wow," she said, quickly raising her hand to flash the family's sign for the word. "Jonathan, that is such a fun team to watch. That offense is pure entertainment. And Brady—how he commands attention without saying a single word." She mimicked his clap-clap. Jonathan followed suit, just like the rest of the offense. Sam then made random hand motions. "It's… it's mesmerizing how they communicate, shift and move. I get goosebumps thinking about it."

Jonathan could only smile. All in all, the team and situation had come together better than he ever imagined. From there, they caught each other up on the day and headed to bed.

On Saturday morning, Jonathan naturally woke, as usual, in the pre-dawn hours. He quietly slipped out of bed, worked out, and got going with his Saturday. It would be a busy, but productive one.

As the first to arrive at the office, he used his access card to raise a special security gate. It jammed a quarter of the way up. After years of use, the mechanism was showing its age. Nothing unusual. Jonathan got out, re-centered the gate by hand, and helped it rise. He muttered to himself, "I need to let Ari know someone needs to look at the gate."

He headed to his office to get organized. Half an hour flew by. Then he was off to meet with Stephenson for several hours. In a small conference room, the two attorneys reviewed the due diligence game plan for the Emerald Medical Far East deal. Stephenson's trip was still a few weeks away, but there was a lot to cover.

Jonathan thanked his colleague for stepping up in his absence. Stephenson responded, "No problem," but there was an uneasiness in his tone. Jonathan could tell he'd been voluntold by *that despicable excuse for a human.*

Ari had arranged for another celebratory treat — chocolate. But this time, he was absent—having left earlier that morning for vacation. Victory cake wasn't quite the same without him, but it was cake, and everyone loves cake. Partners, rank-and-file attorneys, interns, administrative staff—even the weekend security guard stopped in for a piece.

Best of all, the celebration kept *that little rat* away. Warren Scott was off pouting. Where? No one cared. Whenever *that son of a bitch* was around, the tension was palpable. People became guarded—careful with every word and action, knowing it might be used against them.

But with *that embarrassing little butthead* gone, the room loosened. People laughed. They shared. At its core, the firm was a family. And that made working on a Saturday bearable.

After cake, Jonathan made a beeline back to his office to put in another six hours on various client projects. Coaching had brought positive exposure to the firm, but he still had clients to serve and performance metrics to meet.

At the end of a long day, he packed up a few projects to work on at home. As the last to leave, he lowered the security gate—which, unlike on the way in, never had an issue coming down.

Chapter 77

When Jonathan got home from the office, AJ was off playing video games and Sam was reading a book. He grabbed a snack and quietly turned on the television to catch up on the day's college football games. Two hours later, exhausted, he headed to bed.

On Sunday, he managed to sleep in a little—until just after seven. He got up, made coffee and got to work on Emerald Medical matters. His meeting with Stephenson had made it clear: the due diligence process for the Far East acquisition needed to be better systematized.

So, he set about building something—electronic documents using spreadsheets and presentation software. It wasn't techie 1s and 0s programming, and nothing proprietary was developed. But it was relatively complex in how everything worked together. More importantly, it was innovative.

The system would help the firm better serve Emerald Medical and allow Jonathan to assist Stephenson, even from a world away.

At ten o'clock, Sam was up. Together, she and Jonathan prepared a large breakfast. Of course, AJ swooped in to get his fill before heading back to his room to do homework and play video games—though not necessarily in that order.

After cleaning up, Sam went back to reading, giving Jonathan time to continue working on the electronic due diligence setup. It was coming together nicely. But then again, so was everything.

For the first time in over a year, he was home for an extended stretch. That brought comfort to Sam—and was slowly stabilizing his relationship with AJ.

At the office, Jonathan was making a name for himself. While serving clients—and picking up new ones—was important, there was value in simply being present. And on the football field, the Mustangs had everything in place—offense, defense, special teams. They looked poised for another deep playoff run.

It was incredible how things were falling into place.

Monday began like most days. Jonathan arrived early enough to deal with the gate again—sticking two-thirds of the way up. After fixing it by hand, he got to work and stayed productive through most of the morning.

At one point, he called Stephenson in to preview how he was structuring the Far East due diligence system. All Stephenson could do was look on impressed.

At lunch, Jonathan went down to the basement of the Huntington Center to grab a deli sandwich and a bag of chips. When he returned ten minutes later, a document was sitting on his chair—clearly placed there so he wouldn't miss it.

It was a lawsuit, almost certainly set in motion by Sebastian's father. It claimed Jonathan had defamed Sebastian, Noah and Aiden. Worse, the suit named Eisenberg & Anders as a defendant.

And worst of all, *that little shit* had slapped a large yellow sticky note on the pleading that read, *We NEED to talk, ASAP!*

Jonathan glanced at it and muttered an expletive under his breath. Then he slid the complaint to the side of his desk and thought, *ASAP is going to have to wait… preferably until Ari gets back from vacation.*

With that, he refocused on real firm work until it was time to leave for practice.

Chapter 78

AJ continued his daily school routine. He went to class, studied after school, and made sure to be at his car when Casey arrived. After a little infatuated chit-chat, he'd go get ready for practice, riding out with Shea and the water.

As they approached the field, AJ sensed something was up. All the coaches were huddled to the side in serious discussion.

"What's going on?" he asked teammates.

No one knew. Though, like AJ, they were curious.

Soon, the coaches broke their huddle. Their mood lightened. Some joked around, as usual. Whatever it was seemed to pass. Everyone's attention shifted back to the familiar rhythm of practice.

At 6 p.m. sharp, Coach Dad blew his whistle. Practice started like any other under Jonathan Reese. Warmup lap. Stretching. Calisthenics. Then, the team gathered in as Coach Dad reviewed the last game and previewed the next opponent: the New Lexington Panthers. Though the school was up north, this would be a home game for Blacklick.

Then, something changed in Coach Dad's tone. He took a breath and hesitated, signaling he wasn't done.

"As you know, Steve Parker's been dealing with knee issues since the Utica game," he said. "This afternoon, we learned he needs surgery. That'll happen later this week, and he's out for the season."

The team let out a collective gasp. The news was sudden.

"Okay, okay," Coach Dad tried to steady them. "Let's support Stevie—but we've got to move forward, and fast."

He cleared his throat, then turned to Parker's backup.

"Robby, you're his backup. And I hate saying this in front of everyone—this is all happening fast—but I need you to stay in that role. I know that's not fair."

Coach Dad assured Robby he still had a critical role: special teams, scout reps, staying ready. Robby nodded, disappointed but mature.

Then came the real shake-up.

"We're moving AJ from offense to defense. He'll step in at defensive back."

The defensive coaches gave a low but enthusiastic "Yay AJ," trying to be respectful of Robby while welcoming a needed addition. The move explained the pre-practice coaches' meeting. They'd learned about Parker's surgery earlier in the day. Knowing Robby wasn't ready, they pushed hard for AJ. While the offense still had weapons under the A-11 scheme, the defense needed a fix—and AJ had already proven his ability in the Utica game.

The team was surprised, but most understood: this was what winning demanded.

AJ, though, was stunned. Outwardly, he smiled. He liked being valued. He wanted to help.

But inside, he seethed—especially at his dad. That wasn't new, but now, he had a concrete reason.

Not one person—including his father—had spoken to him in advance.

He thought, *did anyone consider how this might affect me? He wondered, what about the scoring record or college recruiting?*

Coach Dad, for all their tension, knew his son well. He saw the flicker of anger in AJ's expression. It made him uneasy. He regretted how the decision played out.

In the coaches' meeting, the defensive staff had made their case. The logic was strong. The timing, urgent. Coach Dad initially resisted—but ultimately relented. The defense needed AJ more than the offense would miss him.

Still, he told himself he'd talk to his son later.

For now, they had a practice to run.

"Let's get to work," he called out.

Everyone broke into their usual groups—except AJ.

Chapter 79

While AJ was bitter and resentful—especially toward his dad—none of it showed. Outwardly, he brought the same energy to defense that he had on offense.

Still, being with the defense felt strange. It was the same field, the same team in name—but the players were different. The coaches were different. The terminology was different. The goals were different.

And the offense was just across the way. He could hear it. Brady's clap-clap echoed, followed by the team's mimic. AJ recognized every signal. When a play unfolded, he knew exactly what call had set it in motion.

He had vowed to confront his dad—just not yet. For now, he did what he was told. As odd and angering as the move felt, sulking wouldn't help. He jumped to the front of the line in drills. He asked questions. He encouraged teammates, especially Robby Sandoval, who was clearly dealing with his own disappointment.

After practice, though, AJ wasted no time. He was first to the locker room, first to shower and change. Normally, he lingered. Today, he was out the door in minutes. The frustration returned in full.

He thought about rushing home, venting to his mom, and recruiting her to confront his dad alongside him. Maybe she could help reverse the decision.

But as he neared his car, he stopped. No, he wasn't going to hide behind his mother. He wasn't a kid anymore. He was technically an adult—and this was his issue to handle.

He turned and headed back toward the practice field. His dad was still out there.

But before he could leave the blacktop and hit the grass, someone stepped into his path—and just like that, his heart rate race.

"Hey, AJ," Casey Kaufman said with her usual bright smile. She placed a light hand on his chest, gently stopping him. "Do you have a minute?"

Her hand was warm. AJ felt a jolt—intoxicating and unexpected. Despite the storm brewing inside him, he smiled back. He couldn't help it.

"Sure," he said.

"AJ, I haven't known you long—and I don't know you well," Casey began, pausing.

AJ's heart raced. *And…?*

She continued, "But today, I can't tell you how impressed I was. They moved you from offense to defense and…"—she searched for words— "…and you didn't even flinch."

AJ was stunned. He'd been gearing up for a confrontation, and now he felt a little guilty. He had nothing to say, so he let her continue.

"AJ, I've been around sports a long time. I've played at different levels. My dad coached. My brothers played. And I've seen it—everyone wants to start, to get the glamour position. And when they don't, they pout, complain—or quit altogether."

AJ shifted uncomfortably.

"But not you," she said. "You're a senior. A starter. A star. And you took the change like… like a real teammate. I'm just really impressed, AJ. Really."

Thank God she can't read minds, he thought.

"That's all," Casey added with a small shrug. "Sorry for stopping you. I know you were headed somewhere."

"Um," AJ stammered. "I can't remember. I guess it wasn't important." They shared a nervous laugh.

"Are you going to your car?" he asked.

"Yes," Casey replied.

With that, AJ gestured that he'd walk with her. They turned and began making small talk as they headed toward their cars. But as they approached, Casey noticed something AJ hadn't.

"AJ, your front tire is flat," she said.

"No way! It's brand new," AJ replied, clearly annoyed. He hurried ahead. "And my back tire is flat too." He placed both hands on his head, exasperated. Then he noticed something else. "Casey, your two tires on this side are flat too."

"You're kidding," she said, catching up to him.

She bent to check and confirmed it. Just then, a lone car rolled past on the road. The driver honked several quick times. Inside were three familiar faces—Sebastian, Noah, and Aiden— laughing.

"Oh, Casey," AJ said with genuine remorse. "I'm so sorry."

"Why? You didn't do anything," she said, confused.

"No, but…" AJ sighed. "It's a long story." He paused, thinking, then added, "Casey, I'll be right back. My dad has one of those portable air pumps in his car."

Without waiting for a reply, AJ turned and jogged toward the practice field—this time with a different purpose.

Coach Dad was still on the field, deep in conversation with the team trainer. Mid-sentence, his phone rang. He checked the screen.

"Ari Eisenberg," he said. "Nathan, hold on a sec. This'll be quick."

He answered with a chuckle. "Ari, what are you doing? You're on vacation."

Ari let out a booming laugh. "Jonathan—"

"Hold on, Ari," Jonathan said as AJ approached fast. "AJ, I know we need to talk. Can it wait until we're home?"

"No, Dad," AJ said, panting. "I need the air pump. Can you unlock your car?"

"Sure," Jonathan replied, hitting the unlock command on his phone. "Why?"

"Sebastian and his crew let the air out of my tires. And Casey's too," AJ said, disgusted.

"Do you need help?" Jonathan asked.

"No, just the pump," AJ said, already heading back.

As Nathan waited patiently, Jonathan returned to his call.

"Sorry, Ari. It seems the Sullivan family is waging war on me from all fronts."

Ari laughed again. "I heard. What did I say? Some people's kids." Another chuckle. "And some people's parents, Jonathan. That's actually why I called."

His tone shifted. "Look, you've got a life. I'm on vacation. Don't worry about the lawsuit. And forget about nervous-nelly Warren. I had Theresa set up a meeting for the three of us when I'm back."

"Thanks, Ari. I appreciate you running interference," Jonathan said.

"No problem. They say it's five o'clock somewhere—well, it's actually five o'clock here. I'm headed to the hotel bar," Ari said with another hearty laugh.

With that, the call ended. Jonathan turned back to Nathan, and the two resumed their conversation, briefly touching on the latest Sullivan-related distractions.

AJ returned to Casey with the portable air pump in hand, fresh from a quick stop at his dad's car. Powered by a lithium-ion battery, the device was one AJ considered a miracle gadget— he'd used it more than a few times to inflate his perpetually leaky back tire.

He went straight to work on Casey's front tire. The pump buzzed and whirred, but the tire didn't inflate.

"What am I doing wrong?" he wondered aloud.

He checked everything—battery fully charged; switches properly set. Still nothing.

To double-check, AJ attached the pump to his own front tire. It immediately began to inflate. Then his back tire. Same result—full inflation in seconds. He moved to Casey's rear tire. Again, no luck. That's when he spotted the problem.

"Casey," he said, pausing with frustration. She looked at him with concern.

"These tires are shot. They're so deflated the seal between the tire and rim is broken. Watch." He engaged the pump again, showing how the air escaped as fast as it entered.

"I'm really sorry."

"Don't be," she said gently. "It's not your fault. I've been meaning to replace them, but… I was just hoping they'd last until graduation and a steady paycheck."

There was a beat of silence.

"I can call my roommate. She can come get me."

AJ sat still, thinking. He didn't want to just give up—not with her. He scanned both cars, counting lug nuts. Five each. An idea hit him.

"Here's what we'll do. You have a spare. I have a spare. I'll put them both on your car so you can drive—just not too fast, OK?"

Casey didn't quite follow but nodded anyway.

AJ had her pop the trunk, pulled out her spare, and got to work on the back tire.

"You'll still need to replace them soon," he said, wiping sweat from his brow. "But I think at least one might be repairable. I know a place—Don's Car Care. They're solid and won't screw you over. I can call first thing tomorrow and get you set up."

As AJ talked, Casey picked up his phone and quietly texted herself from it.

Thx AJ! - Casey

As AJ heard the ding from her phone, his heart skipped a beat. She'd effectively given him her number. The gesture lit a spark, and he quickened his pace to get the spares mounted on Casey's car.

Chapter 80

Jonathan's conversation with Nathan Rogers didn't last long after AJ left. He thought about checking on his son but opted to head straight home, hoping to arrive before AJ and brief — and enlist support from — Sam.

He succeeded. Sitting at the kitchen table, Jonathan gave his wife the full rundown: a season-ending injury, a backup who wasn't ready, and a defensive coaching staff lobbying hard for AJ.

"How did he take it?" Sam asked.

Jonathan shrugged. "Outwardly fine, but I think he was putting on a brave face, honey." He shrugged again. "I imagine he's upset. We'll hear about it."

"I bet," Sam replied. "We'll know soon enough. He just pulled into the driveway."

They fell silent, waiting for AJ to come in. Two minutes later, he did—sweaty, stoic, and with tire grime on his face. He walked straight to the kitchen table, pulled the portable air pump from his gym bag, and set it down.

"It was fine, Mom. How was yours?" he asked calmly.

Caught off guard, Sam blinked. "Fine," she replied, then regrouped. "I heard they moved you to defense."

"Yeah," AJ said, still even toned. "I've got to be a team player."

Jonathan watched silently. It was as if he weren't in the room.

"Are you hungry?" Sam asked, defaulting to a motherly concern. "Do you want me to fix you something?"

"Um, yeah... sure," AJ replied. "But let me shower first. I feel like I've got dirt all over me." With that, he walked to his room.

As he left, Sam shot Jonathan a wide-eyed look across the table. She mouthed, Wow, then raised three fingers — her pinky, ring, and middle — while pressing her thumb and index finger together in the family's sign for the word.

Jonathan said nothing. He just shrugged again, this time shaking his head as well.

Chapter 81

Mid-to-late September in Blacklick, Ohio, is a kind of tweener time. Technically still summer, but signs of the season's change are unmistakable. Morning temperatures dip lower, and red-orange leaves begin to hit the ground.

When students headed off to school, the sun was just cresting the horizon. Sebastian and his crew climbed into his car for the short ride to the high school, moving through long shadows cast by nearby houses and trees. All were a little groggy and none noticed the fading scent of industrial cleaner used to eliminate the stench of pounds of goose poop.

Sebastian let out a big yawn as he started the car. Once alert, he shifted into reverse. The engine revved, but the car barely moved.

"What the ...," Sebastian muttered, throwing it back into park. Something wasn't right. Aiden and Noah stirred from their daze, now alert.

Thinking something might be blocking a tire, the trio got out to inspect. Sebastian exited the driver's side, and Aiden and Noah took the passenger side.

"They're flat," Sebastian said. "Both are flat."
"Here too," Noah added.

Aiden crouched down for a closer look. "They're not just flat. They're slashed." Each tire bore a clean, one-inch horizontal puncture on the sidewall.

The three stared at each other in disbelief.

Sebastian finally growled, "Somebody's dead."

Chapter 82

Living his new normal, Jonathan was up early and racing to the office. He focused on getting work done, continuing to build out the electronic due diligence framework. At one point, he crossed paths with Warren Scott could tell that *that little moron* wanted to say something but didn't. True to his word, Ari had muzzled *that egotistical S.O.B.* Jonathan thought, *Great. The fewer distractions, the better.*

That afternoon at school, AJ was confronted by Sebastian and his crew about the slashed tires. AJ was genuinely surprised.

"What are you talking about? I didn't come anywhere near your car," he said, pushing Sebastian's hand off his chest and stepping through the troublesome trio. As he passed, he looked over his shoulder and added, "I've been too busy dealing with my own tires—thank you very little—to waste time on yours."

The rest of the school day was uneventful. Classes had settled into their curriculum, and senior projects were well underway. AJ and Shea leaned into theirs—neither wanting the other to feel like they weren't pulling their weight, even though the deadline was still weeks away.

Outside of class, when AJ wasn't working with Shea, he spent time with Brady and Tank. The three found clever ways to work around the obvious communication barriers. They texted when they had phone access, and Brady taught them simple ASL words and phrases.

But mostly, they just understood each other. One could point at something and all three would laugh. A glance could convey an entire thought. They were teammates, online gamers—but above all, friends.

After school but before practice, AJ meandered out to his car. Once again, he was conveniently there when Casey arrived. He lit up at the sight of her backing in—with all tires intact.

She didn't say a word at first. Instead, she smiled wide, walked to her trunk, and popped it open. From inside, she pulled out AJ's spare tire and handed it to him, along with a packaged cookie she'd picked up at the Ohio Dominican student center.

AJ's heart raced. He fumbled for words, then settled on the obvious. "So, how did it go?"

"Great, AJ! Absolutely great." She beamed. Then she admitted she'd been nervous walking into Don's Car Care — *What is this going to cost?* — but was pleasantly surprised when Don himself jumped in to handle the fix. Within 30 minutes, he had her on her way, assuring her, "Your tires should be fine until spring." And the bill? Just enough to cover shop supplies.

Casey couldn't have been happier—or more relieved.

She was running late, though, and needed to catch up with Brady. She quickly thanked AJ again, then bounded toward the practice field. About ten yards away, she stopped, turned back, and called, "Hey, AJ!" Then she pointed at him, made two fists, and knocked her right fist against the back of her left.

AJ cocked his head and shrugged as if to say, *"What does that mean?"*

Casey smiled, turned to run again, and shouted over her shoulder, "You figure it out."

At this point in the season, each weekday felt like the last. Warm-up. Drills. Review the upcoming opponent. Talk through issues to address. Even for AJ—now with a new unit and learning a different position—practice had become routine. As a result, Friday, game day, came quickly.

With New Lexington coming to Blacklick, pregame was more relaxed. There was no packing checklist to stress over. No bus to catch. No bumpy ride to endure.

This gave the team a chance to go home after school, get something to eat, and relax before reporting back. When they returned to the high school, they were there in time to see their opponents arrive—having traveled a little over an hour from southeastern Ohio—and go through the same motions Blacklick did on road games.

Unlike schools closer to Central Ohio, New Lexington didn't have competing sports like lacrosse, hockey, or volleyball. If you were an able-bodied young man, you played football, basketball—or both. And in the offseason, you trained for the next one.

This dynamic helped ensure the visiting Panthers had a traditionally strong football program. This year was no different. New Lexington, as well as Blacklick's next two opponents, were on par with Kettering Alter and projected to be in the playoff conversation by season's end.

Fortunately for Blacklick, it was the fifth game of the season. Brady Troy was fully entrenched as the starting quarterback, and the team was more comfortable operating the simplified A-11 offense. That was critical, because New Lexington had a staunch defense.

Brady observed defensive patterns and adjusted formations and plays. He had plenty to choose from and could change calls with his signature clap-clap. He could run, pass, and pass on the run.

Moreover, the deaf quarterback had a stable of receivers and backs he could get the ball to. Spreading the ball around—one of the A-11's key benefits—made New Lexington defend everyone.

And if the Mustangs ever needed just two or three yards, Brady could hand signal "G-Six-H-L or R." That was their goal-line formation. The ball would go to Tank. Left or right. It was nearly automatic. Whenever that play was called, Tank would shout "Hammer Left" or "Hammer Right," a throwback to junior high when Coach Norm called plays at St. Matthew School.

The Mustangs moved the ball well against New Lexington. Scoring, however, was another matter. Instead of touchdowns, they had to settle for field goals. While they had a wealth of offensive weapons, the most experienced one—the one with a nose for the end zone—was now playing defense.

Coach Dad and Norm tried to work AJ in for a few offensive plays. He even caught a pass that secured a key first down. But mostly, AJ was on the sidelines when Blacklick had the ball, huddled with the defense around a dry-erase board, strategizing the next stop.

And that was necessary. New Lexington's offense was dynamic.

Still, AJ couldn't help how he felt. He was torn, confused. He recognized that accepting his new role was a sign of maturity, of leadership. He understood the team-first concept. It wasn't foreign—it just wasn't something he'd ever had to live.

At the same time, another part of him burned with resentment—especially toward his dad and the coaching staff. In AJ's mind, he was making a Herculean sacrifice. He felt robbed. The scoring record was likely out of reach now. And his chances of playing college football? Slim too.

Defense felt foreign. He was an offensive guy. His heart remained with that unit. He still kept tabs on what they were doing—listening in, watching signals, tracking down and distance, even glancing over when Brady issued his clap-clap.

And AJ believed his presence would've made a difference. He would've made key blocks. He wouldn't have dropped the passes others did. He'd have been more elusive. He would've found the end zone.

All of that resentment lit a fire in him. And serendipitously, that fire made him dangerous on defense. He flew across the field. He broke up passes. He stifled drives. He sacked the quarterback. He delivered highlight-reel tackles.

Arguably, his absence on offense cost Blacklick touchdowns. But his presence on defense kept New Lexington from scoring any of their own. While AJ wasn't scoring points, he was preventing them—which mattered just as much.

And with less than a minute left in the game, it was AJ's interception in the end zone that sealed the Mustangs' 15-9 win.

Chapter 83

Winning never gets old, but it can become routine. The same goes for cake.

On Saturday, Jonathan and his colleagues gathered for another round of victory cake—though Ari was still out on vacation.

As everyone enjoyed a unique apple-filling-and-cinnamon-icing combination, one of the senior partners raised a fork and said to Jonathan, "Congratulations."

Jonathan gave a puzzled look and replied, "Thanks?"

The partner clarified with a chuckle, "Not for the win—for being sued."

Word of the Sebastian Sullivan lawsuit had spread and was now common knowledge around the firm.

Jonathan said nothing, his eyes dropping in embarrassment.

The partner went on, "Seriously. Congratulations. Most of us agree—you're not a real attorney until you've been sued a time or two."

Jonathan cracked a wide grin as the room erupted in laughter.

Not everyone shared that sentiment.

On Monday afternoon, Warren Scott grabbed the first opening on Ari's calendar, delighted to usher Jonathan into the "big boss's" office.

Warren was ready. He handed Ari a copy of the legal complaint. *That crafty bastard* had marked various pages with sticky notes and highlighted key passages.

After giving the document a quick scan, Ari nodded. Then Warren launched into a monologue, reprimanding Jonathan as if the lawsuit were an existential threat to the firm. He painted it as a black mark on the firm's reputation and a stain on everyone's work.

Ari patiently let him finish. Then, calm as ever, he said, "Warren, thank you for your work on this," holding up the document. "And thanks for looking out for the firm."

Warren straightened in his chair, beaming. "Of course. Thank you."

Jonathan just watched, expressionless.

Still polite, Ari continued. "Warren, do you know how often this firm gets sued?"

Warren's face dropped. This wasn't going the way he'd hoped.

"If we didn't get sued as often as we do," Ari added with a bellowing laugh, "we might have to lay off a staff attorney."

"But—" Warren started to push back.

"Warren," Ari interrupted gently, still smiling. "You've obviously read this." He held up the pleading again. Warren nodded, now sheepishly.

"Then you know, as I do, there are four or five holes in the case. Honestly, I bet an attorney as sharp as you could have it tossed with a single motion. Right?"

Warren nodded again—this time uncertainly. He couldn't disagree without undercutting Ari's praise, but agreeing would contradict the point of the meeting.

Ari turned to Jonathan. "Now, is this ideal? No. But you haven't done anything reckless."

He then told both attorneys that a litigation intern would handle the matter.

Without missing a beat, Ari pivoted. "So, what else did I miss while I was away?"

Caught off guard, both men looked at each other and shrugged.

"I heard you've been working with Stephenson on the Emerald Medical due diligence," Ari said, looking at Jonathan. "Some kind of electronic system?" He laughed. "I'm always amazed by what technology can do. I can't do any of it—but still amazed."

He walked them both to the door. Warren turned left, deflated. Jonathan started to the right, but Ari called after him.

"Hey, Jonathan."

He turned.

"We still on for Friday night? The game?"

"Absolutely," Jonathan said, perking up. "The boys will be excited. I'm excited."

"Great. I found my old high school jersey," Ari said proudly. "And it still fits ... sort of."

He let out a signature bellowing laugh.

Jonathan smiled. "I'll get the details to Theresa so she can work your schedule around it."

Chapter 84

Ari Eisenberg loved vacations. But he never enjoyed returning from time away. The first few days back were always chaotic — catching up on developments and readjusting to the pace of a large, high-powered law firm.

So, on Friday, he welcomed the chance to leave a little early.

Navigating the usual rush-hour traffic through downtown Columbus, he made it home for a quiet dinner with Alison. Afterward, he changed into something appropriate for a high school football game: walking shoes, khakis, a T-shirt, his old Bexley jersey, and a black windbreaker.

With a kiss goodbye, he headed out.

He arrived at Blacklick High School around 5:30 p.m. The parking lot buzzed with tailgating families and students. The Mustangs were hosting Columbus Academy—a nearby, highly selective private school with a long tradition of excellence in both academics and athletics. The Vikings were undefeated.

Ari held a particular distaste for Columbus Academy.

Early in his legal career at Belden & Schmidt, many of his colleagues were Academy alumni. They never let him forget that he came from Bexley—a public school.

Worse, the two schools had been rivals. In four years of high school football, Ari's Bexley Lions never once beat Columbus Academy. And the neighborhood kids who attended Academy never let him forget that, either.

Following Jonathan's instructions, passed along by Theresa, Ari made his way into the school and down to the locker room. The first person he saw was Jonathan, who greeted him with a warm hug. Jonathan reintroduced him to Norm, who again thanked Ari for helping make key contacts.

Ari took a seat in the coaches' office and watched as players and staff filed in. The sights, sounds, and smells of football filled the air. The hum of excitement was unmistakable. Ari felt his heart rate rise.

Time flew. Once the team was suited up, they jogged out for initial warmups. Ari followed, keeping off to the side. He took in the scene—fans filling the stands, the band tuning up, flags spinning, cheerleaders jumping, kids with painted chests yelling across the rails. He smiled, soaking it all in.

Later, he followed the team back into the locker room for final prep.

Coach Dad gathered the players around him near the equipment lockers. He hit on key points from the week: focus, play through the whistle, trust your training.

Then he turned to Ari.

"Everyone, I want you to meet my friend and mentor, Ari Eisenberg. He runs the firm I work for—and he's the reason I've had the time to coach this season. Tonight, he's an honorary coach. Anything you want to say, Coach Ari?"

Ari gave a slight nod and pulled a note card from his back pocket. Norm's eyes widened. Jonathan just smiled.

"Gentlemen," Ari began, calm and deliberate. "Before you tonight is an opportunity. Not just to play football. Not just to win and take a step toward defending your state title."

The room quieted. Players leaned in.

"No, this opportunity is bigger than that. Tonight, you have a chance to earn something." He slapped his palm on a locker. "Respect."

The word rang out. Everyone jumped.

"They don't respect you," Ari continued, raising his voice. "They think they're better than you. They live in big houses. Drive fancy cars. And look down on you because you go to a public school."

He let that hang in the air.

"You want to know how I know that?" He yanked off his windbreaker, revealing a faded Bexley jersey, #53. "Because I played against them. I lived next door to them. I worked with them." He slapped the locker again.

His face was flushed. His voice rang with fire.

"So tonight—don't just earn their respect." He stepped toward the locker room exit. "Get out there and take it."

He flung the door open and high-fived players as they charged the field.

As the room emptied, Norm turned to Jonathan. "Were you done?"

Jonathan just laughed.

Whether or not the Columbus Academy players respected public school kids was a matter of opinion. There was no question, however, that they came ready to play football. From the opening kickoff, they matched Blacklick's energy. It was no fluke they were undefeated.

The game went back and forth. Each team mounted promising drives, only to see the opposing defense step up—forcing punts or long, failed field goal attempts. The teams battled to a scoreless tie at halftime.

Throughout the game, Ari remained engaged. He paced the edge of the field, bent at the waist with his hands on his knees. He shouted encouragement. He loudly questioned unfavorable calls. And when Brady clap-clapped to change plays, Ari enthusiastically mimicked it with the offensive players on the field.

Starting with their second possession of the third quarter, Columbus Academy began to seize momentum. The Vikings moved the chains repeatedly and pushed the ball just inside Blacklick's 10-yard line. It felt like they were about to score.

On first and goal, the Viking quarterback threw to the far side of the end zone—but AJ jumped the route, intercepted the ball, and took off down the sideline. The Blacklick fans erupted. Teammates and coaches shouted, motioning him on. The cheers only grew louder as AJ sprinted past the Mustangs' bench. No one was in front of him. No one would catch him.

As he crossed into the end zone, the stadium exploded. AJ flipped the ball to the official, then celebrated with the rest of the defense as they caught up to him. Together, they made their way back toward the bench.

Coaches and players crowded as far down the sideline as officials would allow. That invisible boundary didn't stop Ari, though. He stepped five yards onto the field to high-five AJ, then made his way back to the sideline.

AJ was swarmed by teammates and coaches, all eager to slap his helmet or shoulder pads. Just beyond them stood Casey, waiting with a big smile. She pulled him into a hug, adding to the moment. AJ hugged her back.

After the extra point gave Blacklick a 7-0 lead, John Evans boomed the kickoff into the end zone for a touchback. Columbus Academy started from its 20-yard line—but didn't get much further. Riding a wave of momentum, the Mustang defense forced a three-and-out.

Then it was Brady Troy's turn.

Yes, he was hearing impaired—but in some ways, that was an advantage. With Casey standing beside Coach Dad and Norm, Brady had near real-time communication with the sideline.

Ari had been watching from afar and finally made his way over to Casey. Fascinated, he observed the ASL exchanges between her and Brady.

"Are you really talking?" Ari asked.

"Yes and no," Casey replied. "Not every word gets signed. We use concepts, gestures, facial expressions, and body language to convey meaning." As she spoke, she demonstrated a simple sign to Brady. "It's about key ideas, not word-for-word translation."

"Wow," Ari said, clearly enthralled.

"Here, try this," Casey said, showing him a few signs.

Ari did his best to copy her. "What did I just say?"

"'Good job,'" Casey answered, as she watched Brady's response.

"What did he just say?" Ari asked.

Casey smiled. "'Thanks, Coach Ari.'"

"Really?" Ari let out a booming laugh. "I've got to introduce you to my friend Bobby. He runs Emerald Medical. They just announced a new cochlear implant division. You know, those devices that help people like number ten hear. Bobby could use people like you."

"That sounds amazing," Casey replied. "I'd love to meet him."

Before Ari could respond, all eyes turned to the field. From the Ace formation—one running back, two tight ends, two wide receivers—Brady took the snap, faked the handoff, and fired to his right. The tight end got out front and threw a key block, springing the receiver for a big gain.

Three plays later, Blacklick was in the end zone again—14–0.

That fueled the defense once more, allowing Brady and company to get the ball back. This time they managed only a field goal, but the drive chewed more than seven minutes off the clock.

Columbus Academy didn't regain possession until well into the fourth quarter. They managed a late, meaningless touchdown. But Blacklick held on for the 17–7 win.

Chapter 85

For the Blacklick players and fans, beating Columbus Academy was good, but nothing they hadn't done several times before. For Ari Eisenberg, however, the win was epic. As time expired, he stormed the field as fast as his late-70-something body could move. He then carried on as if he'd won a state championship—high-fiving and hugging everyone.

The players were amused by his enthusiasm. It was nice to know their efforts meant so much. What they really appreciated, however, was the pizza. Win or lose, Ari had arranged for 20 large pizzas to be delivered to the locker room.

When the pizza showed up, Ari took another opportunity to address the team. He shared more fire and brimstone. He shared his appreciation for being given a joy he'd dreamed about for 60 years. And he shared well-wishes to keep on their winning ways. Then Ari doled out boxes of pizza to thankful and hungry players.

As kids ate, someone turned on a mix of loud rock and rap music. A few started in with an impromptu dance in the middle. Caught up in the moment, Ari jumped into it. Players cheered the legal matriarch on. He wasn't great, but then no one expected him to be.

Soon Ari was the only one dancing. Others clapped to the beat, further encouraging him. He then grabbed Coach Dad and Norm and pulled them to the center. The moment they made any attempt, players started to laugh and boo. Tank shouted, "Save us. Kill the music." Someone did. And it was back to just eating pizza.

It was Friday night. Players quickly finished the pizza, showered, changed, and headed out the door—thanking Ari first. They were eager to get on with their teen lives. Soon, the only people remaining in the locker room were Jonathan, Norm and Ari.

They sat in silence for a moment, and then Ari broke it. "Hey, Jonathan. Before I forget. That girl who does the hand motion thing." Ari made wild motions to mimic the team's ASL interpreter.

"Yes. Casey," Jonathan clarified.

"Yeah, yeah, Casey," Ari bopped himself on the head, indicating that he knew but forgot. Then he continued, "Remind me to connect her … Casey … with Bobby O. Emerald is working on a new cochlear implant division." He paused, then clarified, "You know, to help the hearing impaired. I'm sure they could use her."

Norm gave a couple of big nods of his head to demonstrate his agreement.

Jonathan chimed in with, "I will. That's a great idea. I'm sure Casey would love the opportunity … and be an asset for Emerald."

Then Ari spoke up again. "Thank you so much for tonight. I cannot tell you how much fun I had." He looked off and shared, "And it brought back so many memories."

"No, Ari," Jonathan said. He paused and then enunciated, "Thank you."

Norm again nodded.

Jonathan continued, "You were an inspiration. You're welcome back any time. The team responded to you."

"Jonathan, thank you." He adjusted his seat on the hard locker room bench. "I intend to come back. This is a special team. The assembly of coaches. The players. The camaraderie. The offense." He then paused and clapped twice, as if to mimic Brady.

Jonathan and Norm laughed.

Norm shared, "Well, it's not like either of us is a great offensive savant. Most everything about our offense sort of found us."

Ari patted Norm on the leg and remarked, "That's okay. No matter how it came to be, you capitalized on it, and that's what counts. The world is full of people who had opportunity knock and they failed to answer."

Jonathan and Norm quietly thought about Ari's sage offering. Before they could respond, Ari continued, "As I was saying, this is a special team. They will go far."

Jonathan interjected, "I hope so. Next week will be a big test. Jonathan Alder is another undefeated team. But they are the real deal. They're number one in the region. Number three in the state."

Ari responded, "You'll be fine. There is something about this group. I can just feel it." A determined look came across his face. "Tomorrow, I'm going to get with Theresa and re-rack my schedule so I can come to the game next week."

Norm chimed in, "That would be great. We can get you a team jacket."

"Norm, two XL please," Ari laughed. "But do you know what I'm really looking forward to?" He didn't wait for an answer. "The state championship game. Assuming I have not worn out my welcome by then." He laughed again.

Jonathan nodded as if to say, "Absolutely." And then spoke, "As you always say, Ari—'From your lips to God's ear.'"

Without responding, Ari added, "And I'm going to be there with this jersey." He patted his number 53. "Old Bexley High is going to be represented." He then let out a bellowing laugh, which Jonathan and Norm joined in on.

When the laughter subsided, Norm spoke. "Ari, I love that. I appreciate your thinking." Then he let out a little giggle and continued, "What I don't appreciate is you getting me to dance and highlighting just how uncool I am in the eyes of my son."

Everyone laughed.

Jonathan added, "Norm, you're lucky. You're only uncool. I'm uncool and hated by my son."

"Oh, Jonathan," Norm protested. "It's not that bad."

"None of those things matter," Ari said in his sage voice, taking control of the conversation. "Your job as a father is not to be cool in your kids' eyes. It's not even your job to get them to like you." He paused as if to gather his thoughts. "No, your job as a dad is to love your kids no matter what."

Jonathan and Norm took in Ari's words. They slightly nodded and quietly listened for more.

Ari continued, "Think about it. You can't control what your boys think. They're kids. Great kids, but they're clueless. They have no appreciation for what it takes to be a parent. They can't even appreciate just how much love you have for them … how you would sacrifice anything … really everything … for them. It's a love that they won't be able to comprehend until they hold their own children for the first time."

Ari paused for a moment, and Norm asked, "Do you have kids, Ari?"

Jonathan knew the answer and wanted to respond for Ari. He was not sure just how much pain that question would dredge up for his boss.

Before he could, however, Ari responded, "Yes. Yes, Alison and I had a son."

Norm caught the past-tense reference and held any further questions. And was content in a brief void of silence.

Ari stared off for a moment, contemplating. He then nodded and continued, "Yes, Alan. Wonderful little Alan." He pondered some more, looking off at nothing, creating a long pause.

Then Ari started in on another sage monologue. "Yes, Alan. What a great kid. He was only with us for just a few days, but in those few days everything changed.

"The moment I held Alan for the first time, I felt a level of love that I never, ever knew existed. I couldn't have. But at that moment … and, of course, we knew Alan was not well and likely would not last long. But at that moment, I was willing to do anything for Alan. Anything!

"I didn't have much then, but I would have given it all to spare his life. I would give everything I have today for his life. I would have literally given my life so he could have his."

Ari continued to stare off. "But in those days, as Alison and I took turns holding Alan … and crying over our fleeting time with Alan … it all came rushing to me. It wasn't a sadness. Rather, it was a wonderful epiphany. As I held Alan, I realized for the first time in my life just how much my father loved me. How much he wanted nothing but the best for me.

"My father didn't nag me because he hated me. No! He did so because he loved me and would have done anything for me." Tears welled up in Ari's eyes. "My father wanted nothing but the best for me. He had hopes and dreams for me that were beyond me at the time.

"In a way, God put Alan in my life for those few days to help me realize my father's love for me. God put Alan in my arms to drive me back into the arms of my own father. And that helped me become the person I am today.

"Little Alan. Wonderful, little Alan." Ari continued to stare off. Silence again filled the locker room, until Ari shared, "That was 50-something years ago. But it still feels like yesterday."

Norm allowed a few seconds to pass, and cautiously asked, "Did you and Alison ever contemplate trying to have another child?"

Ari thought for a second, let out a heavy sigh, and then shared, "Not really. No." After he gathered his words, he continued, "While Alan unearthed a love in my heart, losing him created a hurt that Alison and I were afraid to endure again. And fear of that pain—that awful, indescribable hurt—well, it just lingered. And that fear prevented us from even talking about trying again."

Ari then stopped staring off and quickly looked at Norm, and then took a long look at Jonathan, before continuing. "That pain … that hurt, well, it never really goes away. And so, neither does the fear. In time, you learn to cope, Norm. And in time, you fill that emotional void by channeling that immense love into special people that come into your life."

Ari then looked down at the floor. It was as if the emotion of the conversation had drained him.

After a quiet moment, his head popped up and he gleefully asked, "Norm, do you like cake?"

Caught off guard, Norm took a moment to respond, "Cake? Who doesn't love it?"

Ari laughed. And then answered the rhetorical question, "No one, Norm. That's who." He laughed harder. Then followed up with, "If you're free tomorrow at lunch, you should stop over to the firm. We're having some cake."

Chapter 86

Norm accepted Ari's invitation and stopped over for victory cake—a strawberry shortcake-style sheet cake with whipped cream icing.

As Theresa's twin nieces—Tamara and Tabitha—served the cake, Norm recognized them; his older son had graduated with them and their twin cousins. He engaged them in conversation and complimented them on their cake. But he could not help but commiserate with the former high school soccer phenoms about how their senior season had unfolded—having their veteran soccer coach replaced by a nobody so funds could be diverted to the football Mustangs.

Ari was five minutes late. However, he arrived at the celebration pumping a fist. He shared with Jonathan and Norm, "My schedule is now officially re-racked. Friday night I will be at the Jonathan Alder game."

As Jonathan's mouth was full of cake, he could do little but give a genuine smile and nod.

Ari couldn't stay long. He was off to tailgate with "muckety-mucks" at the Ohio State–Purdue game and then in Cleveland the next day for the Browns–Bengals showdown.

After indulging in cake, Jonathan excused himself, went back to his office, and closed the door. He'd spent much of the morning reviewing and revising documents. He planned to spend the afternoon refining the electronic due diligence framework. He was fixated on remotely helping the firm's due diligence team when they ventured off to the Far East.

As Stephenson's wife now had doctor's orders to be home resting in bed, Stephenson needed to be available more often to help her. It was the perfect situation. Jonathan instructed his colleague to stay home. Stephenson could then periodically test the framework remotely, simulating conditions as if he were halfway across the globe. This also allowed the soon-to-be father to stay home, help out, and log some billable hours—which served to appease *that overbearing turd.*

For Jonathan, Saturday was long but worthwhile. He felt he was getting steadily closer to being able to assist colleagues a world away. Sure, coaching had pulled him out of the typical work routine he'd come to know, but it helped him become more productive.

On Sunday and a portion of Monday afternoon, Jonathan devoted himself to football. He mapped out practices for the week and summarized information that he and Norm had gathered on their powerhouse opponent—Jonathan Alder. This was the last big test before the playoffs. He intended to ensure the team was prepared to meet the moment.

And he was not alone. As he gathered the team around for Monday practice, Jonathan could sense an air of excited anticipation from the team. He didn't need to call them in. Rather, minutes before the scheduled start time, everyone was already there and eager to get started.

As they stood around waiting, Jonathan's phone buzzed to life. The notification indicated "Dr. Samantha Reese." As he had 90 seconds until practice kicked off, he playfully answered, "Jonathan Reese's phone."

"Honey ..." There was panic in Sam's voice.

The next three words caused Jonathan's face to transform from light-hearted to stoic seriousness. A jolt hit his stomach. And his knees buckled.

Chapter 87

Monday morning, Ari gloated about his football weekend. Blacklick crushed Columbus Academy. The Buckeyes romped Purdue for homecoming. And the Browns beat the Bengals to claim bragging rights—at least until later in the season, when the AFC North rivals would face off again. Thanks to his money and connections, he attended all three—even being flown to Cleveland and back on Emerald One, Bobby O's metallic Gaelic green Leonardo AW139 helicopter.

By late afternoon, Ari wasn't feeling well: sweating, nausea, indigestion, fatigue. He laughed off his symptoms as "too much football." And as he headed home early, he shared, "This is nothing that can't be cured by a long hot shower, a heavy dose of vitamin C, and a good night's sleep."

During that long hot shower, Alison went in to check on Ari—he'd become unusually quiet. She found the love of her life collapsed on the bathroom floor. She knew it was something serious, as Ari's lips, fingertips, and face were eerily blue.

She dialed 911. Ari was rushed to the Wexner Medical Center. There was little anyone could do. It was the "widow maker," a heart attack caused by a severe blockage in a main coronary artery supplying oxygenated blood to the entire body. It's aptly named, as it's especially deadly.

One of the ER doctors, knowing Sam was associated with the now-deceased, broke protocol and informed her boss. After gathering herself from the shock, Sam called Jonathan and shared, "Honey … Ari is dead."

After getting other details from Sam, Jonathan sent the team on a warmup lap. In disbelief, he muddled through briefing Norm and the other coaches on the situation. Norm offered condolences and encouraged, "Go. We've got this." Jonathan handed over his notes on Jonathan Alder and then went home — dazed and confused.

Once home, Jonathan was welcomed by Sam with a consoling hug. He quickly changed, and together they drove over to Ari's house.

There, they found Alison on the couch, grieving arm-in-arm with Theresa. In Ari's reading chair sat Warren Scott, crying uncontrollably. And throughout the main living area were other members of the firm, along with a few longtime clients and close neighbors—everyone grieving in their own way.

There was sadness, but also a sense of confusion. Normally, in moments like this, Ari would have been at the forefront, guiding others. Sensing the void, Jonathan stepped up—offering comfort, providing encouragement, and giving direction in the early hours following Ari's passing.

While Jewish law traditionally emphasizes burying the deceased as soon as possible—ideally within 24 hours—Jonathan lobbied for a delay until Friday. Many clients and members of the firm were scattered across the country and beyond. In fairness, they deserved an opportunity to attend the services.

That was just the first of a litany of details and decisions. For that reason, he and Sam were among the last to leave Ari's widow. Knowing there would be more ahead at the office, Jonathan was one of the first to arrive the next morning.

There, mourning and commotion continued. The phone rang continually with conciliatory calls and grief-stricken others asking about arrangements. Floral arrangements flooded the firm's lobbies and halls. But despite the unexpected depth of sorrow, the firm still had client, IRS, and court deadlines to meet. Jonathan and a few others were at the forefront of these business matters.

Warren Scott, however, was conspicuously absent from any of it. This made conducting firm business all the more challenging, as he had worked closest with Ari in recent years.

That poor man didn't make it to work until sometime after noon. Even then, he was no use—just drifting through the firm in tears.

By 3 p.m., Jonathan knew it would not be possible to make it to practice. He wasn't even sure he could make it home that evening. He excused himself to his office, closed the door, and called his football right hand.

"Norm, um," his mouth froze. Words of unreliability were seldom part of Jonathan's vocabulary. Fortunately, they didn't have to be.

"Jonathan, you don't need to say a thing. You deal with things there," Norm comforted.

"But…" Jonathan's mouth froze again.

"But nothing," Norm interjected. "We've got football covered. They need you there. You need to be there." There was a moment of silence. Norm then broke it. "In fact, just try to get to the game Friday night. Everything will be fine with the team. Trust us, dog. Okay?"

Jonathan agreed, thanked Norm, and slumped into his chair, letting the sorrow wash over him.

Chapter 88

After about 10 minutes, Jonathan gathered himself and got back to being useful — comforting, encouraging, coordinating. He, Theresa, and others moved life forward, just as Ari would have wanted.

Shortly after 5 p.m., that core group sent Warren Scott home, arranging for an intern to drive him in his own car. They instructed the junior partner to just stay there: "See you on

Friday at Ari's services." Where they really needed his help—accessing files and understanding firm business arrangements—Warren was of little use. He was mostly in the way and had become a distraction.

Jonathan was one of the last to leave. Then, the next morning, he was one of the first to arrive. It felt as if there was so much to get a handle on. As a result, Wednesday was another late night. And Thursday was no better.

Staying busy was cathartic. It helped firm operations slowly return to a degree of normalcy. While the firm would never be the same without Ari, the deep sorrow softened with each passing moment.

On Friday, however, everyone knew there would be a collective step back. Until about 1 p.m., the firm operated as usual. After that, the offices were closed. Email autoresponders were set. Telephones forwarded to an answering service. Doors shut. Lights out. Gates down. For the first time in firm history, no client work was happening. Everyone was heading to the services for Ari Eisenberg.

By Monday, it became clear that Ari and Alison's synagogue wouldn't be able to handle the expected crowd. While there would be a private Jewish service on Saturday morning, the firm arranged for a more secular memorial at the Ohio Theatre on Capitol Square. It was ideal—just around the corner from the office.

Sam came downtown separately and met Jonathan at the door. She greeted her husband with a warm hug and asked, "How are things?"

"We'll see," Jonathan said with a shrug. They clasped hands, walked in, and found seats in the first ten rows, in a section marked "Eisenberg & Anders."

Sam scanned the crowd. In the front row sat Warren Scott. Keeping to himself, he slouched in a padded seat, staring off. His eyes were swollen and red. His face, ghost white.

She craned her head to see who was there from outside the firm. Almost immediately, she was taken aback by an unexpected but familiar face—Walter Bachman. *What's he doing here?* she thought. Before she could look away, their eyes met. Sam offered an uncertain smile. Bachman nodded and raised two fingers in a polite salute. His entire thumb was wrapped in gauze.

At 2:30, the lights dimmed, signaling the service would soon begin. Though mourners didn't fill the entire performing arts center, it was an impressive turnout for a man who was neither a celebrity nor a public official.

Within minutes, the crowd settled, and the murmur turned to silence. The service began with a reading of *El Maleh Rachamim*, Hebrew for "God full of Mercy." From there, various songs were played, and Psalms and prayers were read. After that, a series of individuals came forward to deliver eulogies.

Each spoke to the life and character of Ari Eisenberg: the football hero, the diligent student, the community supporter, the compassionate leader, the wonderful friend.

Though uncoordinated, the tributes carried a common theme—Ari's legacy of kindness and generosity. He was a man with a blessed life who never hesitated to share his blessings, whether through time, talent, or treasure.

After about 90 minutes and thousands of tears, the program ended. Everyone retreated to the lobby and adjacent pavilion for a celebration of life. There, eyes dried, and laughter pierced the sorrow. People shared stories about how Ari had touched their lives.

Jonathan heard story after story of how Ari had rescued a situation or enriched someone in some way. Usually, he'd swoop into their lives completely unsolicited. And when people thanked him—often in disbelief at their good fortune—Ari would wave it off: "Ah, it was no big deal."

At times, however, Ari would grace people's lives and they wouldn't even realize it—until days, weeks, or even years later.

And when they finally asked, "Did you…?" he'd let out his trademark bellowing laugh and reply, "You can't prove that."

Another 90 minutes passed, and Jonathan and Sam found themselves among the last to remain. Sam asked, "When was the last real meal you had?"

Jonathan stopped to think. As he winced to come up with an answer, Sam interjected, "As your doctor—and your wife—I'm prescribing a decent dinner. You'll be no use to the team if you're malnourished."

Chapter 89

Still dressed from Ari's services, Jonathan submitted to his doctor's orders and followed his wife to her car. Together they drove toward Jonathan Alder High School—a public school in rural Plain City, about 45 minutes west of downtown Columbus. As they drove, they engaged in their usual back-and-forth about where to eat.

Jonathan asked, "What do you want?"

Sam replied, "What were you thinking?"

"You prescribed this," Jonathan fired back, a little ire in his voice.

"I know … but it's your turn to pick," she said, using the statement to shut down the discussion—only to veto his suggestions along the way. "No way! Not that."

Their options dwindled as they got closer to the high school. But the moment they entered Plain City, the choice was obvious: Der Dutchman—a warm, family-style restaurant known for its Amish-inspired comfort food.

Jonathan didn't realize how hungry he was until the food arrived. He powered through his meal while Sam savored hers. As he started to feel full, his thoughts drifted to the game. He fidgeted in his seat.

Sam chided, "Jonathan, just relax. You haven't been there all week. Things have been fine without you. They're fine now."

He knew she was right. Still, the Pioneers were undefeated against strong competition. Jonathan tried to push down the anxiety, but it kept welling up.

Eventually, Sam finished her meal, and they made the short drive—just two and a half miles south on U.S. 42—to the school. As they approached, it was clear the hometown fans considered this a big game. The parking lot was packed, many vehicles still showing signs of tailgate activity.

Sam grabbed the first open spot she could find. After a quick kiss and hug, they went their separate ways—Sam to general admission; Jonathan off to find the team.

Kickoff was fast approaching, and the Mustangs weren't yet back on the field after warmups. Jonathan realized he needed to find the locker room. He wasn't exactly sure where it was, but based on the school's layout, he had a good sense.

As he moved, he saw the home team already on the field. The national anthem had played, and now the PA announcer was introducing starters—rattling off Blacklick names quickly, then elaborating colorfully on the Pioneers.

"Where's the visitors' locker room? I'm a coach," Jonathan asked a young woman who seemed to be with the school.

"Oh, they'll be coming out of that door … hopefully soon," she said.

Jonathan thanked her and quickened his pace toward the door. His breathing was labored, but it drowned out the animated droning: "And our right guard, number 63, a senior, two-year starter…"

When he was about 20 yards away, the door flew open. Dozens of Blacklick players filed out and gathered in a tight cluster. As he approached, Jonathan sensed the intensity. No one acknowledged him. They just stared ahead, focused.

Under each player's eyes were glare-reducing eye black strips. Each was written on. On the right: "ARI." On the left: "53."

No one said a word. Nothing needed to be said. When the pregame countdown ticked under a minute, the Mustangs moved forward in formation and veered toward the visitors' bench.

Blacklick received the opening kickoff but was pinned deep in its own territory. Brady took charge. Using claps and hand signals, he began orchestrating a methodical drive—nothing flashy, just relentless progress. Two yards. Three. Four. Rarely more than five. When they needed short yardage, Brady called the Hammer. Tank would secure the ball and punish defenders with his body. After 16 plays and more than nine minutes, Blacklick led 7-0.

Jonathan Alder responded with a drive of its own, and it looked like they might match the score. Their fans were loud and engaged.

AJ changed that. He intercepted the ball on the 10-yard line and returned it to midfield. The Mustangs got right back to work. Five minutes later, it was 14-0.

On the Pioneers' next possession, Blacklick gave no ground. The defense had even changed its break from "Ready—Break" to "Ready—Ari." They were locked in.

Alder was forced to punt. Brady kept calling the Hammer. Tank kept pounding. And Blacklick took a 21-0 lead into halftime.

In the locker room, there was no celebration—just focus. The Mustangs came out for the second half with the same energy. Alder's offense went nowhere. Another punt. More pounding. With a minute left in the third quarter, the top-ranked home team trailed 28-0.

The game was effectively over. Second- and third-team players from both sides got time on the field. In the closing seconds, David Roberts—using claps and hand signals—led the second unit on a final scoring drive. Final score: 35-0.

It wasn't until this point that the players let themselves celebrate. That celebration spilled into the locker room, but Norm got things under control to address the team. After a few congratulatory remarks, he turned to Jonathan.

"What would you like to add?"

Jonathan stood silently. All those joyful faces, with ARI and 53 under their eyes. It had been a long week. Between grief and work, he hadn't had space to fully process Ari's death. He was sad, but in that moment, he was also incredibly proud. He just stood there. All he could manage was:

"I am… I'm just… I'm just so…"

As he struggled to find the words, Brady stepped forward. He looked Jonathan in the eyes and said, "Toach." Then he held up his hand: palm out, thumb extended laterally, index and pinky fingers raised — *Love*. Then he pointed that same hand at Coach Dad — *You*.

Brady pulled him in for a hug.

Chapter 90

As soon as Brady was done hugging Coach Dad, Casey was there to do the same. Then Tank. Shea. Paul. David Roberts. One by one, every player came up to either hug their coach or give him a warm pat on the back.

Everyone, except AJ. He stayed seated. His head was down. He'd felt a resentment toward his father for as long as he could remember. For the moment, however, that was gone. He'd never seen his dad in such a vulnerable state.

Once players were seated again, Coach Dad was able to muster a heartfelt, "I'm proud of you, and I appreciate you all. See you Monday at practice." He then left the locker room and quickly went to the car, where Sam was waiting, scrolling on her phone.

As soon as he got in the car, Sam drove off. She knew nothing of the locker room situation, but she could tell that Jonathan was distracted. She kept quiet unless necessary, and then remarked, "I will see you at home in a bit," as she dropped Jonathan off just outside the front entrance to the Huntington Center.

Jonathan was not going to the office on Saturday. He didn't think anyone would, as it would likely be a weekend of mourning. Nevertheless, he needed to get his car from the parking garage, and he figured that he would grab work to do while watching football.

He signed in at the security desk and rode the elevator up to the Eisenberg & Anders offices. When he got off, Jonathan was met with low lighting and an unsettling, eerie quiet. He tried not to think about it. He thought, "Just get what you need and leave."

He attempted to raise the security gate. It got stuck halfway up. Jonathan wondered who needed to be notified about it now, as he simply ducked under the half-open gate.

He made a beeline to his office, turned on a light, and grabbed two or three files that he'd need. He then turned off the light and walked down the dark hallway.

Rather than going directly back to the elevator, however, Jonathan detoured. He walked to Ari's corner office. It was dark and quiet. The former head partner's chair faced out toward Capitol Square. As there were no lights on in the office, Jonathan could see for miles into the clear night sky.

He leaned against the door, took a deep breath, and almost sighed. He was going to miss Ari. His laugh. His smile. How he interacted with others. Everything. It hurt to know that he was gone.

Jonathan started to reminisce. How they'd met. How the Belden & Schmidt fiasco separated them. How fate seemed to bring them back together. It was hard to imagine the firm without Ari Eisenberg at the helm.

Just as Jonathan was getting lost in thought, he was startled back to reality. Ari's chair abruptly turned toward him.

Warren Scott sat in it, his head below the top of the black leather chair. He said nothing. He just stared at Jonathan. He no longer seemed sad. Rather, his expression was somewhat demonic.

Jonathan just looked back. As he had nothing to say either, he quickly walked away without a word. He ducked under the gate and lowered it. His heart was racing.

He stepped into the elevator before the doors were fully open. He hit the button for the parking garage level and pressed the button to close the doors. When they did, he exhaled in relief.

Chapter 91

When Jonathan got to his car, his nerves were still shaken. It triggered a primal flight response. The dim, eerily quiet office setting likely contributed to it. Warren's expression lingered in his mind. As he drove home, he hoped this episode wouldn't haunt his sleep. He occasionally took a few deep breaths to calm himself.

By the time he pulled into his driveway, however, he was back to normal. Like the office, he could see that his house was dark. But that was not unusual for this time on a Friday night. As quietly as he could, he pulled into the garage, got out of his car and entered the house.

Though calm, the incident left him craving sugar. As there would be no victory cake the next day, he gave in to the urge.

Grabbing a spoon, he found an unopened half-gallon of ice cream in the freezer. Jonathan sat at the kitchen table and quietly opened the packaging. He then began scooping Moose Tracks into his mouth.

As he indulged, he heard the door to AJ's room open and his son walking toward the kitchen. While they were no longer the pitter-patter of young feet, the sound was familiar and comforting to Jonathan. He paused, spoon in hand, as AJ walked into the kitchen.

It was an unusual setting, and for a moment, awkward. With everything going on relative to Ari, they literally had not seen one another at home all week.

AJ spoke first. "Dad, I just wanted to say how sorry I am about Ari. I know he meant a lot to you, and … well, I feel bad."

"Thank you," Jonathan replied. At a loss for words, all he could add was, "That means a lot."

They just looked at one another, though it felt less awkward. Jonathan broke the silence. "AJ, can you do me a favor?"

"Sure," AJ responded, curious as to what the request might be.

"Grab a spoon and come help me with this," Jonathan said as he ladled out a healthy spoon of swirled ice cream. "That way, if this carton somehow disappears tonight, it won't be entirely on me." He let out a snicker as the spoon went into his mouth.

AJ complied, racing to the utensil drawer and grabbing a soup spoon for serious eating. Together they dug in, laughing about excavating veins of fudge and deposits of peanut butter cups.

At one point, Jonathan said, "Tomorrow … tomorrow, nothing. No work. Just watching football. Eat popcorn. Maybe grill out." He put a spoonful of ice cream in his mouth. Talking through it, he said, "Just us hanging out."

Through his own mouthful of ice cream, AJ murmured, "Sounds good."

Chapter 92

Saturday morning, AJ slept later than usual. The late-night ice cream had made his sleep restless. The house was quiet—quieter than usual, even for a Saturday.

He went to the kitchen. There, he found his mom reading a grocery-store tabloid as she sipped her coffee. AJ looked around. Then he listened. After a moment, he asked, "Where's Dad?"

She responded, "He had to leave town for work. He'll likely be back Monday afternoon in time for practice."

Before Sam could say another word, AJ blurted out, "Are you serious?" His voice was edged with betrayal.

"He wanted me to tell you sorry. But something urgent came up," Sam said, trying to explain.

AJ let out an exasperated sigh and shook his head in disbelief. "What could be so urgent that it came up in the last 12 hours?"

"Honey, I don't know. I'm not in the loop when it comes to his legal world," she said calmly. Sam tried to soften the moment. "He's really sorry, though."

AJ stormed off. As he did, he muttered, "Typical."

Sam knew far more than she let on, however.

At 4:45 a.m., Jonathan's phone sprang to life. Tank's mother, Melissa, was calling. Tommy had been arrested.

After the team returned to the high school, Tommy drove two hours north to North Baltimore, Ohio. He was going to spend the remainder of the weekend with his dad.

Shortly after arriving, his father instructed Tommy to take him to the beer-wine carryout before it closed. He'd been drinking and was running low. En route home, Tommy's father couldn't wait. He cracked open a beer and began drinking.

Tommy chided him, but his father told him to mind his own business and just drive. A heated argument ensued.

This led to erratic driving, which a Wood County deputy witnessed. The deputy pulled Tommy over and was going to only cite them for violating Ohio's open container law, which is a minor misdemeanor—a monetary fine with no incarceration.

But Tommy's father didn't know how to quit while he was ahead. He got belligerent with the deputy. He challenged the law, called it stupid, cursed at the officer repeatedly, and refused to provide identification. And when Tommy tried to provide his, he took it and threw it out the window.

The deputy had no choice but to take the pair into custody, elevating the charges to a fourth-degree misdemeanor. They were now facing more serious penalties, including up to 30 days in jail.

After he was processed, Tommy used his one call to wake his mother in the early morning hours. Melissa, in turn, called Jonathan—the only person she could think of.

Jonathan relayed the entire situation to Sam as he packed. Thinking it through, he knew he might be gone until Monday. He also mentioned his pledge to AJ.

"What should I tell him?" Sam asked.

"The truth, Sam. Just not the whole truth," Jonathan said as he zipped up a suit bag. "Tell him that I got called out of town for work. He doesn't need to know about Tommy. No one does. I don't want anyone to get a whiff of this. Certainly not that butthead—Sebastian's dad, whatever his name is. And Tommy doesn't need this embarrassment looming over him."

By 5:30 a.m., Jonathan was picking up Melissa. Together, they headed two hours north to the Wood County jail in Bowling Green, Ohio. As they drove, she did her own legal research. The phrase "up to 30 days in jail" sent her into a panic. Jonathan implored her to just relax.

When they arrived at the jail, Jonathan presented himself as Tommy's attorney. The arresting deputy was still agitated over what should have been nothing more than a fine. Unable to separate the father from the son, he insisted that Tommy stay in lockup until arraignment on Monday morning. Jonathan had to work against that, as well as the hysterics of Melissa.

By 11 a.m., emotions were tempered. Jonathan was able to get a supervising deputy to agree to release Tommy into his custody. There was, however, a stipulation: they would not leave Wood County until after they faced the judge on Monday. Jonathan agreed and signed various paperwork as attorney of record.

Within ten minutes, a buzzer sounded, and a big metal door opened. For now, Tommy was free. He hugged his mom and then turned to Jonathan.

"Oh, thank you," Tommy sobbed as he hugged his coach for the second time in a day. "I'm so sorry. I didn't do anything wrong." He took an oxygenating breath and continued, "Am I going to have to sit out a game?"

"Tommy, not if I can help it," Jonathan reassured.

Over a late breakfast, Jonathan asked them to just trust him. In so many words, he shared that he was going to work his network to help navigate the system.

They retrieved Tommy's car and checked into a Hampton Inn—Tommy and Melissa in one room, Jonathan in his own. Once settled, Jonathan started making calls. His first was to Joseph Thompson. He needed his help going to bat for Tommy if needed, and also for any insights or connections in the area.

Thompson pledged his support, "wherever; however." The board president indicated that he knew a judge in neighboring Hancock County. While that judge wouldn't be of immediate help, he could offer insight into the judge and prosecutors in Wood County.

From here, there would be lots of waiting. Jonathan did a little research to see what he could find on Wood County cases related to open containers and the implications of fourth-degree misdemeanors. There was little on the internet. He let out a heavy sigh.

He tried to tinker with legal work. He tried watching college football. Nothing could hold his attention. It made him feel guilty for not being at home, as he'd pledged.

He sent AJ a text that read, "I'm really sorry." After an hour, AJ responded with nothing but a thumbs-up emoji. Jonathan could sense teen passive-aggressiveness in it. He contemplated following up—but with what? Nothing came to mind. He decided to let it drop for now.

Coupled with guilt, being alone added to his misery. The past 24 hours had been an emotional whirlwind—Ari's services, the big win, Warren Scott. Now, sitting there, largely isolated, the thought of losing his friend and mentor still hurt. Jonathan hadn't really mourned. He'd been too busy. Now, with the solitude of the hotel, a feeling of sadness and depression seeped in. He just wanted to go home, to be around Sam and AJ. He knew he couldn't, though. The situation with Tank had to be kept quiet.

He fell asleep early and slept later than usual Sunday morning. While he still felt an emptiness, at least he was rested. And that allowed him to get a grip on his emotions. Focusing back on Tank's situation gave him a sense of purpose.

By midmorning, he heard back from Joseph Thompson. The Hancock County judge offered nothing substantive but strongly encouraged, "If this kid is really a good kid, then appear in court as such—and not show up looking like an unruly teen." So, Jonathan and Melissa took Tommy to get a haircut and a presentable outfit.

By Monday at 9 a.m., the trio were in court for arraignment. Fortunately, Tommy's case wasn't first. This gave Jonathan time to find one of the three assistant prosecutors. He wanted to explain the situation and propose a favorable resolution.

Thankfully, the young prosecutor was willing to listen. She was well aware of Tank's father and wasn't surprised to note that he was on the arraignment docket—again. The prosecutor remarked, "That guy is never in big trouble, but he continually seems to find little trouble." Because of this, she knew the sheriff's office tended to overreact when he was involved. She took one look at clean-cut, well-dressed Tommy Frank and understood what she needed to do.

At 9:45 a.m., Tommy Frank's case was called, and the assistant prosecutor stated, "Your honor, we recommend that there be a complete dismissal of the case involving Mr. Frank. He is a juvenile and was simply in the wrong place at the wrong time because he was on a court-ordered visitation with an accused we will be dealing with—yet again—later this morning. As Mr. Frank is a juvenile, we also urge that his name be expunged from our records."

Knowing this was just the start of another long Monday of adjudicating a weekend of alleged wrongdoing, the judge rapped her gavel and said, "So ordered."

With that, the prosecutor closed Tommy Frank's file and stacked it on a small but growing pile. At the same time, Jonathan put away the notes he'd prepared and led his fullback out of the bustling courtroom. In the courthouse hallway, Melissa caught up with them.

Confused, Tommy asked, "Coach, what's happening?"

"Nothing, Tommy," Jonathan quickly answered. Then he clarified, "It's as if this never happened. You are free to go."

"That's it?" Tommy was bewildered. "It took me longer to brush my teeth—and that's saying something."

Everyone chuckled at the levity. Melissa hugged them both.

As she did, Tommy's demeanor shifted. He asked, "Am I going to miss a game?"

"For what? The official record shows this never happened," Jonathan assured. "See you at practice. We've got to keep winning."

"Thank you, Coach," Tommy said.

"Melissa, get him back to school ASAP," Jonathan instructed. As they were about to depart, Jonathan caught their attention. "One other thing. Dr. Reese knows I'm here. Mr. Thompson from the school board, too. No one else does. It's best if we keep it that way."

Chapter 93

After Jonathan parted company with Melissa and Tank, he raced back to Columbus and directly to the Huntington Center. Along the two-hour drive, he checked in with Sam and a few clients. Mostly, he just drove—no radio, no podcasts. Just him and his thoughts of Ari.

There was a lingering sadness that Jonathan couldn't seem to shake. It didn't feel real. It was hard to believe he was gone. It was hard to imagine what life at Eisenberg & Anders would be like without him.

Jonathan, however, didn't have to wait long to get a glimpse of the firm post-Ari. The moment he got off the elevator, he ran into Stephenson. The young attorney was scurrying along, carrying an armload of files. His eyes were wide. His face expressed panic.

"He's back," Stephenson said with an exasperated tone.

"Who's back?" Jonathan asked, confused.

"That maniacal a-hole," Stephenson responded as he double-timed down the hall.

Jonathan wasn't surprised by Stephenson's response. He sensed that what he'd seen of Warren Scott on Friday night was a precursor to nothing good. He rolled his eyes and went to his office.

There, on his desk, was a note: *"We need to talk!"* Jonathan crumpled it and tossed the now-yellow paper ball into the trash. He didn't have the time—he'd already missed half the day. And even if he had the time, he didn't have the energy to deal with *that stupid moron*. He closed his door and set calls to go directly to voicemail. He was going to catch up on work and be at practice for the first time in a week.

Football practice had functioned without Jonathan. The moment he left, Norm called the team in and explained the situation. He said, "This is very sad news—certainly for Coach Reese, but a little bit for all of us. We can let this sadness take us down, or we can use it to drive us forward."

That was all the team needed. Every moment of every practice was focused on playing their best game—not because they were facing the region's top team, but because of their coach and the passing of his friend and mentor.

While the loss of Ari inspired intensity among the team, it evoked sympathy from Casey for AJ. Though he didn't intend to garner sympathy, when Casey offered it — "AJ, how are you holding up?" — he went with it.

It was just too easy to play along when all he had to do was be at his car when she arrived. After all, it was complicated trying to explain that his relationship with his father was somewhat estranged, and that he really didn't know Ari Eisenberg. Plus, the sympathy often came with a hug or other physical touch from Casey.

On the Monday following the win over Jonathan Alder, things were back to normal. Just like any other day, Jonathan and the other coaches raced to practice from their respective jobs. The players gathered on the practice field and carried on like teenage boys do.

That day, Tank was the focus of good-natured teasing for his haircut and for being "MIA" on Monday morning. The beefy former lineman just played along with a variety of outlandish stories—CIA missions and supermodel shoots.

And just like any other day, after his interaction with Casey, AJ hurried back inside to get geared up and ride out to practice with Shea on the ice-and-water-laden golf cart.

As AJ rolled into practice, he saw his dad for the first time since Friday night ice cream. It didn't resurrect any bitterness. He was used to his father being whisked off to work and not being around. Initially there was anger, but it was fleeting. Unreliability was just something he came to expect.

Jonathan, however, felt a sense of guilt seeing AJ for the first time. He knew that, in recent years, he had been absent from his son's life. He intended to do better but making that happen proved complicated. And there was nothing he could do in the moment. It was time to start practice.

He blew his whistle, signaling to players and coaches to gather and listen up. Coach Dad gave a short recap of the three previous games, declaring them as big challenges met. Then he previewed the final three games, describing them as winnable but emphasizing their importance for improvement heading into the playoffs. He then directed the team to break into their respective units—offense and defense—and head to the appropriate areas of the practice field.

AJ was now effectively a permanent fixture on defense, yet he stayed connected to the offense. He eavesdropped when he could. During idle moments, he'd watch the offense drill. Outside of practice, he'd observe—and at times participate in— conversations between Tank and Brady.

Using a combination of play hand signals, ASL gestures and text messaging, Tank and Brady discussed—and at times debated—the Mustang offense. AJ usually listened quietly. At times, however, he was drawn in to share an opinion or act as a tiebreaker in a good-natured dispute.

Shortly after the Utica comeback win, the trio became inseparable. But their conversations weren't limited to the Mustang offense. They talked about football in general and high school playoffs. They talked about school—assignments, projects, quizzes and tests. And they talked about online gaming.

Earlier on Monday, out of the blue, Brady added another discussion topic.

goin 2 this dance thing?

Years earlier, when Blacklick High was formed, one of the early decisions teachers and staff wrestled with was how to handle the equivalent of an annual homecoming. After weighing all the pros and cons they'd experienced at other schools, they decided to hold it the Saturday following the last regular-season football game.

As the timing was somewhat unique, so was the name— Autumn Stampede. It was cute. Perhaps a little trite. It stuck, however. As such, the planning committee of students and staff began promoting it with posters around the school.

To Brady, it was all part of a new experience. AJ and Tank, however, hardly noticed. They'd gone as freshmen, but since neither of them really dated, the dance wasn't on their radar. Tank quickly texted back a thumbs-down emoji. AJ simply shook his head.

Brady made a gesture that both AJ and Tank knew meant "come on." Then he texted:

go in w/ gf, lil help?

Tank and AJ read the same message on their respective phones. Then they looked at each other. AJ mouthed, "Who?" as Tank texted:

who gf

Brady rolled his eyes in playful exasperation. Then, through a volley of generic gestures, ASL words and text messages, he explained that—other than being deaf—he was normal. And that the Ohio School for the Deaf was the same. Boys and girls liked each other, and he'd had a girlfriend for a couple of years: Riley Bennett.

From there, AJ and Tank fired off a litany of questions about "RB," as they now called her. Brady answered some, gave "no comment" to a few, and even shared a photo. AJ and Tank's eyes went wide when they saw stunning Riley Bennett on Brady's phone.

AJ and Tank were totally entertained, carrying on like a couple of fifth graders. They had no idea about this side of Brady's life. Tank texted:

RB, WOW!

Then another thought came to Tank. Out of curiosity, he texted:

joyce ur 3rd wheel, lol

He wondered how it would work with two deaf people at a mainstream dance. He pictured 60-something Joyce interpreting every conversation. AJ and Brady laughed at the shared visual. Brady shook his head and quickly texted back:

no, kc

Then Brady steered the conversation back to its original purpose—encouraging AJ and Tank to attend the Stampede. Whether they had dates or not, it would be a chance to meet Riley.

Tank was noncommittal, communicating through body language: *We'll see.* More than that, he had no interest in lingering on the topic. He changed the subject, mentioning how he liked his new hairstyle.

AJ didn't commit either, but he quietly thought about it—especially the notion that Casey would be at the Autumn Stampede. He thought, *Maybe, just maybe, she'd need a date.*

Chapter 94

Coming off three solid wins, practice spirits were high, and execution was crisp. Though the remaining regular-season games looked favorable on paper, the team remained locked in on getting better each day. Their sights were set on the playoffs—and they envisioned a deep run, hopefully repeating as state champions.

Jonathan's first practice back with the team flew by. In an instant, he was back at home—enjoying dinner with Sam and a brief but tense exchange with AJ. Afterward, he set up at the kitchen table to get organized and reoriented with the electronic due diligence framework. With everything surrounding Ari's passing, he felt behind.

He devoted a couple of hours to firm work, but then felt a wave of exhaustion coming on. He decided to surrender to it and go to bed. His own bed. A place to finally get some real sleep.

It worked. Tuesday morning, he bolted out of bed and raced off to work—arriving before 7. As he lifted the security gate,

Jonathan knew he'd have time to work distraction-free. He got to his office and closed the door. While *that annoying excuse for a lawyer* had left another note demanding a meeting, Jonathan wasn't about to let that slow him down. He pitched it, as he had the first, and got busy.

The firm was coming to life outside his office—people walking by, talking, and phones ringing. He tuned it out.

Shortly before lunch, there was a light tap on the door. Jonathan was sure it wasn't *that little creep*, so he exclaimed, "Come in."

The door opened halfway, and Theresa, Ari's former assistant, slipped in holding a medium-sized, flat, rectangular box wrapped in last week's newspaper.

"I have something for you," Theresa said, speaking softly as she closed the door behind her and remained near it. Before Jonathan could respond, she continued, "I've been with Alison. Crying. Sorting through Ari's things. And more crying." She let out a nervous laugh. "But she asked me to give this to you."

"What is it?" Jonathan asked as he got up from his chair and approached her.

As he gave Ari's former assistant a light hug, she replied, "Jonathan, I don't know. This is how she gave it to me last night."

Without a word, Jonathan took the present. He walked back to his desk and set it down. Theresa joined him. They hovered over the gift in silence. Jonathan looked at her, gave an inquisitive glance, then turned back to the newspaper-wrapped box. He flipped it over and carefully opened it along the taped seams.

Once the newspaper was off, Theresa quickly folded it and put it aside. They again stared—now at a plain white box. After a moment, Jonathan reached under it and delicately broke the clear tape Alison had used to seal the lid. After taking a deep breath, he gently lifted the lid. A lump formed in his throat.

Inside, staring back at Jonathan, was Ari's Bexley High School number 53 jersey. The same one he'd worn at the Columbus Academy game. The same one he'd pledged to wear on the sidelines when Blacklick played in the state championship game.

On top of the jersey was a plain light blue envelope, on which Alison had written *Jonathan*. He picked it up and eased open the unsealed flap. He then removed the single piece of matching-colored stationery, folded in half.

Curious, Jonathan began to read Alison's handwritten note.

As he did, a single tear started to roll down his cheek.

Dear Jonathan,

I want you to have this. Ari would have wanted you to have it.

This jersey meant the world to him. It reminded him of a special time in his life—a time when he felt alive, connected, and full of purpose. And you seemed to mean the world to him, too.

Over the years, he talked about you often. He was always so intrigued by the kid from Toledo: Jonathan Reese—your ups, your downs, and all the hopes and dreams he carried for you.

When you started coaching, I don't think I've ever seen him more proud. Being on the sidelines with you—and finally beating Columbus Academy was a crowning moment for Ari. And that's saying something, for a man who had a lifetime full of great accomplishments.

So please, take this jersey. Hold onto it. Cherish it, just as Ari cherished having you in his life.

With love,
Alison

Jonathan set the note on the jersey. Tears streamed down his face. He bent forward, face in hands, and quietly whimpered. Theresa moved in and gave him a comforting embrace.

After a few minutes, Jonathan gathered himself, stood up straight, and wiped his eyes. Theresa gently rubbed his shoulders and offered some soothing words. Jonathan simply nodded to show he understood.

He then took a deep breath and carefully removed the jersey from the box. Theresa watched as he walked to his door and grabbed a spare wooden hanger perched on the coat hook.

Jonathan placed the jersey on the hanger. He didn't return it to the hook, however. He walked back to his desk and hung it from the top of the bookshelf behind his chair. It was positioned so that sunlight from the windows softly illuminated it. More importantly, it was the first thing someone would see upon entering Jonathan's office.

He stepped back, looked at the jersey, and nodded once, indicating it was perfectly positioned. Theresa looked on and quietly affirmed Jonathan's choice with a single word.

"Beautiful."

As they admired Ari's Bexley 53 jersey, there was a loud, obnoxious knock at the door.

"Reese? Are you in there?" Warren Scott was looking to have a word with Jonathan.

Theresa signaled she'd handle it. She quickly headed toward the door, intending to run interference for Jonathan. She opened it—but only wide enough to let herself out—and then quickly closed it behind her.

"Warren! Yes, he's in there," Theresa said firmly. "But he's not available. Not today, Warren." She continued, her tone emphatic. "We're all still hurting… still mourning. I don't know what's on your mind, but whatever it is, it can wait. Tomorrow is too soon. Maybe next week. Give all of us some peace."

Warren Scott was stunned into silence. Worse, he was embarrassed as others watched Ari's former assistant dress him down. While Theresa was technically subordinate to him and an employee of Eisenberg & Anders, Warren didn't dare cross her. Her twin was the executive assistant to Bobby O, giving her indirect influence with the firm's biggest client.

He turned and walked away, looking down and muttering nonsense under his breath.

Chapter 95

Jonathan sensed that he would be somewhat insulated from *that Napoleonic troll* for the rest of the week—thanks, in part, to Theresa's intervention. This allowed him to lean into work: reviewing documents, drafting language, returning calls, delegating, organizing, and focusing on the electronic due diligence framework.

With the passing of Ari, he'd lost momentum on the framework, but he knew that with a little uninterrupted time, he'd quickly get back on track. He was confident that within a week it would be complete, and he'd be able to help Stephenson a world away—or whoever was there.

Just before 5 p.m., he gathered up work for home, took one last look at Ari's jersey, and headed out to practice.

AJ couldn't shake the thought of Casey being at the Autumn Stampede. Surely, she'd rather be with someone than not. But he wasn't confident enough to talk to her about it. He pondered what to say, how to bring it up, how to ask. He was treading on new ground. Dating was not his thing.

And he really didn't have anyone to ask. His dad? No way. His mom? Maybe—but he wasn't ready for that conversation. Brady? Nay—the communication challenge was too much.

Tank? Nope. He was equally, inept around girls—maybe more. Shea? Negative. She'd be clueless about dating.

This consumed AJ's thoughts. At practice throughout the week, he kept stealing glances at Casey. She'd catch him, smile, scrunch her nose, or wink. He was smitten—and terrified. Why was he so afraid to just ask, he wondered. What more assurance did he need?

On Friday, Casey seemed to help the situation. As the team was hosting Lakewood, the after-school schedule was slightly different. Their not-so-coincidental meetups at her car happened a little later than usual. Nevertheless, they still engaged in small talk.

While AJ wanted to somehow segue into a conversation about the Autumn Stampede, at the same time he avoided anything that might lead there. He knew he was being completely counterintuitive. It made no sense, but in his mind, it protected his ego.

As they were preparing to separate, Casey came out with, "Not now, but maybe Monday, can we talk about this autumn dance?"

The words caught him off guard. He could feel his heart race. A lump formed in his throat. He hardly knew what to say. All he could muster was, "Yeah. Sure."

Chapter 96

The Lakewood football team came into Blacklick thinking they could pull off an upset. Despite their 3-4 record, the Lancers hoped to catch the Mustangs off guard after three big wins. And that felt like a real possibility on the opening possession, as Lakewood easily drove the length of the field in 10 plays to go ahead 7-0. But that was the high point for the visitors.

The Mustangs received the kickoff, and Brady Troy got to work. Four plays—or four clap-claps—later, they'd tied the game. The response lit a fire under the defense, which—still wearing messages of "ARI" and "53" under their eyes—became immovable. The stout unit forced the Lancers to punt the ball back, allowing the Mustang offense to score again.

The Mustangs scored on two more drives before halftime, and twice more in the first five minutes of the third quarter. With the game at 42-7, coaches on both sides conceded that the contest was effectively over. This led to a quarter and a half of back-and-forth, sloppy play by second and third stringers. Each team added a field goal to officially close out the game—45-10.

The Lancers' upset hopes never came close to materializing. They had a 35-minute drive back to Hebron, Ohio, to think about the 35-point drubbing they'd just suffered.

The Mustangs' reaction was subdued by comparison. They were happy with the win, but they didn't celebrate. They knew they were going to win—it was only a question of how much. Coach Dad addressed the team in a very businesslike manner. Then the players quickly showered, changed and moved on with a typical Friday night.

The next day, Jonathan was up early and off to the office. While he felt caught up, in big-firm life there was always a continual flow of hours to bill. After wrestling with the reliably unreliable security gate, he got busy.

Moreover, Jonathan wanted to share with Stephenson where he was on the framework. And Saturday morning—when firm activity was a tad less chaotic—was the best time to do this. He and his younger colleague tested the system from one corner office to another as if they were operating a world apart. The electronic system was almost done. It just needed a few more tweaks.

Firm activity was the same, but the vibe had shifted. Ari and his jubilant aura were missing. There was no celebratory cake to have fellowship around. No small talk about weekend youth sports, upcoming college football games, or who was cooking what for their big Sunday meal.

But it wasn't just that the joyful feeling was gone—it had been replaced by a dark shadow, one cast by Warren Scott. His existence seemed to command a cold, transactional tone. His presence made smiles disappear and all nonessential conversation stop. It was as if personal lives and individual personalities were forbidden. People continually looked over their shoulders for *that doofus*, always ready to feign busyness.

Jonathan crossed paths with *that troll* a time or two each day since Theresa had commanded him to stand down. Each time, he could sense *that spineless leech* was dying to lash out. And Jonathan took great pleasure in knowing it gnawed at *that ignoramus*.

But Jonathan also knew he couldn't avoid *that cretin* forever. Albeit only a junior partner, Warren was still a partner. As such, he'd have a say in whether Jonathan would reach that status.

Moreover, *that knave* had quickly connived the senior partners into allowing him to fill Ari's leadership and administrative void. *That charlatan* made the case that—at least for now—it would be less disruptive to firm operations. And the senior partners were all too willing to go along. Not only were they content simply working with clients, but they also felt this would appease *that crooked S.O.B.*, who seemed to have dirt on a few of them.

So, Jonathan knew that conversations and confrontations were looming—but not today. Shortly before noon, he'd accumulated enough billable hours and Saturday facetime. He packed up and headed home to be a dad, a husband, and a college football fan.

Just before Jonathan started to pack up, AJ was rolling out of bed. His alter ego — A2J9R — had been up until the early morning hours gaming online with the likes of T-Frank, JSevans, and SpartyBT10.

As AJ attacked and defended against zombie hordes, his mind replayed his final exchange with Casey. And that likely continued while he slept. The ruminating certainly started in earnest the moment he woke up.

AJ's mind churned: *Not now, but maybe Monday, can we talk about this autumn dance? Why not now? Why wait until Monday? What's wrong with talking over the weekend? What does maybe mean? And would it be Monday? And if not Monday, then when? And what about the Stampede? Why leave me wondering?*

AJ continued to pore over that interaction as he went downstairs. *We could've talked after the game. We could've talked during it—I was on the sidelines for much of the second half.*

It was all very mentally exhausting. He grabbed a foil pack of Pop-Tarts and headed back to his room to be a student, a college football fan, and A2J9R—and not necessarily in that order.

Chapter 97

Jonathan did very little once he left the office, other than doze off on the couch and eat meals with Sam and AJ. He and Sam had a quick call with Johnny, as they usually did on Sundays. And Kelly called in with a more comprehensive rundown of events since she'd spoken with Sam the day before. But he did essentially nothing related to work. He wondered if that was what made the weekend seem to fly by.

Whatever the reason, it felt like in no time he was back at Eisenberg & Anders early on Monday morning. He wasn't the first, however. The gate was fully up.

As he walked toward his office, he could see that the light was on. Curious, he continued to approach and poked his head around the door frame to look in.

Sitting at his desk was Stephenson, in a hooded sweatshirt, feverishly writing a note by hand.

"What are you doing?"

Stephenson's head shot up. His eyes went wide. He inhaled as he said, "You startled me."

Jonathan laughed, then repeated his question. "What are you doing? Did you get fired?" He laughed again to indicate he wasn't serious.

"Don't even joke about that, Jonathan. This firm has a lunatic at the helm. Anything is possible … and I need this job." Stephenson then resumed focus on the note.

"Okay," Jonathan said more seriously, "but what are you doing?"

Stephenson stopped writing and took another deep breath before saying, "I need help. They're inducing my wife this morning. She's been up all weekend with false contractions, and we've been in and out of the hospital. First, she's in labor, then not. So, they just decided to induce labor at 10 a.m."

"That's great!" Jonathan fired out with genuine enthusiasm. Then he laughed again. "So, what are you doing here? Go home."

"I will, but I need help, Jonathan." Stephenson looked at him, clearly desperate. "I need you to cover for me at Emerald Medical today. There are a series of due diligence planning meetings we need to attend."

"Okay, so—" Jonathan was perplexed and searched for words. "Why didn't you call me? Email? Text?"

"Jonathan?" Stephenson let out an exasperated sigh. "This all came about late last night, and I'm just not thinking straight. I needed to come in to grab some work, and I figured I could just write you a note."

"Stephenson! Stop." Jonathan got the younger associate's attention and continued in a reassuring tone. "I'll cover the Emerald Medical thing today—and whatever else." He motioned for Stephenson to get up. "Leave all your work here. We'll get it done. We might text you with questions. Come on." He gestured toward the door. "I can handle the meetings at Emerald. If I need you, I'll text. But your whole focus today needs to be your wife."

Though still uncertain, Stephenson got up and followed his older colleague. He turned out the lights, and they headed toward the elevators, leaving the gate up. They rode down together, talking through a couple of details regarding the Emerald Medical meetings.

As they departed toward their respective cars, Jonathan smiled and said, "Go have a baby. Make it two—they're small, and they travel in pairs. Congratulations."

Jonathan got to his car and just sat. He had responsibilities of his own—and now he'd taken on Stephenson's, too. He paused for a moment. Before starting the car, he sent out a flurry of texts to his team, to Theresa, and to anyone who needed to be in the loop or working on related firm obligations. After about 20 minutes, he started the car, put it in gear, and headed off to Emerald Medical for the better part of the day.

AJ had ruminated all weekend on Casey's Friday afternoon words—*Not now, but maybe Monday, can we talk about this autumn dance?* As he got ready for school on Monday, he wondered when that conversation might happen. Or if it even would—weekends had a way of changing things.

He didn't have to wait long. Just before he started his car to head to school, his phone lit up with a text from Casey:

can we talk later

AJ felt euphoria rush through his body. He responded immediately with a thumbs-up emoji. But that wasn't the end of it. Casey sent another text:

important! need BIG favor

His heart pounded in his chest—not from exertion, but from sheer elation. He quickly fired back:

got u dont worry

Seconds later, a single heart emoji came through. He stared at it, then re-read the entire exchange. Then again. He pumped his fist, started the car, and drove to school.

When Jonathan arrived at Emerald Medical, he explained why he was filling in for Stephenson, and the security guard quickly produced a visitor badge for him. He was then ushered to a large conference room to meet with the company's accounting and in-house legal team.

There, Jonathan ran through the entire plan for Eisenberg & Anders to support the Emerald Medical acquisition due diligence. He was met with looks of astonishment—and then laughter. Lisa Kaye, the legal team lead, verbalized it: "You'll be sending a guy to the Far East who has a set of twins ... what ... a few weeks, a month old? You guys are cutthroat."

"Yeah," Jonathan replied, feeling a twinge of guilt. He knew it was his coaching responsibilities that were driving the plan. "It wasn't my decision." He paused, then added, "But we've been working hard on some technology that will allow us to support Stephenson from the firm's office in Columbus."

The group looked on with curiosity, and Jonathan continued. "On our end, it'll require some very early mornings and some late nights, but we're confident we can provide the same level of service."

Lisa seemed intrigued. She asked a litany of questions, and Jonathan answered the best he could. Toward the end of the informal Q&A, he qualified his presentation. "I wish I'd known I would be here—I could have set up a demonstration."

Lisa responded, "No, no, that's okay. We trust you, Jonathan. You've been around us for a long time. My question is—if this thing, this technology, works as you say, why are we sending anyone from your firm?" She looked around the room, clearly posing the question to everyone.

She was met with a chorus of uncertain shrugs. No one had an immediate answer. Jonathan seemed to speak for the group when he said, "I don't know. It's above my pay grade."

Collectively, they determined that the question needed to be addressed by higher-ups at Emerald Medical, Eisenberg & Anders, and the company's auditors. The conversation then shifted back to substantive matters on the agenda.

AJ hadn't told anyone about his upcoming conversation with Casey—or how he felt about her. All of it just made him feel vulnerable in so many ways. As a result, no one knew of his internal anguish as he quietly endured the slow passage of time. He drifted through the day—classes, lunch, even study table— barely registering any of it. The waiting was excruciating.

Eventually, time passed, and AJ was at his car, fiddling in his trunk as if there were something he needed to tend to. Then, like any other day, Casey arrived—backing into the spot next to his.

When she got out, AJ could see a visible uneasiness in her. She offered a nervous smile.

"AJ, thanks for meeting me." She let out a deep breath. "I'm so nervous. I can't believe how nervous I am."

"Relax, Casey," AJ said in a calm, reassuring voice. "Whatever you need, I'm here for you. I'll come through. I promise."

"Oh, thank you, AJ. That's very sweet of you," Casey responded, relaxing a bit.

"No problem, Casey. Whatever. Just ask." AJ was brimming with confidence.

Then Casey said it. "AJ, would you ask Shea to the Autumn Stampede?"

Immediately, AJ's eyes went wide. He heard what she said—but he wasn't expecting it. His mind struggled to process. He didn't know how to respond. He'd pledged to help Casey, but what she asked wasn't what he had in mind. He was embarrassed. He was hurt. He felt dizzy, as if the blood had drained from his head.

Weeks earlier, as Casey and Shea worked to simplify the Mustang offense, they struck up a friendship. Casey had become the female role model Shea never had—and in many ways, needed. They talked about all kinds of things during that first evening, and in the many others that followed—over dinner, while watching *The Bachelor*, or just hanging out.

Through those encounters, the student trainer began to open up to her first real female friend. Casey asked big-sister-type questions. And through that, Shea revealed her feelings toward AJ. Casey had pledged to help bring them together.

But now, as she waited for AJ's answer—confidently hoping her matchmaking had worked—she saw the confused, pained look on his face. She quickly realized she'd misread the situation. She had unintentionally misled him. AJ had feelings for her. And that realization made her feel awful.

"Oh, AJ," she said, struggling to find the right words. She wanted to hug him, but she knew that might only make it worse. "I'm so sorry. I don't know what to say."

She searched for more words, as AJ looked down, his face flushed with embarrassment.

"I'm sorry. I like you. I do. And if I were in high school, I wouldn't let you out of my sight. You're awesome. But I'm not in high school, AJ. And I don't say that to put you down. We're just at different stages in life right now."

AJ said nothing. He just stared at the ground, thinking, *how foolish could I have been?*

"AJ, you don't have to ask her. I just thought—" Casey paused. "You're really nice. And she's really nice. And ... well ... AJ!"

She stopped talking, waiting for him to look up. "You just need to know one thing: Shea really likes you. She really, really does. She thinks you're smart, funny ..."

Casey was about to continue, but AJ raised his hand to stop her mid-sentence. She went quiet, braced herself, and waited. She didn't have to wait long.

AJ looked her in the eye and said, "I'll do it."

He wasn't defiant. He wasn't angry. He was simply committed—intentional with his words.

"I'll ask her. I'll ask Shea to the Autumn Stampede."

"AJ, you don't have to," Casey replied gently.

"I know," he said. "I know. But I said I'd help you, and I will."

Casey searched for the right words. "AJ, you don't have to. You really don't. But if you do ... AJ Reese, if you do ... I promise you—it will be a great evening. I promise you that."

Chapter 98

Like anybody, AJ Reese had his own temperament when it came to the uncomfortable things he faced. When eating, he would simply devour what he liked least—usually vegetables.

When helping around the house, he'd tackle the nasty job of scrubbing the toilet first. And when he had to remove a bandage, he'd just rip it off.

So, as soon as he arrived in the training room to help Shea, he came out with it.

"Would you go to the Autumn Stampede with me? You know, like a date?"

Shea, though hopeful, was taken off guard. They'd talked, worked on projects, and been connected through football. And while she'd wished for this, with each passing day she'd stopped believing Casey could actually make it happen—but she did.

Coached by Casey, she replied, "Yes! Of course! I'd love to."

She gave him a hug. He reciprocated in a half-hearted fashion, using the excuse that he didn't want to get her dirty from his soiled practice uniform. Then they rode out to practice together like any other day—except this time, Shea was driving with a smile from ear to ear, and AJ was a dazed and confused passenger.

Shea dropped AJ off with the team and rode off to tend to her student trainer duties. However, as soon as Coach Dad sent the team off on their warmup laps, she caught up with Casey. In a giddy fashion, she shared the news.

During practice, AJ tried to stay locked into football. He focused on defensive adjustments and drills. He listened in on the offense whenever he had the chance. Football made sense. Everything else didn't.

There was a tinge of feeling duped. There was acknowledgment of his own delusion and stupidity. And it all compounded into an internal cringe.

While AJ and Casey usually made eye contact during practice, now he avoided it. This created a tension they both felt. AJ was sick with confusion and didn't want to be reminded of why. Casey felt horrible. She wanted to make amends. But there were no easy answers as to how.

As practice ended and players were walking off, Casey called out, "Hey, AJ."

Not wanting to be mean-spirited, he stopped, looked back, and acknowledged her.

She pointed at him, made two fists, and knocked her right fist against the back of her left.

AJ gave her an uncomfortable smile and shrugged. He still didn't know what she meant.

Casey smiled and shouted, "You figure it out."

He then casually turned and continued walking away.

Chapter 99

When AJ arrived home, his dad was already there. Seated at the table, Jonathan and Sam were working on half of a pizza, intending the second half for their son. AJ politely said, "I'm really not hungry." He then went directly to his room without another word.

Closing his door, Sam gave Jonathan a look as if to ask, *what happened at practice?* Jonathan simply shrugged and made a facial gesture as if to respond, *I don't know.* They then continued with the conversation they'd been having.

After dinner, Jonathan got a few work things done and then went to bed. Sam was already asleep, though she had to get up to work through the night at the emergency room. When he got up the next morning, Jonathan went about his day — working out, getting showered and dressed, and then heading to the office.

When Jonathan arrived at Eisenberg & Anders, he again was not the first — the gate was up. As he walked toward his office, again his light was on.

As he approached, he spoke aloud, "Stephenson, what are you doing here now? You should be home with your wife and twins."

When he entered his office, Jonathan didn't find Stephenson, however. Rather, sitting at his desk was Warren Scott. And seated in the other two office chairs were two senior partners.

"Jonathan. Close the door. We need to talk," Warren calmly said.

Jonathan complied without a word. He could feel his heart racing. He'd never experienced anything like this in his professional life.

Warren continued in a businesslike fashion, "Did you make a court appearance last Monday in Wood County?"

"I did," Jonathan quickly replied.

"Why? Who?" Warren fired back.

"Just a *pro bono* matter that doesn't involve the firm at all," Jonathan calmly said.

Warren slammed his hand on the desk. "Damn it, Reese. You're going to tell us what this is all about."

"Really? It was just a simple matter. I was asked to make an appearance, representing one of my players. There was nothing to it. It was promptly dismissed." Jonathan remained calm.

"Players? As in football players?" Warren asked. "Is that the same player or a different one from this?" The junior partner held up a copy of the lawsuit Sebastian's father had filed weeks earlier.

"No, Warren. That's a different matter." Jonathan paused to look at the two senior partners, hoping for one of them to become the adult in the room, as Ari would have. "We already talked about that — me, you and Ari. Remember? We have an intern dealing with it. Remember?"

"Why are we wasting valuable intern time on this, Jonathan?" Warren fired back. "We could be using intern time to make money. You know — money? The stuff that pays for things around here, including your salary."

"Yes, I understand," Jonathan responded. "But it makes less sense for me to work on it at my rate."

"Are you arguing with me, Jonathan?" Warren slammed his hand on the desk again and stood up. His face was beet red. "What makes no sense is you leaving here every day at 5 to coach football, when you could put in two or three more hours for the firm."

The senior partners remained seated; their lips pursed.

"Jonathan, there is a theme running through all of this." Warren paused, then raised his voice for effect. "Football!" He paused again, then continued. "Your hours are down because of football. We're getting sued because of football. You're chasing off to places to make appearances for juveniles because of football." Warren then slammed his hand on the desk three times as he shouted, "Football, football, football."

Jonathan said nothing, though he worked through responses in his mind.

Then Warren stood tall, pointed his finger at Jonathan and said, "Enough."

"What do you mean, Warren?" Jonathan calmly asked.

"No more coaching. We're in agreement on this." Warren motioned to the two senior partners for a quick nod, though neither did so with conviction.

"Warren, haven't we been through all of this? Back in August, Ari gave his blessing. Actually, he wanted me to coach as part of my community involvement." Jonathan remained calm, though he could feel sweat rolling down his back.

Warren responded, "Ari's not here anymore. We need to move on from him and his decisions. And to be honest, I had a few private conversations with him, and he was having second thoughts about you coaching anyway."

"Warren, I don't believe that," Jonathan said.

Warren got an angry look and glared at Jonathan. "Are you calling me a liar?"

"No, Warren," Jonathan fired back. "I just don't believe that Ari had any second thoughts. You can connect the dots from my opinion to your statement however you'd like."

"Whatever, Jonathan." Warren got back to the subject at hand. "The fact remains, however: Your coaching days are over. We need you to go to the Far East in a few weeks."

"Wait! Isn't Stephenson going?" Jonathan was confused.

Warren raised his voice again. "No, Jonathan. Stephenson is not going to work out for us. He's going to be too distracted with his family situation. I can't believe you ever suggested him."

"Warren, I never …" Jonathan began to protest. "Never mind. I'm not sure anyone needs to travel to another hemisphere for this, to be honest. Or anywhere."

"What do you mean?" Warren was perplexed, caught off guard by Jonathan's comment.

Jonathan boldly spoke. "Warren, we've been working on an electronic interface that could minimize — maybe eliminate — our need to travel around to conduct due diligence."

"Are you kidding me?" Warren protested. "We make a lot of money chasing our young attorneys around conducting due diligence. Why would we want to undertake anything that would undermine that?"

"Maybe to be better stewards of our clients' money? Maybe so we don't burn out young attorneys?" Jonathan paused to let his rhetorical questions sink in. "The technology is there. We just need to use it. Ari would have been all about this."

"Whatever, Jonathan. Again, Ari is no longer here," Warren said. "The bottom line is that your coaching days are done if you want to continue working at Eisenberg & Anders — and maybe, just maybe, one day make partner."

Chapter 100

After AJ went to his room, he just sat and stared. He was confused and wounded. He questioned his own judgment and kept thinking: *How did this happen? How do I explain it to others?*

He didn't want to communicate with anyone. He turned the notifications on his phone off and put it away. He muddled through homework and went to bed without gaming — unusual for him. Despite this, his tormented thoughts kept him up.

Eventually, however, he dozed off and slept well, oversleeping a bit. But AJ woke up refreshed. For a moment, he was carefree. Then all the mental anguish came rushing back. He was not looking forward to school, but he was going to go. He had to go.

He got out of bed and ventured out of his room. His dad was already gone, and his mother was not home from work yet. Being somewhat late, he quickly showered and got dressed. As he was racing off to his car, he felt some hunger pangs, so he grabbed a couple of slices of leftover pizza.

He started his car and then turned the notifications on his phone back on. A flurry of beeps and dings sounded. While he might not have wanted to communicate with others, others were hopeful of communicating with him. He didn't want to look. He took a bite of pizza and drove to school.

Out of habit, he headed toward his usual parking spot. Before he got there, however, he stopped. He contemplated changing his routine — where he parked, where he'd enter the school, how he would go about his day.

While he was still confused and emotionally bruised, he reminded himself that no one knew about the embarrassment he felt. Nor did they need to. And no one needed to know what led to him asking Shea to the Stampede. The fact was that he did.

He needed to conduct himself as normally as possible, even if it didn't match how he felt. With that, he parked in the same space, backed in, and walked into school through the door he always used.

As AJ started down the hallway, he felt as if all eyes were on him, and students whispered to one another about what he'd done. It was hard to act normally as his face felt flushed and his ears burned. He walked deliberately; eyes fixed straight ahead.

As AJ neared his locker, Brady greeted him with a big, friendly smile. The team's quarterback put his arm around First Friend and patted him on the chest in a playful, friendly manner. It helped knowing a familiar face would be at the Stampede.

Through an unsure smile and a shoulder shrug, AJ communicated back, *Yeah, I'm going.* He was not comfortable at all. And he didn't know what to say, which was fine as there was no one to hear anyway.

That changed, however, when Tank came walking up. But the beefy fullback verbalized nothing. Rather, his facial expressions said everything. He pursed his lips and rolled his eyes slowly from left to right as if to say, *I don't understand.* He just stood there. There was a tension in the silence.

Brady motioned that he had something to do and walked away. The moment he did, AJ couldn't help but say to Tank, "What?"

"What do you mean, what?" Tank responded. "You're the one with something to say."

AJ shrugged his shoulders. Yes, he had lots to say, but he wasn't going to say a thing.

"I don't get it," Tank broke the silence. "Of all the people, AJ."

"Don't say it," AJ quietly protested.

"I know. I won't, but ..." Tank said, then went silent. He looked at his friend and teammate, whose face was expressionless. "But I still don't get it."

"Tank, there's nothing to get," AJ calmly responded. There was no conviction in his voice. "It's just someone asking someone else out. It happens all the time."

"I know, but," Tank searched for words, "but it's you — Mr. Everything — asking her — Ms. ..." He stopped as AJ glared at him. "I know. I know. I know."

AJ grabbed what he needed from his locker as Tank just stood there. All he could respond with was, "Well."

"AJ, this school is going to be buzzing over this," Tank said.

"I feel that it already is," AJ responded.

"Do you know what the worst part is?" Tank asked, almost rhetorically. AJ gave him a curious look, as if he didn't know the answer. "Now I feel like I need to find a date too. If you're going and Brady's going, I guess I will too."

AJ let out a little chuckle and a genuine smile, then said, "The school will be buzzing over that too."

Chapter 101

Shortly after AJ left for school, Sam arrived home. Working nights still didn't feel normal. But she appreciated at least one perk: guilt-free sleep midmorning. There was something comforting about sleeping when the house was empty and quiet.

She needed time for the chaos of the emergency room to leave her system. A cup of chamomile tea tended to do the trick. Within an hour, she was in loose-fitting pajamas and in bed. In mere minutes, she started to drift off to sleep.

Before she could, however, Sam was startled by a commotion downstairs.

As her heart raced, she put on her robe and slippers. She stepped to the top of the stairs and called down; her voice unsteady. "Hello." She had no idea what she might hear back.

"It's just me," Jonathan called back almost immediately.

"What are you doing home?" Sam asked as she hurried down the stairs. Her anxiety was replaced with genuine confusion.

Jonathan didn't respond, focused on the box in front of him. When she caught up with her husband, he was engrossed in removing a new laptop from its packaging.

After a minute, Jonathan looked up and started with, "Well …"

Standing in his office, surrounded by Eisenberg & Anders leadership, the words "your coaching days are done if you want to continue working" didn't sit well with Jonathan. He knew if he allowed Warren Scott to have this moment, it would lead to more moments like this. It was just how *that maniacal little imp* operated.

In a defiant tone, Jonathan announced, "I'm not going to stop coaching." Ari's jersey, behind where Warren was sitting, reminded him that Ari would have wanted him to take this stand. And Jonathan believed the senior partners sitting around would step in and take control, the way Ari once would. But Jonathan was wrong.

"If that's your decision, so be it," Warren said as he worked the intercom on Jonathan's phone. Without another word, he barked out, "Security, please."

Within seconds, two unarmed security guards appeared at the door. Jonathan stood, stunned. One security guard calmly asked Jonathan to come with them. Together, they escorted him to his car. There, they collected his office credentials and parking pass.

In the office, word of Jonathan Reese's dismissal spread almost as fast as news of Ari's passing. This news, however, evoked fear in some and anger in others.

As Warren walked back toward Ari's office, where he was now quasi-permanently operating, Theresa followed him, her steps quick and full of fury.

"Shame. Shame on you, Warren Scott. How could you?"

Warren just walked, completely ignoring Ari's former assistant. When he got to Ari's office, he turned, looked at Theresa, and closed the door in her face. He was in control — and answered to no one.

"So, I lost my job. Or I quit. Or I don't know." He continued to work.

Sam snapped as Jonathan finished speaking, "That %&$#!"

Jonathan looked up, mildly surprised. "That's a new one." He stood up and added, "Hon, I don't know what to say. My mind is numb."

"But all that time invested in becoming partner," Sam said, her voice laced with confusion.

"I know, Sam. If I really think about it, I'll want to cry. But I'm not sure Eisenberg & Anders is the place to be anymore," Jonathan said.

"But you could help right that ship, couldn't you?" Sam asked.

"I could. Absolutely, that could happen in time," Jonathan said. "But at what cost? Partner, associate, admin — it's all just a job. Being here," he said, pointing downward, "being a husband, a father … and even coaching — that's life. That's what matters."

He paused for a moment, then motioned toward the high school. "I'm not letting that team down." He made a circular motion with his hands. "And I'm not letting this team down."

Jonathan walked over to Sam and gave her a hug. "What's the point? We work to live. We shouldn't live to work."

He pulled her close. Sam said nothing.

"Sam, we're not hurting for money. And if things get bad, you can get a second job." He chuckled.

Sam pushed away and playfully hit him on the chest with the back of her hand.

"Seriously, Sam, it's going to be fine," Jonathan said. "I was an attorney in private practice before. I can do it again. Everything is going to work out."

Chapter 102

Sam went back to bed. She was exhausted — and there was nothing she could do at the moment anyway. In the ER, crises are short-term and often life-or-death. Jonathan's crisis, while unsettling, wasn't that. And its solution would take time. Building a law practice wouldn't happen overnight.

Jonathan knew this. His impatient side wanted clients now; his rational self understood he had to get situated first. Still, as he worked to set up his new laptop, his mind spun with the question: *Who can I network through to find clients?*

It wouldn't be easy. For years, he'd focused almost entirely on one client — Emerald Medical — which needed a powerhouse firm like Eisenberg & Anders to manage its broad legal needs. The same was true of the other half-dozen clients he'd brought in. They chose the firm, not Jonathan Reese.

Finding clients on his own would be tough — but not impossible.

There were upsides to his new reality. No more rushing to make football practice. No last-minute client calls or workplace distractions. No traffic jams leaving downtown Columbus. His commute to Blacklick High was barely two miles. And now, he had time to focus on the team.

AJ was completely distracted. He felt as if everyone was looking at him and talking about him. And whenever someone talked to him, the topic of the Stampede and Shea would eventually be the focal point. In those moments, he tried to change the subject in a less-than-obvious way. It was mentally exhausting, and he could not wait to get to practice.

Nevertheless, AJ stuck to his routine, even though at times he felt compelled to do otherwise. He moved between classes as usual, sat at the same table at lunch, and tried to act normally when he encountered Shea.

He didn't want things with her to feel awkward. They were friends. They were going to a dance together. It was no big deal.

At least, that's what he told himself. Outwardly, he kept going through the motions. But inside, he couldn't ignore the reality — there was more going on than he wanted to admit. And that truth felt a little humiliating.

Despite his efforts to keep everything feeling normal, parts of his world weren't cooperating. One in particular was Shea. She looked at him differently. She smiled at him differently — more often, and in a friendlier way. AJ tried to match her energy, but it felt unnatural. He didn't want to be misleading.

The same awkwardness colored his daily encounter with Casey. He wanted that interaction to feel routine, too. Doing otherwise would only reveal how confused he was. More than anything, he wanted it all to seem like no big deal.

Their conversation was pleasant, though noticeably cooler. Casey didn't want to lead AJ on any more than she already had. And AJ didn't want to show how torn up he felt inside. So, their exchange was shorter than usual and steered clear of Shea, the Stampede, or anything related.

It was mentally exhausting. He couldn't wait to get to practice, vowing to help Shea with the water and ride out with her.

Practice was an oasis of normalcy for both AJ and Jonathan. The team was riding a seven-game winning streak, and barring a complete collapse, they were on track to finish the season nine and one. While the focus needed to stay on the next game, it was hard not to talk about playoff seedings and matchups.

By this point in the season, practices tended to run shorter — and felt a lot faster than the dog days of August and September. In no time, AJ and Jonathan were home, having dinner with Sam.

AJ didn't talk about the situation surrounding the Stampede. Jonathan didn't mention no longer working at Eisenberg & Anders. These were two seismic shifts in their lives, yet all that seemed to matter was who got what Chinese food from Mr. Wok's and how good it tasted.

The surface-level normalcy carried into the next day. Jonathan vowed to stick to his routine. He was up early, worked out, and left the house — even though he had nowhere specific to go. He ended up at McDonald's, sipping coffee and mentally brainstorming who he could reach out to for potential legal work.

After a few hours, he'd return home. AJ was at school. Sam was home, but asleep. Jonathan would sit down and begin emailing contacts, letting them know he was available for legal work — anything. Somehow, having no work at all was more stressful than being overwhelmed by it. Becoming busy again would take time.

Thank God for football, both AJ and Jonathan separately rationalized. For a few brief hours on Wednesday and Thursday, life felt relatively carefree. And on Friday, that feeling was extended as the team traveled to Bloom-Carroll High School for a game.

The Bulldogs didn't put up much of a fight. Brady clap-clapped the offense methodically down the field, scoring 35 points. AJ led the defense in shutting out the home team. Everyone pledged to continue honoring Ari with eye black patches.

On Saturday morning, Jonathan was up and at it. He stayed home and enjoyed a mug of home-brewed coffee. He felt the need to keep working. While waiting for responses to his outreach, he kept busy creating forms and procedures and catching up on aspects of the law he hadn't touched in years.

Around 9 a.m., there was an odd but quiet knock on the front door.

No doorbell, AJ thought as he went to see who it was.

Standing on the doorstep were four young women — two sets of identical twins. One of them held a small sheet cake that read: *Congratulations. 35–0. Go Mustangs Go.*

Knowing it was somewhat early for a Saturday, the one holding the cake quietly said, "Good morning, Coach Reese. We brought you something."

"Oh, wow," Jonathan said reflexively. "Everyone loves cake. Thank you. What kind?"

"Well," another twin spoke up, "this is a new one — white cake with spearmint frosting."

Jonathan held the door, ushered them inside, and offered everyone coffee. As he poured, he got their names: two were Theresa's daughters, Tatiana and Talia. The other two were daughters of Theresa's twin sister, Tessa — Tamara and Tabitha.

As he poured the coffee, Jonathan said, "That's a lot of T's. I'll do my best to keep it straight." Everyone giggled, and the quiet morning shifted into cheerful commotion.

Turning to the girl who'd brought the cake in, he said, "Thalia?" He got it right. "I'll let you cut and serve." He handed her a knife and grabbed a stack of paper plates and plastic forks.

Thalia gave Jonathan the first piece. Everyone waited for him to take a bite. Just as he shoveled a forkful of cake and frosting into his mouth, Sam walked into the kitchen. She didn't say a word, and all eyes stayed on Jonathan.

After a pause, his eyes rolled back, and he said, "Oh … my … God! Sam, you have to try this."

Everyone broke into laughter. Thalia continued serving cake while Jonathan tried to brief Sam: "Thalia, Tatiana, Tabitha, and Talia. Wait, no — Talia and Tabitha."

Within a minute, everyone had cake. Then AJ walked in, smiling sleepily, hair a mess. Sam handed him a slice of victory cake and attempted to recite the twins' names correctly.

With no chair open, AJ stood at the counter and took a big bite. He nodded enthusiastically as he chewed. Everyone laughed.

"Hey AJ," Talia said, "I hear you're going to the Stampede with the team trainer."

AJ paused mid-chew, eyes darting between his parents. A flush came over his face.

"This is news," Jonathan said.

"Oooo, AJ. I like her. She's a smartie," Sam added.

AJ neither confirmed nor denied but asked, "How do you know?"

The twins laughed. Tatiana answered, "We're not in high school anymore, but…" — then the rest of them finished in unison — "we're not out of the loop."

As everyone laughed, AJ quietly confirmed, "Yes. Shea and I are going to the Stampede together." The group nodded their approval as they kept eating cake.

Jonathan shifted the spotlight: "So, what do we owe you for the cake?"

"Nothing," Tatiana protested. "Nothing at all, Coach. It's our pleasure." They all nodded. "We love what you're doing and hope you win it all."

"Us too," Sam said.

"I bet," Tatiana replied. "But a year ago, we were hoping the team would lose every game. In fact, this is the first time in years we've rooted for Blacklick football."

Sam looked at Jonathan, puzzled, then turned to the girls. "Why?"

Thalia answered calmly. "For years, Gary Studer made football king — which is fine — but it came at the expense of other sports." Everyone stopped eating.

Talia continued, "That cost us our senior year. We were returning a great soccer team — the four of us and several other strong players. Then Studer dismissed our coach — a great coach — for some nobody. Why?"

Before anyone could answer, Tabitha said, "No one knows for sure. But it felt like the money was being used to keep football fully staffed."

"Or buy new equipment. Or fund a camp," Tatiana added.

"Look at Blacklick sports now," Tabitha said. "Football's still great — but other sports are doing well too."

"Dr. Reese," Thalia added, "we know you worked hard for the levy, and you might not agree — but to us, Walter Bachman was the savior of Blacklick sports."

Chapter 103

The cake party didn't last much longer after the duo twin's declaration of support for Walter Bachman. There was nothing controversial. They felt what they felt. Rational minds can disagree. The subject simply changed — being twins, the cake business, career aspirations. It came to its natural conclusion.

Once they left, AJ found himself on the hotseat regarding Shea. His mother had a litany of questions about how AJ asked Shea, their plans, and whether there was more to the relationship than just the Stampede. His father instructed him on being kind, respectful, etc.

AJ was annoyed. It was still early on a Saturday, and he had nothing to share. He tried not to let it show, giving short responses.

"Mom, we're just going together."

"There's no story."

"There are no details."

He let out a heavy sigh. "Dad, I know."

The inquisition didn't last long. They all had things to do — sleep, game, and rebuild a career.

By Monday, Tank also had a date to the Stampede — Kaylee Dawson — a younger cheerleader. This took some focus off AJ and Shea. Yet there was still a buzz, which made AJ uncomfortable. He did his best to ignore it. He intended to go. AJ planned to be all the things his dad chided him about. But he didn't want to think about it. He certainly didn't want to talk about it.

While he didn't want to talk about it, the situation required some communication. AJ assumed he would drive. He assumed he would pick up Shea. When? Where? Would they go straight to the Stampede? Or might they go to dinner like most others — with or without dates? There were details, and he didn't want to deal with them. Maybe if he didn't, the situation would go away.

But the situation was not going to go away. Casey had worked to set this up. And as bad as she felt about hurting AJ, she pledged to help Shea make it happen. But how? While she and AJ still met up in the parking lot each day, there was an edge to the encounter.

AJ was there, but he couldn't look her in the eye. His presence lacked warmth. In the past, he was eager to share a comment about anything. Now, he had little to say. His answers to questions were short and to the point. And he seemed to steer clear of any conversation related to the Stampede.

Nevertheless, Casey knew a plan had to be made. The Stampede was Saturday night. As they were about to go their separate ways, Casey grabbed his attention.

"AJ!" She waited for him to briefly look up. "About Saturday night. The Stampede?"

"Yeah," AJ half-heartedly responded.

"Here's an idea," Casey said, pausing. "Pick up Shea at my place. Brady and Riley are coming there too. You can meet my boyfriend. We can do pictures. And we'll go out to eat."

AJ looked up and said nothing. Then he nodded, indicating he was onboard with the plan. No, he was not thrilled about going with Shea. He was less thrilled about meeting Casey's boyfriend — or even knowing she had one. But like it or not, this was happening. He just needed to make the best of it. He thought for a moment and asked:

"Would it be okay if I included Tank in these plans? He has a date now, too. One of the cheerleaders."

"AJ, that's a great idea. It'll be fun." Casey smiled. "Actually, it'll be great. You'll see."

AJ looked up and shared a spiritless smile. He looked back down and started to walk away. Casey caught his attention.

"AJ!" She pointed at him, made two fists, and knocked her right fist against the back of her left.

Chapter 104

While Joyce Yocheim didn't enjoy being dragged up and down the football sidelines, she loved moving from classroom to classroom at Blacklick High School serving Brady Troy. Being among all the teen energy didn't make her younger, but it made her feel more vibrant.

The only downside was that she was often tethered just a few steps from Brady, ever ready to bring the speaking world to him. She got brief breaks when he moved between classes or needed the restroom.

During those moments, Joyce would stand in the hallway near Brady's next classroom and happily people-watch. She'd observe, make eye contact, smile, and say hello. From there, conversations sometimes blossomed.

On Friday morning, a student carefully approached from the side and said, "Mrs. Yocheim." He didn't want to be too obvious.

She quickly recognized him and replied, "Oh, AJ. Please, call me Joyce."

"Okay, Joyce," AJ said. "Can you help me? I'm trying to understand the meaning of a sign. I can go online and find signs for words or phrases, but I'm not sure how to do it in reverse."

"Why didn't you just ask Brady? Or even Casey?" Joyce asked, curious.

"Ahhh," AJ hesitated. He needed a plausible answer — just not the truth: that Casey told him to figure it out and he didn't want Brady getting curious about what she said. "I've been meaning to, but I saw you and figured ... go to the expert."

Joyce chuckled at the word *expert* and replied, "Sure, AJ. I'd be happy to help. And I appreciate your interest in ASL."

"Great," AJ said, quickly glancing around to see who might be watching. Confident no one was, he quietly asked, "What is this?" He then pointed, made two fists, and knocked his right fist against the back of his left.

Joyce smiled broadly. "Oh, that's an easy one, AJ. Assuming the finger is pointed at someone..." She pointed at AJ. "You," and then knocked one fist against the other. "Rock." She nodded. "It means someone is telling another person they're great. They rock. Understand?"

"Yes. Thank you, Joyce," AJ replied quietly, still worried someone might be watching.

"No, AJ," Joyce said. She placed her hand near her chin, palm facing her body and fingers pointed up, then moved her hand forward and slightly down in a short arc.

AJ tilted his head, confused.

Joyce repeated the motion. "This is how you sign *thank you*, AJ."

"Oh," he said, and mimicked the motion.

Joyce smiled and nodded. "And to say *you're welcome*—"

AJ raised his hands in a polite gesture to cut her off. "I'm happy to learn more another time, Joyce. But I have to get to my next class." He signed *thank you* again and quickly walked away.

Chapter 105

While Jonathan was no longer at Eisenberg & Anders, he was still consumed with work. He was no longer consumed with doing the work, but with finding it. As he put it, "I'm busy trying to get busy."

The difference wasn't going downtown or traveling the globe. Other than a few early morning hours at McDonald's, he was at home, trying to convert connections into clients.

On Friday, he took a short break. Sam was home, up and about. That was a perfect distraction from what seemed like pointless networking.

As they sat at the kitchen table, Sam gave Jonathan a curious look and asked, "Did you just hear a car pull up?" She leaned back to see the driveway.

Jonathan stepped onto the stoop and asked, "Where's your sister?"

"What are you talking about?" Theresa shot back.

"I figured you twins traveled in packs," Jonathan said, laughing. "Your daughters and nieces were here on Saturday — and they brought cake."

Theresa joined the laughter. "No, just me. But I also have something for you." She opened her trunk and lifted out a copier paper box.

Jonathan took the box from her. "Let me help you. What is it?"

"Jonathan don't get too excited," Theresa replied. "It's just your personal items."

"Okay. That's something." Jonathan smiled. "Why don't you come in and visit for a bit? Sam will be happy to see you."

At that point, Sam was at the front door, reiterating what Jonathan said. She went out to greet Theresa with a warm hug and walked Ari's former assistant into the house. Sam set her up at the table with coffee.

Jonathan placed the copier paper box on the table and opened it. He rooted around a bit, looking for something. After a minute, he stopped. He looked disappointed.

Theresa said, "I know. I'm sorry. I couldn't get it."

"Get what?" Sam asked.

"Thanks for bringing this, Theresa," Jonathan said sincerely. He then looked at Sam and explained, "Remember, Alison gave me Ari's jersey. It's not here."

Theresa attempted to explain, "Warren said that—"

Before she could finish, Sam jumped in. "Oh, don't get me started on him…"

"Okay, okay, Sam. Relax," Jonathan interjected, laughing.

"Warren says the jersey belongs at the firm," Theresa explained, as Sam quietly cursed.

"Oh, I can hear him," Jonathan remarked. "Sharing his illogical logic, woven to serve his own needs." He took a deep breath. "I'm not going to worry about it now, Theresa. Thanks for bringing this stuff."

"Jonathan," Theresa said confidently, placing her hand on his. "Things will work out for you. Everyone is hoping and pulling for you. Be patient, and trust that the relationships you've built will come through for you."

Chapter 106

The Mustangs hosted the Licking Heights Hornets for their final regular-season game. Though, it wasn't much of a game. By halftime, the Mustangs were up 35–0.

Brady ran for a touchdown and passed for another. Tank scored twice, pounding into the Hornet defense — hammer after hammer after hammer. AJ rounded out the scoring, intercepting a short pass and returning it for a score — his first since the Columbus Academy game and now only 21 points from the scoring record.

The Blacklick halftime locker room was full of jubilation. The game was in hand. They were headed to the playoffs. Nothing was going to change that. Coach Dad announced, "The second half is going to be about giving the second team opportunity."

Tank immediately started advocating for his favorite second-teamer. "Coach, we can get AJ the scoring record today. We can."

"Tank!" Coach Dad tried to get a word in.

Tank continued, "Do the math. Seriously. Four touchdowns. We could do that against these losers."

"Tank!" Coach Dad tried again.

"That gets him 24 points. Coach, he only needs 21. Right, AJ?" Tank looked to AJ for confirmation.

AJ, unsure, slightly nodded.

Then Tank looked around the locker room for allies. "We've done the Hammer all day. We just do that a few more times, and then I'll flip the ball to AJ, and he'll zip around end the other way. Hammer Reverse. Hammer Reverse. Hammer Reverse.

They won't catch on. Remember, AJ? Like the St. Agatha game back in sixth grade. We could get AJ the record by the fourth quarter."

"Tanks! Tank! Tank!" Coach Dad shouted. When that didn't work, he clap-clapped loudly like Brady. Everyone laughed, as it took that to stop Tank's rant. "We're not going to do any of that. Chase a record. Hammer whatever. We can't."

"But—" Tank tried to fire up his argument again.

"Tank," Coach Dad calmly cut him off. "We can't risk injury on that. Not today. We need AJ for the playoffs. We need everyone. Let's just finish this game out and be smart."

Tank, defeated, looked toward AJ and flashed disappointment.

AJ just shrugged and shook his head in disgust.

AJ and Tank spent the second half watching the second team rack up three touchdowns.

"That could be … should be … yours, AJ," Tank commiserated. "I tried."

"Appreciate it, Tank," AJ replied. "I've given up on that record, to be honest."

While AJ may have given up on the record, he wasn't done venting. He shared his disappointment with his mom after the game. She just listened, but encouraged him, "Trust your dad, AJ. None of this is purposeful."

AJ patiently listened before going to his room.

Sam then relayed the message to Jonathan when he arrived home 20 minutes later. Again, she just listened.

"Sam, I feel bad. I do." Jonathan searched for words. "I remember our conversation from earlier in the season. I'm aware of AJ's goals. Scoring. Repeat. Scholarship, for even just…"

"A pencil," Sam added.

"Yes, a pencil. I remember. But I can't control everything. I can't even control my own aspirations." Jonathan let out a heavy sigh.

After a moment, he continued, "But Sam, I agreed to coach the team, not just my son. I need to look after everyone. Those bench players work hard too. They deserve their moment. So do their parents in the stands. I was happy for them." Thinking about it, Jonathan smiled.

Then he started in on a different thought. "And say for an instant we went after the record tonight. What would our conversation be right now if someone got injured? AJ? Paul? Brady? Or Tank... performing some middle-school reverse stunt we've never even practiced?"

Sam got up, walked to Jonathan, and hugged him. "Honey, I'm not taking sides. I'm just sharing AJ's frustration." She kissed him on the cheek. "None of this is easy."

AJ heard his parents talking, but he couldn't understand what was being said. It didn't matter. He put on his gaming headset and watched videos of others playing video games.

He quickly became tired and bored, put everything away, and went to bed, needing rest. Tomorrow was going to be a long day.

They hadn't really talked about the Stampede since AJ asked Shea, even though they'd driven the water to practice every day. For AJ, it was a quiet form of denial. As for Shea, she didn't know what to expect.

But before AJ left the locker room after the game, he found Shea and said, "I will see you tomorrow night."

Peering through her glasses and disheveled hair as she busily performed her team trainer duties, she responded, "Yes! I'm looking forward to it."

Chapter 107

Saturday morning, Jonathan was up and off to McDonald's. The coffee wasn't free, but it was easy to come by. That, and the hustle and bustle of people coming and going, now jump-started his day. He wasn't certain what he needed to be doing to re-establish a private law practice, but he knew that doing nothing wasn't the answer. As he hunched over his laptop, investigating the small and mid-sized business scene of central Ohio, his phone rang. It startled him. Jonathan wasn't expecting a call. He quickly glanced at the phone to see who it was. He felt compelled to. He had no clients.

Whoever was calling wasn't part of Jonathan's contacts, so only a number came up on the small phone display. He didn't recognize the number, but the area code and prefix were familiar.

"Good morning. This is Jonathan Reese."

"Hello, Jonathan," the caller started in. "This is Lisa Kaye, from the legal department at Emerald Medical." She briefly paused, then continued. "I hope this call is not too early."

"Oh no, Lisa. I'm up. How can I help you?" Curious, Jonathan sat up, not wanting to miss a word.

"Simple. We want you to take the lead on the due diligence for this pending acquisition over in the Far East." Lisa was matter of fact.

"You do know that I'm no longer at Eisenberg & Anders, right?" Jonathan clarified.

"We do. Quite frankly, we don't care," Lisa shot back. "Everyone here agrees that you're the person with the most familiarity and experience. You know what needs to get done and how we operate."

"Okay!" Jonathan was stunned. "Sure, however I can help."

"Jonathan, we're especially interested in this electronic system you spoke of," Lisa clarified.

"Oh, that." Jonathan was confused. "I don't have that. It's still at the firm."

"Hmmm?" Lisa went quiet. "Warren Scott said you might. He can't find any record of what you were talking about."

"Well, Lisa, I don't have anything," Jonathan defended. "Pardon my French, but Warren is full of…" He caught himself and quelled his anger. "When they walked me out, I left with nothing. No files. No technology. Nothing."

"Could you rebuild it?" Lisa quickly inquired. "From what you described, that could help us with this acquisition and others we're considering."

"I could," Jonathan responded. "But I'm not sure I could meet your timeline. It's just me. I'd be starting from scratch, and I don't have the foundational material, which is at the firm. And…"

"Jonathan," Lisa cut him off. "I have been instructed to secure your help at all costs. This acquisition is vital to lots of people here. Bonuses. Stock price. You get it. We'll get you some support here. And we'll get you what we can from Eisenberg & Anders."

"Okay, then. Count me in." Jonathan sat up even taller. "Warren Scott might not be happy about this, but…"

Lisa cut him off again. "We don't care, Jonathan. We're the client, and lots is riding on this. I'm going to get my assistant connected with you to get your firm in our system so we can get you paid. Thanks for your time. I must get to another meeting. Thanks." She ended the call.

Jonathan's heart was racing. He opened his laptop and started to think through how he might recreate his electronic due diligence system.

Chapter 108

Like most Saturday mornings, AJ woke up to a quiet house. To him, it was just another Saturday. His dad was off working, and his mom was milking as much sleep out of the weekend as she could. He got up and left — he had things to do.

While he wasn't looking forward to the Stampede, he was committed to seeing it through — looking respectable and being respectful. He got his hair cut and went to a florist for a corsage.

The woman helping him was very helpful. They settled on something basic with hints of the school colors — navy and gray. But she made it clear that, in the future he shouldn't wait until the last minute — and he should know basics like the type and color of his date's dress. Duly admonished, AJ thanked her, paid, and headed home.

When he returned, he found his parents engaged in another conversation about Eisenberg & Anders and Emerald Medical. He didn't interrupt. Instead, he went to his room to occupy himself until it was time to get ready.

When that time came, he got cleaned up. His mom helped him pick out a tie, and his dad helped him tie it. After a few obligatory pictures on the back deck, AJ was off to Casey's house.

When he arrived, he discovered he was the last to show up. Brady was there, and AJ awkwardly got acquainted with Riley Bennett. Tank looked uncomfortable suited up, but proud to have Kaylee Dawson as his date.

AJ also met Casey's boyfriend, David Quinn. In that moment, AJ knew just how far out of his league Casey really was. David was a grad student in engineering at Ohio State and sported a full half-inch beard.

Shea was there but still upstairs with Casey and her roommate, getting dressed. While everyone waited, they made small talk — as best they could — mainly through text messages and obscure gestures.

After a few minutes, Casey came bounding downstairs, carrying her dress shoes. She wore a black dress. It was not too formal but fashionable for the moment. It accented her athletic figure.

As she cleared the last few stairs, Casey excitedly announced, "Shea will be down soon." She then signed a few short messages to Brady and Riley.

A few minutes later, a door opened and closed. AJ heard footsteps — likely Shea coming downstairs. He pondered: *What should I do? What should I say?*

Within seconds, the footsteps reached the stairs. They were attached to tennis shoes and jeans. A lump formed in his throat. Not good. But a split second later, he realized it wasn't Shea, but rather Casey's roommate, Aubrey.

Aubrey appeared to be a free spirit — streaks of red-dyed hair, multiple but subtle piercings, and a small symbol tattooed behind her ear. Like Casey, she was excited. "Okay, okay. Are you ready for this?"

Moments later, a single navy high heel appeared at the top of the stairs. Then the second landed on the next step. Above the shoes were slender bare legs. After a few more steps, the legs were attached to someone wearing a dress that matched the shoes. A few more steps, and Shea appeared — but not as the girl AJ thought he knew.

Weeks earlier, when they were reconstituting the offense, Shea remarked to Casey,
"I wish I were as beautiful as you are." That single comment not only set in motion Casey's efforts to fix up AJ and Shea, but also served as a starting point to help transform the student trainer into the woman she could become.

Casey responded to Shea's aspiration with, "Oh, Shea. Honey." She then reached over, removed Shea's thick glasses, and pushed her hair behind her ears. "You are beautiful." With the simplified Mustang offense in place, the new friends devoted hours to playing dress-up.

To Shea, Casey was the right friend at the right time—an encouraging female influence who cared about her, a role model to show her the way of womanhood. Casey filled a void created when Shea's mother left, and it was a void her father could never fill.

Casey applied makeup to Shea and reworked her hair in various styles. The impact, however, Shea couldn't see without her glasses. So, Casey would take a picture, allowing Shea to put them on and view the transformation.

"Oh Shea, let's get you some contacts," Casey remarked. "And we can get them with a slight blue tint to really enhance the blue you already have."

Shea went along with it all. As sharp as she was in math and science, she was clueless when it came to beauty and femininity—she didn't know what she didn't know.

But Casey recognized her own limits as well. She was a college athlete, not necessarily a girlie girl. Knowing that, she suggested, "You should come back when my roommate Aubrey is back in town. She's a pro with these makeovers. And you're about her size too."

When Aubrey returned a few weeks later, she took charge. She had Shea strip down to her bra and underwear, then stepped back to size up her body. "Oh, love it. Lots to work with."

"Thanks?" Shea replied, her tone uncertain.

"First things first: We've got to shave the pits," Aubrey said in a matter-of-fact tone. "You aren't French, and this isn't Paris." She paused for a second, then commanded, "Now turn around. Let me see the backside."

Shea instinctively covered up but spun around without a word.

Aubrey sized her up again, then enthusiastically said, "Okay, let's get to work."

That set Casey and Aubrey in motion—concocting a makeover plan. There was lots of work to be done: playing with hairstyles, tinkering with makeup, trying on outfits. And once the

date with AJ was set, Project Shea—as Aubrey referred to it—
went into overdrive.

Within seconds, the full manifestation of the makeover was
standing at the base of the stairs. The transformation was
stunning. No one said a word.

Shea had never made herself up and didn't know how.
Nevertheless, the foundation for beauty was there, waiting for
the likes of Casey and Aubrey to bring it forth. While her dad
couldn't help with any of that, he could financially underwrite it.

Scrolling through lifestyle magazines and Pinterest, the trio
settled on a sleeveless navy dress. When it arrived, Shea raced
over to Casey's to try it on. It hung down to her mid-calf. Seeing
her, Aubrey raced off and returned with a gray cropped jacket to
accent the look. From there, they rounded out the ensemble
with metallic-tone heels, a matching clutch, and other
accessories.

Then around noon, Shea showed up at Casey's, and Aubrey
got to work. Shower. Shave legs. Trim and shape eyebrows.
Highlight hair. Press-on, polished nails. Style hair, pulled back
with a medium clip. Then Aubrey tastefully applied makeup,
finishing up just as people were arriving downstairs.

As everyone just looked at Shea, Aubrey broke the silence.
"It's not my best work." Then, pridefully, she added with a
chuckle, "But it's damn close."

Chapter 109

Everyone laughed at Aubrey's comment — except Shea. She
shared an uncomfortable smile. While she enjoyed the fresh
feeling of being beautiful, she was not confident how others saw
the change. And she was unsure whether the laughter was
directed at her.

Tank chimed in with, "Girl, you are all woman, now." Again, laughter filled the apartment.

Almost simultaneously, Kaylee gave him a quick, playful elbow, and Casey similarly hit him on the shoulder — each as if to say, *not appropriate*.

AJ stepped forward, in front of the others. "Shea, you look really nice. I mean, *wow*. Really nice." He then offered the corsage. "This is for you. But I'm not sure where it goes." Uncomfortable himself, he chuckled.

Aubrey stepped in, taking the flower. "Don't mess with my art." She began to pin it to Shea.

Casey came up to help and encourage. "That's really nice, AJ. It goes well with Shea's look."

AJ didn't acknowledge them. He was transfixed on Shea. He couldn't stop looking. Admiring. His mouth was slightly ajar. His heart raced, and he felt a flush come across his body.

Once Aubrey had the corsage appropriately secured, Casey organized the group and asked Aubrey to take a series of pictures — various iterations of groups, couples, and individuals. They then departed for dinner reservations in four separate cars, leaving Aubrey behind.

On the drive to the restaurant, AJ kept stealing glances at Shea, even at dinner as they sat next to each other around an eight-top table. Shea had been in front of AJ before. Actually, many times. Tonight, he really noticed her.

Shea's deep blue eyes, albeit aided by slightly tinted contacts. The shape of her face — eyes, nose, and cheeks. And the curves and contours of her body. It had all been there before, but it had been partially hidden and totally unobserved.

After dinner, they drove to the high school, where the gym had been transformed into a dance hall. Before they entered, Shea separated from AJ. She followed the others into the bathroom to freshen up their look — whatever that meant. It was all a new experience.

When she emerged, AJ was not there. So, Shea walked into the dance. The bleachers were retracted but covered with decorations. The lights were low. The music loud. Couples and individuals were dancing.

Shea watched people dance. As she did, she could feel people watching her. They were pointing. And then questioning, "Who is that?" And then remarking, "I think it's Shea Brooks." And then questioning again, "Really?" And remarking, "You're kidding!"

All this made Shea feel uncomfortable. She tried to ignore it, but the quiet attention was piercing and unsettling. It was not something she was used to. She was in an environment she'd never been in before, nor thought she'd ever be. Part of her wanted to go home. While home was lonely, there was a comfort to it.

Just as Shea was about to turn and exit, AJ came up from behind. He reached in, grabbed her hand, and squeezed it twice — as if to say, *I'm here. I'm with you. We're together.* Nothing was said. She returned the grip and leaned in. With that gesture, all of Shea's anxiety disappeared.

Chapter 110

More relaxed, Shea began to enjoy herself. Talking. Laughing. Dancing. And AJ was with her.

A couple hours into the Stampede, Casey and David came up to them. They were leaving. Ironically enough, the dance was not loud enough for Brady and Riley. While the deaf community enjoys music they experience it differently—often through vibration, rhythm, bass, and visual components rather than hearing melody or lyrics in a traditional sense. Without those two, there was no reason for college graduates to be at a high school dance.

Casey and David said their goodbyes, and everyone exchanged hugs. Then the ASL interpreter and her date moved towards the exit. When they were about 20 feet away, AJ called out, "Casey!" When she turned back, AJ signed to her, "You rock!"

A big smile came across Casey's face. She walked back towards AJ, and when she was close enough for him to hear, she said, "AJ, I'm glad we're friends. You are a really special person."

AJ smiled, nodded, and then signed, "Thank you."

Casey let out a chuckle, "Look at you. Soon Brady won't need me." She then turned and left.

Thirty minutes later, for AJ and Shea had enough. It was a long day filled with anxiety and discovery. They said goodbye to Tank and Kaylee, who seemed to be permanently on the dance floor, and then hand in hand they walked out of the Stampede and towards AJ's car.

From the moment Shea revealed herself, AJ's heart raced. As they slowly walked, touching one another, AJ could feel the pace of his heart quicken.

When they got to his car, AJ opened the passenger car door and let Shea get in before closing the door for her. He then walked around the back of the car and got himself in. She was looking forward out the windshield, lost in her own thoughts. AJ was about to start the car, but then turned to Shea and asked, "Are you buckled in?"

Shea broke from her trance. She didn't immediately comprehend what AJ had asked. Then she quickly looked left and right almost confused, trying to understand what she needed to do. The moment was intoxicating to her too.

Before she could get a grip on the seat belt, AJ quietly said, "Let me help you." Then he reached across her with his left arm across her body towards the passenger side seat belt.

For a moment, they were almost face to face. They both stopped and looked at one another. Frozen in that moment, Shea asked, "You don't really care about this seatbelt, do you?"

Quietly and sincerely, AJ responded, "No. No, I don't." With that, he moved closer. He stopped searching for the seat belt, put his left hand on Shea's shoulder, gently pulled, and kissed her on the lips.

Shea responded. Throwing both her arms around AJ, she pulled him in and kissed him back.

Chapter 111

Much of Saturday afternoon and into the evening, Jonathan devoted mental energy to thinking about the Emerald Medical due diligence opportunity. He'd put a lot of time into creating the electronic framework. It would be great to have. Though it wasn't completely done, it was 90% there.

Without it, the situation would be a challenge — especially without the related documents and underlying work papers. Thinking through all he needed, and what he needed to do next, was draining. Other than finding other clients, however, that was all Jonathan had to focus on. And while it was exhausting, he knew he couldn't relax enough to sleep. So, he kept after it.

Just before midnight, his son came home. "How was it, AJ?"

"It was good, Dad. It was really good." There was a different sort of energy in his voice.

Though AJ didn't offer any more, Jonathan didn't press. That was Sam's *forte*. AJ had shared much more than his usual "fine," so Jonathan just replied, "Good."

Shortly after AJ disappeared to his room, Jonathan pushed his work aside and went to bed.

AJ and Shea remained in the school parking lot for another 20 minutes. As the Stampede neared its conclusion, however, there was a lot of commotion and interruption. So, they left and found themselves in the parking lot of Wendy's, sharing a Frosty. They recapped their first date and planned others.

As midnight approached, Shea playfully remarked, "If there's going to be a second date, you need to get me home before I turn back into a pumpkin." As much as she was enjoying her time with AJ, her father had given her a curfew, and she intended to adhere to it.

AJ drove her home. He kissed her once more in the car. Then he got out and walked her to her front door. Standing on the small porch, he kissed her again.

On Sunday afternoon, AJ invited Shea over for a "study date." While she was now sporting more casual attire, she wore her slightly tinted blue contacts, had devoted attention to her hair, and mimicked some of the makeup tricks Aubrey had taught her.

They sat across from each other at the kitchen table, working on their team projects for Advanced Scientific Methods and Senior English. Beneath the scholastic business, however, their feet were intertwined.

On Monday, Jonathan reached out to contacts at Eisenberg & Anders to get what he needed for Emerald Medical. He left a few voicemails for former team members and followed up with detailed emails. In each message, he added, "If you're up for it, we can grab coffee. Most mornings I'm at the McDonald's on Hamilton Road in Gahanna."

Part of him just wanted to drive to the firm and retrieve what he needed. But he knew that, despite support from Emerald Medical's legal team, his involvement would pull client billings from his old firm — enough to antagonize Warren Scott on its own. He didn't want to make things worse by showing up at the office only a week after leaving.

He decided to let his connections at Eisenberg & Anders work for him. Besides, he needed to focus on finding other clients. No attorney — or law firm — could survive long-term on a single client.

At school, things felt different for AJ. Shea had always seemed like part of the background at Blacklick High. Now she was center stage. He looked for her, talked whenever possible, and at a minimum, casually brushed up against her. He felt an energy around her.

While AJ had been on Shea's radar for some time, things felt different for her too. She loved the attention, blushed whenever they talked, and felt a spark with even the slightest touch.

On the Monday after the Stampede, they were hauling ice and water out to practice again. As AJ pressed the accelerator, Shea shouted, "Hold on," as if she'd forgotten something.

"What?" AJ asked, glancing over with a concerned look.

She opened her left hand and bounced it on the back of AJ's right thigh. He gave her a confused look. She bounced her hand again. Then he caught on — and placed his right hand in her left.

She grabbed it firmly and squeezed twice, as if to say, *"I'm here. I'm with you. We're together."* Then she leaned in to kiss him. He moved in too. Their lips lightly met, and they shared a moment.

Shea slowly pulled back just inches. Her face was flushed, eyes glossy. She softly said, "I've been waiting all day to do that."

Chapter 112

On Monday, Jonathan didn't hear back from anyone at Eisenberg & Anders. He didn't hear back on Tuesday either—

nor Wednesday, Thursday, or Friday. Not a call. Not an email. Nothing.

That was unsettling. On Friday, he contemplated reaching out again. Maybe his message hadn't gone through, but he didn't want to be a pest. He recalled times when he was overwhelmed and didn't respond to people in a timely fashion. He resolved to follow up next week.

Besides, hearing back from his former colleagues wasn't the only thing he had going. Several people he'd contacted the week prior had responded. Many replies were just emails, which still needed to be acknowledged. But some responses came through actual calls. While generally short and meant to reestablish contact, each required time and documenting a plan to follow up. Jonathan's days were busy.

Beyond his professional life, Blacklick football filled more of Jonathan's time, giving him more opportunities to plan practices and think ahead to their next opponent. And that was important now. After all, they were in the playoffs—the second season. Win or go home.

The first round was a rematch against New Lexington. The playoff game differed from the Week 5 contest in one important way — the game wasn't even close.

During the regular season, AJ effectively ended the game with an interception. In the playoff matchup, his interception set up the Mustangs to score early and often. They routed the Panthers 28–3.

There was little celebration. They expected to win. And they needed to refocus on their next opponent—Columbus Bishop Ready. Coach Dad and the other coaches knew little about the Silver Knights, other than that they'd stymied a potential rematch with Jonathan Alder on a late field goal. They did know they'd have one final home game under the OHSAA playoff format.

On Saturday, Jonathan was up early and out of the house again. He went to McDonald's for coffee and to continue thinking about how his private law practice might come together. He wanted to do work related to Emerald Medical's due diligence—but it was hard to motivate.

Jonathan faced a circular dilemma. He could create an outline of what needed to be done from scratch, but that felt like wasted effort. After all, he and his team at Eisenberg & Anders had already done it. He just needed to coordinate with them.

Then Jonathan pondered: *But what if they don't get back to me? I'll need something to show when I meet with the Emerald Medical legal team next. So, I should do something. But…*

His thoughts spun in circles. He knew if he could get his hands on the electronic framework he'd created, it would solve a lot of problems. But that still required communication with his old firm. The frustration was maddening.

There was nothing he could do about it today. He finished his second cup of coffee, packed up, and headed to the high school to meet with the other coaches. It was clear who they were playing and that they had another game. They needed to plot and scheme what the Mustangs had to do to advance.

AJ, once again, woke to a quiet house. Like the previous Saturday, he had things to do. Unlike last week, however, he was looking forward to it. Shea had invited him over to meet her dad, work on their school projects, and spend the afternoon hanging out and watching football.

AJ's response to the invitation wasn't a straightforward "yes." Instead, he playfully said, "Okay. It's only fair you get home field advantage." He let out a chuckle to make sure she knew he was joking, and she responded with a good-humored rap on his shoulder with the back of her hand.

AJ didn't know what to expect at Shea's house. Every household is different, and that made him nervous. But he was getting to spend time with Shea—and that made the anxiety worth it.

On Monday, Jonathan resumed contacting colleagues at Eisenberg & Anders. He called direct lines and left voicemails, asking them to respond or meet him at McDonald's.

He fired off text messages—he could see they were read, but none drew a reply. He sent emails and got the same result. He even called the firm's main number several times, asking for different people. Each time, the receptionist assured him they'd pass along the message.

On Tuesday, Jonathan tried again. Still, radio silence. Then again on Wednesday. And Thursday morning, he called Theresa. While Ari was gone, the firm had confirmed she still had a role.

She recognized the number and picked up. "Hello, Jonathan."

After some pleasantries, Jonathan got to the point. "Theresa, be straight with me. Is there a reason no one is getting back to me? I mean—no one. Nothing."

Ari's former assistant let out a heavy sigh. "Yeah." She paused, scanning the room to see who might be listening. When she determined she was alone, she continued, "That imp has given everyone strict orders not to communicate with you."

"Oh boy," Jonathan replied with his own sigh. "Emerald Medical has asked me to lead the due diligence for the Far East acquisition." He sighed again. "It's hard to do that without communication."

"I don't know what Warren's deal is," Theresa said. "He's not like his father, and Ari certainly didn't rub off on him either. I don't know what to say. How can I help?"

"You can't. Don't," Jonathan replied, clearly frustrated. "It's not your problem. I'll figure something out." She offered some encouragement, and after a few more pleasantries, they ended the call.

Jonathan set his phone down and muttered, "Now what?" He considered calling Lisa Kaye at Emerald Medical to respectfully bow out of the assignment. He simply didn't have the information or support to deliver. Before he could decide, however, his phone rang. Lisa was calling.

"Good morning, this is Jonathan Reese."

"Hello, Jonathan. This is Lisa Kaye from Emerald Medical." She paused, then continued. "I'm following up on our conversation from the week before last. I know you're set up in our system to be paid, but I wanted to touch base on the project itself."

Jonathan hesitated. Saying Warren Scott was actively blocking him felt unprofessional. But admitting he'd made no progress didn't sound great either. His voice lacked confidence when he offered a polished half-truth. "Well, I'm trying to gather information and coordinate people."

"Really?" Lisa replied, surprised. "I just got off the phone with Warren Scott. He said you've never contacted anyone at the firm." Jonathan was stunned and silent. Lisa continued, "In fact, he said he's called you several times and you haven't responded."

"Lisa," Jonathan began, trying to stay composed, "that's not accurate. I've made multiple attempts to contact my old team, and no one has responded—yet." Lisa listened. "As for Warren calling me, I can't say whether he has or hasn't. I can't speak to his actions. But I can say with confidence that I've received no calls. And if I had, I would've responded."

"Um," Lisa muttered. She paused, then continued more firmly. "I don't want to be in the middle of some law firm tiff. We've got enough drama here—trust me. All I know is this acquisition is critical, and I've been instructed to have you lead it."

"Lisa, you sound frustrated," Jonathan said gently. "I am too. I want to be involved. You don't need to be in the middle of anything. We just need to get the job done. I'm trying to communicate. Trust me."

"Jonathan, I believe you," she replied. Her tone softened, though concern remained. "You have a great reputation here. That's why leadership is insisting on your involvement."

"Thank you," Jonathan said. He was slightly relieved—but he knew there was still a problem.

Lisa continued, "But can you see where I'm at? We've relied on the Eisenberg & Anders firm since—well, forever. And they're telling us you haven't been in touch."

"Lisa!" Jonathan interjected. He wanted to expose Warren Scott but stopped himself. There was no value in that—just the possibility of personal satisfaction. "Can I suggest we do this?"

"I'm listening," Lisa responded calmly.

"Call a meeting," Jonathan said confidently. "Invite me and the team from Eisenberg & Anders to a meeting at Emerald Medical. We can sort out whatever's going on."

"That's a good idea, Jonathan," Lisa conceded.

They compared calendars and scheduled it for first thing Monday morning—November 13. Lisa had out-of-town travel, and the timing gave the Eisenberg & Anders team time to coordinate.

"At some point, we're going to have to meet anyway," Jonathan added. "But it would be great if I could get my hands on the electronic framework I mentioned."

"You know, Jonathan, we've pressed Warren on that," Lisa said. "He says he's never heard of it. To be honest, he kind of implies you made the whole thing up."

"Lisa, I'm not. Trust me—it's there." Jonathan paused. He wanted to call Warren a bold-faced liar but didn't. "Let's meet on the 13th and go from there."

Chapter 113

Bishop Ready came to Blacklick High brimming with confidence. Sure, the Mustangs were the No. 1 seed in the region. However, they had a hard time taking seriously a team that had an unorthodox offense, a deaf quarterback, and communicated using rhythmic clapping and hand signals. In practice leading up to the game, one of their assistant coaches remarked, "It feels like we're headed into a dance competition more so than a football game."

Immediately after the Silver Knights kicked the ball off, they realized how wrong they were. The Catholic high school from the west side of Columbus didn't have a prayer. Midway through the third quarter, they were scoreless and behind by 31 points. They only managed a field goal late in the game when second- and third-string players were squaring off for mop-up time.

Again, on Saturday, Jonathan was up early and off to McDonald's. He felt that this daily cadence gave him a sense of stability as he worked to build his practice. And then, after a few hours, he met at the high school with the coaches to discuss Blacklick's next opponent — East Liverpool High School.

The meeting stretched into the evening. They had little information on East Liverpool, no common opponents, and the scout report from their blowout second-round win was of limited value. With the school located three hours away near the Pennsylvania border, the coaching staff relied on internet research to piece together a game plan.

It was time well spent. On Monday, Coach Dad presented to the team a coherent overview of the game ahead and an optimistic plan to prevail. This led to a spirited, enthusiastic practice.

Coach Dad gathered the team, shared his usual encouragement, and finished with, "Remember to help Shea."

To which Tank wisecracked, "Especially you, AJ!" Everyone laughed as the herd of Mustang players and coaches dispersed in all directions.

Jonathan was left in the middle of the field preparing to talk to Nathan Rogers. With 11 games played and hopefully four games left, Jonathan wanted a rundown of where various players were with their aches and pains. As Nathan shared details, Jonathan noticed Casey talking with a stranger. The ASL interpreter pointed in their direction, and the man began walking toward them.

He looked to be in his mid-70s — fit, well-dressed, confident. His only visible imperfection was a gauze wrap around his right thumb.

Jonathan and Nathan continued talking as the man approached. When he was close enough that he didn't need to shout, the man said, "I believe that one of you is Jonathan Reese."

"Yeah, that's me," Jonathan said, stepping forward. "How can I help you?"

"Great to meet you, Jonathan," the man said.

Before they could continue, AJ came running up, out of breath. "Hey, Dad, somebody broke into Brady's car and stole his backpack." He added, "Actually, it wasn't just anybody. We think it was Sebastian and his crew. Someone said they saw them hanging around Brady's car."

"Shocking," Jonathan said dryly. "What was in the backpack?"

"Um? I think some notes, a couple textbooks, and maybe his playbook," AJ replied. "Nothing else. He had his wallet, keys, and phone."

Jonathan laughed. "Okay, then I'm not too concerned. The playbook is useless at this point, and the textbooks are used less than they should be. Whoever stole it got nothing. I'll talk to the office, AJ. We'll get Brady new books."

At this point, Nathan interjected, "Jonathan, I got this. I'll go talk to the office for Brady."

As Nathan left, Jonathan turned back to the man and offered a quick explanation. "Sorry about that. We've got a former player who's become a bit of a pain in our backside."

The man smiled. "Sounds like someone's dad needs to take his boy out to the woodshed."

"Well," Jonathan laughed, "believe it or not, the father is worse than the son." Realizing their introduction wasn't complete, he added, "I'm sorry. I didn't get your name."

The man offered his hand. "Walter. Walter Bachman."

Jonathan shook it and said, "Oh, I know of you. You and my wife squared off over the tax levy?"

"Yes, Dr. Reese," Walter said. "She is sharp, feisty, and formidable."

"Trust me, Walter, I know." Jonathan then asked, "So what brings you here? To me?"

"Jonathan, word has it that you're an attorney in private practice," Walter said. "And I need some estate planning done."

"Really?" Jonathan didn't expect that response.

"Yeah, I tried to get it taken care of earlier this year, but—" Walter paused, then continued, "but that didn't work out. Long story. Could you help me?"

"Not now," Jonathan replied. "I mean, not right now, but sure."

"Great," Walter said. "What's next?"

"Well, we'll need to meet." Jonathan was caught off guard. "What works for you?"

"I'm busy tomorrow," Walter said. "And Wednesday. And Thursday, too. How about Friday? Earlier the better."

"Friday works. 8 a.m.?"

"Perfect. Where's your office?"

"Well," Jonathan hesitated, a little embarrassed. "I've been an attorney for years, but I'm just getting started in private practice. So, I don't have an office yet. I've been hanging out at McDonald's. The one near the high school."

Walter laughed. "You need to spin that better. Say you've got a thousand offices worldwide. Right now, you're using the one on Hamilton Road."

They shared a laugh, smiled, and shook hands.

Chapter 114

After meeting with Walter, Jonathan was elated. He finished up what he needed to at Blacklick High, raced home, and bounded into the house.

"I think I just landed my first client," Jonathan announced to Sam.

As AJ had already come and gone from dinner, Sam was seated alone behind a half-eaten pizza. Without a word, she stood, raised her right hand, and extended three fingers. "Awesome! WOW!" She was excited for her husband.

"You'll never guess who it is," Jonathan blurted out. "Actually, forget it — you'll never guess." He paused for a second and proudly said, "Your buddy, Walter Bachman."

Immediately, Sam's enthusiasm evaporated and was replaced by disgust. "Jonathan, you're not seriously thinking about taking him as a client, are you?"

"I am. In fact, we're meeting Friday morning," Jonathan said, confused.

"You can't," Sam protested. "Of all the people in the world, I can't think of someone I trust less than that man."

"Warren Scott?" Jonathan asked quickly.

"Okay, Walter is a close second to that loser, but still," her words trailed off. "You can't."

"Sam," Jonathan said firmly, signaling he was going to stand his ground. "In the ER, you and your Hippocratic oath serve any and all who come through the door, right?"

"Yes, but that's different," Sam argued. But before she could elaborate, Jonathan continued.

"Yes, it is different. I agree, Sam." He gathered his words. "It's different because there will always be a steady flow of people having life-threatening situations."

"So, what's your point?" Sam asked.

"My point is that there's not a steady flow of legal work out there," Jonathan said. "I don't know whether I trust Walter Bachman. But I know I can serve him as an attorney — and I need a client. So yes, I'm taking this client."

"Fine. Whatever." Sam grabbed a piece of pizza and dropped it on her plate. "But don't expect me to trust him."

Chapter 115

It was another typical Tuesday morning for the former foul tip club. Noah Turner and Aiden meandered over to Sebastian Sullivan's house. Then, together, they drove to school.

Riding on new tires and the scent of a professionally cleaned interior, they laughed about stealing Brady Troy's backpack the day before. They mused about how it might impact him and lamented that there was nothing of real value inside — though they found the playbook interesting.

About a mile from the high school, on a short, straight stretch of rural, quasi-suburban county road, Sebastian applied the brakes to slow his car. The Franklin County sheriff had unofficially marked this stretch for heightened enforcement, with a cruiser posted here each school day.

Everyone knew it. And Sebastian didn't need any more trouble in his life. He wanted to be sure he was below the posted speed limit before he passed the cruiser. He quickly glanced down to confirm he was.

Nevertheless, a few seconds after Sebastian passed, the deputy pulled out and raced to get directly behind his car. Moments later, the deputy activated his light bar and gave a short burst of the siren, signaling that Sebastian should pull over immediately.

Sebastian complied but quickly shot a confused look at Aiden and Noah. Then he added, "What did I do?" Everyone shrugged.

After a minute, the deputy got out of his cruiser and walked up to Sebastian's car. There were no polite pleasantries. The deputy simply said, "License and registration, please."

"Sure," Sebastian responded. "Officer, what did I do?"

The deputy repeated himself: "License and registration, please."

Sebastian handed over his license and registration. As he did, he again asked, "Officer, can I ask what I did?"

The deputy didn't respond, instead instructing, "Stay here. And stay in the car." He walked back to his cruiser and started his investigation.

Just then, a second cruiser arrived and parked directly in front of Sebastian's car. The former foul tip club exchanged concerned looks.

Minutes later, the first deputy exited his cruiser and stood behind Sebastian's car. The driver of the second cruiser quickly joined him. Together, they looked at Sebastian's license and registration, then pointed toward the license plate area on the back of the vehicle.

Moments later, a third cruiser arrived. Sebastian and company were completely confused.

The first deputy then walked up to Sebastian's door and commanded, through the open window, "Please get out."

Sebastian got out. The deputy frisked him, cuffed him, and read him his rights. Nothing else was said. The deputy walked him back to his cruiser and put him in the back seat.

Then the second deputy cuffed Aiden. The third did the same to Noah.

Chapter 116

"Not funny, Reese!" Sebastian Sullivan shouted at AJ across the hallway. "Not funny at all." He was mad — and had good reason to be, as did Aiden and Noah.

The moment they drove by the first deputy's cruiser, the vehicle's automatic license plate reader — ALPR— system buzzed to life. Like many law enforcement organizations across the country, the Franklin County sheriff's office had installed ALPR systems on all its cars. These scan license plates and compare them to a list of stolen vehicles or plates.

The system instantly flagged Sebastian's car, triggering the deputy to pull him over. What escalated the situation, however, was that the back plate on Sebastian's car didn't match the vehicle's registration. In fact, the plate wasn't even from Ohio — it was from Mississippi.

That prompted the first deputy to call for backup so the alleged thieves could be interviewed individually. In the end, deputies declared the situation a prank. The so-called stolen plate only looked real; it was plastic, 3D-printed. Still, sorting out the prank took a couple of hours.

Missing school was not the problem. The real damage was that photos of the trio being taken into custody flooded social media, turning them into a laughingstock across the high school.

AJ shouted back at Sebastian, "What are you talking about?"

As AJ walked away, Sebastian shouted, "I will get you back, Reese. Count on it."

AJ just waved him off and kept moving to his next class.

Chapter 117

In addition to his networking efforts and preparing for the meeting at Emerald Medical, Jonathan got reacquainted with Ohio's laws on probate and estate planning. He had known them well when he was first in private practice, but over the years his knowledge had atrophied — and the law had changed.

By Friday morning, he was ready — at least enough to get through the meeting with Walter Bachman. He arrived at McDonald's 15 minutes early, got his coffee, and reviewed the notes he'd created from his research.

As he did, a quiet voice called out, "Jonathan."

Jonathan looked up but saw no one.

Again, the voice rang out, "Jonathan. Behind you. But don't look back. It's Stephenson."

"Stephenson? What are you doing? Come sit with me." Jonathan was partially confused and somewhat amused.

"I can't. Don't look back. I can't be seen with you. I need my job. If Warren finds out I'm here, he'll fire me." Stephenson's voice was loaded with concern.

"Then what are you doing here?" Jonathan was empathetic but concerned.

"Listen carefully, Jonathan." Stephenson took a deep breath. "In a moment, I'm going to get up and leave. Under my coffee cup and some napkins will be a thumb drive. On it is the electronic framework you created."

"What? Why?" Jonathan was confused.

"Jonathan, no one can know that I'm here," Stephenson said.

"I get that. I appreciate you. But…" Jonathan had a dozen questions, yet only one came out. "Where did you get it? Who sent you here?"

"Ari," Stephenson replied quickly.

"What? Ari's dead," Jonathan blurted.

"I know. It sounds crazy, but I got an email from Ari last night." He paused. "It simply said to get to the office ASAP for further instructions. So, I did. On my desk was a typed memo to get you this drive. I know what's on it because, well, I peeked."

"Okay, but…" Jonathan didn't know where to start.

"Jonathan, please don't tell anyone I was here or that I gave you this." Before Jonathan could reply, Stephenson added, "I can't lose my job. I've got twins now." He paused. "I'm leaving. Count to 10 and then get the drive."

Stephenson made a beeline to the exit. Jonathan took a few deep breaths, then got up after what felt like a 10-count. He found the drive under the cup and napkins, then tossed the trash.

When he turned back, Walter Bachman was there, standing tall and smiling. "What are you doing? Busing tables? Did you get a job at McDonald's since we last spoke?" He laughed.

Jonathan laughed too, slipping the drive into his pocket. "Thanks for meeting me here, Walter. My home office isn't much."

"And I'm sure Dr. Reese isn't a huge fan either," Walter added with a smile.

"Well, there is that too," Jonathan said, motioning for him to sit.

Before Walter did, he noticed four men conversing on the other side of the dining area. "In a minute, Jonathan," he said, walking over to greet them. They shook hands like old friends, laughing.

Jonathan didn't mind. He was eager to see what was on the drive. Opening it on his laptop, he found the framework file exactly as it had been a couple of weeks earlier.

No doubt Warren Scott had gone to great lengths to keep it from him — and to make sure Emerald Medical never knew it existed, even if that meant lying. The question was, who sent the email from Ari's account and left the memo?

"Jonathan, come over here," Walter called from across the room. "There are some people I'd like you to meet."

Jonathan closed his laptop and joined him. Walter introduced him as not just his attorney but a great attorney, then one by one introduced four men — each an owner of a prominent area small business.

With each introduction, Walter suggested how Jonathan's skills could help.

"Tim, you've been talking about selling your company to your employees. Helping you make that happen would be child's play for Jonathan."

Jonathan smiled, nodded, blushed a little, and handed out business cards.

Once the introductions were done, they sat down.

"Wow, Walter," Jonathan said with pleasure. "I've been working the phone and email for weeks and haven't come close to introductions like that. Thanks."

"No problem, Jonathan. Happy to help," Walter replied. After a pause, he added, "So, tell me about Jonathan. I've heard great things, but no details."

That led to more than 90 minutes of small talk. Jonathan was comfortable — he now had leads on a few other clients and the recovered file, which eased his mind.

They traded life stories. Jonathan explained how he and Sam met, and spoke about Johnny, Kelly, and AJ, even touching on AJ's budding romance with the team trainer, Shea.

"Ah, young love. Isn't it wonderful?" Walter remarked.

Walter had more history to cover, but less detail in each era. He talked about why he enlisted in the Army in college, how he got into electronic security and surveillance, and how he later used that in private-sector consulting.

"Jonathan, do you have any hobbies?" Walter asked.

"No, not really. Unless you count work and coaching football. You?"

"The past and the future," Walter replied quickly. "As for the past, I enjoy learning about the rise and fall of nations and detailed accounts of wars — from the Spanish-American to the Gulf Wars — and lesser-known conflicts."

Jonathan nodded. "Interesting. And the future?"

"The future," Walter said dramatically, "I love exploring uses for technology, computer science, programming, and artificial intelligence."

Jonathan's eyes widened. "Wow. Does that dovetail into your work helping companies with security and surveillance?"

"Oh, sure," Walter said. "But that's not my true passion."

"What is?"

"I love working with stained glass."

"As in windows?" Jonathan asked.

"Absolutely," Walter said, brightening. "But stained glass isn't just for windows — crafters make sun catchers, candle holders, picture frames, even jewelry. I'm hardly an experienced artisan, but I enjoy it. I find it relaxing."

"Sounds like it," Jonathan said.

"And dangerous too," Walter added with a laugh, holding up his gauze-wrapped thumb.

Jonathan raised his eyebrows.

"Yep, I was careless a few weeks back and sliced my thumb pretty good," Walter said, chuckling. "It's healing fine, but I'll have a scar shaped like New Jersey. Want to see?"

Jonathan laughed and waved his hands. "No, no. I'll take your word for it."

Eventually, they got to the purpose of the meeting — estate planning. But time was short. Rather than go through it, Jonathan gave Walter questions to answer and a list of needed documents.

Walter suggested meeting again at McDonald's on Monday morning. That wouldn't work for Jonathan — he had the Emerald Medical meeting.

"Okay, then. I'll bring them to you after practice Monday," Walter said. "I have every confidence you'll win tonight."

"I appreciate that," Jonathan said with a smile.

"If something changes, text me," Walter said. "Give me your phone and I'll text myself, so you have my number." Jonathan complied.

Walter glanced at the phone. "Man, you've got a ton of apps open."

"I know. I'm not great with technology," Jonathan admitted.

"No worries. I know my way around," Walter said, tapping on the phone. "Let me do this, this, and this." After a pause, his phone dinged with a text message. "We're all set. I'm programmed into your phone and you in mine."

They shook hands and went in opposite directions.

Chapter 118

When Jonathan got home from his meeting with Walter, he was elated — the exhilaration of making a new friend, the euphoria of being connected with prospective clients, and the thrill of getting the file. It was a near-perfect morning.

Once Sam was up, she was excited for Jonathan — except for the part about Walter. She scrunched her nose at his mention and declared, "I just don't trust him. I don't think I ever will."

Jonathan calmly replied, "Sam, you just need to give him a chance. There's an energy about him — a resourcefulness. My sense is that he's a good person to know."

According to Ohio high school playoff rules, once the field is whittled down to 16 teams in a division, all games are played at neutral sites. This meant Blacklick High would be traveling a little over an hour east to play the Potters of East Liverpool High School.

East Liverpool is located on the Ohio River at the extreme eastern edge of the state, near where Ohio, Pennsylvania, and West Virginia converge. The city has a rich pottery and ceramic history — hence the Potters mascot — and its football team has a reputation for being hard-nosed and blue-collar in approach.

After eight straight losing seasons, this year marked the Potters' return to the playoffs. They had the size and strength to sustain offensive drives against the AJ-led defense, and that brawn could somewhat contain Tank's bruising, off-tackle hammer runs.

The Mustangs, however, had Brady Troy. While the Potters fought valiantly, the deaf quarterback's versatility ended their miracle season. Walter Bachman's confidence was well placed, as Blacklick advanced with a 24-14 win.

On Saturday, AJ once again ventured over to Shea's. And on Sunday, he had Shea "be the visiting team." They studied together, he introduced her to the video game world — which she rolled her eyes at — and she enjoyed talking with Dr. Reese over the family's takeout pizza dinner. As they geeked out over medical terms, AJ rolled his eyes.

On both Saturday and Sunday, Jonathan was up early and becoming a regular at McDonald's. He'd run into people Walter had introduced him to, and they would introduce him to others. His network was building.

However, his main objective was to pore over and finalize the electronic framework, then create an understandable presentation for the Emerald Medical meeting on Monday morning. He intended to have everything ready and be fully prepared to talk through it. The work consumed his every thought throughout Saturday and into Sunday — so much so that he was completely oblivious to Shea and Sam's science banter.

On Monday morning, Jonathan was up and headed to his meeting. He stopped at McDonald's briefly for coffee to stick with his routine. Despite the detour, he arrived at the Emerald Medical campus and the appropriate conference room 10 minutes before the 8 a.m. meeting. He was the only one there and sat at one end of a large conference table.

A few minutes later, members of the Emerald Medical legal team entered, led by Lisa Kaye. One by one, they introduced themselves, shook Jonathan's hand, and took seats together on the side of the table opposite the door.

At the top of the hour, a receptionist held the door open for the Eisenberg & Anders team — Warren Scott, Stephenson, and two other associates from Jonathan's old team. None of them acknowledged Jonathan; they didn't even look his way. It was as if their former colleague were invisible. They sat opposite the Emerald Medical team, as far from Jonathan as possible.

Being neither with Emerald Medical nor his old firm, Jonathan remained alone at one end.

"Where do we want to start?" Lisa asked, immediately taking charge.

Warren spoke first. "Before we talk about anything, I want to go on the record saying it's a bad idea to involve in this due diligence process anyone from outside Eisenberg & Anders."

"Yes, Mr. Scott. Noted. You've made that clear in your emails," she said, emphasizing the plural, "to me — and to my boss — and her boss." She leaned in slightly. "And," she added, stressing the word, "in your voicemails to all of us."

After a pause, she continued, "I'll explain this one last time — and this comes from well above any of our pay grades — Mr. Reese will be involved and will be leading your team. We do not care about his employment status at Eisenberg & Anders. Is that clear?"

Warren pressed on. "Yes, I understand what you're saying. But it's nearly impossible for us to do our job if he will neither initiate communication nor return ours." He still refused to address Jonathan by name or look at him. "And I'm not sure he brings any value to the situation."

Lisa turned toward Jonathan, feeling as though she were refereeing children.

Jonathan took a deep breath. "As to Mr. Scott's concern about communication, as I've shared, I've made attempts to contact the Eisenberg & Anders team. I can't speak to where those messages have gone. And I can't dispute that they've made attempts to contact me, but for whatever reason I've not received them. Going forward, I suggest that all communication include someone from the Emerald Medical legal team."

Lisa thought for a moment, then nodded in agreement.

Jonathan continued, "As for bringing value, I believe I have plenty to offer." From his small stack of materials, he pulled out his laptop, powered it up, and asked, "Is there a way for me to connect to that screen?" He motioned to a large television monitor at the other end of the table.

"Lucas, would you please?" Lisa said.

A young staff attorney turned on the monitor with a remote, then came over. "Can I?" he asked, gesturing toward Jonathan's laptop.

Jonathan nodded and turned it toward him. Lucas made a series of keystrokes, and within seconds Jonathan's screen appeared on the monitor. He turned the laptop back toward Jonathan, who thanked him with a nod.

With the tension in the room, Jonathan's hands weren't steady, and he fumbled before locating the framework file. Once he found it, he clicked to open it.

As the program launched, Jonathan said, "The whole due diligence process is necessary. But with technology, I'm not sure travel to far-off places is as necessary as it used to be."

The framework file appeared on the screen. Warren's eyes bulged. Before he could speak, Lisa asked, "Is this the program you mentioned to us, Jonathan?"

"Yes," Jonathan said with confidence.

"Where did you get that, Reese?" Warren erupted, jumping to his feet and pointing. "How did you get it? Who gave it to you?"

"No one," Jonathan said carefully.

"Then you broke into our offices or hacked our server?" Warren shot back.

"Wait a minute," Lisa interrupted. "Mr. Scott, you told me this file never existed. Now you claim Mr. Reese stole it from your firm?"

"Umm…" Warren broke his glare at Jonathan, scrambling to cover for his earlier statement.

"You lied to me," Lisa said, her frustration boiling over.

"No, I didn't," Warren protested. "I thought you were referring to something else."

Lisa threw her hands up and rolled her eyes. She knew this was exactly the file she'd asked about. *I can't believe Eisenberg & Anders would have such an annoying liar,* she thought.

Warren looked back at Jonathan, ready to resume his interrogation. Stephenson shifted uneasily, worried his role might come out. Jonathan stayed silent.

Lisa abruptly stood. "Enough. I don't care where this came from or any of that." She turned to Jonathan. "Mr. Reese, will this work as you described a couple of weeks ago?"

"Yes," Jonathan said. Then he added, "More or less."

"More or less?" Lisa pressed, as Warren smirked.

"It's 95 percent," Jonathan explained. "If I could borrow your tech genius here," he said, pointing at Lucas, "I'm confident we could clean up some rough edges and enhance the functionality. From there, I have every confidence this will work."

Warren began, "Again, I must go on record—"

"Shut up and sit down," Lisa snapped. "Lucas, please work with Mr. Reese. Help him however he needs it."

Lucas smiled at Jonathan.

Jonathan smiled back. "Call me Jonathan, please."

Chapter 119

AJ's booming voice filled the tiny smartphone speaker: "Hey, it's AJ. I'm probably ignoring responsibilities. Leave something intriguing or funny, and you might get a call back."

Noah Turner hung up without a word, then protested, "Sebastian, let's just let it go."

"Oh, don't be a sissy, Noah," Sebastian shot back as he continued driving to school. "Call it again."

"Why?" Aiden Davis asked. "I'm with Noah on this. We don't know who was behind any of the things that have happened to us."

"Us?" Sebastian fired back; his tone sharp. "My trunk, my tires, my plates — I'm not letting this go."

"Sebastian?" Noah said, concern in his voice. "Why?"

Before Sebastian could respond, Aiden added, "We got them. They got us."

"You guys are something else," Sebastian said in disgust. "In case you've completely lost track of current events, we got kicked off the football team."

"True," Noah conceded. "But we almost burned down a whole city block."

"So what?" Sebastian shot back. "It doesn't justify getting booted from the team." No one responded — there was no reasoning with him. "Just call again."

"What if he answers?" Noah asked.

"I hope he does," Sebastian said with a sinister look. "Talking to him will be even better."

Chapter 120

"How did it go?" Sam asked Jonathan as he walked into the kitchen. Dr. Reese was busy mapping out her schedule for the next few weeks, hoping and assuming the Mustangs would continue to advance in the playoffs.

Jonathan stood expressionless, then broke into a huge grin as he raised his right hand and extended three fingers — the little, ring, and middle — while holding his index finger and thumb against his palm.

Sam rose to her feet, smiling. She was excited. "Tell me all about it. Does this mean you can cut loose Bachman as a client?"

"No, Sam," Jonathan laughed. "Walt and I are tight. In fact, he texted me another introduction about an hour ago."

Sam scrunched her nose in displeasure. "I still don't trust him." Then her excitement returned. "So tell me all about it."

Jonathan told her about the cold nature of the Eisenberg & Anders team, the clash between Lisa Kaye and Warren Scott, Warren being caught in a lie, the tech attorney Lucas, and how Lisa had set the date and time for when the due diligence would take place simultaneously in three locations — the Far East, Emerald Medical, and Eisenberg & Anders.

"Friday, Dec. 1?" Sam asked. "That's the day of the state championship game. How are you going to make that work? Did you say anything?"

"No, I didn't," Jonathan confessed. Sam looked concerned. "Sam, amidst all the tension in the room, things were working in my favor. I didn't want to spoil that over something that wasn't for sure yet."

"Plus, it might jinx the team," Sam added with a smile.

"Exactly," Jonathan said. "And I'm not sure it's going to matter."

"What do you mean?" Sam asked, wincing with curiosity.

"Well," Jonathan said, "because we're going to be conducting this due diligence examination from opposite sides of the world, each team is going to compromise on the time. The Far East team will start at 2 p.m. local time, and the U.S. team will start at 2 a.m. local time, same day. The goal on both ends is to be done within eight hours."

"Oh, okay," Sam said, indicating her comprehension. "So, where are you working from? Home? Emerald? The firm?"

"Well, that's the bad news," Jonathan replied. "I'm headed downtown." He let out a heavy sigh. "But I can stomach it for one day. The hard part will be getting up and being down there by 2 a.m."

Sam laughed and replied sarcastically, "Oh, you poor baby. Two a.m.? One day? You get no sympathy from me."

Chapter 121

While AJ often seemed at odds with his dad, he shared his father's work ethic, discipline, and love of routine. He rarely missed class, stayed prepared, and after school followed a steady rhythm: study table, a quick meet-up with Casey, helping with ice and water for practice, and stealing a romantic moment with Shea before leaving. Life was going well.

Life was going well for Jonathan too. His client list was growing, he no longer had to fight downtown traffic, and—though Sam didn't necessarily approve—he had a new friend and mentor in Walter.

Beyond texting Jonathan about a prospective client during the Emerald Medical meeting, Walter and Jonathan exchanged a few messages Monday afternoon, mostly about getting Jonathan the documents he needed.

Off to the side, Sam listened to the steady ding of Jonathan's phone. Each time she asked, "Walter?" Jonathan would just nod and smile before laboriously typing a perfectly worded reply. All Sam could do was shake her head and mutter, "I sure hope you know what you're doing."

Walter arranged to deliver the documents before practice. Jonathan spotted him in the distance chatting with Casey and a few early-arriving players helping Shea. As Jonathan headed that way, Walter excused himself and began ambling toward him.

Almost immediately, though, an out-of-place figure emerged from the parking lot: Warren Scott, striding fast with an angry scowl. He intercepted Jonathan well before Walter could reach him.

"How did you get that file?" Warren shouted, eyes blazing.

Jonathan said nothing.

"I'm going to find out," Warren fumed. "You're working with someone on the inside—or you broke in. Or hacked in. I'm going to get you."

Walter arrived in time to hear the last of it. He stood calmly until there was a pause, then asked with a slight chuckle, "Jonathan, who is this twit?"

Warren blinked, stunned. "W-w-what'd you say?"

Walter didn't flinch. "Unlike you, I don't stutter. You heard me."

Warren squared up to the taller man, incredulous at being disrespected so openly. "Do you have any idea who I am?"

"No," Walter said, still chuckling. "That's why I just asked Jonathan, who is this twit?"

Warren leaned in aggressively. "I'm the acting managing partner of the largest, most prestigious law firm in Columbus—Eisenberg & Anders. We're some of the top lawyers in the country. And with the snap of a finger, I can have a team sue you so hard your ancestors feel it."

Walter didn't respond—just grinned and turned to Jonathan. "Sounds like somebody wasn't breastfed as a child." Then he pulled a black thumb drive from his pocket. "Here, Jonathan. Let me know if you have questions." Once Jonathan had the drive, Walter walked away.

Warren turned back to Jonathan, searching for his next attack.

Jonathan cut him off. "Warren, this is not the place for any of this. And I refuse to engage with you."

Just then AJ and Shea pulled up with the water. Jonathan blew his whistle twice, calling players in for the start of practice.

Before long, Warren was being jostled by players crowding around Coach Dad. Still, he managed to shout, "This isn't over, Reese. I will get you. Know that."

Chapter 122

Jonathan couldn't wait to get home and tell Sam about the Warren–Walter showdown.

"How do I root for them both to lose?" she asked.

"Sam"— Jonathan paused to get her attention — "you've got to trust me. There's something about Walter. When things seem dark, he's the guy to turn to."

"Whatever, Jonathan." Sam waved him off. "I don't trust him."

For the second week in a row, the Blacklick Mustangs were headed to Zanesville High School for a neutral-site game — the regional championship against Ridgewood High School.

For a fourth straight year, the Generals had won the large-school division of the 14-team Inter-Valley Conference, which spans six counties in east-central Ohio. While that usually led to a playoff berth, this was the first year they'd advanced this far.

Though seeded higher than East Liverpool, the Generals weren't as big or bruising. Whenever the Mustangs needed three or four yards, Brady Troy would read the Ridgewood defense, clap-clap, and send Tank hammering off-tackle in the opposite direction. It kept drives alive and almost always ended in points.

Those long drives also kept the Generals' high-powered offense sidelined, and when they did take the field, they faced a well-rested Blacklick defense. Time and again, Ridgewood had to punt.

Their only promising drive came late in the third quarter, when they pushed deep into Mustang territory and earned a first down at the 11-yard line. Already down 17-0, they weren't playing for a field goal. The quarterback aimed for a seemingly open receiver in the end zone—until AJ closed fast, arriving just as the ball did. He had as much right to it as the receiver, and after a brief midair tussle, came away with the interception.

It ended Ridgewood's lone scoring threat but not without consequences. In the struggle, AJ jammed his right little finger. It hurt at first but soon went numb, stuck in an awkward position—just like in the Utica game earlier in the season. Remembering that incident calmed his initial panic.

As AJ came to the sidelines, he called out, "Shea, Shea, Shea." Keenly interested in what was happening in the game, especially as it related to her boyfriend, she was there waiting.

She fronted up to AJ. "Relax," Shea calmly grabbed AJ gently by the wrist and repeated, "Relax." And again, "just relax," tenderly caressing AJ's hand. As Shea did, she maneuvered her body so that her back was against AJ's chest. She continued to gingerly examine the hand.

AJ could only feel her warm, gentle touch. Seconds later, Shea reversed the position of her body, facing AJ again. AJ's finger was back in a normal position. She then quickly taped the little finger to AJ's ring finger and caringly remarked, "We need to ice that later."

Before Shea released AJ's hand, he looked her in the eye, whispered thanks, and then squeezed her hand twice, as if to say, *I'm here. I'm with you. We're together.*

Chapter 123

Blacklick stomped Ridgewood, 27-0, to win the regional championship. None of it was surprising—they were playing their best football and were the No. 1-ranked team in the region—but they still celebrated like it was an upset. Loud music. Yelps and cheers. High-fives. Hugs.

Despite all the carrying on and commotion, Shea had a job to do—cutting athletic tape, doling out ice packs, tending to minor abrasions. It was a challenge.

As the celebrating carried on, Shea quietly excused herself. She needed to use the bathroom. While she knew when to avert her eyes, she was not comfortable trusting that 50-some high school football players would return that courtesy. She left the locker room and found a girls' restroom in another part of Zanesville High School. She wasn't alone, however.

Hanging out in the washroom was a clique of Blacklick varsity cheerleaders. Their chatter stopped the moment Shea entered. They just looked at her and then giggled when she entered the stall. Their nonsensical exchange continued as Shea took care of her business.

When Shea was done, she came out and squared up to an open sink to wash her hands. The gaggle of cheerleaders went quiet again. A lone cheerleader came up and stood behind her. Shea didn't need the reflection in the mirror to know who it was—it made her stomach tighten.

While Sebastian was no longer part of the Blacklick football equation, in a sense, he still had a presence. His girlfriend, Jessa Harroway, was a cheerleader.

Jess was the kind of person other girls aspired to be. She was tall and attractive. While she had an athletic build, she had no interest in sweating, as that might mess up her platinum-blonde hair, signature winged eyeliner, and always photo-ready appearance. She carried herself with confidence and was known to be incredibly charming and sweet.

While many aspired to be her, they also feared her. Jess was the alpha cheerleader and ran the squad like a CEO. She dictated every move, every cheer, and every outfit. If you crossed her, outshined her, or took any attention from her, you'd better watch out. Those who did proclaimed that she became "like liquid evil poured into skin."

"Have you heard the latest, Shea?" Jess sneered, holding her phone as if she was ready to play something.

Shea didn't answer. She just wanted to wash her hands and get out. That was not on Queen Jess' agenda, however.

"Don't do it, Jess," Kaylee Dawson pleaded.

"Shut up, Kaylee," Jess snapped back. She wasn't interested in feedback, certainly not from an underling on the squad. With that, the alpha hit play on a recording and held out the phone so that the audio would be clear. Standing with a hand on her hip, she watched Shea's reflection, looking to see her reaction.

Sebastian: "So, AJ? What's up with you and Sheasquatch?"
AJ: "Yep."

Shea looked up the moment she heard AJ's voice.

AJ: "Let's just say I lost a bet and had to take the ugliest girl in school to the Stampede. Just paying up on that."

Shea's eyes darted from herself to Jess and then back.

Sebastian: "You seem to be overpaying on it, AJ."
AJ: "How was I supposed to know she'd get a makeover? This is an inside joke that somehow got out of hand."

Shea just stared into her own face.

Sebastian: "Really? Are you guys serious?"
AJ: "No. Hardly. Let's just call it a pity play. You know, play it out and see what I can get."

Shea felt all alone. A sickening lump formed in her throat as she watched tears well up in her own eyes.

Sebastian: "That's cold. And that says something coming from me."
AJ: "Thanks! Yeah, let's be real. She's cleaned up a bit since then—but let's not pretend she's not still her. Deep down, she's still Sheasquatch. Always will be."

"Stop it, Jess," Kaylee stepped forward and protested. "Enough. Don't do it."

"Too late, Kaylee," Jess snarled as she worked her phone a bit. "You can't un-ring a bell."

Shea took the opportunity to move to exit the bathroom. As she did, Jess called out, "Go ahead. Run away. But you can't run from the fact that you'll always just be Sheasquatch."

In the locker room, the celebration was interrupted by a symphony of chimes and dings as players' phones lit up with text messages and social media notifications. The joyous air became somber as, one by one, they played the recording Jess had shared.

Even AJ got a notification. When he heard it, he jumped to his feet and looked for Shea. He didn't see her and panicked. Spotting Casey, he raced over and pleaded, "I didn't say this," as he played the message. Casey immediately became concerned for Shea as well. She knew her friend had gone to the bathroom, so she went after her, leaving AJ in his bewildered denial.

Casey quickly found Shea, sobbing in the hall halfway between the bathroom and the locker room. Other Blacklick students were around and had also received the notification. Shea couldn't escape the recording. Her hurt was amplified by humiliation.

"Who did this?" Casey asked. While the recording was bad, in her mind the distribution was the bigger sin. Through her tears, Shea indicated Jess and pointed to the bathroom.

Casey headed in that direction and stormed into the bathroom, demanding of Jess, "Why did you do that? You had no right."

In a flippant manner, Jess replied, "Sure I did. Let's call it a public service announcement. Everyone needs to know that wonder boy is not so wonderful, and Shea is still Sheasquatch."

Casey stepped forward aggressively, but then stopped herself. She made a guttural sound indicating her frustration. "Why do people like you have to be so mean?"

Still flippant, Jess replied to Casey's rhetorical question, "Because we can be."

Casey sarcastically replied, "That's great. Real nice." She turned to go back to console Shea, but added, "This isn't over."

As she did, Jess called out, "Hey." Once she had Casey's attention, she remarked, holding up her middle finger, "Read this, bitch."

Chapter 124

Moments after Casey left the locker room, so did AJ. He went in a different direction, however, so he didn't find Shea. Eventually, he gave up and returned to the locker room.

By now, Shea was back. She had a job to do, and she was committed to doing it. She pushed her hurt aside, swallowed the humiliation, and got busy. Replacing those feelings, however, was anger—an anger toward AJ.

"Shea," AJ uttered, half out of breath.

Before he could say anything else, Shea shut him down. "Get away. I don't want to talk to you." She worked double time, maneuvering around AJ as if he wasn't there—never making eye contact, her posture tight with fury.

AJ had never seen her like this. He understood it, based on what she thought she knew—but what she knew was completely wrong. He wanted to explain, but she didn't want to listen. That was clear. AJ quietly walked away, feeling his own hurt and a growing bewilderment, hoping she'd reconsider.

The ride back to Blacklick High was quiet. No one knew what to say, so no one said anything. Players knew something was off but couldn't reconcile their thoughts. On the recording, it was clearly AJ's voice, yet the words were uncharacteristic. AJ's consistent denials complicated things. Still, he was a teammate and friend—you don't turn on someone for one ugly transgression.

Then again, Shea was also a teammate and friend. She didn't deserve humiliation, especially at the hands of Sebastian and his crew, who had never been anything but mean-spirited toward her. Compassion poured out for her.

Brady was mostly oblivious. He'd never heard First Friend's voice and couldn't hear the recording. Even with a transcript, he couldn't track who said what. But he could sense the tension and mirrored the team's unease.

The coaches also sensed something was off. It didn't feel like a team that had just won a regional title, but they didn't know about the recording. They assumed the team was looking ahead to the state semifinal—a rematch with Dayton-Kettering Bishop Alter.

As for AJ, he felt sick. He believed every whisper on the bus was about him. His mind raced, searching for a way to reconnect with Shea. He texted her—once to say sorry, once to check in, and once to ask to talk. No response. Maybe her phone was off. Maybe she'd blocked him.

She wasn't on the bus and wouldn't be at the high school when the team returned. She'd found a ride home with team parents, leaving others to cover her duties.

Once back in Jefferson Township, AJ went straight home and to his room and collapsed on his bed. He tossed and turned, ruminating until exhaustion took over.

When he woke, the anguish rushed back. At a reasonable time, he texted, "Good morning." No reply. An hour later, he suggested meeting to work on their Senior English or Advanced Science project—or both. Again, nothing.

By Saturday and into Sunday, AJ still felt unsettled but began to rationalize: they had classes together, shared hallways, group projects, football practices, and at least one more game. They would cross paths. And if not, Casey might help; she had introduced them, after all.

These thoughts let him relax a bit. He just needed to get to Monday.

But it was not to be. Monday, Shea wasn't in the hallway—or in class. Rumor was she was home working on college applications, same for Tuesday. It was Thanksgiving week, so those were the only two school days.

In Advanced Science, the teacher congratulated AJ—and Shea, in her absence—for turning in their joint project. AJ felt a sickening twist in his stomach. In Senior English, Mrs. Makowski praised their other project. AJ realized Shea had single-handedly completed both assignments over the weekend to avoid him. The work was done, but the spirit behind it stung.

He couldn't blame her. Given what she thought she knew, her actions made sense. Somehow, they needed to clear the air.

That wasn't going to happen at practice. AJ skipped talking to Casey and went to the training room to wait for Shea. She never arrived. Alone, AJ filled the water jugs and drove them to practice.

It felt odd. Eyes on him. Whispers. A crime he didn't commit and couldn't prove he hadn't. His mind was in a fog. This carried over into how he practiced — lethargic movement, messed-up assignments, blank stares. Worst of all, he had no skillset for reorienting himself.

After practice, he caught Casey, hoping for advice. She saw his pain but didn't know how much was self-inflicted. The voice was his, but the words didn't fit.

She knew Shea's hurt was real. "Time heals all wounds," she said, "but it doesn't necessarily create amnesia. Give her space." Casey revealed Shea wasn't coming back to practice and was likely done with the team. "Who could blame her?"

As Casey drove off, AJ stood there — dazed, confused, out of answers. He didn't think he could feel any worse.

Chapter 125

After Warren Scott showed up at practice, Jonathan was a bit unnerved. He had to wonder what that bastard might try next.

Still, he couldn't dwell on it—there was too much work to do. Beyond coaching the Mustangs in their playoff run, he needed to ride the momentum building in his law practice. He felt bad for not making progress on Walter's estate plan, but Walter bore some of the blame; his new friend, mentor, and frequent texting buddy had already referred him to at least a half-dozen new clients.

Right now, though, Jonathan's focus was Emerald Medical. The stakes for the Far East acquisition were enormous — shareholders expected a boost in stock price, which meant everyone down the chain was invested in success. Jonathan treated it with the seriousness it deserved, working daily with Lucas — Emerald Medical's tech-savvy legal whiz — to blend the technical nuances of computers, the internet, and digital security with the realities of corporate acquisitions.

All this left Jonathan with even less time for family life than when he'd been at Eisenberg & Anders. But he told himself it was temporary: take the work while it's there, do the work while it's there—because the day will come when it's not.

Chapter 126

For AJ, the week of Thanksgiving was horrible. Too much alone time left him stuck in his head, obsessing over the situation.

He kept running scenarios for how to prove it wasn't him on the recording. Sebastian seemed the obvious culprit, but AJ knew he'd never admit it—publicly, anyway. Privately, Sebastian was probably celebrating the damage.

AJ also replayed moments with Shea, wondering how he'd ever overlooked her. That first date at the Stampede kept looping in his mind. He longed for even a single word from her, and the fact that he couldn't see her felt like a physical ache.

AJ was not the only one to miss Shea, however. While they lacked the emotional connection, AJ's teammates felt her absence too. She had become a fixture within Blacklick Mustang football. And they appreciated how she treated injuries and helped them work through the various bumps and bruises of the long football season.

While they were confused and divided as to AJ's culpability, the team was unanimous in their disdain for Jess and her cheerleading minions. The broadcasting of the recording was a bullying tactic aimed at one of their own. And they planned retribution.

Before the state semi-final game against Kettering Bishop Alter at Springfield High School, the cheerleaders went all out. Wanting to mark the occasion, they crafted a dramatic run-through banner—two oversized sheets of paper taped together and stretched tight at the end of a gauntlet of cheerleaders and band members. With extra prep time that week and creative direction from Jess, the banner became a true work of art. It featured the Mustang name, vivid imagery, and bold slogans—designed not just to impress but to inspire. The goal was clear: fire up the team, energize the crowd, and set an electric tone for the game.

Like a proud mother, Jess stood on the exit end of the run-through banner with her phone intending to capture the spectacular moment when the team came tearing through. She beamed as she imagined how the video would play on social media as 50 pairs of legs raced toward the banner, led by Brady, Tank, and AJ.

Only a few yards before, however, the trio veered 90 degrees to the right, avoiding the banner and slipping through the gauntlet. One by one the team followed, leaving the banner completely untouched. Jess looked on in humiliation and horror.

The final person to the banner was Casey. She simply trotted up to it and used her hands and fingers to gesture in ASL, *read this bitch*. Clueless about the message, Jess simply fired back a one-finger salute. To which Casey followed up signing, *this is not over*.

"AJ! Focus! Get your head in the game!" Coach Dad shouted from the sidelines.

AJ had just dropped his third potential interception of the game. The first, late in the second quarter, seemed minor at the time—but it gave the Archbishop Alter Knights a chance to open the scoring with a field goal.

Alter came in believing they could beat Blacklick a second time, and they had reason. Their only loss all season was by a single touchdown to perennial Division III power Trotwood-Madison, and they'd only improved as the season went on.

But this was not the same Mustang team they faced in week one. Blacklick now had a revamped offense, a deep coaching staff, a legitimate quarterback, an actual kicker, and the discipline to execute on the X's and O's.

That discipline showed. The Mustangs answered Alter's field goal with a touchdown to take a 7–3 lead, then forced a punt and let Brady Troy march the offense—*clap-clap*—down the field. When the drive stalled, Brady got it going again with handoffs to Tank, hammering left or right for steady yardage. With the clock running, Brady scrambled in for another touchdown, sending Blacklick into halftime up 14–3.

The momentum carried into the third quarter. The Mustangs added ten more points, stretching the lead to 24–3. The game looked all but over—until AJ missed an assignment. An Alter receiver slipped wide open for a long catch-and-walk-in touchdown. The Knights missed the extra point but closed to 24–9, sparking hope.

Alter quickly forced a punt and took advantage of good field position to add a short field goal, making it 24–12.

Blacklick drove to the Alter 20 but missed a long field goal with under seven minutes left. The Knights started a methodical march—five- and six-yard passes—until their quarterback got careless with a throw to the flats. AJ read it perfectly, ready to take it to the house, but bobbled the ball and let it hit the turf. Alter kept the drive alive, scored, and pulled within five, 24–19.

Hoping to close it out, Brady and Tank tried to hammer the ball downfield and bleed the clock, but two penalties stalled the drive. The Mustangs had to punt, giving Alter just over a minute to pull off a game-winner.

"AJ! Focus!" Coach Dad barked again as AJ dropped yet another easy interception, letting Alter's drive continue.

After a shaky, distracted week of practice, AJ was playing the same way on the field. Fortunately, his teammates stepped up. The rest of the defense held, stopping Alter's final desperate push and securing Blacklick's chance to defend its state title.

As they waited for the team to change and head back to Blacklick High, Jonathan and the other coaches admitted they were lucky—the season could just as easily have ended that night.

Instead, they turned their attention forward. They fully expected a rematch with Cardinal Mooney, but they were wrong—and shocked. Mooney had been soundly beaten by Coldwater Bluff, 35–7.

A look at the box score revealed why: Coldwater Bluff's offense ran heavily through one receiver, who racked up 250 yards and scored four of the team's five touchdowns. The coaches knew they had a long week of preparation ahead. They knew little about the Wolves, a relatively new high school formed through the consolidation of four adjacent county districts in northwest Ohio.

Chapter 127

"Is there anything liquid, fragile, perishable, or potentially hazardous?" the man behind the counter asked.

"It's just a binder," the teenage postal patron replied, his tone edged with snark.

"Anything liquid, fragile, perishable, or potentially hazardous?" the man repeated.

"No," the teen said, this time with an aggravated sigh, before adding his own question: "Will this get there tomorrow?"

The postal employee glanced at the address on the USPS Priority Mail Express label and replied, matching the teen's tone, "Yes. But this is going to a school, so no one will be there on Sunday." After a pause, he added, "It'll be delivered Monday before 10 a.m."

"Okay, fine," the teen muttered. "What do I owe?"

"The amount's right here. Sign here. Insert your card here." The postal worker pointed to the screen and the payment device. "Your receipt will have a tracking number."

Without another word, the teen signed, paid, and tore off the receipt before exiting the small Blacklick postal facility.

The moment he stepped outside, Aiden Davis called out, "Did you get it mailed?"

Sebastian Sullivan didn't answer. He simply raised the receipt high over his head in a clenched fist and gave Aiden a look that made his intentions clear—he was up to no good.

Chapter 128

"Could I talk to Shea, Dr. Brooks?" AJ could barely get the words out, even though he'd rehearsed them over and over on the short drive.

Shea's father stepped onto the porch—where AJ had kissed Shea on their first date. "Let's talk. Please, take a seat, AJ," Dr. Brooks said calmly, gesturing to a pair of chairs off to the side.

Without a word, AJ complied. He swallowed hard; his heart was pounding.

"AJ, I'm sorry," Shea's father began, then paused. "But I'm not going to let you talk to Shea. I don't know what this is all about, and I'm not sure I want to. I do know this—it's my job to protect her. Over the years, as a father, I've failed her in plenty of ways—things dads just aren't equipped to do."

His tone hardened slightly. "But I will not fail in protecting her. That's my job as a father. One day you'll understand."

AJ's shoulders slumped. His reason for being there was gone, but he stayed respectfully seated.

"I'm sorry, AJ. I am. But I also feel your pain," Dr. Brooks went on. He hesitated, as if deciding whether to share more. "Years ago, someone I loved very much walked out of my life— our life. It was painful. The pain I see in your eyes is the same I once saw in my own."

He went quiet for a moment before continuing. "For years, I searched for answers. What did I do wrong? What didn't I do? How could I have been more? I asked myself those questions over and over, but I came up with nothing. Then I realized—as an astronomer—it's my job to look to the sky for answers." He pointed toward the pale daylight sky. "And you know what, AJ? Some things just can't be explained. We know gravity pulls two objects toward each other, but we don't fully understand what creates gravity."

He met AJ's gaze. "Love is much the same. We know attraction pulls people together, but we can't explain what creates attraction. It's just there—or it's not. You can't manufacture it. It just happens. So I'm not telling you to give up on Shea. But I am suggesting you not waste too much time and energy trying to figure it out. If it's meant to be, somehow the Universe will correct itself."

Chapter 129

"9-1-1, what's your emergency?" The operator's voice was flat, worn down by twelve hours of saying the same words at least fifty times.

"I think I just saw a man abduct a young woman and drag her into a house," a panicked young man blurted.

The operator straightened in her chair. This was not routine. "Stay on the line. Can you give me an address or location?"

"Sure," he replied quickly, then rattled off the necessary information.

"Order whatever you want—it's our treat," Casey Kaufmann said, flashing a grin and gesturing toward her roommate, Aubrey.

"Thanks," Kaylee Dawson replied. It might have only been Applebee's, but free food and a chance to hang out with college women was a win.

"We heard you tried to stand up to … what's her name?" Casey tilted her head, like she was fishing for something unpleasant.

"Jessa. Just Jess," Kaylee filled in.

"Bitter nag," Aubrey said without missing a beat. "That's what I call her." The table broke into laughter.

"Seriously, though," Casey said once the laughter ebbed. "We appreciate you going to bat for Shea. So, order whatever."

"Yeah, whatever," Aubrey added. "I'm declaring this a cheat meal, so join me. Misery loves company—and French fries." More laughter followed.

When it faded, Kaylee hesitated, glancing between them. "Do you … do you think Shea will come back to the team? I mean, it's not the same without her."

AJ returned to Shea's street but parked halfway down the block. He got out, carrying a blue, medium-sized bucket he'd decorated with a Blacklick Mustang theme. Walking casually to her front porch and set the bucket down with care. He then headed quickly back to his car. Once inside, he pulled out his phone and sent two text messages—each containing only a single bucket emoji.

"Kaylee, trust me—we're working on that," Casey said with a wink. Just then, her phone buzzed with an incoming text. "Oh, I've got to take this. Sorry." She glanced at the screen and replied with a thumbs-up emoji.

"So, if you weren't slumming it with us, Kaylee, what would you be doing tonight?" Aubrey asked, making small talk.

Down at the opposite end of the street from Shea's house, Tank sat in his car with the engine off. Brady was in the passenger seat, and two younger teammates were in the back. Tank's phone buzzed with a text. He glanced at it, said nothing, and replied with a thumbs-up emoji. Then he started the car— prompting a dozen other parked cars in the area to do the same.

"Well, Jess—" Kaylee started, then caught herself. "I mean, *that bitter nag*, as you put it—pretty much ordered us to go to a party at one of the … well, a former football player's house. She's not happy with me, but I told her I had plans."

"It's good to know we rate," Aubrey said.

"Of course. Not even close," Kaylee replied with pride. "Plus, this former player—Sebastian—is kind of a magnet for trouble. He almost burned down a building on the OSU campus."

"Yep," Casey chimed in. "Sounds like nothing good will come from that party. We're glad you're here."

"So, what would you guys be doing if you weren't here?" Kaylee asked. "Aubrey, do you have a boyfriend?"

"Nope. Not at the moment," Aubrey said. "Either my standards are too high, or the quality is too low. I'm still figuring that out."

"How about you, Casey?" Kaylee asked. "Where's David tonight?"

"Oh, he might join us," Casey answered. "Right now, he's running an errand for me."

"What's your name, son?" the deputy sheriff asked. "You're the one who called this in, right?"

"Yes. It's David Quinn," the young man replied, his tone still a little hurried. "Do you need a statement from me?"

"No," the second deputy said with a half-chuckle. "Turns out it was just a party with some high school kids."

"Yep," the first deputy added. "No human trafficking—just underage drinking."

David let out a breath and pressed a hand to his chest in exaggerated relief. "Oh, that's… good to hear. I'm sorry to sound the alarm. It just looked wrong from where I was."

"No, no. It's David, right?" the second deputy said. "See something, say something—you just never know. We need more people like you speaking up."

"So, what happens now?" David asked. "I mean to the kids. Slap on the wrist? Warning?"

"Nope. Doesn't work like that anymore," the first deputy said. "We've got to write each of them up for underage drinking. Anyone under eighteen needs a parent to come get them."

"Really? Write them up? Do they go to jail?" David asked, feigning concern.

"No jail," the second deputy laughed. "Just a fine, an embarrassing moment—and probably an honor code violation if they're in sports or other extracurriculars at Blacklick High."

Casey interrupted the conversation, "I'm sorry, I need to send a text." She picked up her phone and fired out a quick message.

Shea sat cross-legged on her bed, lost in the world of the romantic characters on the pages before her. Alone in the room, her mind wandered, weighing the truth of Alfred Lord Tennyson's famous line from his 1850 poem *In Memoriam A.H.H.*: *'Tis better to have loved and lost than never to have loved at all.*

Just then, her phone buzzed with a text from Casey.

look outside ft door

Curious, she got up, quietly left her room, and followed Casey's instructions. Opening the door, the first thing she noticed was the street—littered with a dozen or so cars, haphazardly parked, headlights on, engines still running.

On the porch sat a decorated bucket, no longer empty. One by one, the players had filled it with dozens of long-stemmed white carnations.

In the front yard stood the football team, each holding a small sign of support and encouragement. At the center, Brady and Tank held a large banner that read, *Would You Please Go to the State Championship Game with Us?*

The moment Shea opened the door, AJ sent Casey a second text—this one with a bucket emoji and a flower. Catching it out of the corner of her eye, Casey said to Kaylee and Aubrey, "Sorry—one last text."

Standing on her front porch, completely touched, Shea received another text from Casey.

see ya @ practice

Chapter 130

Jonathan tried to balance all the new client prospects Walter had referred with the due diligence project. But as the Emerald Medical opportunity drew closer, it began consuming more and more of his waking hours.

On top of preparing for the Coldwater Bluff game, he poured his time and mental energy into making sure the due diligence framework worked flawlessly and the people behind it were ready to execute perfectly. He drafted instructions, ran tests, and performed mock troubleshooting.

This meant several daily exchanges with Lucas and Lisa Kaye at Emerald Medical—via video calls, phone calls, emails, and texts.

The same was not true of his former colleagues at Eisenberg & Anders. They never replied to his emails or texts or made time to join video calls.

The saving grace was Stephenson, whose support Jonathan had always appreciated. Stephenson would make quick calls to confirm they'd received the information, understood it, and were ready. But his tone was guarded—clipped sentences, lowered voice, as if he were constantly watching the door.

It was the kind of wariness that made Jonathan suspect Stephenson wasn't just worried someone might be listening, but that someone *was*. Still, it gave him a small measure of comfort about showing up at Eisenberg & Anders in the early hours of Friday morning.

All this work pulled him away from Sam and AJ, leaving his personal life on hold yet again. He told himself the Emerald Medical situation was just a one-off—and once it passed, his workload would finally stabilize.

Nevertheless, he remained largely out of the loop on AJ's funk. Jonathan knew about the bad week of practice that carried over into the Alter game, but he was oblivious to the broader picture of AJ's demeanor. In the context of the last decade, that wasn't unusual—he was still completely unaware of just how badly AJ was moping around the house.

Moving into Monday, AJ was still really down. Talking with Shea's father helped, and so did being part of the effort to recruit her back to the team. But being at school was not fun. The odd looks and random whispers he sensed were about him bothered him.

He was fortunate, however, as he was no longer the main topic in the rumor mill. The student body was buzzing with the news that the cheerleaders were caught in an honor code violation. They would not be permitted to cheer at the state championship game, but one member — Kaylee — was strangely absent from the infraction. She would lead the junior varsity squad in cheering on the Mustangs.

Nevertheless, the situation at school for AJ was not great, but it was much improved. Shea was back, roaming the halls and sitting in class with him. There was still much to be desired. She still avoided eye contact, sat where AJ had no direct line of sight, and kept her distance — even getting the ice and water to practice before AJ could help. But just seeing Shea gave AJ a small dose of hope that "somehow the Universe will correct itself."

"Are you Jonathan Reese?" the stranger asked.

Being incredibly busy, Jonathan stuck with routine — getting up early, working out and dashing off to McDonald's to jump-start his workday.

"Yes," Jonathan said, looking up from his laptop.

"Consider yourself served," the stranger said, laying an oversized mailer on Jonathan's lap. Then he spoke into his phone: "It's 8 a.m. on Thursday, Nov. 30." Then the stranger just walked away.

Jonathan could feel his stomach tighten. He didn't need to be an attorney to know that nothing good came from being served like this. He closed his laptop, carefully opened the envelope, removed the contents and scanned them.

It was a series of official filings with the Franklin County courts. One requested that Eisenberg & Anders be removed as a defendant in Sebastian Sullivan's defamation case against Jonathan. Another was a dozen or so pages long and requested that Jonathan produce various documents and provide written answers to a series of questions related to the lawsuit. The final filing was a request to allow the law firm of Eisenberg & Anders to become the attorney of record representing Sebastian.

Jonathan could feel the tension building in his neck. While he knew he didn't need to do anything in the moment, it was still one more thing to do. Moreover, he was being pitted against the legal might of his former employer. It was clear that Warren Scott intended to join forces with Sebastian's father to make Jonathan's life hell.

Jonathan slid the filings back into their envelope, dropped them on his laptop and stared out the window. He knew he still had final prep work to do for the Emerald Medical project —

which would be kicking off in less than 24 hours — but the court filings distracted that focus. He just needed to go home.

Chapter 131

"I'm sure you're busy with school and everything, Casey. I appreciate you making the time," Dr. Samantha Reese said as she poured the ASL interpreter a cup of coffee. Jonathan was oblivious to AJ's recent mood change. Sam was not. Concerned, she turned to someone who might have insight.

"Of course, Dr. Reese," Casey responded.

"Sam, please. Call me Sam. Even the 3-year-old neighbor kid calls me Sam," AJ's mom clarified with a smile.

"Okay, Sam. I'm happy to meet with you," Casey replied.

Just then, Jonathan arrived home and walked into the kitchen. "This is a surprise. I didn't expect to see you here," he said to Casey. "And I didn't expect to see you up already," he added to Sam with a laugh.

"Oh, hey, Coach. I figured you'd be downtown, at work," Casey said.

As he sat at the table, Jonathan responded, "Well, I don't work downtown anymore. I'm sort of between things. But I'm trying to figure everything out. The working world is not easy."

"I understand that," Casey replied. "I'm still trying to figure out what comes next for me, too. I graduate soon, and I'm not sure where I'm headed."

"I'm sure you'll be fine," Sam interjected. "You've got a lot going for you."

"Thank you," Casey replied. Then she continued, "But I'm sorry for you. What happened?"

"Well, Casey, it's complicated," Jonathan said with a heavy sigh.

"You might as well tell her, Jonathan," Sam encouraged.

"You don't have to, but I am curious. You worked there a long time," Casey said.

"Yeah, I did," Jonathan started. "Things changed after Ari passed." He then launched into a summary version of events — the who, what, when, etc. And ended with, "The straw that broke the camel's back was when I represented a friend who got in trouble with the law near Bowling Green."

"That guy doesn't sound very nice," Casey said when Jonathan was finished.

"He's not. He's a %#$#%#^," Sam interjected.

"All right, all right," Jonathan said as he motioned with his hands for calm. Everyone laughed. Then he inquired, "So, what are you guys talking about?"

"AJ," Sam stated. "He's sort of out of it, and I was hoping Casey might know something."

"What's wrong?" Jonathan asked. "I haven't noticed anything."

Sam rolled her eyes and said, "Jonathan, you're lost in your own little world, aren't you?"

"Well, Sam," Casey started, "how much do you follow social media?"

"Lately, not at all," Sam responded. "I was fed up with it after the tax levy election. I'm somewhat detoxing from it." She then looked at Jonathan, and so did Casey.

"Don't look at me," Jonathan said defensively. "I've never really been on it. We couldn't have it on our firm computers, and it's too much work typing on the little phone keyboard."

"Honey!" Sam said with playful exasperation. "That's because you communicate in full sentences with perfect English."

"So?" Jonathan defended, and everyone laughed.

When the laughter subsided, Casey warned, "This might be a little tough to hear." With that, she tapped a button on her phone, and the infamous recording started to play.

Sam and Jonathan casually listened as Sebastian began with, "So, AJ? What's up with you and Sheasquatch?" The moment AJ remarked, "Yep," they each leaned in and listened intently.

When the recording was done, Sam confessed, "That's bad. I have to be honest. I'm a little disappointed in AJ. It's embarrassing."

"I know. I'm sorry you had to hear that," Casey said empathetically. "But as a result, Shea was crushed. That's why she wasn't at the Alter game. As you can imagine, she doesn't want anything to do with AJ anymore."

"I don't blame her," Sam asserted. "No one deserves that." She then looked at her husband and asked, "Jonathan, what do you think?"

"Casey, can you play that again?" Jonathan requested.

Casey complied, and they all focused on the recording again.

When it was complete, Jonathan remarked, "Yeah, that's really bad." After a moment of silence, he added, "Except that's not AJ."

"Jonathan?" Sam blurted, looking at her husband to see if he was serious. Casey shot Jonathan a confused look as well.

"It's not. It's just not," Jonathan asserted. "No, Sam, I don't know AJ like I should. And I can keep straight that he'll settle for a pencil as a scholarship. But I know the voice on that recording is not AJ."

"Honey!?" Sam said. "You're either not listening or totally biased."

"Sam, I'm neither," Jonathan responded defiantly. "Sure, you talk to AJ far more than I do, but I hear him all the time talking to the guys," Jonathan said, using air quotes. "I'm telling you, that is not AJ. It's not."

"Are you sure?" Casey asked.

"I can't say exactly why, Casey, but that's not AJ," Jonathan said with even more confidence.

Sam challenged, "Jonathan, I'm not sure denial is how we should play this."

"Sam, that voice is not AJ," Jonathan said, growing annoyed. "I can't prove it," he admitted, "but—" He picked up his phone and began typing a text message. "I know someone who probably can."

"Let me guess. Walter?" Sam said skeptically.

"Walter!" Jonathan responded.

"Oh boy," Sam scoffed, rolling her eyes.

"Casey, can you forward me that recording?" Jonathan asked.

"Sure." Casey quickly operated her phone, and moments later Jonathan got a notification. Then she asked, "What's wrong with Walter?"

"Nothing, Casey," Jonathan said, laughing. "Sam just doesn't like him. Thanks for the file."

"You're welcome, but Walter? Why? He's great," Casey said.

"It's not that I don't like him, Casey. I just don't trust him," Sam clarified.

Chapter 132

"You were behind that recording, weren't you, Sebastian?" AJ rhetorically asked as he had his former teammate cornered at his locker.

Initially, Sebastian was startled but quickly morphed from a defensive posture to someone in control. With that, he gave an ominous smirk and offered a non-denial denial. "Oh, it wasn't me. That was horrible. I'm just as mad as you, AJ."

"You're so full of it," AJ angrily fired back, moving aggressively closer.

"So, what are you going to do?" Sebastian stood his ground. "You can't prove anything." He let that statement settle. "Are you going to beat me up?" He laughed. "I'm already suing your dad. It would be no problem at all adding you to that suit."

Realizing he had no real recourse, AJ relaxed his posture but kept an angry grimace.

Sebastian let out a little chuckle and said, "That's right, AJ. Back off. There is nothing you can do. Get used to losing. You lost the girl. You're going to lose against Coldwater Bluff—no, you're going to get killed by them. Let's see what other losses you're going to endure."

Sebastian then pushed AJ aside as he walked through his position.

Chapter 133

"Can I get you a cup of coffee?" Walter Bachman asked Jonathan. It was just after noon on Thursday, and this was the soonest he could meet.

"Oh, hey," Jonathan responded, looking up from the pages of court filings he'd received earlier. He was so engrossed that he didn't initially comprehend the question. But once he did, he said, "No, thanks. I've got to get to bed early tonight. It's too late for any caffeine."

"Are you okay?" Walter sat down across from him at the McDonald's table.

"Yeah, I'm fine," Jonathan said. "I'm just… I'm just…" He searched for words and then added, "I'm a little frazzled. There's a lot going on."

"Football?" Walter guessed.

"Yes, but football is the least of my issues, Walter."

"So, what do you got? Share your woes with me," Walter coaxed. "I'm all ears."

"Well, I just got this gem this morning." Jonathan lifted the stack of court filings. "I'm being sued for not letting a certain troublemaker back on the football team."

"I was at the meeting," Walter replied. "I remember. That dad is a piece of work."

"Yeah, that dad is," Jonathan said. "Now, my old firm is taking on the case for them."

"They can't do that," Walter said. "Isn't that a conflict?"

"Arguably, yes," Jonathan replied. "But one of the partners — well, you encountered him."

"Mr. Never-been-breastfed," Walter inserted.

"Yes, him," Jonathan confirmed. "He's using this as a weapon against me."

"Why?" Walter leaned in.

"He's always seemed to have it out for me," Jonathan said with an exasperated tone.

"Obviously, there are court rules to prevent these legal system abuses," Walter reasoned.

"Yes, but that all takes time and mental energy, Walter. And that's just not productive." Jonathan paused, then continued, "And I'm supposed to be down at that firm — the firm he runs — at 2 a.m. I have no idea what sort of stunt he's going to pull. It's so stressful."

"Really? Wow. That's early." Walter was incredulous. "But it's a major law firm. Surely, he'll have a level of professionalism."

"You'd think," Jonathan said. "But his M.O. is to do something underhanded. Like, I'm afraid he'll have the security gates locked so I can't get in. Or something like that. And then I just look stupid in front of the client."

"Well, you'll know soon enough, and you'll deal with it. Worrying about things won't change them, however," Walter said.

"You're right," Jonathan conceded.

"But what else, Jonathan?" Walter asked. "You texted about a recording?"

"Yes, the recording," Jonathan confirmed. "A recording was released on social media of my son, AJ, saying some not-so-nice things about… well, his girlfriend. Maybe a former girlfriend now."

"And?" Walter prompted. "That's not good, but how can I help?"

"Walter, I don't think it's AJ," Jonathan said. "In fact, I know it's not. Every fiber of my being says it's not. But I can't prove it."

"Do you have the recording? Can you play it for me?" Walter asked, leaning forward with interest.

"Sure." Jonathan opened his laptop and launched the file. "Lean in, please. I don't want to play it too loud."

Walter bent closer as the recording played. He winced, grimaced and shook his head. When it was done, Walter said, "No, that's not a good look."

"No, it's not. But that's not AJ. It sounds like him, but it's not," Jonathan said firmly. Then he asked, "Is there a way… I mean, you're into these electronic things. Can you somehow determine, or reverse-engineer, or whatever, to prove it's not AJ?"

"Jonathan, I'd be happy to try. Can I get a copy?" Walter pulled a black thumb drive from his pocket and handed it to Jonathan. Then he asked, "If it's not AJ, who do you think is behind it?"

As Jonathan inserted the drive into his computer, he said, "If I had to bet, I'd say it's the ringleader of the kids I kicked off the team. Apples don't fall too far from the tree, you know?"

"No, they don't," Walter said with a laugh. "I will get after it as soon as possible."

As Jonathan worked, he said, "Oh, no rush. I don't need it today."

"Well, right now I don't have much else to do," Walter said. He then showed Jonathan the well-healed, Jersey-shaped wound on his thumb and added, "I'm taking a break from working with stained glass for a bit."

Chapter 134

"Good week of practice," Casey encouraged. AJ needed the affirmation.

"Thanks," he replied as he stood next to his car, talking over the top of it at Casey.

AJ needed to have a solid week of practice. Beyond it being the last week of practice — maybe forever — he and the other defensive back had to somehow stop Coldwater Bluff's ace receiver. As one of the defensive coaches playfully remarked, "No pressure, but the game might rely on you guys."

"How are things on the Shea front?" Casey followed up.

Not wanting to talk about this across cars, he walked toward Casey and said, "Not great, but better. In an odd way, by avoiding eye contact she acknowledges I exist. It's a start."

Just then, Tank came over to join the conversation. "Let's go get pizza," he said.

"Sure," AJ said. "But before we do, I wanted to let you two know — again — that recording is not me. It's not."

"AJ," Casey started, "at first I didn't know what to believe. Now I'm starting to believe you."

Tank added, "Hey, I'm Team AJ. I always have been. Always will be."

"Thanks. That means a lot," AJ responded in a heartfelt manner.

"Do you know who really believes it's not you?" Casey asked. Before AJ could answer, she said, "Your dad."

"My dad? How do you know?" AJ asked, confused.

"I played the recording for him today," Casey replied, then added, "and your mom."

"Wait a minute. When? Where?" AJ was even more confused. "Downtown?"

"No, at your house," Casey said, showing a hint of confusion. "Your dad doesn't work downtown anymore."

"Wait? What are you talking about?" AJ was now completely perplexed. Tank just watched, amused by the back-and-forth.

"You seriously don't know?" Casey asked, carefully studying AJ's face, trying to answer her own question. "Your dad was let go by the firm," she said directly.

"What? When did this happen?" AJ was astonished.

"It was a few weeks back, I think. The tipping point was something about representing a friend for something criminal in a Bowling Green court," Casey said, trying to recall the conversation.

"Oh no. I feel horrible. I think I'm to blame," Tank blurted out, shame consuming his face.

Casey and AJ were further confused. They looked at one another and then each asked Tank a form of, "Why would you think you're to blame?"

"Remember when I got that really short haircut?" Tank said.

"Yes. So?" AJ responded.

Tank quickly told the story of being arrested. "Your dad drove up to get me out," he said, looking genuinely distraught. "You don't know because he told me not to say anything — and clearly, he didn't tell you."

"No, he didn't," AJ said, annoyed. "I still don't understand, Tank. Why would he get fired for that?"

"AJ," Tank said, exasperated, "he missed work to get me out of trouble. Your dad probably got fired for that."

"No, Tank," Casey interjected. "It wasn't that. That was just one think, as I understand it. It was really about football. The firm — well, one person in the firm — gave him an ultimatum to quit coaching or lose his job."

Bewildered, AJ said, "I can't believe I didn't know — but I guess I shouldn't be surprised." Disgust edged his voice. "My dad and I don't communicate. Never have. At least not in a good way. He's always working."

Casey interjected again. "AJ, that's not unusual. It doesn't make your dad a bad person."

"Bad person? No way!" Tank chimed in. "AJ, I wish my dad were half the person yours is."

Casey said, "AJ, maybe you feel shut out — from information, from your dad's life — because he's always working. But here's another perspective." She paused. "I see a man working hard for his family. I see someone who stepped up to coach when no one else would, who gave up his weekend to help Tank, and who faced a choice — his career or the team — and chose the team. Those are sacrifices."

AJ had nothing to say. He just listened and thought.

"And without those choices, none of this happens," Casey added. "The season never starts. Brady probably goes back to OSD. We never meet. You're not playing for a state championship tomorrow. All of it hinges on a series of sacrifices. Think about that."

AJ still had nothing to add. He could only nod his head in uncertain agreement.

Casey added, "And you and Shea never connect."

AJ remained quiet but shared a look that said, "Well, that's nothing now."

"AJ, that's not over. I think your dad is trying to prove it's not you on the recording," Casey said. "Again, sacrifice."

Chapter 135

"Johnny! What are you doing?" AJ greeted as he accepted the incoming call on his short ride home. After the conversation with Casey and Tank, he decided not to get pizza with Tank.

"A-J!" Johnny replied. "We haven't talked in forever. How are you doing?" Almost a decade older, he and AJ still had a brotherly connection.

"I'm fine. Football and school take up all my time," AJ said.

"And Mom tells me you have a girlfriend too. Fill me in," Johnny Reese prodded.

"Um… well, I might have had a girlfriend," AJ said with a slight sigh. "It's complicated. Can we not talk about that right now?"

"Sure," Johnny said in an upbeat manner. "We can talk lots this weekend."

"Are you coming to the game?" AJ asked excitedly.

"Of course!" Johnny matched AJ's energy. "I'm flying into Cleveland, meeting Kelly, and we're going to drive down to the game. Then we'll spend the weekend at home."

"That's great. It'll be great to see you. And I appreciate the support," AJ said.

"Oh no, we wouldn't miss this," Johnny replied. "I want to see you and Dad win a state championship together. And I get to see you break the scoring record."

"Well, Johnny, we have a chance, but it's going to be a tough game. And there's no chance I'll break the record — I need 21 points. And Dad has me playing defense now," AJ explained.

"Well, it's probably because he needs you there, AJ," Johnny reasoned. "Don't worry about it. Ten years from now, no one will care. It's the championship that matters. Nothing else."

"I suppose you're right," AJ replied, though not entirely convincingly.

"AJ, come on. Be positive," Johnny said, then asked, "If you had a choice between being on offense or winning a state championship, what would you pick?"

"Sheesh, Johnny! You sound just like Dad, you know?" AJ said with a chuckle.

"Maybe I do. But do you know what?" Johnny paused for a moment, then said before AJ could respond, "Dad's right."

"Right about what?" AJ asked, confused.

"About everything," Johnny replied. "Hard work matters. Reliability is everything. Everything he's said that you've rolled your eyes at — that I rolled my eyes at — he's right about."

AJ didn't say a word. Instead, he pulled over and parked so he could focus on listening.

Johnny continued, "You don't know it in the moment when you're right under your parents' thumb. But Dad set us up for success. Mom too. But Dad was hard-nosed about it."

For the second time in the last 10 minutes, AJ was rendered speechless.

"Listen, I know Dad can be a pain. But looking back at all the things he did and said to drive me — and even Kelly — it's ingrained in who I am. And it's empowering me to find success in lots of ways. Once you realize it, you'll appreciate it."

Chapter 136

"Do you have a minute?" AJ asked as he stood in the doorway of his dad's home office.

On the short ride home, AJ had time to reflect on the conversations with Casey and Johnny — two people he had great respect for. They had different messages, but both were aligned in seeing his dad in a different light.

When he got home, he sat with his mom to get confirmation on his dad's situation. "So, is Dad's work nemesis that guy you two have all those disparaging references for?" AJ asked.

"Well… yes," Sam stammered and paused. "But it's not nice to call people names."

The irony of the situation was not lost on AJ. "Mom, you don't have to convince me of that." He laughed and continued, "I didn't say what I'm accused of saying, and I'm in trouble for it."

Shortly thereafter, AJ moved on to talk with his dad. "I know you're busy."

"Actually, I'm wrapping it up, AJ," Jonathan responded. "I've got an early day tomorrow."

"That's what Mom told me," AJ said. "Two a.m. downtown, huh? Mom said in her world that's considered sleeping in." He laughed.

Jonathan joined the laughter. "She said that? Nice." Then he added, "Tomorrow is going to be a long day, but hopefully a great one."

AJ nodded, then said, "Thanks for coaching, Dad. I know leading this team was not on your bucket list, but the season doesn't happen without you. That's a fact. I appreciate it. Everyone appreciates it."

Jonathan responded, "Thanks. No, it wasn't on my bucket list, but this experience makes my lifetime highlight reel for sure."

"Also, I heard about how you broke Tank out of jail," AJ said, making air quotes.

Jonathan smiled broadly at how AJ characterized the events near Bowling Green. That was a secret he had almost forgotten about, as it seemed to have happened a lifetime ago.

AJ followed with, "Tank told me to tell you and Mom that if you're ever looking to adopt someone, he'd like to be considered." They both laughed at the thought.

When the humor passed, AJ said, "And thanks for believing in me."

Jonathan gave AJ a curious look, as if he didn't know what he was talking about.

AJ clarified, "Casey told me how she played the recording for you and Mom. You're right. It's not me. I just can't prove it."

His father responded, "AJ, I don't want you worrying about that — or the Shea situation. Put your focus entirely on having a great game — your best game ever. No matter what happens, know that you gave it your all."

For a third time that evening, AJ had no response. He could only listen.

Jonathan continued, "Zero your energy in on the state championship game. Don't give the recording another thought. I've asked a favor of someone I'm confident will be able to definitively prove it wasn't you."

AJ didn't know what to say. He sensed that everything would be fine.

"I've got to get to bed. I'll see you tomorrow at the send-off assembly. You get some rest too," Jonathan said as he turned out the light in his office and walked past his son.

Chapter 137

"Tell me again, Sebastian, why we're here at oh-dark-thirty?" Aiden Davis asked, still sporting bedhead. "It's freezing, and pitch-dark in these woods. Gives me the creeps."

The sun would not crest the horizon for another 90 minutes, and its impact would be minimized by a dreary early December cloud cover that filled the sky.

Sebastian responded, "Quit whining. I already told you. I got a text late last night from someone telling me to meet them here if we *really wanted to get AJ and Coach Reese.*"

Through a yawn, Noah Turner inquired, "Who's it from? Are you sure they meant here?"

"Noah, the number is a 614 area code, but I don't recognize the number," Sebastian replied. "And yes, whoever said the Boehnke Nature Preserve … just inside the parking area. I can show you the text if you don't believe me."

The Boehnke Nature Preserve is a 23-acre township park with walking trails through woodland areas and across meadows. The preserve was established in 2017 when the Boehnke family donated the property to Jefferson Township for conservation purposes.

"Well, this might be the right place and the right day and time, but this is likely a joke," Aiden remarked. "No one's here. No one in the whole county is up right now, Sebastian."

"Yeah, let's go home," Noah added. "Or go get a donut. They're really fresh now."

"Oh, just be patient," remarked a shadowy figure emerging from one of the trailheads near the parking area. He walked past Sebastian's car, clicked on a tactical flashlight, and blinded the three Blacklick students. "You can get fresh donuts any morning."

"Can you turn that off?" Sebastian asked as he shielded his eyes from the piercing light.

"Sure," the shadowy figure said.

With a click, the light was out. The trio's eyes readjusted to the dark. They blinked several times to clear their vision. Once they had, the shadowy figure came into focus.

"Who are you?" Sebastian asked boldly, though his heart was pounding.

"It doesn't matter," Walter Bachman replied, brimming with confidence as if he'd been in similar situations many times before. "All that matters is our respective interests."

"You said you were going to help us get Coach Reese and AJ. How are you going to do that?" Sebastian demanded.

Calmly, Walter responded, "Young man, I never said that. I simply said, meet me here if you really want to get them. Re-read my text." He then said, "You're here, so I assume you do."

"Not funny, old man," Sebastian fired back. "We're not amused by your survey."

"Oh, I didn't intend it as a survey. I just wanted your attention," Walter said, still calm.

"Well, you got our attention. The question is why?" Sebastian asked.

"That's simple. I have a question for you," Walter responded.

"What is it?" Sebastian was losing patience.

Walter didn't immediately respond. He let the silence hang for a moment, then said in a playful manner, "How did you get the smell of goose crap out of that car? Or are you just nose-blind now? Tires can be replaced, plates reissued—but that stench? How'd you do it?" He stopped and shared a guilty smile.

"You! It was you!" Sebastian growled. "You must be some dumb old man with a death wish, meeting us alone here."

The former quarterback then lunged toward the old man. Walter calmly stood his ground, but at the appropriate moment, he pulled a hand from his pocket and hit Sebastian in the face with a short blast of pepper spray. Sebastian was able to knock the pepper spray canister out of Walter's hand before he went to his knees, trying to comfort his eyes, which were searing with pain.

Aiden and Noah immediately swung into action, aggressively moving toward Walter. Aiden arrived first, swinging wildly. Walter deflected the punch and jabbed a thumb into the soft notch above his sternum, connecting with the windpipe. Aiden's attack turned into a desperate gasp for air.

Within seconds, Noah also attempted to best the old man, grabbing to neutralize his arms. Walter, however, grabbed a fistful of the former lineman's fingers and bent them back. The pain was intense, but Noah fought it. Walter quickly popped Noah in the upper part of the nose. Noah collapsed in pain. His nose started to bleed, and his eyes swelled shut.

Walter quietly let the troublesome trio writhe in pain for a bit. Then he addressed everyone: "Okay. Relax. No one is going to die."

Then one by one, he gently helped each of them sit against the base of a large oak and began tending to their wounds.

To Noah, he said, "Pinch here to stop the bleeding. Ice it as soon as you can."

To Aiden: "Hands over your head. Breathe deeply."

And to Sebastian: "Stop rubbing—it only makes it worse. Wash with mild soap and cool water when you get home."

Once everyone was situated, he directed his comments: "Sebastian, regarding your car, your beef is with me. I'd be mad too. But you had your shot—three versus one. Well, it didn't work out, did it? Take the loss and move on."

"Now let's talk about this recording business. You're behind it," Walter said.

Sebastian sat up, intending to challenge that assertion.

"Sebastian, you are. You can't deny it. You used a starter package on the Eleven Labs platform to mimic AJ's voice."

Sebastian's composure softened as he now realized that somehow Walter knew.

"Actually, your work is quite good, Sebastian," Walter complimented. "You should use your talents for good. You really should. But you didn't, and you hurt people who had done nothing to you. And you're going to make it right. All of you. And that sassy-mouthed girlfriend of yours—Jessa Harroway, right? Don't be surprised. I've done my homework."

"Why should we do anything?" Sebastian fired out, not willing to concede anything.

"I can't make you," Walter said. "But I've been on your computers—yours, Aiden's, Noah's. I know exactly what you've been up to."

Aiden and Noah's heads popped up from their conquered, seated positions.

"Yeah, that's right. I've got stuff on each of you. How do you explain to your parents, Aiden, the cheating? Maybe you graduate next year. Maybe you just go to community college." Aiden's head dropped in impending shame.

Walter paused briefly. "And you, Noah. Oh my God, you've got to ease up on the porn. Sheesh. I'm embarrassed for you."

Noah's eyes darted between his friends, hoping they didn't catch what was said.

"Listen, there's more. But enough on that. AJ wasn't your enemy, and you know it. And Shea—yes, that's her name, nothing else—she's been through hell because of you."

Walter then reached into his pocket. He held up a black thumb drive. "This one's yours. I have another. If you don't undo what you've done, I'll send it everywhere."

Sebastian started to openly challenge Walter but was cut off by Aiden, who asserted, "Shut up, Sebastian. Enough! We're going to do what he says."

Noah confirmed, nodding his head. "What do we need to do?"

"Great question. I appreciate the enthusiasm," Walter responded. "On the drive are detailed instructions as to how you will undo what you did. It's really pretty simple. A public wrong deserves a public apology—from each of you, including Jessa."

"What if I can't get Jess to comply?" Sebastian asked. "I can't control her."

"Sebastian, I've been all over your digital footprint, including your phone," Walter nonchalantly shared. "You and your girlfriend have some fiery text exchanges. I'm sure she won't be happy if they become public. I know her dad won't."

Sebastian could only conjure up images of Jess' dad coming after him.

"Enough talk, guys," Walter continued. "I must get to a meeting. You know I'm serious. And you have instructions as to what you need to do." Walter then lifted his arm to look at his wrist. "You have 12 hours to make this right, or the information comes out. That's 6 p.m. tonight."

As Walter began to walk away, Sebastian shouted to him, "My dad is going to get you."

Walter stopped and calmly turned back. "No, he won't. In a few hours, he's going to have his own issues to deal with. I promise you that."

Chapter 138

"Okay! Now can we get Coach Reese, his coaches, and the football Mustangs up here?" Kaylee Dawson nervously yelled into the microphone.

The band struck up a tune, settling the crowd for the team's send-off to the state championship. After a few quick announcements from the principal, Kaylee was handed the microphone to run the program, with one instruction—keep things moving so the team could board the bus by 11.

Normally, this emcee role was Jess' job, so Kaylee had no experience and little prep time. Nevertheless, she stepped up to embrace the opportunity. After a brief welcome to those heading to the game, she called the coaches and players to the stage.

Everything was moving along nicely—except for one thing: Coach Reese still hadn't arrived. He was expected earlier, but other coaches were trickling in late, and no one seemed worried. When the band began playing, AJ raised a skeptical eyebrow.

When Kaylee called up the team, he grew more concerned. He spotted his mother standing with other parents in the back of the auditorium. They caught each other's eye and shrugged, as if to say, *I don't know*. As Coach Norm—completely unprepared—was trying to address the gathering, AJ motioned to his mom that he was sending a text.

Ur late u owe us a lap

The moment he hit send, the entrance doors at the back of the room flew open. AJ turned with anticipation. It was only Sebastian, Aiden, and Noah, and they were behaving erratically. They scanned the crowd of students, teachers, and parents for someone. AJ couldn't care less. His first text had been read, but there was no response, so he quickly fired out another.

coming? norm needs res-q

"Kaylee, where is Jess?" Sebastian asked, out of breath and in a complete panic. After the encounter with Walter, he, Aiden, and Noah opened the thumb drive—and were immediately motivated to comply with the instructions.

Startled, Kaylee responded in complete shock, "Sebastian what happened to your face?"

"I don't have time to explain. Where is Jess?" he repeated.

"She didn't come to school today. None of the varsity cheerleaders did," Kaylee said.

Sebastian immediately fired back, "Where is she? She won't pick up her phone."

Annoyed, Kaylee replied, "I don't know. I'm not her keeper." She was busy with the assembly. Then a thought hit her. "Wait, I know, Sebastian—she's in Cincinnati. Well, actually across the river in Newport, at some spa."

"Oh, this is not good," Sebastian said with a sigh. "I need her back here, like now. Who can we call?"

"No one," Kaylee replied. "They went to this place called Song Spa. It's holistic, relaxation oriented. Strict phones-off policy."

"You said Song Spa, right?" As Kaylee nodded, Sebastian typed the name into his phone. "Come on, guys. We have a road trip."

Coach Norm muddled through as best he could, and players helped fill time. As planned the assembly was over almost precisely at 11 a.m. AJ sent one more text to his dad.

ya gonna mak it to the game

When the assembly ended, he made a beeline toward his mom.

"Mom, I heard from Dad," AJ said, out of breath and panicked.

"What did he say?" Sam asked.

AJ swallowed hard. "He said he's not coming."

Assuming AJ would be disappointed, Sam replied, "Oh, AJ, I'm sorry. Something important must have come up."

"Except there's one other thing," AJ said, showing her the text.

not com'n good luck

"Mom, there is no way Dad sent that. No way," AJ said in a panicked tone as his mom examined the text and nodded in agreement. "Where is Dad? Mom, something's wrong. We have to help him."

Sam saw genuine terror in her son's eyes—something she'd never seen before. Nevertheless, she took a deep breath, suppressed her own anxiety, and replied, "AJ, just relax. You need to go with the team. Let me worry about Dad, okay?" She looked him in the eye and said, "Everything will be fine. Just go get ready to play."

AJ hugged his mom and said, "Keep me posted." He then headed toward the team buses.

While telling AJ to relax, Sam felt fear welling up inside. Years of marriage told her something was wrong, but she didn't know what to do.

Then, out of nowhere, a thought came to her. She looked around, spotted another parent—a JV cheerleading mom—and made a beeline toward her. "Marie, would you please give me Walter Bachman's phone number?"

Marie was taken aback by the request and by who was asking. They'd been on opposite sides of a contentious tax levy campaign. Even so, she quickly gathered herself and replied, "Dr. Reese, um, I'm really not comfortable giving you Walt's number. I'm sorry."

Stung by the rejection but undeterred, Sam asked, "Well, would you at least call him and let me talk to him? This is an emergency related to my husband—the team's coach."

Though Marie was further taken aback by the persistence, she sensed deep concern in Sam's demeanor and gave in to her empathy. Without a word, she pulled out her phone and made the call. When it began to ring, she handed the phone to Sam. "Here."

"Hello, Marie. How are you doing this Friday?" Walter answered.

"I'm sorry, Walter. This is not Marie. She called you for me," Sam said. "I'm Sam Reese—Jonathan's wife."

Caught off guard, Walter said, "Hello, Sam." After a slight pause, he added, "This is an interesting surprise. How can I help you?"

Rushing her words, she said, "Something is wrong. Jonathan is missing, and I don't know what to do."

Sensing her panic, Walter calmly said, "Please take a deep breath and start again."

Sam slowly breathed in and out. "Jonathan was supposed to be at the high school an hour ago. He hasn't shown up. We texted him, and we got a reply…" She paused, as if unsure how to say the rest.

"And?" Walter prompted.

"This is going to sound strange, but it wasn't Jonathan," Sam blurted.

"What do you mean?" Walter asked.

"Jonathan has a habit of sending perfect text messages—capitalization, spelling, punctuation," Sam explained.

"Oh, I know—he's such an attorney," Walter chuckled. "I've been meaning to stage an intervention."

Walter's humor made Sam briefly smile, but she quickly said, "The text we got wasn't even a sentence. Not one capital letter. Misspellings. No punctuation. It wasn't Jonathan."

"Sam, I agree. This is very odd. Even him being an hour late is odd," Walter said.

Sam started to get choked up but pushed through her tears. "Jonathan recently told me that if there was trouble, he would turn to you." Tears streamed down her face. "Walter, I'm turning to you. I need help."

"Sam, I know we've not always seen eye to eye," Walter said. "But one thing we have in common is that we both care about Jonathan." He paused. "I want you to know this: I will find him, and everything will be fine. Trust me."

Sam fought to hold back full-on crying. She turned away from Marie, closed her eyes, and spoke words from her heart that conflicted with what she'd previously said. "Walter, I trust you."

Chapter 139

"You don't need to escort me out this time. I know the way," Jonathan said with a chuckle to the same two unarmed security guards who had walked him out eight weeks earlier. He was leaving the due diligence project at 9:55 a.m., and they had just shown up outside the conference room where he and the Eisenberg & Anders team had conducted remote due diligence.

Jonathan was in a good mood. All in all, the morning at Eisenberg & Anders had gone well. At 1:15 a.m., he turned off the alarm quietly, annoyed with himself for forgetting to charge his phone, but figured 50 percent was enough to last until the team bus.

He made quick work of showering, reached downtown in record time, and parked near his usual spot.

Getting off the elevator on the firm's main floor was unsettling. Front and center hung Ari's No. 53 jersey between his picture and the firm's co-founder, Richard Anders. Putting aside his feelings about how he was ousted, Jonathan felt the jersey belonged there. Still, it was strange seeing it, knowing Ari had talked about wearing it to the very place Jonathan was heading later.

Jonathan's mood lifted as he rounded the corner toward the main conference area. The security gate—which never seemed to work—was now completely broken, one side lodged into the ceiling and the other hanging low.

When Jonathan walked into the large, well-lit conference area overlooking the still-night city, he chuckled. "What happened to the gate?"

With Warren Scott absent, the Eisenberg & Anders team broke into laughter. One attorney said, "I know. Looks like someone broke in. That bozo is going to have a cow—he just had it fixed."

That got the super-early morning off on the right foot. The Eisenberg & Anders team could not have been more welcoming. And they followed Jonathan's lead, just as when he worked at the firm. Together, they coordinated the entire due diligence process among three locations — their operation, the Emerald Medical crew, and the Far East team.

While everyone appreciated being able to sleep in their own bed, they jokingly lamented not being able to be in it longer. "Next time, we let the Far East take the early shift," one attorney quipped. But that shared pain of having their circadian rhythms pushed out of whack made them hyper-focused and productive.

By 9:45 a.m., the effort was wrapping up. One by one, attorneys left the now day-lit conference room—most heading home to get some sleep. Stephenson left just ahead of Jonathan, who wanted to text Lucas one last time to make sure there were no lingering items. There weren't.

The project was a success. Maybe there would be other opportunities with Emerald Medical. For now, Jonathan's mind was clear. He was carefree enough to joke with the security guards.

The joke didn't seem to land. One of them said, "Come with us."

Jonathan complied, unconcerned. There was a buzz of activity around the broken gate as they turned toward it, but the guards steered him away from the commotion.

"Where are we going?" Jonathan asked. They didn't respond, directing him into an interior conference room a few yards down the hall.

Inside sat Warren Scott and a well-dressed man, who said, "Mr. Reese, have a seat."

Jonathan complied, though his instincts told him otherwise.

"My name is Theo Vance. I'm a detective with the Columbus police, and I work nonviolent and white-collar crimes." Vance paused to let that sink in before continuing.

"You're being detained as part of an ongoing investigation into allegations of unauthorized physical entry and unlawful access to confidential electronic records belonging to Eisenberg & Anders."

"None of that is true. And holding me is completely unnecessary," Jonathan calmly replied.

"Perhaps, Mr. Reese. But we do have the right," Vance said.

Looking on with delight, Warren couldn't contain himself. "Aren't you going to cuff him and read him his rights?"

Vance shot Warren a look that said, *I know my job.* Then he looked back at Jonathan. "Jonathan, I'm going to have to place you in restraints while we sort this out. It's procedure. Stand, please. Hands in front."

Again, Jonathan complied. He knew Vance was operating within the law. He offered his hands. As he did, Vance methodically said, "You have the right to remain silent ..."

"Before we get started, would you like an attorney, Mr. Reese?" Vance asked.

"Detective Vance, there is nothing to any of this. In fact, it's malicious. The sooner I can establish that, the better. So, no, I'm not going to wait around for an attorney. Let's get on with this."

Vance directed Jonathan to be seated, produced a small recorder, turned it on, and set it on the table. He began questioning Jonathan, starting with full name, date of birth, and address, then moving to employment and whereabouts.

Jonathan answered carefully. He wanted to cooperate, but his mind was on where he should be—where he'd promised to be.

At one point, Jonathan's phone chimed with a text notification. Then a second. He was surprised it still had power. Removing the phone from his sports coat pocket, Jonathan asked, "Can I respond to these?"

Before Vance could answer, Warren jumped up, raced over, and snatched the phone from Jonathan. "No. No communication. He's working with someone. No coordinating."

"Warren," Jonathan said with a laugh. "I didn't do anything. And there is no one else. You're delusional."

"Yes, you did," Warren angrily shot back. "You got that file—whether you broke in or hacked in, we'll find out. So you might as well tell us now." He slammed his hands on the desk.

"Mr. Scott," Vance said calmly. "I suggest you leave. This is not how we work."

Warren shot Jonathan an angry glare before walking out, still carrying the phone.

Warren Scott stormed off to what had been Ari's office, where he tended to operate. He could barely contain his anger. He sat, fiddled, stood, and paced. At 11 a.m., Jonathan's phone received another text. Warren looked at it and surmised it was from Jonathan's son.

ya gonna mak it to the game

Warren desperately wanted retribution, but it wasn't coming fast enough. To hasten it, he replied to the text.

not com'n good luck

He then dropped the phone into the small trash can, which already held some discarded materials. Removing the liner, he walked out of the office and asked the nearest staffer to deposit it into the trash chute leading to the basement.

Once Warren was gone, Vance worked to restore calm and questioned Jonathan for any sign of guilt but found none.

Jonathan tried to cooperate, but his mind stayed on AJ and the team—where they were, where they should be, and the quickest way to reach them.

A forensic tech hurried in with a potential breakthrough. "Let me examine your right thumb, sir."

With nothing to hide, Jonathan raised both shackled hands for her to examine.

"Negative," she said, somewhat disappointed.

"What were you looking for?" Vance asked.

"We found one unusual print, Detective," she replied. "There is one print with a scar that looks like a fat comma—or maybe a misshapen peanut, or the state of New Jersey."

Chapter 140

"Jess, gotta go," Sebastian said loudly, completely out of breath, as he walked unannounced into the massage therapy area.

"Ssshhhh," one of the massage therapists responded. Song Spa in Florence, Kentucky—just across the Ohio River from Cincinnati—was known for its candlelit, feng shui-inspired silence.

Sebastian repeated, but this time in a whisper, "Jess, we've got to go."

"What are you doing here, Sebastian?" Jess whispered back without lifting her face from the massage table's cradle. After years of on-and-off dating, she recognized his voice instantly.

"I've got to get you to the state championship game," he whispered in reply as he moved toward the sound of her voice among the half-dozen massage tables.

"Why would I want to go there?" Jess whispered, her tone rhetorical.

Not wanting to share the answer aloud, Sebastian went to the table where Jess was getting a full-body massage. He leaned over near her face cradle and murmured in her ear.

She responded with a quiet but audible whisper, "That's horrible, even for you."

Sebastian murmured more.

"You should fix it," Jess said in a low voice. "Why should I be any part of this?"

Sebastian murmured again.

Immediately, Jess sat up, covering her nearly naked body, and declared to the other three cheerleaders, panicked, "We gotta go." As she gathered herself, she looked at Sebastian, her eyes widening. "Sebastian, what happened to your face?"

Chapter 141

"Any word, Mom?" AJ asked Sam. He had searched her out among the tailgaters just outside Canton's Hall of Fame Stadium.

The drive from Blacklick to Canton was filled with anxiety for AJ. His mom had told him to focus on playing and let her worry about his dad. How could he, though? The last text message from his father was unnerving.

He fidgeted with his phone. His parents tracked his location—it was a condition of having his own phone. He had never bothered to track their location in return, something he now regretted. He searched online for ways to track someone else's phone, but found nothing viable in the moment.

When they arrived at Hall of Fame Stadium, he quickly unloaded his equipment and had a light pregame meal. He tried to focus on football but couldn't. He needed information. So he sought out his mother among the other team parents.

"AJ, what are you doing here?" Sam chided. "Go be with your team. Get ready to play." Then she added, "I have someone finding Dad. I trust him. Things will be fine."

Chapter 142

"Jonathan Reese! You're not an easy person to find," Walter Bachman playfully remarked.

Before hanging up with Sam, he took her phone number and confirmed Jonathan's last known whereabouts at the Eisenberg & Anders law firm. In downtown Columbus, Walter parked near the Huntington Center.

Upon entering, he checked his phone. The information on it directed him away from the Center's main foot traffic. Slipping past the elevators toward a service area, he picked a lock that gave him access to the loading dock. From there, he worked his way into the section where the building's trash accumulated.

It didn't make sense to linger there. He decided instead to head up to the floors occupied by Eisenberg & Anders. Moving from floor to floor while posing as a safety inspector, he eventually located the windowless conference room where Jonathan was being held.

Jonathan was alone. Finally. After a long interrogation, Detective Theo Vance had left to consult with his forensic team. Then Stephenson stopped in and brought Jonathan a sandwich and a soda.

As Jonathan ate, Stephenson said, "We know you're here. We don't know what to do. That lunatic is now actually a lunatic—drunk with power." The young attorney swallowed hard. "Jonathan, I need this job, or at least a job, but if you need me to take the fall…"

Jonathan motioned for him to stop. "I have no idea what you're talking about." With an obvious wink, he added, "I built the electronic interface, and Lucas jazzed it up with programming. That lunatic has it all wrong—there's nothing to this." He sipped his soda. "Could you do me a favor?"

"What are you doing in here?" Warren Scott barged into the conference room, disrupting the conversation. His eyes looked maniacal, his face a dark red.

Stephenson was silent. Jonathan had no response either. Before either could speak, Theresa made her own grand entrance. "I told Stephenson to bring him lunch." Ari's former assistant got in Warren's face and said firmly, "This is Jonathan, not some common criminal. I don't know what you've got cooked up, but the man gets lunch. And he gets to enjoy it in peace and quiet. Now everybody out of here."

That commotion tipped Walter off to Jonathan's location. He waited for people in the area to disperse, then he slipped into the conference room.

Jonathan was surprised that anyone had come back so soon. He was floored to see Walter. "Did you break into here last night, Walter?" he asked after swallowing his food.

"No," Walter quickly replied. "I didn't break in. I did break the gate, though."

The humor didn't land. Jonathan was too dumbfounded to realize there was even an attempt at it. "Who are you?" he asked.

"Jonathan, I am exactly who I told you I was," Walter replied calmly. "Why am I in your life? Well, that's a little more complicated. But I'm here now because your lovely wife..."

"Sam?" Jonathan interrupted.

"Yes, Sam," Walter continued. "She asked me to find you, and I have—though it wasn't easy. Where's your phone?"

"Sam? Um, I'm so confused," Jonathan muttered. "My phone? I don't know. They took it." He held up his cuffed hands. "I'm being detained."

"I can see that," Walter said. "I need to call Sam and let her know I found you."

As Walter reached into his coat pocket for his phone, Warren barged back in. "One quick question, Jonathan…" He saw Walter and immediately called out, "Detective Vance! Detective Vance!"

Seconds later, Vance arrived. "What is it?"

"This is the man. This is Reese's accomplice," Warren said eagerly. "Frisk him. Cuff him."

"Mr. Scott," Vance said with exasperation, "this is America. We follow the Constitution. Okay?"

Warren said nothing, though the enthusiasm remained in his posture.

Vance turned to Walter. "What's your name, sir?"

"It's Walter Bachman," Walter replied calmly.

"Could I see your right thumb, Mr. Bachman?" Vance asked. Walter complied. Vance's eyes went wide. "Can you explain why your thumbprint is on the gate outside?"

Walter chided, "Detective, you're getting ahead of yourself."

Vance gave him a curious look. Walter clarified, "You need to read me my rights."

With that, Vance began, "You have the right to remain silent…" He cuffed Walter's hands behind his back. After sitting him down, Vance asked again, "Can you explain why your thumbprint is on the gate outside?"

"I would like to confer with my attorney before I say anything," Walter said.

"Okay," Vance replied. "Allow Mr. Bachman to make a phone call."

"Detective, that won't be necessary," Walter said smugly. He motioned to Jonathan. "He is sitting right here."

Vance was momentarily confused and speechless. Per the Constitution, he had to comply.

To Warren, however, this was unacceptable. "Detective, no. We can't allow this. They're complicit in the same crime."

"Allegedly," Vance said. "But at this point, neither has been charged. As we did not catch them in the act of an alleged crime, I will need to get a warrant from the prosecutor. That might take 30 to 40 minutes." He turned to Walter. "Would you please surrender your phone?"

"Certainly," Walter said calmly. "It's in the right pocket of my sport coat." He turned to give Vance easy access.

Chapter 143

"Get dressed. Get focused. Get your mind prepared to play," Norm encouraged the team. "Coach will get here when he gets here. Whatever the case, each of you has a job to do today. Get ready to do it." Once he'd spoken, he turned and rolled his eyes, unsure if he was ready to take on the role of head coach.

At first, only Sam and AJ noticed Coach Dad was missing. By the time the team reached Canton, everyone knew—but no one knew why.

Players told themselves a coach didn't affect the X's and O's, but without Coach Dad, their energy was off.

Chapter 144

"What do we do, Jonathan?" Walter asked after Detective Vance cleared the room.

"You tell me," Jonathan fired back, frustration in his voice. "I have no idea what's going on. They think I—we—broke or hacked in. What did you do?"

"Jonathan, relax," Walter replied. "Everything is going to be fine."

"Fine? Fine?" Jonathan snapped. He checked his watch; it was closing in on 12:30 p.m. "I need to get out of here now.

And we're in handcuffs. What's fine about that?" He held up his hands.

"No, Jonathan. You're in handcuffs," Walter said, sliding the shackles that bound him across the table, landing them in Jonathan's lap.

Jonathan was dumbstruck. He looked at the cuffs that Walter had slid across the table. In a calm, quiet tone that conveyed both confusion and curiosity, he asked, "Who are you?"

Walter matched Jonathan's tone. "I told you. I'm exactly who—"

"No, why are you here?" Jonathan cut him off.

"Again, Sam—"

"No. I know that. I understand all of that." He paused, searching for the right words. "Right now, I'm so confused. I have a ton of questions. There's got to be more to your story than what you're telling me. If you broke the gate, you did it in the wee hours today. How did you know this was the firm I was talking about? I don't ever remember mentioning it. And it wasn't Sam—she called you long after the gate was broken."

Walter stayed silent.

"And why did you ask me to be your attorney? There are dozens of attorneys out there. I'm trying to understand. It wasn't random, was it?"

Again, Walter said nothing.

"And what's your interest in the Jefferson Township schools? And defeating the tax levy? What brought that on?"

Walter finally spoke. "Well, the tax levy situation is a long story, Jonathan."

"Well," Jonathan said, holding up his hands, "we don't seem to be going anywhere."

"It's pretty simple, really," Walter began. "The athletic department was corrupt." He pressed a finger into the table to emphasize his point. "Defeating the tax levy forced the school board to gut the athletic department."

"Corrupt?" Jonathan mused. "Why do you say that?"

"Not criminally corrupt—morally," Walter clarified. "Studer might have been good for football, but he was bad for sports overall." He detailed abuses and how Studer was enriching football at the expense of other sports.

"But your approach effectively threw out the baby with the bathwater. Why take sports away from the kids because of one person?" Jonathan asked.

"We didn't, did we?" Walter replied. "Parents stepped up. We knew they would. Sports are arguably better than ever now. And football hasn't missed a beat."

"But Walter, why do you care? You're not from here. You have no kids in the system. Why not just move? Or not move in to begin with?"

"Jonathan, you're not wrong," Walter said. "There is more to me than I've shared."

"So, who retained you?" Jonathan asked, leaning forward.

"Can't say," Walter replied quickly.

"Can't or won't?" Jonathan pressed. Walter shrugged.

"What about me? How—or why—did I get on your radar?"

"I was retained to keep an eye on you. Help you. Protect you."

"Why? By who?" Jonathan demanded.

"I'm not at liberty to answer—either of those, Jonathan." Walter checked his watch. "Besides, you'll know soon enough."

"Before or after we go to jail?" Jonathan asked dryly.

"Jonathan, trust me. Things will be fine. We're not going to jail."

"Well, if you're so sure of that, there's nothing else for us to talk about."

Jonathan fell silent. He checked his watch and did some quick math. *If I leave now, I might make it before kickoff.* But leaving anytime soon didn't seem likely. He felt hopeless, helpless, and as though he was letting the team down.

After several minutes, Walter said, "One other thing and I'll shut up. You were right about AJ—it wasn't his voice on the recording."

Jonathan gave Walter a curious look.

"I've been retained to protect you and yours, Jonathan," Walter said. "The wrong against AJ is being righted. Trust me."

Chapter 145

"Jess, we can give you a ride," Sebastian shouted to his on-and-off girlfriend.

She snarled through clenched teeth, racing around the hotel room to pack. Sebastian's news had wrecked their plans.

"Seriously, Jess! You shouldn't drive when you're this mad," he tried to reason.

"No, I'm fine," she fired back in his face. "I just don't want to be anywhere near you right now—certainly not for a four- or five-hour car ride."

"Just forward the instructions to me," she sneered. Then, with sarcasm: "Is that too much to ask? Or are you going to screw that up too?"

"Okay, okay," Sebastian said, motioning at Aiden to forward Walter's instructions. "What are we supposed to do then?"

Jess stopped her frantic packing and faced him, her cheeks red with anger. "I don't care. Go get a pedicure—they're already paid for. And you're going to pay us back." She motioned to the other three equally displeased cheerleaders in the room. "But whatever you do, stay away from the game. You've screwed things up enough."

Sebastian swallowed hard, staying silent.

Jess zipped up her bag, swung it over her shoulder, and glared at him. "You better hope we get this done in time—or my dad is going to kill you."

Chapter 146

"I'm sorry, gentlemen, but we're taking you in for booking," Detective Vance said. He needed to follow procedure, so he instructed, "Jonathan, please stand so we can reposition your handcuffs behind your back. And to play it safe, I'm going to read you your rights again."

After he left the conference room to allow Walter and Jonathan to confer, Vance consulted with his own team and then reviewed those findings with an assistant prosecutor. The case wasn't solid, but it was enough to convince a judge to issue a warrant — especially with Warren Scott working his connections to exert influence.

As Vance began to recite, "You have the right," a well-dressed man with a commanding executive presence entered the room talking on the phone. "Yes, he's right here." The man then handed his phone to Vance, saying, "It's for you."

Startled, Vance stopped issuing Miranda warnings, took the phone, and said in an uncertain tone, "Hello." He just listened. Then he stood taller and replied, "Yes, sir. I understand. Yes, sir. We will. I appreciate that. Thank you, sir." He then handed the phone back to the well-dressed man.

"Thank you, Judge Clausen. Give my best to your wife," the man said.

Vance said, "Officers, please remove the handcuffs from these men. The judge just revoked the warrants. They are free to go."

Walter stood and remarked, "Mine are already off."

"Of course they are, Walter," the man said with a laugh, adding, "I'm not surprised."

"No, no, no," Warren protested. He had been savoring the moment of formal arrest. "Mr. O'Farrell," Warren appealed to the CEO of Emerald Medical. "These two are being arrested for physical and cyber trespass."

"Excuse me," Bobby O said, then asked Warren, "What's your name?"

"Warren Scott, sir. We've met a couple of times. I was with Ari," he replied.

"Thank you, Scott. I think I remember," Bobby O replied.

"No, it's Warren, sir," he interjected.

Without acknowledging anything, Bobby O continued, "These men didn't trespass," he said, pointing to Walter. "This man works for me and Emerald Medical, the primary tenant in the offices occupied by Eisenberg & Anders."

Jonathan just looked. He sensed that things were working in his favor, but he continued to be confused.

Bobby O then turned back to Warren. "If you read the sublease agreement, you will see that the primary tenant — Emerald Medical or its representatives — can come in at any time to conduct inspections or make repairs. There is no trespass. There is no crime."

"What about going into Ari's computer account?" Warren protested.

"Scott, Ari's wife — who technically is still a shareholder in the firm until she's bought out — gave us his login credentials," Bobby O said in a matter-of-fact tone. "No trespass, right, Detective?" Vance nodded in agreement. "No trespass. No crime. And that's the end of it."

Warren's shoulders slumped in disappointment.

Bobby O turned to Jonathan and said, "Jonathan, it's nice to see you. You're free to go."

Jonathan started toward the door, then realized, "Wait, I need my phone." He then asked Warren, "Where's my phone?"

Walter interjected, "It's down in a trash area, I believe." He then looked at Jonathan and sheepishly said, "Sorry. Yes, I was tracking it. When I added my number in your phone, I added an app."

"Scott? Why is this man's phone in the trash?" Bobby O was annoyed.

"Um, I think … maybe it fell in a garbage can — by accident — and somehow went down the trash chute."

"Go get this man's phone," Bobby O admonished Warren, then added, "Now."

Warren dashed out the door, and shortly thereafter Vance and his team departed. Walter and Bobby O took a seat at the table and encouraged Jonathan to do the same.

Looking at Walter, Jonathan asked as he motioned toward Bobby O, "So is this who retained you?" Walter said nothing but smiled and nodded.

"I'm sure you have questions, Jonathan," Bobby O said. "We have a few minutes. Ask away."

Jonathan sat quietly for an uncomfortable moment, then said, "I don't know where to begin." He thought a bit, then asked, "Why? Why defeat the tax levy? I don't understand. Blacklick is the school that Bobby O built."

"You may not agree, but Studer could not be reasoned with. And he was hurting kids in the process. What he did to Theresa's daughters and Tessa's was …" Bobby O searched for words.

"Morally corrupt? Ethically bankrupt? Lacked conscience?" Walter offered.

"Yes, any of those," Bobby O confirmed.

The Emerald Medical CEO gave other examples — times they tried to reason with Gary Studer, but he resisted, lied, or reneged. The school board, he added, was compromised and lacked the conviction to do what was right.

"Jonathan, we had to get Studer out. Given the popularity of football and lack of board support, there was no easy solution. All in all, defeating the tax levy seemed like the cleanest way. It was far from perfect, sure, but it was going to be messy no matter what."

Jonathan just listened. Every bit of information seemed to lead to more questions.

Bobby O continued, "Jonathan, it was never part of the plan for you to coach. That just sort of unfolded. Just like I never expected to lose my good friend, Ari. You can plot and scheme life, and you work toward hopes and dreams. But sometimes fate has other plans."

Now better understanding the tax levy situation, Jonathan asked, "So why keep an eye on me?" He then playfully glared at Walter. "Track me?" Walter simply winked. "Why help me?"

"Jonathan, years ago, Ari helped me." Bobby O went on to explain all that Ari did for him — helping him through school, getting him started in business, and assisting Emerald Medical in the early days. He concluded with, "I wouldn't be who I am today without Ari Eisenberg. I owe him everything. And I will never forget that."

Jonathan, still confused, asked, "But what does that have to do with me?"

"Everything, Jonathan. Everything." Bobby O looked Jonathan directly in the eye and continued, "I still remember the day that Ari first met you. He referred to you as *the kid from Toledo*. In that interview, there was something about you — something that reminded him of someone he lost years earlier. This was years before I met Ari."

Bobby O then shared what he knew about Alan, the infant child that Ari and Alison lost and the hole that loss created in their hearts — one they didn't dare try to fill. "You might not have known, but you were close in age to what Alan would have been. But there was something about *the kid from Toledo*," Bobby O made air quotes, "you were someone Ari could imagine Alan growing up to become."

Jonathan just listened. But thoughts of Ari and Bobby O's words stirred his emotions. He couldn't help it. Tears started to well up in his eyes, overflow, and roll down his cheeks.

Bobby O continued, "Jonathan, he couldn't stop talking about *the kid from Toledo*. He lobbied — I mean hard — to get you into that Belden firm. And when he decided to leave, he wanted you to go with him. And when you didn't, it crushed him. But he understood. He did. He was taking a massive risk, and you couldn't — you had a young family."

Tears began to roll down Jonathan's cheeks. He wiped them away, but they kept flowing.

"When the Belden firm imploded, Ari quietly kept tabs on you. He wanted to reach out but didn't know how you felt — the firm blamed him for their failings, and he didn't know what side you were on. So he helped from a distance."

Jonathan couldn't keep up with the tears, so he lowered his head and watched as they dropped into his lap one by one. As they did, Bobby O shared about all the ways that Ari unknowingly helped Jonathan over the years — sending him clients that seemed to come out of nowhere, working his contacts and growing political influence to get the Ohio Attorney General's Office to recruit him. And when the time was right, recruiting Jonathan into Eisenberg & Anders, but ensuring that Sam got a promotion so that family could manage the demanding big firm requirements.

"Jonathan, when you accepted the position here — at this firm — Ari couldn't have been happier." Bobby O then chuckled. "He referred to it as *the prodigal son* coming home, which is funny — a good Jewish boy quoting *New Testament* stuff."

Jonathan briefly stopped crying to join the humorous moment.

When the laughter settled, Bobby O continued, "Shortly after that, Ari and I were having dinner. He asked me to keep an eye out for you should something happen to him."

Just then Warren Scott interrupted, storming into the room. He was out of breath, sweaty, and his hair was a mess. His shirt was noticeably soiled from digging through trash. But he had the phone, and he set it down in front of Jonathan without a word.

Walter then instructed as he flicked his fingers, "You can leave."

But not before Bobby O added, "Please gather the senior partners in the main conference room for a meeting."

Jonathan examined his phone and tried to reboot it.

"Jonathan, is it OK?" Walter asked.

"Yeah, the battery's just dead, though," Jonathan responded.

"Do you want me to call Sam, or do you want to use my phone?" Walter followed up.

"That's OK, Walter. Thanks." Jonathan then rationalized, "I'll charge it in the car."

"Jonathan," Bobby O started, intending to get back to his narrative. "Know this — Ari loved you like a son. You meant the world to him. And he would have done anything for you. He may have never said any of this, but it was truly in his heart."

Those words again triggered the tears in Jonathan's eyes.

"And he asked me to keep an eye out for you should something happen to him." Bobby O paused briefly, then emphatically added, "And that's a favor I intend to see through."

Walter smirked. "For starters, that Sullivan lawsuit? It's cooked." He explained that Bobby O was a major player in a private equity firm, and Sebastian's father was learning his biggest competitor and customer were merging. "The bully's about to be bullied — he won't have the time or resources for a baseless lawsuit."

Bobby O then asked, "So what else? What do you need? Do you want your job back here? Consider it done. Do you want to work at Emerald? You can start on Monday. Whatever."

Jonathan was overwhelmed — with emotions and questions. But that state was quickly overridden with thoughts of where he needed to be and how to get there — hopefully by halftime. He stood up and muttered, "I've got to go. I'm sorry, I just have to be somewhere."

Bobby O said, "I understand. Think about it. Maybe you and your wife can come over for dinner soon. My daughter just finished culinary school. Our kitchen is now a bit of a concept restaurant, but she's got promise. We can talk then."

Jonathan nodded. He then wiped his eyes one last time, grabbed his phone, and walked out of the small conference room with his head down. Almost immediately, he bumped into someone.

"Oh, I'm sorry," Jonathan said as he looked up at Stephenson.

Jonathan had a thought. Without a word, he grabbed Stephenson by the arm and said, "Come on." Jonathan dragged him into the conference room. "Bobby O? This is Stephenson. I'm not sure what's going to happen here, but I want you to know that through everything, this man helped me — at great risk to his career and his family's security. Please take care of him."

"Sure," Bobby O gleefully replied. "Stephenson, what's your first name?"

Jonathan's face indicated he shamefully didn't know, but Stephenson responded, "Robert."

Walter asked, "Is your middle name Louis?" Stephenson nodded, and everyone laughed.

The Emerald Medical CEO then asked, "Does anyone call you Bobby?"

"Yes. My mom. She still does to this day," Stephenson remarked.

"Well, you're Bobby to us," Bobby O said. "Come have a seat, Bobby." He then moved over to put a chair between himself and Walter.

As Stephenson was seating himself, Warren re-emerged in the conference room and said, "The senior partners are gathering in the main conference room. Do you want me to join you? To take notes? Get things?"

"Scott, that won't be necessary," Bobby O replied. "We've got Bobby."

"Bobby? Who's Bobby?" Warren asked, completely confused.

Almost in unison, Walter and Bobby O loudly said as they gestured to Stephenson, "Bobby!" Everyone laughed with amusement except Warren, who quietly left.

Bobby O then added, "Ari devoted his life to this firm. It will continue. But the senior partners need to step up and lead."

"Also," Jonathan indicated he had more. "There's a young woman helping our team. Her name is Casey. She does that sign language stuff." Jonathan briefly waited, ensuring he had their attention. "Bobby O, just before we lost Ari, he was going to introduce Casey to you. I believe Emerald is going to be starting a cochlear implant division. At any rate, Casey is a wonderful person and has great energy. She'd be good for Emerald and Emerald good for her."

"What's her name?" Bobby O asked.

"Casey Kaufman," Walter answered, adding, "She is great."

"Wonderful," Bobby O replied. "Let's set up a meeting."

"I'll take care of it," Stephenson chimed in, taking notes on his phone.

"Yes … Bobby will handle it," Bobby O remarked with a laugh.

Jonathan just stood there. It was clear by his posture that there was something else. When he had everyone's attention, he came out with it.

"Could I get a ride?"

Chapter 147

"You'll never amount to anything" was something Travis Carrick heard from almost everyone growing up — neighbors, parents, classmates. Seemingly everyone, except his dad.

His dad proclaimed, "I believe in you," and encouraged, "Just find that thing you're passionate about and pour yourself into it."

Whatever the case, Travis needed an escape from the loser label his small Nebraska town gave him. So he enlisted in the Army. He knew immediately it was his "thing," roaring through basic training, volunteering for Airborne School, and earning a spot with the 75th Ranger Regiment.

After rising through the ranks, he set his sights on Army aviation, earning a place in Warrant Officer Flight Training at Fort Novosel.

After 25 years of service, Travis moved to his wife's hometown near Columbus, Ohio, and became a chauffeur of sorts.

His phone lit up with his next assignment:

NCH - ALT. Airborne ASAP.
Usual plan. Ping confirm.

If *never amounting to anything* included shuttling one of America's richest men in a metallic Gaelic green Leonardo AW139 helicopter known as Emerald One, he'd accept that they were right about him.

Chapter 148

"Go to your car and get what you need," Walter instructed. "Then meet me out front. We'll get you there by game time."

Once Travis Carrick confirmed his instructions, Walter swung into action. He arranged for special transport by police for the two-mile ride from the Huntington Center to Nationwide Children's Hospital, where Jonathan would rendezvous with Emerald One.

Jonathan raced to the elevator. As he waited, Theresa hugged him and wished him well. When the doors opened, he said, "Hold that a second." She did, giving him a curious look.

Jonathan ran to the wall with Ari's picture and grabbed his No. 53 jersey. Returning, he said, "I'll return this tomorrow. You arrange for cake." The door closed, and he was off to meet Walter after a quick pit stop at his car.

As soon as he reached High Street — downtown's main drag — Walter asked, "Jonathan, do you want to use my phone?"

Jonathan waved him off. "I'm sure a multi-million helicopter has a charging port. I'll call from there."

Just then a Columbus police patrol car pulled up. Walter got in the front and Jonathan in the back. As soon as the doors closed, the car sped away, lights and sirens blaring. As they sped through downtown, Walter casually discussed the tax levy and football coaching. "Yeah, our big mistake was giving that dumbass Maven and his clown assistants payment in full upfront. They got stupid with all their money, you know."

Jonathan could hear over the siren but didn't comprehend much. His focus was on bracing himself in the back seat with a white-knuckle grip on whatever he could grab.

Thankfully, the trip was quickly over. The cruiser pulled up to the emergency entrance at Nationwide Children's Hospital.

Walter let Jonathan out, and together they briskly walked to the security desk. Walter flashed credentials to a guard, who summoned someone to take Jonathan to the heliport.

As they waited, Jonathan extended his hand. "Thank you. I think this is it. I'm not sure I need watching over anymore."

Walter shook Jonathan's hand and laughed. "Perhaps. But I still need that estate plan done. I was never a great husband, Jonathan. But I will be a good dad and leave my kids something."

Walter winked as a second security guard whisked Jonathan away and led him to the Tower Elevators. The guard keyed the elevator to the 12th level, where the mechanical penthouse and heliport were. When they arrived, the guard led Jonathan down a short corridor and up a few stairs to the helicopter deck. As they stepped outside, Travis Carrick was landing Emerald One.

From there, the flight operations team took over, briefing Jonathan on protocol for safely approaching and boarding. Once the helicopter was secured, a crew member escorted Jonathan into the front passenger seat of his ride.

Jonathan quickly secured the single-point release lap belt and shoulder restraint, then put on headphones. He located a charging port for his phone and plugged it in. The moment it powered on, he began to call Sam.

Travis grabbed his hand and shouted over the roar of the rotor blades, "Charge, OK. No calls. It can wait 45 minutes."

Jonathan sheepishly put the phone down and settled in for the flight.

Travis then spoke into his headset: "CMH approach, AW139 at Children's helipad, request transition through Class C for Canton-bound flight."

An air traffic controller at John Glenn International Airport quickly replied, allowing Emerald One to cross controlled airspace.

With clearance granted, Travis gently lifted the bird a few feet off the deck, spun 180 degrees, and pushed forward. Once Emerald One cleared the building, he executed a dive takeoff – plunging the helicopter downward in a controlled fall to pick up speed and letting the blades bite into the air with greater lift.

Jonathan entered a state of sheer terror as he felt the freefall sensation and saw the ground rushing toward him through the front canopy.

Within seconds, Travis leveled out and pushed northeast toward Canton, Ohio.

Chapter 149

"Oh, hi, Daddy," Jessa Harroway said sweetly — a daddy's girl playing it up.

Moments earlier she was in her "liquid evil poured into skin" persona. She barked at her fellow cheer mates, "One of you make yourself useful. I paid. You pump. Those handles are gross." Jess voluntold her crew to ditch their spa day and join her at the state championship game.

But with her dad, the sassy, vinegar approach didn't work. Daddy had money, and using a honey strategy was much more effective in keeping it flowing. But the money also let her dad keep tabs on Jess. He knew the moment she swiped his card at the Sheetz gas station 45 minutes south of Columbus that she was no longer in Newport, Kentucky.

"Yes, we left the spa. Sebastian convinced us we need to go to the state championship game to support the team," Jess pleasantly answered her dad. "Yes, we'll be careful. Love you, Daddy."

Just as soon as the call started, it was over, and Jess's personality reverted. She barked to the one manning the pump,

"Don't just stand there. While the gas is pumping, squeegee the windows."

The girl promptly acted, wanting to be in good graces and get a ride home.

Jess then walked toward the gas station entrance carrying her purse. She quickly turned back and shouted, "If I've got to do this, I'm putting my makeup on."

Chapter 150

"Look," Emerald One's pilot said to Jonathan, tapping him on the shoulder and pointing north to Hall of Fame Stadium. It was easy to spot — bright lights cut through the late autumn cloud cover as the sun, due to set in a few hours, hung low over Canton, Ohio.

After Travis Carrick leveled out Emerald One following departure, Jonathan's heart kept racing for a few minutes before he settled into the flight. With no access to his phone and communication with Travis nearly impossible, Jonathan got lost in thought. His mind replayed Bobby O's words over and over — how Ari Eisenberg had impacted his life.

"Ari loved you — like a son." Jonathan found that phrase emotionally powerful. A lump formed in his throat as it reran in his mind.

"You meant the world to him." His eyes teared up. He turned away from Travis to hide the ones that rolled down his cheek.

"He would have done anything for you." Jonathan reflected on all that Ari had done — or might have done — to help him live a life rich in love and happiness.

"He may have never said any of this, but it was truly in his heart." Jonathan contemplated that and tried to reconcile it with the words he'd never spoken.

Ruminating on this made the 45-minute flight seem much shorter. Travis broke the white noise of the blades overhead: "Canton traffic, Emerald One, medevac helicopter, ten miles southwest at 2,000 feet, inbound for Aultman Hospital helipad. Request landing clearance. ETA five minutes."

Moments later, helipad operations responded, "Emerald One, Aultman helipad is clear. Wind 270 at 6. You're cleared to land. Advise on final."

At this point, Travis pointed out the lights at Hall of Fame Stadium. Jonathan checked his watch. It would be close, but he might make it before kickoff. Once they landed, Aultman Hospital was only two miles south of the stadium.

As Emerald One closed in on the helipad, Jonathan spotted a somewhat overweight officer standing outside the operations room, hat in hand. Bracing against the downwash, the man stood his ground.

When Emerald One touched down, the officer cautiously approached, opened the door, and shouted over the roar, "Jonathan Reese? I'm Deputy Sheriff Hank Crayton. Walter Bachman asked me to escort you to Hall of Fame Stadium. Please come with me."

Jonathan thanked the pilot, unbuckled, grabbed his phone, and stepped out. He moved away from the helicopter as the downwash intensified. Travis Carrick had to get back to Columbus quickly — his eight-year-old had a birthday party he was determined to make.

Crayton took Jonathan by the arm and led him to the main elevator. Together they rode seven levels down to the emergency department entrance. "This way, Jonathan," Crayton said.

Jonathan stopped. "Hold on. I have to make a quick phone call."

He found a quiet spot a few yards away, pulled out his charged phone, and hit speed dial. Within a ring, Sam answered. "Jonathan?"

"Yes," he said. "It's me."

"Where are you? Are you coming? Where have you been?" Sam asked in a rush.

Jonathan took a deep breath. "Oh Sam, have I got a story. No time now — tell them I'm five minutes away."

"Just get here," Sam replied. "Things will be underway soon."

"Is Johnny or Kelly there?" Jonathan asked.

"Yes. They're both right here."

"Please put one of them on."

Sam handed the phone to her oldest son, who said, "Dad?"

"Johnny, quickly — thanks for coming to the game. I really appreciate it. I just wanted to tell you how proud I am of you, and…" Jonathan choked up. "And just how much I love you. Now, please give the phone to Kelly."

Johnny, half-stunned, handed the phone to his sister. "Dad wants to talk to you."

Kelly said hello, and Jonathan repeated the message for her.

When the call ended, Kelly looked at her mother with concern. "Mom?"

Sam took the phone, trusted her intuition, and said, "Don't worry. Everything is fine."

Chapter 151

"TOACH!" Brady Troy shouted and pointed. Uber-observant, the deaf quarterback spotted a familiar face as the team took the field before game time. He grabbed AJ's arm, and the two ran toward Coach Dad, prompting a stampede of Mustangs to follow.

After Jonathan ended his call to Sam, he and Deputy Crayton double-timed it to a Stark County sheriff's cruiser, which was already running. Crayton flipped on the lights and sirens and sped away, quickly reaching I-77. While it wasn't the shortest route, it was the safest way to maximize speed.

Crayton raced past Hall of Fame Stadium on the interstate going north, took the first exit, and doubled back. Foot traffic thickened near the stadium, slowing them down.

"Come on, people," Crayton said aloud in the cruiser. No one could hear, yet he continued to mutter, "This isn't Bangladesh. Get out of the streets." He made short bursts on the siren.

Eventually, they reached the stadium and drove into a ground-level area for emergency vehicles. But they could only go so far. They had to get out and walk the last 20 yards. A security guard stopped them just before they entered.

"You need to bring him in via the main entrance," the guard said.

"Ralph, he's a coach. That's his team right there," Deputy Crayton barked back.

"Hank, I don't care. Take him to the main entrance — you've got no authority here," Ralph said.

At that moment, the Blacklick players came thundering over, shouting a varied chorus of "Hey, Coach."

"See," Crayton pointed. "That's his team, Ralph. Come on. Let him in."

"Yeah, come on, Ralph," Tank playfully shouted, catching on. Other players joined in.

"Okay, okay, okay," Ralph said, relenting amidst the commotion. He opened the gate, and the team cheered loudly.

Jonathan quickly thanked Deputy Crayton and entered. Looking at his players made him emotional. Over the season, they'd built a bond. It was good to see them. But under each of their eyes was a reminder of where he'd just been — and the jersey he had in his bag: "ARI" and "53."

Almost immediately, he and AJ locked eyes. Jonathan was happy to see him, and he sensed AJ felt the same.

Jonathan announced, "Look what I have." He pulled Ari's jersey from his pocket. The team erupted. Coach Dad slipped it on.

Collectively, they headed back to their sideline. As they did, Coach Norm caught up.

"Ah, dog, I'm so glad you're here," Norm said. "I'm out of my depth without you."

Chapter 152

"Eyes on me. Everyone. Everything has led up to this. Everything. Put whatever distractions aside and focus on the next four quarters," Coach Dad shouted.

He had to compete with the screams, cheers, and bells from thousands of fans on each side. The crowd was especially rambunctious as the national anthem had just wrapped up. The Mustangs players gathered in close to listen. Having missed the pregame buildup, he felt compelled to inspire.

Jonathan's words seemed to work. Blacklick — in home navy jerseys with light gray numbers — pinned Coldwater Bluff deep. The Wolves — in Vegas gold with forest green trim — started on their own 12.

As AJ and the rest of the defensive backs headed onto the field, a defensive coach shouted, "Don't let him torch us for a long play," referring to Coldwater Bluff's star receiver, Tanner McCoy.

For the championship, Mustang coaches reached out to talk with teams that had faced Coldwater Bluff. On McCoy, there was little intel. They knew he'd transferred in for his senior year from a Chicago high school and kept hearing, "He's good — really good."

The Blacklick defense needed a stellar game. They were confident they could rein in Coldwater Bluff's run game and had the athleticism to get to the Wolves' quarterback. But McCoy was the big unknown. They had to slow him and avoid the deep ball.

To do that, the coaches set the defensive backs in zone coverage. If McCoy entered your zone, you went man-to-man. If you covered an adjacent zone, you had to be ready to help if the ball went his way.

The strategy worked to a point. They contained the deep threat but didn't stop him. The Wolves' quarterback hit McCoy for a string of short gains — three, five, eight yards — and mixed in short runs.

On its opening drive, Coldwater Bluff scored on a four-yard pass to McCoy. Following the point-after, the Wolves led 7-0.

Blacklick was disappointed but not discouraged. It was a championship game — they expected ups and downs. Besides, Coldwater Bluff had just kicked off to them, and they were confident of an equalizing score.

But moving the ball was harder than expected. Coldwater Bluff's defense was ready. When Brady Troy clap-clapped, they keyed on the Mustangs' shifts and formations. The Wolves seemed to have a rudimentary signaling system — hand motions and one-word calls.

They couldn't match the Blacklick offense perfectly, but they weren't a half-step behind like most opponents. That allowed them to slow the Mustangs and hit Brady — "the head of the snake," as their coaches referred to him.

Brady felt like he was taking a hit on every play — not simple touches, but hard contact. Defenders hammering his waist and thighs, wrapping his torso, dragging him down, slamming him to the ground.

Despite this, Blacklick managed three first downs and reached near midfield before facing fourth and long. They punted.

Coldwater Bluff picked up where it left off — methodically moving the ball in chunks of three, five, and eight yards.

For the Blacklick defense, stifling big plays felt like a win. But each small victory was really a loss, with their backs edging closer to the end zone.

Eventually, those incremental losses led to more disappointment: McCoy caught his second short touchdown. The only bright spot — the Wolves' kicker shanked the extra point wide right. Blacklick trailed 13-0 instead of 14-0.

After the kickoff, Brady and the offense returned with optimism. On the sideline, they adjusted the play sequence.

At first, the tweaks worked. In five plays, they gained 40 yards and three first downs. Then Coldwater Bluff adjusted and again stymied the Mustangs, hammering Brady. At the end of the first quarter, facing fourth down in Wolves territory but too far for a field goal, they punted again.

Between quarters, the defense resolved to be more aggressive. "When McCoy is in your zone, give him no cushion."

On the whiteboard, it worked. In live action, not so much. On the second play of Coldwater Bluff's third drive, a miscommunication between two Mustang defenders let McCoy cross from one zone to another. They collided, and McCoy caught the ball and went untouched for an 83-yard score.

This time, the Wolves' kicker made the extra point. Blacklick trailed 20-0 only minutes into the second quarter.

Chapter 153

"Enough!" AJ shouted as he stormed onto the sidelines after Coldwater Bluff's third touchdown. He ripped off his helmet, considered smashing it, but slapped it hard and shouted, "Enough!" again.

A defensive coach grabbed him and said firmly, "Okay, okay, AJ. Just relax."

"What we're doing is a slow death," AJ shot back. "Coach, I want him. Shadow McCoy. The others can adjust, but I'm lining up where he lines up and going where he goes. I played receiver for years — I can think like he thinks."

The defensive coaches sensed AJ wasn't asking — he was telling. And he was hard to argue with. What they'd tried wasn't working, and they had to adjust quickly as the Mustang offense faced third and long.

They gathered the defense and reworked the coverage based on AJ's plan. "Don't lose sight of other receivers. Be ready to support AJ. Coming back starts with us — on this next series."

"Is he okay?" Coach Dad asked Casey as she greeted Brady coming off the field.

The offense had gone three-and-out. Coldwater Bluff had landed solid hits on the Mustang quarterback every play.

"He's fine. A little beat up, but I think it's more bruised ego than anything," the ASL interpreter replied. "They're just all over him. It's frustrating."

Blacklick punted the ball back, and AJ ran onto the field with the other defenders. AJ's heart raced. He'd stepped up to defend the Wolves' big threat with bravado, though doubt lingered. After a quick defensive huddle, he located McCoy and lined up across from him. They were equal in size and stature.

McCoy instantly noticed the coverage change. He smirked, confident it wouldn't matter. At the snap, he darted right. AJ matched him, but McCoy cut back left and caught a five-yard pass. AJ recovered to make the tackle, but cursed himself — unacceptable. He stayed undeterred.

Coldwater Bluff lined up without a huddle. AJ chased McCoy across the field and reviewed in his mind ways he'd been stopped as a receiver. An idea formed.

McCoy, waiting for the snap, looked AJ in the eyes and winked.

AJ didn't react. Energy built inside him. At the snap, AJ slammed two hands into McCoy's chest, jolting him upright, then jammed him again.

The receiver couldn't run his route, forcing the quarterback to look elsewhere. No one was open. The pass was thrown away.

Coldwater Bluff lined up again quickly. AJ and McCoy squared off once more. McCoy's confidence had faded; his torso still stung.

At the snap, AJ engaged him again. It wasn't as solid as before, but enough to disrupt his route. The quarterback's throw sailed off McCoy's fingertips. For the first time, Coldwater Bluff punted.

The Mustangs celebrated as the defense came off. They still trailed by 20, but the small victory gave them hope.

The inspiration didn't carry over to the offense. Another three-and-out, another punt. Coldwater Bluff's defense mirrored Brady's moves and manhandled him.

The Wolves' offense was also stifled: incomplete pass, short run, quarterback sack. Another punt.

Coach Dad decided to simplify the offense and give Brady a reprieve: Give Tank the ball left, then right, opening short passes. The Mustangs marched downfield for a touchdown. After John Evans' point-after, they trailed 20-7.

More important than the score was the momentum. After Evans forced a touchback on the kickoff, the defense hit the field intent on a quick stop.

AJ again locked onto McCoy, but Coldwater Bluff had adjusted to free its star. Still, AJ followed and harassed him every play, limiting him to seven yards on 37 total.

After another Wolves punt, Blacklick stuck with its low-risk runs. The problem was the clock — the half was running out. Coach Dad opened the offense slightly, but that fed into

Coldwater Bluff's defensive scheme, which keyed on Brady's clap-claps and pressured him relentlessly.

The pressure led to a mishandled snap and a delay of game. The promising drive stalled, and Blacklick settled for a long John Evans field goal, going into halftime down 20-10.

Chapter 154

"We're still in this," Coach Dad shouted in the locker room as the Mustangs settled in.

The other coaches stood in various spots while players sat near their lockers, listening. They'd gotten none of this before the game, so they took all they could at halftime.

"Brady, hang in there," Coach Dad said, waiting for Casey to sign. "Your time will come."

After taking in the message, Brady gave an unsure nod, his eyes showing his distress.

Jonathan scanned the room. "Where's Tank?" He found him and continued, "Tank, until we figure things out, you're our offense. Stay hydrated."

"AJ?" Coach Dad spotted his son. "Way to go. Stick on him. Don't let him breathe."

Jonathan called out other players and units — even those unlikely to see action. Everyone mattered.

He wrapped up: "Give. This. Half. Everything. Don't do it for me. Don't do it for the guy next to you. Or anyone in the stands. Do it for you. Because a lifetime is a long time to deal with regret."

The team stormed out with renewed enthusiasm, which carried into the opening drive. Even though Coldwater Bluff knew it was coming, Tank battered into them, opening chances for simple plays. The gains weren't big, but they moved the ball.

Unfortunately, the Wolves were in Brady's head. Distracted, he mishandled a snap. While he fell on the ball, the drive stalled deep in Wolves territory. They settled for a field goal, cutting the deficit to 20-13.

It didn't last. John Evans sent the kickoff deep, but the return man took it out, raced up the middle, found a seam, bounced left, cut right, then broke outside for a touchdown.

The Blacklick sideline deflated as Coldwater Bluff's roared. Their long, grinding drive had been erased – and then some – in seconds. Now they trailed 27-13.

Blacklick returned determined. They were finding success with power football, but it was time-consuming, and they couldn't rely on it completely. Coldwater Bluff occasionally stacked the right defenders to stop Tank, forcing passing situations.

The Wolves keyed on Brady's clap-claps, making their own adjustments before the snap. The constant reaction, combined with a game's worth of hits, overwhelmed him. He forced a pass into coverage and was intercepted. Brady made the tackle after 30 yards, but Coldwater Bluff had prime field position.

The defense limited them to three yards, and AJ batted away a pass to McCoy, but the Wolves still kicked a 34-yard field goal to make it 30-13. Less than two minutes remained in the third quarter.

Coldwater Bluff's side buzzed with excitement. The lead was growing, and their offense had barely been on the field. The kickoff went deep for a touchback.

Coach Dad sent the offense back out with trepidation. Down 17 with roughly as many minutes left, running wouldn't cut it.

They needed to open the offense, but Brady was off his game and Coldwater Bluff had his number. Still, Jonathan had little choice but to stick with the plan they'd used since the third game.

Brady surveyed, clap-clapped, signaled adjustments — and Coldwater Bluff adjusted too. No time for another audible. He took the snap, found no open receivers, and scrambled for seven yards before being swarmed.

The next play was worse: Wolves blitzers poured through from all angles. Brady had no time, and he was dropped for a five-yard loss.

The clock ticked down to what would likely be the last play of the quarter. Brady ran the cadence again and took off immediately, shedding two tacklers. Near the sideline, he pushed for the first down marker with a defender yanking his arm. Just as he was about to get there, another defender hit him, knocking the ball loose.

A Wolves player scooped it up and ran it back for a score — 37-13.

Two defenders carried Brady out of bounds, crashing him into a bench. As he got up, something caught his eye: a binder. Not just any binder — his binder. The one stolen from his backpack, holding Blacklick's signs and plays. Inside was his handwriting on a school lunch menu from earlier in the semester.

He reached for it, but a Coldwater Bluff manager snatched it away and walked off.

Chapter 155

"Thorry," Brady Troy choked out, weighed down by how responsible he felt. He shook his head, disappointed in himself. Then he added, "Weally thorry," as he signed a litany of other words to Casey.

"It's okay, Brady," Coach Dad tried to console. "We're in this together."

"No," Casey interrupted. "What he's trying to say is that they — Coldwater Bluff — have his playbook." Casey continued as Brady signed, "It was in the backpack Sebastian stole." Then she mused, "And he sent it to them?"

"That …" Tank caught himself. "No wonder we can't get any traction on offense. I'm going to kill him when we get back."

"Okay, okay," Coach Dad said, trying to rein everyone in. "Whatever the case, we just have to play. There's nothing we can do about that now."

The team was silent, sharing their dejection. The situation felt hopeless.

"There might be something we can do," Shea chimed in, breaking the silence. Everyone gave her a curious look. She clarified, "The other day, I was reading a game theory article on the concept of deception, signaling, and Occam's Razor."

Everyone stared at her in total confusion.

She tried again. "And what it said …"

"Shea," Jonathan politely interrupted, "I'm not alone in saying we're so happy you're part of this team. But you have about a minute to dumb down whatever you've got. Please."

"Oh, okay," Shea replied. "Here's what we do. When Brady claps to call the play, he should call two. Two actual plays. One play is live — that's the one we run. The other is a ruse."

"But how do we know which is which, Shea?" Coach Dad asked.

"Simple," Shea said. "Brady adds a signal at the start of each sequence — a show of fingers: one, two, three, or four. If the number is odd — one or three — and the down is odd — first or third — that's the live play. If the signal is even — two or four — and it's first or third down, that's the ruse."

Everyone looked at her in stunned silence — not confused, but amazed at the simple brilliance of her strategy.

She added, "It'll work. It will. Unless …" Her voice trailed off.

"Unless what?" Jonathan asked.

"Unless they happen to read the June–July issue of the *Journal of Forensic Information and Security*," Shea answered seriously.

As everyone laughed, Coach Dad quipped, "Shea, we'll take our chances on that." Then he addressed the team: "We're going with this. Any questions? None? Good."

Chapter 156

"Casey, tell Brady to shake it off — he needs to relax and refocus," Coach Dad instructed.

Shea had devised a great counteroffensive — the Wolves were scrambling in confusion. But Brady squandered the opportunity. After three quarters of harassment from the Coldwater Bluff defense, he'd lost his usual focus and confidence, leading to miscues.

In three plays, he mishandled the snap and lost yardage, threw a wild pass out of bounds, and scrambled just to get back to the original line of scrimmage. Blacklick had to punt again.

"Jonathan, we should think about giving Brady a break," Coach Norm whispered.

Before Jonathan could respond, his attention shifted. "Come on, D," he yelled. "We need a stop — and quickly."

Coldwater Bluff had every incentive to bleed the clock. The Blacklick series had taken a minute off — only 11 minutes remained. If the Wolves sustained a drive, especially with their running game, a comeback would be impossible.

The Mustangs knew that. With AJ locking down Tanner McCoy, stopping the run could be their sole focus. And they did — holding the Wolves to no gain on first and second downs.

Under 10 minutes remained. The Wolves needed to keep the drive alive. Passing was their best option. They sent McCoy in motion, and AJ mirrored him across the line. Once McCoy cleared his down linemen, the Wolves quarterback set the play in motion. The receiver headed downfield with AJ on his shoulder.

The quarterback aimed for a tight window, hoping to keep it out of AJ's reach. But the pass was off. Both players got hands on it, each fighting for possession. AJ wanted it more — ripping the ball away and knocking McCoy down.

AJ not only had the interception, but he was still on his feet, with momentum toward the end zone. Just 30 yards away. No one was going to catch him. Six points.

He dropped the ball in the end zone and headed to the sideline, mobbed by teammates. In his head, he briefly calculated, *only 15 points from the record.* But AJ wasn't in a celebratory mood — the tussle with McCoy had again dislocated his little finger.

"Shea," AJ called out, racing toward her for help.

Shea saw him coming. Avoiding him wasn't an option — she had a job to do. But anger surged as their eyes met. She seized his wrist and snapped the dislocated finger back into place.

"Oh my God, Shea — what are you doing? Can we please just talk?" AJ cried out in pain.

Still glaring at him, she shot back, "No. I have nothing to say to you." She quickly taped the injured finger to his ring finger and stormed off.

As she did, Casey arrived. "AJ, just let it go. Focus on football. Deal with this later."

Chapter 157

"We're not benching you," Jonathan told Brady, with Casey relaying the message. "Just take a series or two to get your head right."

Brady nodded, but disappointment filled his eyes.

"David Roberts, get warmed up — we need you to step up," Coach Dad shouted.

As Roberts prepared, the defense held strong, fueled by John Evans' extra point and a touchback on the kickoff. They forced a punt quickly — they had to. Blacklick still trailed by 17, and Coldwater Bluff was content to run, punt, and defend. With a little under eight minutes left, the defense headed off.

"Still remember the offense?" Jonathan asked AJ, grabbing is son who was heading to the bench.

AJ began working through the 18 hand motions: "Motion, unbalanced, shotgun, trips, ace, naked. Right…"

"I'll take that as a yes," Jonathan cut in. "Go in. Roberts will take a series or two at QB. We need your leadership."

Without a word, AJ tightened his chin strap and jogged on after the punt.

"Hey, who's the new guy?" Tank joked in the huddle, drawing laughs.

Roberts ran the offense as Brady would — clap-clap, wait, signal two plays. Coldwater Bluff was confused, and Roberts capitalized as Blacklick drove.

AJ's addition helped. Though mostly on defense all season, he had offensive experience — moving without the ball, finding space, and knowing when to fight for yards or step out to save time.

Five plays gained 50 yards, three first downs, and took just 90 seconds. Coldwater Bluff called timeout. Their coach barked, "Number 29 is a backup! He's making you look like the JV. Tackle him!"

Staying in the huddle, Blacklick signaled plays quietly. Tank broke the silence: "We need to score fast. AJ, remember the St. Mathias semi-final in 7th grade?"

AJ hesitated, then nodded.

"David, call unbalanced pitch right. I'm throwing to AJ."

Roberts frowned — that wasn't the called play.

"If it fails, it's on me," Tank said.

"Desperate times, desperate measures," AJ agreed. "Let's do it. David, call anything for the ruse."

After the timeout, they lined up. Roberts clap-clapped, the team mimicked, he called two plays, then he took the snap and pitched it to Tank.

Tank swept right, drawing defenders. AJ feigned a block, then sprinted past his man. Tank pulled up and threw. The pass wobbled, but AJ ran under it and pulled in the ball.

AJ cut left, stopped short, let the defender fly past, then raced right down the sideline for the touchdown. He briefly noted he was now nine points from the scoring record — but winning mattered most.

As they lined up for the extra point, Jonathan yelled, "What was that? No blueberries!"

"It wasn't a blueberry — everyone knew," Tank shot back with a grin. "Besides, it worked."

After the PAT, it was 37-27 with 6:23 left. Evans kicked another touchback. The defense had to get the ball back.

Coldwater Bluff faced third down, likely passing to seal the drive. Blacklick called timeout at 5:46 to plan: "AJ, lock down McCoy. Everyone else blitz."

Lining up, AJ found McCoy. The others disguised their intent, then blitzed at the snap.

The QB rolled right, searching for McCoy, and fired into a narrow window. McCoy caught it — one of few since AJ shadowed him — but wanted a big play. He cut right, AJ closing fast. McCoy stopped, doubled back left, and shook free.

AJ was beaten but spotted the ball in McCoy's right hand. He swiped — enough to jar it loose. Scooping it up, AJ tucked it and pushed forward.

The Coldwater Bluff crowd went silent; Blacklick's roared. Wolves defenders closed in, but AJ protected the ball. Possession was more important than extra yards. When hit, he went down. The Mustangs had the ball, prime field position, and 5:29 to work with.

Chapter 158

"We need to score quickly — but can we think ahead?" AJ asked his dad as the Mustang offense huddled during Coldwater Bluff's timeout after his fumble recovery.

"What's on your mind?" Jonathan asked.

AJ turned to Tank. "How's your arm?"

"Fine. Why?"

"Your *left* arm. Can you throw with it?"

"Yeah — just not as far," Tank replied.

"Perfect," AJ said. "Remember in 8th grade when we set up St. Paul all season and sprung the trap in the championship? Coach Norm's idea?"

Tank and Coach Norm grinned. "Worked like a charm," Tank said.

AJ faced the team. "David, keep signaling fake plays to keep them honest. We'll pound unbalanced pitches, right and left. Tank — right side, you throw to me. I'll get yards and step out. Left side, you run and get out. Simple."

Coach Dad raised an eyebrow. "Not sure where this is going, but I trust you."

"We're going to pick them apart and mix in more deception," AJ said.

After the timeout, the Mustangs executed: David pitched to Tank. On left runs, Tank took four or five yards and went out. On right runs, he passed to AJ for whatever he could gain before stepping out.

Except on the fifth play — AJ cut inside and scored.

That made him three points shy of the scoring record, but more pressing was the scoreboard: 37–34 after the extra point.

Coach Dad thought about an onside kick but chose a touchback with 4:20 left and his defense playing well. The Mustangs still needed the ball back fast.

First and second downs went well: two- and three-yard stops, costing Blacklick its last two timeouts. But on third, Coldwater Bluff gained six for a first down. The clock rolled.

The next set brought no gain, then one yard, then a seven-yard sack. But the real loss was time. Coldwater Bluff punted with 1:31 left.

The kick avoided the returner, rolled dead at Blacklick's 10. Ninety yards, 79 seconds, three points down.

Chapter 159

"Okay, same plan," AJ told the offense in the huddle. "Unbalanced pitch right, pass. Unbalanced pitch left, run. Got it?"

"Yes, AJ," Roberts replied. "But we might have to abandon that depending upon the clock."

"David ... everyone," AJ started and paused. "We will be fine. Trust me."

Though reluctant, David Roberts followed instructions — pitching to Tank right or left. After five plays, the Mustangs were at the 42-yard line with 34 seconds remaining.

As the line of scrimmage was within the player sideline area, the Coldwater Bluff coaches were shouting, "When they go to your right, it'll be a run. Attack it. When they go to your left, back off to cover the pass."

"AJ?" Roberts said. "They're onto us. We need to go with something else, like, soon."

"Agreed," AJ responded. "This time we're going unbalanced pitch right. Tank, run the ball toward the sideline, then cut inside. Don't worry about getting out of bounds. Everyone after the play race up to the line of scrimmage, so we can spike the ball."

The Mustangs lined up on first down. David Roberts clap-clapped, waited for the mimic, then signaled two plays and set the live one in motion.

Tank received the pitch from the quarterback. He immediately put the ball in his right hand as if he were going to pass, as he'd done several times in the last two series. The moment he sensed that the defense was backed off, expecting a pass, he tucked the ball and began to run. He swept toward the sidelines and then cut back in.

The deception let Tank gain 21 yards. The clock stopped as the officials moved the yard markers. David Roberts used this to hustle everyone to the new line of scrimmage and get in position. The moment the officials re-set the down-and-distance chains, the clock continued to tick downward — 20, 19. The quarterback took the snap and spike the ball, stopping the clock with 18 seconds left.

"We need another 20 to 25 yards to give John a chance," David stated as they huddled.

"Or we could just finish this now," Tank responded. "How many points are you from the record now?"

Everyone shot Tank a look that inquired, *Are you serious?*

AJ answered, "Three points." After a short pause, he continued, "But my primary objective is to get us well within field goal range. Given a chance, though, I'll go for it."

Everyone nodded in agreement.

Then AJ continued, "Okay, are we ready? David, we're going unbalanced pitch left. Tank, warm up that left passing arm. I will be open."

Again, the Mustangs lined up. At this point, the down didn't matter. It was all about time and distance. David Roberts clap-clapped, wait for the mimic, signaled a ruse and live play and set things in motion. He pitched the ball to Tank, who was going left — 17.

With the ball, Tank barreled ahead as if he were looking to only get five or six inconsequential yards — 16, 15. He could sense Coldwater Bluff defenders tentatively moving in, satisfied with containing but not over pursuing. With that cushion, Tank stopped, cranked his left arm back and threw the ball — 14, 13, 12.

AJ again feigned blocking and slipped beyond the Wolves' defenders. He didn't go too far beyond, however. He wasn't certain of Tank's left-arm strength. As it turned out, his arm was stronger than he gave himself credit for. Although the ball floated and wobbled, AJ would have to race to get under it 20 yards beyond the line of scrimmage — 11, 10. AJ hauled in the pass and began running — 9, 8.

Because Tank's pass hovered a bit, two Coldwater Bluff defenders were able to re-adjust their direction and pursue AJ — 7. They needed to hustle, as AJ had a head start and was 20-or-so yards from the end zone — 6.

AJ could see the end zone, and there was nothing in front of him — 5. He knew that getting there would end the game and give him the scoring record — 4. But he could also sense pursuers closing in — 3. The decision was his — 2.

Chapter 160

"John, get in there and tie it up," Coach Dad shouted at his kicker.

AJ stepped out of bounds at the 12-yard line with a single second left. As he raced down the sideline with defenders in pursuit, he quickly considered his options. Maybe he could score, but it wasn't a certainty. What was a certainty from this distance, however, was John Evans.

The kicking team poured onto the field, including John Evans and his holder, Brady Troy. This necessitated that David Roberts exit, along with a litany of others. AJ and Tank remained so they could continue to flank to the left and right of Brady.

After a quick huddle, the kicking team lined up, and with little fanfare, John Evans split the uprights with the tying field goal — 37-37.

As the teams went to their respective sidelines, the public address announcer shared with the fans in attendance:

"Alright, folks, the Blacklick Mustangs and Coldwater Bluff Wolves are headed to overtime here. Now, under the rules set by the Ohio High School Athletic Association, here's how it works:

"Each team will get one possession per overtime period, starting from the opponent's 20-yard line. They can score with a touchdown or a field goal, and after a touchdown, they'll have the option to go for one or try a two-point conversion.

"The offense stays on the field until they score, turn the ball over, or fail to convert on fourth down. So, every play matters here.

"Now, before the overtime begins, there will be a coin toss. In fact, the captains are headed out now. The winner gets to choose whether they want to play offense or defense first — or which end of the field they want to use. The other team picks from the remaining options.

"If we're still tied after the first overtime, we keep going — no new coin toss. Instead, the team that lost the first toss gets first choice in the second overtime. After that, the right to choose just keeps alternating back and forth.

"And it's also worth noting — each team gets one timeout per overtime period. Just one. They don't carry over from regulation or earlier overtimes, so they've got to use them wisely.

"It appears that the coin toss is a wrap. Coldwater Bluff won and is electing to go on defense. Blacklick will start with the football on the 20-yard line, heading toward the north end zone toward the scoreboard and video screen. Good luck to both teams."

Coach Dad gave the Blacklick offense final instructions before sending them onto the field. While they felt as if they had momentum toward the end of the game, overtime would be different — mainly because the field was shorter. Additionally, they felt as if they needed to move away from the strategy AJ had concocted to get them back in the game.

Coach Dad opted to go with a simple and safe approach. They'd have David Roberts continue to command the offense — clap-clap, wait for the team to mimic that, and then call two plays. No matter the live formation the Mustangs went with, there would be nothing fancy. No passes. Just get the ball to Tank and have him sweep, dart, or hammer left or right.

Tank's body was taking a beating, but it was nothing compared to the bruising toll his body was taking on the Wolves' defense. Eventually, Coldwater Bluff could drag him to the ground, but he managed to plow ahead reliably for three or four yards — enough to continue the possession and eventually score.

On the scoring play, however, while trying to block for Tank, David Roberts got caught up in the chaos. While it wasn't clear who it was — friend or foe — a cleat crashed down on his lower leg, rolling his ankle.

As he writhed on the ground, it temporarily stopped the flow of the game and muted the celebration. Nevertheless, they were able to get him carried to the sidelines and allow the field goal team to convert the extra point. The Mustangs now led for the first time — 44-37.

The Mustangs would find out soon enough, as Coldwater Bluff was now getting its chance at scoring. The Wolves had their own simple, safe overtime strategy — quick, short, outside passes to Tanner McCoy.

These plays could go left or right, and the Coldwater Bluff quarterback would throw the ball to places where only Tanner could catch it. The strategy was nothing spectacular — just short, reliable passes that the Wolves could use to advance the drive a handful of yards at a time. Within six plays — four passes to Tanner McCoy and then a run up the middle — Coldwater Bluff had tied the score, 44-44. This forced a second overtime.

For the second overtime, things worked in reverse. Blacklick opted to go on defense first, and Coldwater Bluff would start with the football on the 20-yard line. What remained the same was that the Wolves would continue to head toward the north end zone. That allowed them to see the scoreboard as they operated. Plus, many of their fans had now flooded the area, cheering and generally creating a deafening commotion.

The Wolves continued with their successful strategy — unremarkable, short, outside passes to Tanner McCoy. The approach seemed unstoppable, but it didn't account for human error. After gaining an initial first down, on their second set of downs, the quarterback threw the ball too far outside. Tanner couldn't get to it, and the ball sailed out of bounds, incomplete.

On second down, Tanner bobbled the ball. While he was eventually able to make the catch, this allowed AJ to tackle him for minimal gain.

On third and goal, an offensive lineman moved too soon. The illegal procedure penalty forced a change in approach — they needed to complete a longer pass. The Mustangs were ready. AJ locked down Tanner McCoy, and the defense sacked the Wolves' quarterback. Faced with a long fourth and goal, Coldwater Bluff opted to play it safe. They kicked a 24-yard field goal, going ahead 47-44.

As the Blacklick defense did its thing for two consecutive series, the injury to David Roberts created an unspoken question: *Now what?*

Chapter 161

"Brady, you've got this," Jonathan told Brady via Casey. He wanted to believe it, but the uncertainty flickered in his quarterback's eyes. Maybe a couple of successful plays would bring back the Brady of old, but for now he could only wait. However, he wouldn't have to wait long.

Brady took the field, lined the team up, and took his position three or four yards behind Paul Mandrake. While he couldn't hear it, he could see the Coldwater Bluff fans growing increasingly rambunctious.

The deaf quarterback stood still for a moment, trying to shake off the recent past. He sized up the defense and then clap-clapped. The team heard and mimicked. They then looked to him as he called two plays — one live and a ruse. He allowed the team to shift before getting under center and taking the snap.

When he had the ball secured, he turned to the left, took two steps back, and handed it off to Tank, who hammered it off tackle, securing it with both hands. Six-yard gain. Second and four at the 14.

With short, quick claps of his hands — clap, clap, clap, clap — he ushered the team up to the new line of scrimmage for the next play. His teammates responded. Time wasn't an issue but keeping the Wolves on their heels helped.

Coach Dad relaxed a bit on the sidelines, watching a bit of confidence return to Brady.

Brady stood still for a moment. He ignored the wild behavior from the Coldwater Bluff faithful. He scanned the defense, clap-clapped, and waited for the team to mimic and look. When they did, he hand-motioned a truth and a lie. After the team shifted, he got under center and took the snap.

When he had the ball secured, Brady spun to the right, took two steps back, and handed it off to Tank again. The beefy back hammered off tackle to the right for five yards. That was enough for a first down, nine yards from victory.

Again, Brady shepherded the team to the line and blocked out the antics from the Coldwater Bluff fandom. He examined the defense. They were pushed up, anticipating another run. Brady clap-clapped, waited for his team's response, and then called the plays. The team shifted, and again he got under center.

He took the snap and spun left. The ball, however, came loose in his hands, and he was unable to hand it off to Tank. He continued to juggle the ball as he slowly moved away from the goal line. Three yards later, he lost control of the ball.

The ball bounced twice — left, then right. Brady raced after it. He bent at the waist and tried to pick it up so he could make something positive out of the developing debacle. In that effort, he inadvertently kicked the ball, sending it careening downfield.

Brady chased after it. Wolves defenders were in pursuit, encouraged on by their fans going wild. He caught up to the ball at the 29-yard line. He went three yards in the wrong direction, hoping for space to turn and maneuver — but it didn't work. Three Coldwater Bluff players took him to the ground.

First and goal from the nine became second and goal from the 34. Coldwater Bluff fans went berserk, the noise thunderous. They could feel the game slipping away from Blacklick.

As the Mustangs retreated to the unfortunate new line of scrimmage, Brady patted his chest, motioning, *that was my fault.* Everyone attempted to reassure him; after all, they just needed to get back into field-goal range.

Brady quickly lined everyone up. Whatever confidence he'd reclaimed was gone. He scanned the defense, but his mind struggled to process information. Everything was a distraction. The last down replayed in his head. Defenders coming in and out of the game clouded his thoughts. And the antics from the Coldwater Bluff crowd created a chaotic background.

It was overwhelming. He contemplated using their timeout, but he didn't — they might need it. Brady was just going to soldier on. He got in position and took a deep breath. Then he took another. He clap-clapped.

Nothing. With the noise from the Coldwater Bluff crowd, his teammates couldn't hear. He clap-clapped again. Again nothing. He started to panic, running up and down his line to alert his teammates by tapping them on the bottom.

As they started to stand, the head official threw his flag and motioned for a delay of game penalty. Things had gone from bad to worse.

Chapter 162

"Should we call a time out?" Norm asked Jonathan.

"No," Jonathan quickly responded. "I have an idea to buy some time so Brady can settle down. Norm, get the team to mimic Brady — *everyone*."

Norm nodded and got to work.

Coach Dad walked five yards onto the field and called out, "Hey, ref. Wait a minute."

The official, now finished marching the ball back to the 39-yard line for second and goal, came walking over toward the Blacklick coach. While this was unusual, it was the tail end of the state championship, and he wanted to be sure that he wasn't missing something.

Jonathan barked out, "How can you make that call? Their fans are making too much noise. We can't hear."

"Coach," the lead official started as other officials and linesmen gathered around, "this is high school football. Not college. Not pro. There is no such provision in the rules."

"Well, there should be," Coach fired back.

"Maybe," the official replied, "but your QB is deaf. Hearing shouldn't be an issue."

"I know," Jonathan conceded, then continued, "but if he could hear, such a rule would apply. And then, under the rules, you'd need to make special accommodations for him to ensure a player with disabilities had the same opportunities as any other players."

Jonathan's twisting logic caused the officials to stop and think. One back judge, slightly dim, replied, bobbing his head, "That sort of makes sense."

"No," the lead official replied. "It makes no sense at all."

Under his breath, Jonathan said, "I know. I'm just trying to buy some time." He then spoke up and asked, "Can I just have a moment with my quarterback?"

Realizing that this was a unique situation with a special-needs player, the head official replied, "Coach, you have 15 seconds while I fill in the opposing coach as to this exchange."

Jonathan wasted no time. He walked toward Brady, and at the same time motioned to his deaf quarterback to come over. When they met, Jonathan realized that he couldn't communicate much verbally. He put his left hand on the quarterback's shoulder and his right hand over Brady's heart. He then looked him in the eye, patted his right hand on his chest, and enunciated, "Don't worry, Brady."

Jonathan then backed away and turned toward the sidelines. As he walked, he shouted to Casey, who was now also standing on the field, to send in two plays. She did, designating one as the ruse. Jonathan then asked her, "Tell him he's got this. He's got this."

As Casey signed that encouraging message, Jonathan turned back toward Brady and attempted to do what the ASL translator had just done. Coach Dad wasn't even close, but Brady understood and appreciated the sentiment.

When the officials got back in position, they signaled for the play clock to start its countdown, and the Blacklick Mustangs got in position to run the play.

In that moment, the Coldwater Bluff fans began shouting and cheering louder than before. They knew their commotion was creating chaos and amplifying it would make a difference. It was impossible for anyone on the field to hear.

While Brady couldn't hear it anyway, he could see their movements and outcries. Nevertheless, he took his position and clap-clapped just as he'd done several hundred times over the season.

While his on-field teammates didn't respond, a couple of thousands of others did — sideline players, coaches, cheerleaders, and fans. As Jonathan was stalling with the officials, Coach Norm quickly told the other players and coaches to mimic Brady. Then he instructed them to "get EVERYONE" to do the same.

With that, players shouted and motioned to classmates what to do. Those students and fans quickly passed the directions on. A wave of the message moved through the student body.

Shea understood the assignment. She raced over to Kaylee Dawson to enlist help from the cheerleaders. Kaylee was on board. Her squad fanned out, sharing from the bottom up.

Casey signed the instructions to Brady's classmates from the Ohio School for the Deaf, who were sitting near the top of the stadium. Those students then communicated the instruction with their ASL interpreters, who then verbalized it to others from the top down.

In less than 30 seconds, hundreds and hundreds of fans knew what to do. The moment Brady clap-clapped, the Blacklick faithful shared out a thunderous — CLAP-CLAP.

It caught the attention of the opposing fandom, who were temporarily silenced by the show of unity. The Coldwater Bluff players looked up in awe. The on-field Mustangs took note as

well. They stood to look toward the stands in amazement —
Tank let out a "Whoa!" Then they turned to Brady.

Brady Troy couldn't hear the mass mimic, but he saw it out
of the corner of his eye. When he turned to look, an almost
imperceptible acoustic wave hit him — one created by
thousands of hands banging together in a familiar cadence. It
made the hair on the back of his neck stand. A charge raced
through his body. Tears formed in his eyes, and endorphins
started to flow.

He turned back toward his opponent. His mind was clear.
His confidence revived. Brady got a sense as to what the defense
was looking to do. He raised his hands over his head and clap-
clapped again — this time as if he were in control. Everyone
gave another awe-inspiring mimic. Brady then went through a
new series of hand signals.

"Dog, he's changing the plan," Coach Norm remarked.

Coach Dad replied, "I know. I can't wait to see what he goes
with." Jonathan bent at the waist, put his hands on his knees,
and watched intently.

Brady Troy quickly got everyone in position and directed
Paul to snap the ball. He dropped back to pass. AJ and other
receivers raced off the line of scrimmage downfield. Tank got in
position to pass block.

The moment Brady saw an opening, he took off running. He
dashed up the middle. When two Wolves converged, he darted
left, took two steps, and then right. Then he bounced further to
the right, down the sidelines. When Coldwater Bluff closed that
off, he headed back to the middle of the field. By the time the
Wolves had him cornered, wrapped up, and on the ground,
Brady Troy was on the 11-yard line.

Coldwater Bluff fans collectively swallowed hard. Their
confidence dissipated. For the Blacklick faithful, the play
breathed life into their hope.

Brady quickly got the team lined up. He didn't want to give Coldwater Bluff any more time than necessary to re-group. He stood still for a moment. He again sized up the defense, raised his hands over his head, and clapped twice. A split second later, thousands of hands repeated it. As the team looked to him, he called two plays — one live and a ruse. He then allowed the team to shift a bit before getting under center and taking the snap.

When he had the ball secured, he turned to the left, took two steps back, and handed it off to Tank, who hammered it off tackle, securing the ball tightly with both hands. Eight-yard gain. Fourth and goal at the three.

Jonathan quickly sent on the field goal team. It was the safe, smart decision — tie the game and play on in a third overtime. From this distance, John Evans was a sure thing.

John Evans stepped back from where the ball was placed and showed Brady where to set the ball. He then backed himself up and over to position himself for the kick. Everything was ready. Everyone waited for Brady Troy to give Paul Mandrake the signal to snap the football.

Brady hesitated, however. He quietly called out to First Friend, "Eh-jay."

AJ looked over at Brady. Their eyes locked. Brady nodded once. AJ understood, and then called out, "Tank."

Tank looked at AJ. Their eyes locked. AJ nodded his head slightly and scrunched his nose. Tank understood.

Almost in unison, AJ, Brady, and Tank stood and signaled time out.

Chapter 163

"What's the matter?" Coach Dad asked as the entire field goal team came to the sidelines.

"Dad, we want to go for it," AJ responded as he stood to the right of his father.

Tank stood to Coach Dad's left and quipped, "We're Blacklick. We don't go for two. We go for six."

More seriously, Brady Troy added, "Leh' finess dis."

"Okay," Jonathan replied. "Does anyone have a problem with this?"

No one responded verbally, but everyone answered with a determined look.

"Well, then what should we do? Does anybody have any ideas?" Jonathan asked.

At this moment, AJ caught a glimpse of Shea off with a group of cheerleaders. She was looking right at him and their eyes met. She wasn't mad. Her face held a sadness or longing. Something about the scene was off. But before AJ could determine what it was, the team huddle caught his attention.

"Whatever we do, let's get the ball to AJ," Tank fired out. "Let's help him break the scoring record."

Coach Dad looked over at AJ for a response.

AJ replied with a sincere tone, "This isn't about me. This is about us. Let's do what's going to get us the win." He thought for a moment and added, "Let's get the ball to Tank and hammer left, right down their throats. They can't stop that."

"Tank?" Coach Dad looked to his beefy fullback.

Tank secured his chin strap, and responded, "You get me the ball; I will get in the end zone."

"Okay," Coach Dad said. Then he added, "This is what we're going to do ..."

When the timeout ended, the Mustang offense raced onto the field. As they did, the Blacklick faithful and Coldwater Bluff fandom rose to their feet and collectively made a deafening racket.

As the Mustangs quickly huddle, AJ shouted over the noise, "You all have a job. Be sharp about it."

Brady then got them lined up in a formation. He scanned the defense and then quickly clap-clapped — allowing their fans to mimic again. He made hand signals and the Blacklick offense quickly changed formations. When Coldwater Bluff adjusted, Brady quickly clap-clapped again.

The offense quickly moved into the unbalanced formation, so that Tank could properly hammer through the Wolves defense. The moment they did, the Coldwater Bluff coach stepped onto the field and called time out.

The entire Mustang offense returned to the sidelines. Once again, AJ was to the right of his dad, and Tank to the left. Coach Dad firmly grabbed the back of the openings in their shoulder pads. Everyone else gathered around.

Shea was there, standing to the right of AJ. He could sense it. The scent of her hair stood out among the smelly football players.

Jonathan remarked, "Well, I think they're on to us. They know what's coming."

"What should we do?" AJ asked.

"Nothing," Coach Dad replied. "But let's let them think we're doing something different."

Everyone laughed, as they took a moment to hydrate. Shea handed AJ a water bottle. He took it, squeezed a quick swig, and then handed it back with his right hand. She took it with her right.

Coach Dad looked around, meeting the eyes of each player staring back at him. Then he spoke. "Well, this is it. Quite a ride, huh? Win or lose, I can't think of anywhere else I'd rather be — or anyone else I'd rather be doing this with. Let's go make it happen."

He sent the offense back onto the field. Again, fan from both sides erupted into deafening cheers. The team was already huddled when Tank arrived ten seconds later and AJ five seconds after that.

Immediately Paul asked AJ, "Are you okay?" AJ had tears streaming down his cheeks.

AJ immediately shouted an upbeat, "I'm fine. I just want to win. I just want to win." Then he gritted his teeth and implored, "Everybody block for Tank. Push them back."

Brady then got them lined up in the same formation as before the timeout. He feigned scanning the defense and then clap-clapped — again their fans mimicked. He made hand signals and the Blacklick offense quickly changed formations. When Coldwater Bluff adjusted, Brady quickly clap-clapped again.

The offense moved into the unbalanced formation to execute the hammer. As soon as the Mustangs started to shift, the Coldwater Bluff started shouting in an animated fashion. Their timeout had been in preparation for this. Defenders started to overload that side.

Brady could see it. But they had to go with what they'd called. The play clock was winding down and they had no time out. He got under center and took the snap. With the ball firmly in hand, he turned to the left, took two steps back and handed it off to Tank.

As he watched Tank hammer toward the line, he could see that something was not what it was supposed to be. It wasn't off or wrong. It was just something not planned.

At this point, only four people knew what was about to unfold.

Chapter 164

"Hold on, you two," Coach Dad said to Tank and AJ, just after sending the offense out for the final play. He still had a firm grip on their shoulder pads to ensure they stayed put.

Tank and AJ complied.

Jonathan pulled them in close, leaned them forward a bit, and said with a half-whisper, "Do you think you can blueberry into a hammer reverse?"

While the question was met with momentary silence, Tank broke it by saying, "Heck yeah we can," as he playfully slapped an open hand on AJ's chest. "It's about time I got to do one. It was my own idea to begin with."

AJ was taken aback and asked, "Are you sure, Dad?"

"Yes, absolutely," Coach Dad confidently answered. "They know what's coming, and they're going to be ready for it. They will be totally blindsided — unless four years ago they were scouting the Saint Whoever game."

"Come on, AJ, we can do it," Tank added. "It will be legend."

Coach Dad added, "AJ, go get the scoring record and win us a championship."

Jonathan then sent Tank and AJ off to catch up with the offense. Before they got too far along, he shouted, "AJ!"

AJ stopped and turned back. Tears were starting to well up in his eyes. The emotion of the last few minutes was overwhelming.

"AJ," Jonathan shouted over the fan noise. "No matter what, I'm proud of you. Do you understand?"

AJ couldn't speak. He simply nodded. The first tear rolled down his face.

Jonathan could see the emotion on AJ's face. It was causing him to get choked up too. He had more to say, but all he could get out was, "No matter what."

Then he held up his right hand, made a fist, and raised his pinky finger — "I."

Keeping his pinky finger up, in a quick, smooth motion, he pointed his index finger up as well and extended his thumb outward laterally — "Love."

Then, Jonathan pointed at AJ — "You."

He then choked out, "AJ, do you understand?"

All AJ could do was nod while battling full-on tear flow. He then turned to catch up with Tank. Once in the huddle, he redirected his emotions by telling everyone to "block for Tank."

AJ then went about moving through the various formations like the other Mustang players. When they got into the unbalanced formation, AJ could see that the Coldwater Bluff players were stacking up in anticipation of Tank hammering in their direction. That made him cautiously optimistic, but he didn't want to do anything that might give away the deception.

When Brady set the play in motion, he stepped forward as if he was going to block. He made contact but used that to push off and doubled back toward Tank.

AJ could see the confused look on Brady's face. The quarterback had just handed the ball off to his fullback, and AJ — his main blocker — was headed in the wrong direction.

Just before AJ got back toward Tank, Tank flipped him the football. The exchange was near perfect, as if they'd done it a hundred times before. And they probably had — if you counted all the times they'd actually done it in games and practices, playing around in the backyard, and talking about something like this very moment.

As AJ raced past Brady, the deaf quarterback stumbled trying to whip around to see how the plan was unfolding.

AJ arched deep into the backfield, five or six yards behind the line of scrimmage. He was in the open field, moving effortlessly. Off to the left, he could see a tangle of players either looking to tackle or block for Tank — who didn't have the ball.

Despite this, there was one lingering defender moving in on AJ. His entire role was to protect the backside against just this very thing. And he was intent on being successful.

AJ knew he might not get into the end zone untouched. As he and the Coldwater Bluff defender closed the distance between one another, AJ considered his options. To evade a tackle he'd have to outmaneuver, overpower, or simply outrun the defender.

Before he had to decide, however, a fourth option presented itself. Brady, who'd recovered from his initial stumble, rolled in and blasted into the defender. AJ now had a clear path into the end zone.

As AJ crossed the goal line, he let the ball drop to the ground and quietly rejoiced. As he did, he heard a familiar voice shout. It was the fourth person to know about the blueberry.

Chapter 165

"Jess! You aren't supposed to be here," Kaylee Dawson exclaimed as Jessa Harroway and three other suspended cheerleaders made their way into the cheering area behind the player bench. Brady Troy had just made his big run, getting the ball down to the Coldwater Bluff 11-yard line, and Tank got them to the three. The Mustangs were lining up to tie the game in the second overtime.

Jess fired back, "So sue me." She continued to strut forward like a boss, then added, "Besides, I'm not here to cheer, and I'll be gone in a minute. Shea, honey, would you please come stand by me?"

Shea was still standing with Kaylee, as together they'd helped get the entire Blacklick faithful to mimic Brady. She was frozen in place, completely unsure as to what she should do. Her eyes darted back and forth.

As Jess walked up to Shea, she said, "I know I'm not someone you want to see—ever—but just trust me for 30 seconds." Jess then stood shoulder to shoulder with Shea and looked toward another disgraced cheerleader who was working the camera on her phone.

The phone-holding cheerleader quipped, "Lights, camera, and we're recording."

Jess flicked her hair back and started. "Two weeks ago, I posted a recording of AJ Reese and Sebastian Sullivan having a not-so-nice conversation about this person—Shea Brooks."

Shea listened but didn't know where to look—at the camera, at Kaylee, down at her feet. Then she immediately changed her focus to Jess when she heard Jess say, "But it was a fake."

Jess then went on to clarify, "Well, not a total fake. It was dumb-ass Sebastian's voice. But AJ? Well, his was created using AI. He didn't say what you heard. He's probably not capable of saying anything like that. He's probably never even thought it." Jess then paused, as if at a loss for words, but finished with, "So, well. I guess that's it."

Then the phone-holding cheerleader said, "And cut."

"Okay, let's go find decent Wi-Fi to post it up," Jess ordered.

"Jess!" Kaylee declared. "That's horrible."

Jess pursed her lips, put a hand on one hip and pushed out the other, then said, "What can I say?" She then turned to Shea and sincerely added, "I'm sorry."

Shea just looked back at her in stunned silence.

"Shea, I'm just jealous of you. You're so smart." Then Jess swallowed hard and added, "And now so beautiful. And you've got AJ. And all I have is Sebastian."

At that moment, the other cheerleaders who had their spa day cut short jumped in, almost in unison, and declared, "HAD! Had. Had."

"Yes, *had*," Kaylee added. "You're forbidden from dating him anymore."

"Okay, okay, okay," Jess relented. "*Had.*"

At this point, Shea was looking toward the team as they were settling in on the sidelines for the first timeout. She felt a sense of guilt and sorrow. She and AJ shared brief eye contact before he was brought into the team's conversation. She continued to look, wanting to go to him.

Jess added, "My point, Shea, is that AJ really likes you. I mean a lot. He's a good one. Don't let him get away."

Without a word, Shea started to move toward the team, but the huddle broke before she could get there. But she stood next to Coach Dad as the Mustangs went through their series of adjustments—mimicking Brady Troy's clap-clap with the hundreds of others.

Once Coldwater Bluff called its timeout, Shea moved to her right a bit to allow AJ to stand next to his dad. But she was brushed up against him.

With her right hand, she handed him a water bottle. After a quick swig, he handed it back, still not fully acknowledging her. When he dropped his right hand to his side, she reached in with her left hand and gently grasped his. It momentarily startled him, but he quickly maneuvered to pull her hand in. She then squeezed his hand twice, as if to say, *I'm here. I'm with you. We're together.* AJ then quickly reciprocated the grasp.

In the moment, her focus was elsewhere. She was fixated on getting back what she'd almost let get away. Shea heard the dialogue but really wasn't listening. After the huddle broke, she knew that AJ and Tank remained behind, but she didn't comprehend why.

After AJ and Tank were gone, she stood next to Coach Dad, watching the team line up. She asked, "Coach, what's going on?"

He quietly replied, "It's a secret. The whole play is going left, but AJ will come shooting out to the right with the football for the game."

As Jonathan bent at the waist and placed his hands to watch, Shea excused herself. She dropped off the water bottles and hurried to the end zone to stand with reporters and officials.

As her boyfriend crossed into the end zone and the referee signaled touchdown, she called out, "AJ."

As AJ turned toward her, she ran to him on the field and jumped into his arms.

They shared a moment, but it wasn't private for long. Seconds later, Brady arrived and joined the hug. Then Paul. Then others. Finally, before the whole team arrived, Tank became part of the celebration, declaring loudly, "Group hug!"

Chapter 166

"Congratulations, Coach," a random official from the Ohio High School Athletic Association said to Jonathan as they both wandered onto the field following the game.

The official was working to set up for the awards ceremony. Jonathan was simply looking for one person — his son. He walked onto the field and looked on as celebratory chaos ensued in the end zone. He was bewildered, trying to sort out who was who. He spotted this player and that, but no AJ.

After a few moments, the mass started to dissipate as players migrated to various other places on the field and sidelines. AJ emerged, walking out of the end zone.

AJ had his helmet off, and Shea was carrying it in her right hand. In her left, she had AJ's hand. Together they casually wandered onto the field, heading toward the awards presentation at midfield.

Jonathan smiled and began walking in their direction. As he did, he could see Casey race ahead and excitedly engage the couple in conversation. Obviously, there was a story to be filled in on, and the ASL interpreter was eager to hear it.

As Shea shared, AJ spotted his dad. He told Casey and Shea that he'd catch up on the details later. He left their conversation and began walking toward his dad, matching his father's smile.

When they were about ten yards apart, AJ raised his right hand and extended three fingers—the little, ring, and middle—

while holding his index finger and thumb close to his palm. Jonathan chuckled—gentle and full of warmth—as he mirrored AJ's gesture and quietly said, "WOW, indeed."

They continued toward one another, and when they met, AJ went in to hug his dad. Jonathan returned the embrace.

As they hugged, Jonathan let out, "I love you, AJ."

To which AJ replied, "I love you too, Dad."

Chapter 167

"Save the excuses, Dad. You were late. You owe us a lap," AJ chided toward his dad.

The game was long over. The awards had been doled out, and pictures had been taken.

Before they headed to the locker room to change for the victory ride back to Blacklick High, much of the team stayed out on the field to witness Coach Dad serve out his penance.

"Really, guys?" Jonathan jokingly asked, then added, "I was practically kidnapped."

Tank quickly responded, "No excuses. Next time, get kidnapped a little faster."

With that, Jonathan started to jog around the field. When he was 20 yards away, AJ and others caught up to Coach Dad and joined the run.

Chapter 168

"AJ, you disappointed a lot of people today," the stranger said to the new scoring record holder. AJ returned a confused look, so the stranger explained, "There were no less than 50 college scouts here to watch that McCoy kid, and you pretty much shut down the show."

AJ smiled and nodded his head, as if to say, "Yes, I guess I did."

"Do you mind if I sit down?" the stranger asked but was intending to regardless. Once seated, he reached out a hand and said, "I'm Coach Connor, from Case Western."

"Do you know my dad?" AJ quickly asked.

"We didn't play together at Case," Connor replied. Then he continued, "He'd graduated just before I arrived, but I heard a lot of stories about him from my coach — who was his coach."

"Oh," was all that AJ could say.

"But we've talked a lot this season regarding drills, tactics, and other X's-and-O's stuff," Connor shared. Then, changing the subject, he added, "After today, I have no doubt that there will be lots of colleges interested in you. So, I want to be the first to throw my hat in the ring."

AJ's eyes lit up as he let out, "Really?" This was not something he'd expected.

"You have some footwork things to work on, but I think you'd fit in nicely in our program," Connor said. "Not a starter from day one, but a contributor with a chance to really grow into our system."

AJ quietly listened. His eyes were wide open.

"Plus, at Case you'll get a great education," Connor added. "And that matters most."

AJ nodded in agreement.

"That's enough for now, AJ. Congratulations. Celebrate. You've earned it. I'd like to get you to campus for a visit soon. Okay?" Connor finished, stood, and started to walk away.

Two steps later, he stopped and turned back to AJ and added, "The one thing about Case, however, is that we're D-3. We can't offer scholarships." Connor then reached into his jacket pocket. As he did, he said, "But I can give you this." He then pulled out and handed to AJ a single pencil, emblazoned with the name *Case Western Reserve University* and the team colors. Without another word, Connor left.

AJ took the pencil and looked at it. He then broke into a big smile as he glanced over toward his dad.

About The Author

Frank Agin is the founder and president of AmSpirit Business Connections, an organization that empowers entrepreneurs, sales professionals, and other businesspeople to get more referrals through structured, relationship-based networking.

In addition, Frank hosts the Networking Rx podcast, where he shares insights on professional relationships, referral marketing, and business networking best practices.

He is also a prolific writer, having authored numerous books.

Fiction

- *Out of the Comfort Zone*
- *Rival*

Personal & Professional Development

- *Foundational Networking: Building Know, Like and Trust to Create A Lifetime of Extraordinary Success*
- *LinkedWorking: Generating Success on LinkedIn … the World's Largest Professional Networking*
- *The Champion: Finding the Most Valuable Person in Your Network*
- *Networking Rx: Age-Old Prescriptions for Developing Healthy Relationships*
- *The Giving Journal: Achieving Success Through Focused Generosity*
- *Chase Greatness: Life Lessons Revealed Through Sports*
- *Networking Fore Success: A Short Course For Aspiring Franchise Consultants*
- *The Successful Franchise Broker's Ultimate Networking Compendium*

- *The Three Reasons You Don't Get Referrals*
- *101 Essays to Empower You to Rise & Thrive*
- *101 Essays to Empower You to Up Your Game*
- *101 Essays to Empower You to Build Momentum*
- *101 Essays to Empower You to Limitless Reach*
- *101 Essays to Empower You to Elevate Your Influence*
- *101 Essays to Empower You to Peak Performance*
- *101 Essays to Empower You to The Winning Edge*
- *101 Essays to Empower You to Live Unstoppable*
- *101 Essays to Empower You to Achieve Greatness*
- *101 Essays to Empower You to Break Barriers*

Frank grew up in Houghton, Michigan (in the Upper Peninsula) and holds an undergraduate degree from Beloit College in Wisconsin. He also earned both a law degree and an MBA from The Ohio State University and became a CPA while working as a tax consultant with what is now PricewaterhouseCoopers.

He currently lives in Blacklick, Ohio (just outside Columbus) with his wife, Linda. Together, they have three great kids—Lucas, Logan, and Chase.

Stay tuned, as he's working on other novels and professional development books.